MOONSICK

MOONSICK

TOM O'DONNELL

HODDER

HODDER CHILDREN'S BOOKS

First published in Great Britain in 2025 by Hodder & Stoughton Limited
First published in the United States in 2025 by Wednesday Books,
an imprint of St. Martin's Publishing Group

1 3 5 7 9 10 8 6 4 2

Designed by Devan Norman

A CIP catalogue record for this book
is available from the British Library.

ISBN 978 1 444 98515 3

Typeset in Electra LT Std.
Printed and bound in Great Britain by
Clays Ltd, Elcograf S.p.A.

The paper and board used in this book
are made from wood from responsible sources.

MIX
Paper | Supporting responsible forestry
FSC® C104740

Hodder Children's Books
An imprint of
Hachette Children's Group
Part of Hodder & Stoughton Limited
Carmelite House
50 Victoria Embankment
London EC4Y 0DZ

The authorised representative in the EEA is Hachette Ireland, 8 Castlecourt Centre, Dublin 15, D15 XTP3, Ireland (email: info@hbgi.ie)

An Hachette UK Company
www.hachette.co.uk

www.hachettechildrens.co.uk

FOR MY MOM, WHO I MISS EVERY DAY

SOME OF THE THEMATIC MATERIAL IN *MOONSICK*
CONTAINS DEPICTIONS OF BODY HORROR, GORE, AND VIOLENCE.

MOONSICK

1

". . . As the plague ends, our narrator concludes his journal with a poem: 'A *dreadful plague in London was; In the year sixty-five, Which swept an hundred thousand souls; Away; yet I alive!*'"

Mr. Hirsch looked up from his copy of Daniel Defoe's *A Journal of the Plague Year* and surveyed the young faces staring back at him. It was the spring of their senior year, the last period of the day. They were bored. Checked out. Their eyes were deader than a seventeenth-century London plague victim. These kids had already applied to college and, to be quite honest, even those who didn't attend would be absolutely fine. Green Valley was just that kind of school—median family income was almost $200,000. With or without AP English, they would be all set. Which is perhaps why Mr. Hirsch still felt like he ought to try to teach them something.

"So . . . what do we think he's getting at?" asked Mr. Hirsch.

No hands went up. Of course no hands went up. Mr. Hirsch closed his eyes and took a deep breath. He imagined fly-fishing on the Sauk River. Then he picked someone.

"Heidi."

Heidi Mills blinked, a little startled. Heidi was a smart, pretty, popular girl who had, unfortunately, been secretly scrolling on her phone under her desk. She cursed herself. This was the type of thing she never did. Heidi always paid attention in class, no matter how insanely boring it was.

"Um . . ." said Heidi.

"Um," repeated Mr. Hirsch, to the class's mild amusement.

"I think he's happy to be alive but he's, um, looking for a reason why," said Heidi. "Like, why did some people live and others die? He doesn't want to accept that it's just random so it's got to be, like, the hand of God or something."

Mr. Hirsch gave a nod. Good answer, apparently.

"He survived," said Mr. Hirsch. "Ergo, he *deserved* to survive."

"Exactly," said Heidi, relieved she'd been able to pull something out of thin air.

Mr. Hirsch pressed on. "Well, it may have seemed random at the time, but it wasn't. We know now that *Yersinia pestis*—the bacteria that causes bubonic plague—is carried by fleas. Specifically, fleas that live on rats. So, who do we think would have been hit hardest by the Great Plague of London?"

"People with rats in their house?" asked Katie Lackey.

"Sure," said Mr. Hirsch. "And who would that have been?"

Again, no hands rose. Mr. Hirsch's eyes narrowed as he saw Luca Spiro turn a full 180 degrees in his desk, whispering something to Peter Kavanagh.

"Luca," said Mr. Hirsch.

Luca slowly turned back around, as though the maître d' at a fancy restaurant had just told him his table was ready. The boy brimmed with the absolute confidence that comes from being eighteen years old, naturally handsome, and born rich.

"What's that?" said Luca. "Oh. Who's got rats in their house? Hmm . . . I'm gonna say . . . Goth Steve."

The entire class burst out laughing.

Steve Hale, the misfit who was the butt of Luca's joke, glared. "Fuck you," he said through clenched teeth.

"That's sweet, Steve. I'm actually spoken for." Luca nodded in Heidi's direction.

Even though it was a punch line, Heidi felt a flutter in her stomach as their relationship was publicly acknowledged.

"All right, all right, enough," said Mr. Hirsch, whose feeble efforts to restore order were shattered by the ringing of the final bell.

Instantly, the class was on their feet and jostling for the door.

It was the usual pandemonium in the halls, as the collective student body of Green Valley High School made their way toward the exits. The sound of a few hundred simultaneous conversations rose to the level of a dull roar.

Heidi shook her head as she watched a group of boys take turns trying to jump and touch the lunar cycle countdown clock—00:05:47:29 to moonrise—mounted near the ceiling. What were they trying to prove, exactly? Out of the corner of her eye, she saw a tenth grader get pantsed by one of his friends. Idiots.

"Oh my God, Heidi, *such* a cute skirt!" Marcie Love, another senior girl, locked arms with Heidi as they walked. "My mom has one *just* like it."

Marcie was pretty and popular too. She was two inches taller than Heidi, and her hair was incredible. Heidi hated her, and she was 99 percent sure that Marcie hated her back. But neither girl had ever said a (provably) unkind word to the other. Mutual loathing was expressed in backhanded compliments.

Heidi returned an even brighter smile. "I *love* that for your mom. Maybe she'll finally land another husband. I mean, stranger things have happened, right?"

Marcie ignored the jab and regarded Heidi's skirt once more.

"*I* don't think it's too short at all," she said, somehow subtly implying she might be the only one who held that belief. "Okay, gotta run, girl. Really looking forward to Saturday. Ciao."

Marcie blew Heidi air-kisses and broke off in a different direction.

Heidi blew her a kiss back. "Ciao, bitch," she said under her breath.

"Heidi!"

Heidi turned to see Olivia Zeiman-Parr, her best friend since the third grade, nudging her way through the crowd to catch up.

"I got into Kenyon," said Olivia.

"Oh my God, that's awesome," said Heidi. Kenyon was ranked thirtieth in National Liberal Arts Colleges.

"Is it?" asked Olivia. "Kenyon's in Gambier, Ohio. I looked on Wikipedia and it says the town's only got 2,391 people. Could I honestly spend four years in Gambier, Ohio?"

"You spent four years in this place," said Heidi, nodding toward the still pantsless tenth grader, who was now trying to do a handstand to make his buddies laugh. "You'll be fine wherever you end up."

"Easy for you to say," said Olivia. "You'll be at Harvard with your boyfriend."

"Do *not* jinx it," said Heidi. This was what she was supposed to say. "You know I haven't gotten in yet."

"Please," said Olivia. "You're salutatorian. All-state cross-country. French club president. Fifteen eighty on your SATs. You *know* you're getting in."

Heidi shrugged and didn't smile. She wanted to be humble, but . . . maybe she did know she was getting in.

"Ladies, my ears are burning," Luca said as he caught up to them.

Olivia rolled her eyes. "Somebody says 'Harvard' and you appear like Candyman."

Luca ignored Olivia and gave Heidi a wet kiss on the mouth.

"You get your letter yet, babe?" asked Luca.

"Not yet," said Heidi.

"Should've done early decision like I did," said Luca.

"Should've had an uncle who donated a new library like Luca did," Olivia said.

"Olivia, c'mon," said Heidi.

Luca gave her an exaggerated smile. "Ha. You're super funny, dude. You'll be, like, the funniest person at community college."

"Fuck you," said Olivia. "I got into Macalester, Colby and Kenyon."

Numbers twenty-seven, nineteen, and thirty, respectively, thought Heidi.

"Wow. Those are all great schools," said Luca. He slapped the custodian, Mr. Santangelo, on the back as they walked past him. "Watch out, Mr. Santangelo, Olivia's coming for your job."

Mr. Santangelo stared at Luca and said nothing.

"You're such a fucking dick," said Olivia.

"Oh my God, be *nice*!" said Heidi.

Luca threw an arm around Heidi's waist. "You know what, Olivia, maybe you could actually work for Heidi. Every doctor's office needs somebody to, like, clean up the used syringes and crusty Band-Aids."

Olivia was taken aback. "Doctor's office? What is he talking about?"

Heidi shrugged. She didn't want to get into it.

"I thought you wanted to major in art history," said Olivia.

"I don't know," said Heidi. "I've been thinking about it and, like, the world needs doctors more than ever right now. Who else is going to find the cure?" It sounded right. You couldn't really argue with it.

"And more importantly," said Luca. "Doctors are rich as *fuuuuuck*."

"There it is," said Olivia. "Pressure her into something she doesn't want—"

"Who says I don't want it?" protested Heidi. She *did* want it. Right?

Olivia pressed on. "—while you focus on your quote-unquote 'rap career.'"

Luca darkened. "I've got flow, Olivia. I don't expect a little white girl from the suburbs to understand what that means."

"What the hell are you talking about?" cried Olivia. "*You're* white! *You're* from the suburbs!"

The two of them kept on arguing about Heidi's future all the way out to the parking lot.

"You know what, maybe I won't even have a job," said Luca. "Maybe I'll just lay by the pool all day, working on my tan, looking pretty. Olivia, after you graduate from Macolbyster, I'll pay you minimum wage to freshen my mojitos."

"Asshole," said Olivia.

They stopped at Luca's BMW.

"Ooh, speaking of drinks," said Luca. "Just remembered there's gonna be a little change of plans re: Saturday."

Heidi and Olivia stared back at him.

Luca cleared his throat. "Turns out I can't actually get the booze. I forgot it's lockdown tonight and tomorrow night, and I've got practice."

"Okay," said Heidi. "So who's getting it?"

Luca smiled his thousand-watt smile. Slowly, it dawned on Heidi what he had in mind.

"What?" said Heidi. "No!"

"Afraid yeah," said Luca.

"Buy it on Saturday then," said Olivia.

"Saturday's my great-uncle's ninetieth," said Luca. "I'll be stuck in Centralia with my fucking parents."

"Luca, I can't *buy alcohol*." Heidi looked around to make sure no one overheard her.

"We'll get in trouble!" said Olivia.

Heidi saw a flash of something in Luca's eyes. At times, he was capable of great anger. But a split second later he was all smiles again.

"Guys, I don't love to say this, because I *do* consider myself a feminist," said Luca, "but please don't be pussies."

And with those parting words, Luca hopped in his car and drove off, blaring drill music.

Apparently, that settled it. Heidi and Olivia were now responsible for getting all the alcohol for the senior party at Heidi's house on Saturday. The girls made their way toward Heidi's new Audi—an eighteenth-birthday gift from her mom—in nervous silence.

"I don't know," said Olivia as they pulled out of the student parking lot and onto the street. "Luca picked your college. He's picking your career. And now, he's got you, like, doing crimes for him."

"Crimes?" said Heidi, defensiveness overcoming her fear of breaking the law. "You're being *so* dramatic. I'm not some, like, kept woman. Everyone wants to go to Harvard. And how is you telling me I *shouldn't* be a doctor any different from Luca telling me I *should* be one?"

"I don't know, it just is," said Olivia. "And look, I know you think you and Luca will be together forever, but he's your high school boyfriend and high school is basically done. You can't count on—"

"Admit it," said Heidi, cutting her off, "you've just never liked him."

Olivia looked like she wanted to say something. But she didn't. Then Heidi's phone rang.

"Oh shit, it's my mom," said Heidi. "Be quiet."

Heidi answered the call on Bluetooth. As she spoke, her voice was suddenly weak and scratchy. "Hi, Mom."

On the other end, Heidi's mother Madeline spoke. She sounded loud and clear, perfect enunciation, as always: "Hello, sweetie. How are you feeling?"

"A little better. I actually made it to school today. How's Oahu?"

"Not as fun without you," said Madeline.

"I'm so sad I'm not there," said Heidi.

"I know," said Madeline. "We went scuba diving and Ron saw a reef shark!"

"Wow, that sounds super neat," said Heidi.

At "super neat" Olivia gave Heidi a look. Heidi shook her head.

"I'll send you a picture," said Madeline. "We wish you were here, sweetheart."

"Me too," Heidi said sorrowfully. "Me too." Then she added a short fit of fake coughing for good measure.

"Oof," said Madeline. "You sound bad."

"Sorry," croaked Heidi.

"Don't apologize. Oh, before I forget, did Dagamara ever show up?"

Madeline was referring to their family's elderly Polish cleaning lady. Dagamara came every Tuesday to tidy up the house.

"Nope," said Heidi.

"I've been texting her all week. No answer," said Madeline.

"I don't want to be harsh because, of course, I understand her circumstances are different from ours. But this sort of thing isn't acceptable."

"I'll let you know if she comes," said Heidi.

"Okay. Rest up and we'll see you on Sunday," Madeline said. "Oh, and text me if you hear anything from Harvard. Love you."

"Will do, Mom. Love you too."

Heidi turned onto Wyngarde Street, and an upscale shopping center soon came into view. It was completely surrounded by a ten-foot steel security fence topped with loops of razor wire. A tasteful sign that read EASTLAKE COMMONS rose above the fence with a brass clockface mounted beneath it. Under that, they'd even installed a smaller lunar cycle countdown clock with the days, hours, and minutes in Roman numerals.

Heidi drove through the security gate and into the parking lot. Neither girl gave a second look to the homeless encampment abutting Eastlake Commons, a half dozen tents in an alley pressed up against the outside of the fence.

Heidi parked and she and Olivia joined the end of the line to enter Glenmarket Wine & Spirits.

Ahead of them, a bored security guard used a long cotton swab to gather saliva from inside the cheek of patrons going into the store.

"I can't believe you faked sick to get out of a Hawaiian vacation," said Olivia. "Must be nice."

Heidi shrugged. "We went to Hawaii two years ago. It's fine but it's, like, so touristy."

"My family exclusively vacations in Western Pennsylvania," said Olivia darkly. "Does it still count as your graduation present if you didn't even go on the trip?"

"It fucking better not!" Heidi laughed.

They made their way to the front of the line. Yet another saliva test. Heidi, like most people, barely noticed them anymore. She opened her mouth, and the guard slid the cotton swab in, made a few perfunctory circles, and then yanked it out and plunged it into a small plastic vial filled with clear liquid.

There was a good fifteen seconds of awkward silence as the guard and Heidi tried not to look at each other. The vial didn't change color. The guard tossed it into a trash can that was overflowing with them.

"Welcome to Glenmarket Wine and Spirits," he said for approximately the nine hundredth time that day.

Heidi walked through the automatic doors, and Olivia stepped forward and opened her mouth.

Inside, the choices were overwhelming: vodka, bourbon, gin, rum. Heidi didn't really know anything about liquor so she picked out top-shelf bottles of each one and put them into her cart. Hopefully it would be enough to make everyone happy. She and Olivia had a brief debate over whether or not boys drink port, but they ended up grabbing a bottle just in case. By the time they made it to the checkout line with $300 of assorted booze, their latent fear was starting to rise to the surface.

"We're gonna get caught," Olivia whispered as the cashier rang up a bottle of Riesling for a grandmother in activewear ahead of them.

"Shh," said Heidi. She was nervous too, but she knew that in most situations, confidence was everything. Something she'd learned from her mom.

By the time she made it to the cash register, Heidi was nonchalantly looking at her phone. Just buying alcohol. No big deal. Out of the corner of her eye, she saw Olivia staring at the floor. Sweat was beading on her forehead. She looked ill.

The liquor store clerk appeared to barely be older than Heidi herself. "ID, please," he said.

Heidi made a subtle gesture as if to indicate how ridiculous it was that she, a grown woman, was being forced to present her ID to make such a routine alcohol purchase.

"Sure," said Heidi. With a wry smile, she handed the clerk the fake Nevada driver's license of one Dawn Suppley, age twenty-seven.

Olivia's posture had subtly shifted. She was hunched slightly forward. Was her stomach cramping? She looked like she might throw up.

Heidi did not react at all. She went back to her phone. Simply browsing social media while making an absolutely normal and legal purchase. After this, she, Dawn Suppley, would probably go to the bank, or perhaps to a kitchen-and-tile showroom.

The clerk stared at the ID for a long time. The longer he looked, the more Heidi felt her confidence eroding. Why, exactly, was she doing this, again? Couldn't Luca have gotten one of his older friends to buy the booze? If Heidi got caught, what was the penalty? Was this a misdemeanor or an actual felony? She'd resisted the urge to google it beforehand and now she regretted not knowing the answer. Would having a criminal record make it harder for her to get into a top-ten medical school?

"Hang on," said the clerk.

The clerk walked a few checkout lanes down and spoke in hushed tones to his tired-looking manager. At the end of the conversation the manager gave a fatalistic shrug. Heidi thought she could lip-read the words "not even worth it."

The clerk returned to his post and handed Heidi her ID back. "Fine," he said.

He knew. But he rang Heidi up anyway.

Heidi was grinning ear to ear as she and Olivia stepped out of Glenmarket Wine & Spirits pushing a shopping cart full of booze. They'd done it. They'd gotten away with it.

Suddenly, the girls heard sirens.

2

Two hundred feet across the parking lot, on the other side of the security fence, a BearCat armored vehicle screeched to a stop—sirens blaring—in the alley beside the homeless encampment.

Six officers of the Viral Containment Task Force burst out of the vehicle. They wore heavy tactical body armor. Under their helmets, black balaclavas concealed their faces. Most had added personal touches to their official uniform, decorating their gear with macabre imagery: death's-heads, demons, fire-breathing dragons, avenging angels.

A recorded announcement began to repeat through the BearCat's loudspeakers: "Due to public health violations, this unauthorized encampment will be dismantled. Please vacate the area immediately. Thank you for your cooperation."

The affectless female voice of the recording was at odds with the violence with which the VCTF officers kicked down the tents and tossed the residents' personal belongings into piles to be destroyed.

Those who lived in the encampment stood by and watched in grim resignation. It wasn't the first time this had happened to them. It wouldn't be the last. On the edge of this small crowd was a woman in a leather jacket. She was neither young nor old, powerfully built, with a short, severe haircut and piercing gray eyes. This gray-eyed woman wasn't one of them. Not really. She was an interested observer. And she wasn't resigned to what was happening.

Loud yelps suddenly came from inside a tent. A VCTF officer pushed through the zipper flap dragging a terrified mutt by her leash.

"You really gotta do this?" said a man in a dirty Adidas T-shirt. He had tears in his eyes.

"Dogs are passive carriers," said the officer. He jerked the leash toward the vehicle. The dog whined as its claws scrabbled uselessly on the asphalt.

"C'mon, you're hurting her!" cried the man in the Adidas shirt.

He took a step forward and, almost too quick to see, a second officer bashed him across the face with a truncheon.

The man in the Adidas shirt hit the ground, blood gushing from his broken nose. At the sight of her master in pain, the dog's whines rose to frantic howls. The man tried to get up off the ground and another VCTF officer kicked him in the gut. Two more officers quickly joined in with their clubs.

"Jesus," Olivia said as the girls watched the beating unfold from a distance.

"Yeah," said Heidi. "It sucks that they have to do that. But, you know, that's how they keep us safe."

"Right," said Olivia. She sounded unsure. "Right."

As Heidi watched, she couldn't help but notice the woman in the leather jacket who now seemed to be staring back at her through the gaps in the fence.

Heidi turned away. The girls did their best to ignore whatever was happening on the other side as they loaded liquor bottles into Heidi's trunk.

They got in the car and Heidi pulled out of the parking lot

and onto the street. She turned on the radio to the obnoxious baritone of an announcer speed-reading ad copy: ". . . today's economy, owning silver is a no-brainer for every smart investor! If you'd purchased just a thousand dollars of silver five years ago, your portfolio would be worth ten thousand dollars today. Don't miss out again! At Argento Rare Metals we sell silver at below market val—"

Heidi changed stations until she landed on a pop song she recognized. By the time they reached the condo complex where Olivia lived, a succession of earworms and commercials had all but erased the grim scene in the alley from the girls' minds.

There was always a moment of awkwardness when Heidi dropped Olivia off at Tower Grove. She didn't want to be rude, but Heidi just couldn't imagine living like this: families stacked on top of each other like so many Lego blocks. Sharing a common yard? Hearing your neighbors talking through the walls? But Olivia's mom was divorced and this was apparently all she could afford.

"Thanks for the ride," said Olivia as she climbed out of the car.

"Anytime you want to commit another crime, you know where to find me," said Heidi. She pantomimed shooting and then blowing the smoke away from a finger gun.

Olivia laughed, and then went quiet. She looked uncomfortable. "Heidi, I'm thinking maybe . . . I'm not going to prom."

"What?" cried Heidi. "No. You have to come. Olivia."

"I don't have a date," said Olivia, "and—I don't know. The whole thing is kind of bullshit, right? It's stupid."

"No, it isn't! I mean, it *is* stupid, yes, but it's *supposed* to be stupid. It's our last hurrah. When you look back on high school in ten years, you're going to want to have gone to prom."

"But me, right now, *doesn't* want to go, so—"

"Olivia, you have to. For me. Please. Pleeeeeeeease."

"Heidi—"

"Remember when you made me eat a bug?" asked Heidi.

"We were in fourth grade!" said Olivia.

"You made me eat a bug." Heidi crossed her arms, much like a fourth grader might. "So now you have to do this for me."

Olivia sighed. And then she gave a little smile. "Okay. Fine. Jesus."

"Yes!" cried Heidi.

For the drive home, Heidi cranked up the radio even louder than before and sang along to the music. Top 40 was, of course, a misnomer. They only played around fifteen to twenty songs at any given time, and Heidi always knew all of them. Between hits, there came a loud protracted beep. It was an emergency broadcast.

"This is a special message from the Viral Containment Task Force. This lunar cycle's supermoon will cause the moon to appear full for two nights in a row. On the nights of April fourth and fifth, please remain indoors and take all necessary precautions. If you know anyone who's been exposed to *Rabies lupinovirus* or appears to be symptomatic, don't hesitate to call our toll-free hotline at 1-800-555-4949. Your call could save a—"

Heidi changed it to the local R&B station. She knew all those songs too.

As Heidi drove, the houses she passed became older and bigger. The lawns became greener and the trees more lush and dignified. She reached the tall security fence that surrounded Cascadian Estates, the gated community where she lived.

Heidi pulled forward and the triple-reinforced titanium gate noiselessly rolled aside. The guard in the gatehouse, clad in an uncomfortable-looking Kevlar vest and an ill-fitting helmet, waved her forward with a friendly smile.

"Afternoon, Miss Mills," said the guard.

Heidi smiled and waved back as she rolled past. "Thank you!" she said. She could never remember the guy's name.

Heidi drove down a street of large multimillion-dollar houses and pulled into the driveway of her family's beautiful two-story Tudor-style home. She grabbed the mail from the mailbox and punched the security code into the front door.

In the kitchen, Heidi spread the mail out onto the marble countertop: electric bill, credit card bill, *The New Yorker*, Restoration Hardware catalog. She picked up a glossy cream-colored envelope made of thick paper stock.

It was Madeline and Ron's annual invitation to the Gray Ribbon Gala, a charity event at the Gaines Museum of Fine Art. Emblazoned on it was the Gaines Foundation's perennial slogan: A CURE WITHIN REACH.

Heidi had never wanted to go before, but maybe she would this year? A fancy charity ball seemed fun. Maybe Luca could go too. As she was considering proper evening attire, her phone pinged.

It was an email. It was an email from Harvard University's Department of Admissions. It was *the* email.

Heidi took a deep breath. Then she opened the message. As she read it, her excitement curdled into despair. Tears began to roll down her cheeks.

* * *

Hours later, night had fallen. Heidi was still sobbing on the couch under several fleece blankets. She tried to distract herself by watching TV—a silly streaming drama about doctors working on the cure. It was called *Project: Hope.*

On-screen, two incredibly attractive actors—more attractive than any real virologists had ever been—stared at one another with burning intensity.

"Have you seen the antibody levels in the latest samples?" said Dr. Hadrian Pierce, holding up a test tube to the light. "I don't want to jinx it but . . . think this could be the one, Kim."

"That's not why I'm here," said Dr. Kimberly Torres, her voice heavy with emotion. "I want to talk about what happened that night at the lake house—"

Heidi muted the TV. The show wasn't distracting her like it was supposed to. Only reminding her that she would probably never become a doctor now. She'd be the one picking up the used syringes and crusty Band-Aids.

Her phone buzzed. It was Olivia, calling like she did pretty much every night. Heidi ignored the call. Then she ignored a second one. The third time, Heidi answered and told her best friend about the rejection letter.

Olivia tried to console her. "It's not that big a deal. You'll be fine wherever you end up."

"No, I won't," said Heidi, sobbing. "My life is over. This is so fucking embarrassing. I don't even know how this happened. How am I going to tell Luca? You think it was the C that I got in tenth-grade gym?"

"I don't know," said Olivia. "Maybe there's some way to, like, talk to the admissions people or—"

"That's not how it works," snapped Heidi.

Just then, she heard a beep. It was an incoming call from "Mom."

"My fucking mom's calling again," said Heidi, "I have to go."

Heidi hung up and looked at her phone, silently ringing. She couldn't bear to answer. Heidi sent Madeline straight to voicemail.

A moment later, Heidi's phone pinged. It was a text message from her mother:

> Archana Bhagat's mom says she got
> her Harvard letter. Anything in the ✉?

Heidi snarled and felt a strong impulse to fling her phone across the room as hard as she could. But no, that wasn't the kind of thing she did. Instead, she gently placed her phone, face down, on the coffee table.

Immediately, there was another ping. Heidi turned the phone over to see yet another text message. This one was from Luca:

> yo you get in yet boo?

"Leave me the fuck alone!" screamed Heidi as she smashed her phone against the corner of the coffee table.

She instantly regretted it. The screen was now spiderwebbed with a big psychedelic rainbow-colored crack.

"Fuck," said Heidi.

She knew Luca would be pissed if she didn't text him back. He hated being left on read. But she just couldn't bring herself to do it. Instead, she hid the phone in the cushions of the couch and started to cry again.

She heard a muffled buzz from her phone, a push notification from the Lunar Cycle Countdown app, a half second before the smooth voice of the house's automated security system spoke: "Lunar Cycle lockdown will commence in one minute. For your safety, please step away from all doors and windows."

Heidi watched the hot doctors making dramatic faces on the muted TV as the suite of preprogrammed security features began to activate.

A metal roll-down gate descended from its housing above the front door. Titanium bars slid down to cover every window. At exactly 8:07 PM, Heidi's home, like every other home in the neighborhood, became an impregnable fortress.

Except, unnoticed by Heidi, a rubber shim had been inserted into the track of the roll-down gate over the house's back door. The security gate silently slowed to a stop, about halfway down.

3

Heidi's eyes popped open. She turned to look at her bedroom clock. 2:31 AM.

The house was quiet. Except . . . it wasn't. Heidi heard something. Movement. From down the hall. She reached for her phone.

Fuck. No phone. Heidi felt sick when she remembered it was stuffed in the couch cushions downstairs. She lay in bed, staring up at the shadows on the ceiling. Listening. Maybe . . . maybe she'd imagined the sound?

No. She heard it again. Someone was in her house.

Heidi felt a surge of panic. She tried to push the feeling down. She couldn't lose her head. She had to get out of the house before the intruder found her.

Quietly, Heidi rolled out of bed. She crouched on her bedroom rug for a moment and tried to control her breathing. Her hands were shaking and she couldn't get them to stop.

Heidi silently opened her bedroom door and watched and listened. A moment later, she saw the indirect beam of a flashlight at the end of the hallway. Someone was in her mom's room. She heard the sound of a drawer being dumped out and its contents being picked through.

Maybe, while they were occupied, she could escape.

As quickly as she dared, Heidi crept down the carpeted hall to the stairs. Trying not to make a sound, she carefully lifted herself over the nineteenth and the fourth steps, both known to creak. As she got to the ground floor, she heard a male voice swear upstairs. Apparently, he hadn't found what he was looking for. She hoped he wouldn't give up yet, that he would keep looking.

Her plan was to get out the back door and run to the Washburns' next door. Keeping as low as she could, Heidi started to inch across the living room on all fours. As she moved through the darkened room, her hand touched something that shouldn't be there—hard leather. It was a boot.

Heidi looked up. She saw the faint silhouette of a man standing in her living room. Two people had broken into her house. In the slanting moonlight, a revolver glinted in his hand.

"Not so fast, bitch," he whispered.

The man grabbed Heidi by the hair and dragged her back up the stairs to the master bedroom, where his accomplice was tossing out the contents of her mother's armoire.

In the eerie, indirect glow of the flashlight, Heidi could see the other burglar was roughly her age. He wore a ski mask pulled up onto the top of his head like a knit cap. She had the strange sense she recognized him from somewhere.

"Can't find the silver," he said without looking up.

"We got a bigger problem," said the man with the gun.

The one with the flashlight turned. As he finally noticed Heidi, he did a double take and quickly yanked his ski mask down over his face.

"What the fuck?" he said.

The man with the gun, who also wore his ski mask up on his head, shoved Heidi to the floor.

"Scream and you die," he said, pointing his gun at her face.

"Please don't hurt me," Heidi managed to whimper.

"Stop that," snapped the burglar with the flashlight at his partner. "And pull your mask down, for God's sake."

The one with the gun fumblingly pulled his ski mask down over his face and then had to adjust it because the eyeholes were in the wrong place.

Meanwhile, Flashlight crouched beside Heidi and spoke in a calm voice. "Forget him. He's an idiot. We're not here to hurt anybody, okay? You're gonna be fine."

"I didn't see anything," said Heidi, deliberately looking at the floor now. "I didn't see your faces."

It was the wrong thing to say.

"Goddamn it," cried the one with the gun. "She can ID us!"

"One moment, please," Flashlight said to Heidi.

Then he and his partner with the gun stepped aside to confer. Heidi had a sickening feeling that this conversation, these next few moments, would decide her fate. They were trying to whisper, but she could hear every word.

Flashlight took a deep breath. "Let me repeat: What the fuck?"

"Look, the house was supposed to be empty," protested Gun. "I follow the mom on Instagram. The whole family's in Hawaii right now!"

"Well, obviously not the *whole* family," said Flashlight through gritted teeth.

"I don't know! I guess they Home Alone'd this bitch," said Gun. "I can't account for every contingency!"

Flashlight rubbed his forehead. "I knew this job was fucked," he said almost to himself. "I knew I should've stayed home and—"

"We've got to kill her!"

Heidi winced.

"Are you out of your goddamn *mind*?" said Flashlight. "Turn a burglary charge into first-degree murder? I know you're new at this, man, but it's not a fucking video game."

Gun was panicking. "She saw our faces! We have no choice!"

"It's dark. She won't remember us," said Flashlight. "We cut our losses and leave."

Gun went quiet. He almost seemed persuaded. Then, despite commanding Heidi not to scream, he bellowed at the top of his lungs: "Where's the fucking silver!" as he pointed his gun at Heidi's face again.

Heidi closed her eyes tight. "Downstairs in the safe."

She led them down to the living room. Behind the fake Chagall that hung over the mantel (the real one was in secure storage in Utah) was a wall safe. Heidi punched in the digital code—the date her mother passed the bar—and the safe door swung open.

"See?" said Flashlight. "All's well that ends well." It sounded like he was trying to reassure his jittery partner as much as Heidi.

Just then, there was a crash from the back of the house.

"Fuck!" cried Gun. "It's the cops!"

He grabbed Heidi and pressed his revolver to her temple. Then he roughly frog-marched her into the kitchen.

"Don't shoot!" he yelled. "I have a hosta—"

The thing that was now standing in the opening of the back door wasn't a cop.

It looked *wrong*. Its shape, its proportions, even its movements didn't match what the brain expected to see. And no matter how much footage you'd seen on TV, that never changed. It was ropy and fleshy, covered in patchy tufts of coarse fur (or hair). Its eyes gleamed in the darkness, but they weren't the eyes of an animal. The lips were pulled back to reveal a mouth full of sharklike teeth, a snarl that was also a smile. It was an amalgam that shouldn't exist. And yet the fundamental awkwardness of its form belied an ungodly speed—the speed that all killers possess.

In half a second the creature had closed the distance from the back door to the kitchen. As it charged, the burglar barely had time to point his gun away from Heidi and toward the beast.

BANG! BANG! BANG! BANG! BANG! BANG!

As he unloaded all six shots of his .38 special into the thing, Heidi wriggled out of his grasp.

Whether any of the six bullets hit, the creature was unfazed. With a huge swipe of its claws, it ripped open the burglar's stomach and the soft, wet mass of his intestines spilled out onto the kitchen floor. He was dead before he hit the tiles.

Heidi ran for her life. But the werewolf had turned its attention to the other thief. It pounced on him.

Behind her, Heidi heard the sounds of a savage mauling as she raced through her darkened house. In the dining room, her foot caught on a corner of the rug and she fell hard onto the floor.

An instant later, she felt the weight of the beast land on her back, smashing the air out of her lungs and cracking her ribs.

The werewolf violently flipped her over. She smelled the stench of its breath, now tinged with the sharp iron of blood. It was going to tear her throat out.

"Fuck you!" bellowed Flashlight as he came barreling out of the kitchen and shoulder-checked the werewolf, shifting its weight off Heidi.

But the beast was far stronger. With a snarl it spun and flung him across the room. He landed in a heap on the other side of the dining room table.

This bought Heidi a second to act. She squirmed away and made for the living room. She groped into the safe and came out with a fork—part of a forty-six-piece set of Grande Baroque flatware that had been a wedding gift to her great-grandmother. The family silver.

She could feel the werewolf bearing down on her. Heidi screamed and spun, stabbing wildly with the fork. By luck or by miracle, she stabbed it into the soft flesh of the thing's neck.

The beast let out a squeal of pure agony. In an instant, it had fled out the open back door and into the darkness beyond.

4

Every muscle in Heidi's body was trembling from the adrenaline coursing through her. Miraculously, she was alive. She wanted to cry, but somehow her body wouldn't comply.

She realized the antique fork was still clutched in her fist. *I should really wash this fork*, Heidi thought before realizing how absurd that was. Instead, she wiped it on the back of the couch and shoved it in her pocket.

Just then, Heidi heard a moan. Flashlight was lying in a heap of broken furniture in the corner of the dining room. Apparently, he was still alive too. For a moment, Heidi didn't know what to say. The man had broken into her house with the intention of robbing her family. But—but he'd also just saved her life.

"Are you . . . okay?" she asked.

"My legs," he said from the floor. "Fucking thing got my legs."

Heidi inched close enough to see that, indeed, his legs were covered in bloody wounds where it had savaged him with its fangs and claws.

She gasped. A thousand public service announcements and CDC press conferences about how the virus spreads were suddenly echoing in her mind.

"Okay," said Heidi, "let me just . . . I think we have bandages in the medicine cabinet. Hang on."

Instead, Heidi ran to the living room. She dug into the couch cushions and fished out her phone. Despite the big spiderweb crack, it still worked. Discreetly, she started to punch in a number that had been relentlessly drilled into her subconscious for the last five years. She didn't even know she knew it by heart: 1-800-555-4949.

"Who are you calling?"

Heidi turned to see the burglar. Somehow, despite the wounds on his legs, he was on his feet. He leaned heavily on the wall, but he looked deadly serious.

"That thing—when it attacked you, it broke the skin," said Heidi. "Saliva is how lupinovirus spreads."

"I know that."

Heidi took a step back. "So I'm calling the VCTF hotline so—so we can get you some help."

"Put the phone down." He took a lurching step toward her.

"What?"

"Heidi, put the phone down, now!" He stumbled forward and almost fell, catching himself on the back of the couch.

Heidi backed away farther. "No."

"Look," he said, as he pointed at Heidi's arm.

Heidi did. Somehow, she hadn't noticed it, but the werewolf's fangs had left a bloody bite mark on her biceps.

The burglar pulled his ski mask off to show his face again. He looked scared but his voice was calm. "I'm infected," he said. "You are too."

Heidi's mind began to race. *Infected?* Intellectually, she knew there was a pandemic. Of course she knew there was a pandemic—it was on the news every single day. It was all some people could talk or even think about. But getting infected was . . . it was the kind of thing that happened to others. She'd never even known a single person who'd contracted *Rabies lupinovirus*. People at her school didn't get infected. People in this neighborhood didn't get infected.

"If anybody is exposed," said Heidi, "what you're supposed to do is—you're supposed to call the hotline."

The burglar took a deep breath. "Seems like you need a reality check, so let me lay it out for you: Once you have the virus, the Dogcatchers—the VCTF—they don't give a shit. You may think because you're rich, and you live in this house, it'll make a difference. It won't."

"You're *supposed* to call the hotline," said Heidi, doubling down.

"If you call that number, I promise you, we'll either get a silver bullet to the head, or we'll get quarantined for the rest of our lives."

"How do you know?" asked Heidi.

"I just know," said the burglar.

"Quarantine is just until they find a cure," said Heidi.

"How long's it been?" he asked. "Almost five years now? Quarantine is prison."

"There are state-of-the-art facilities—"

"Yes, maybe *your* prison will have nicer wallpaper than mine. Vegan options on the menu or whatever. But it will still be prison. They're not going let you leave. You'll never come home. You won't be allowed close to anyone you love—not your mommy, or your daddy, or your little boyfriend—ever again. So why don't you just put down the phone, and—and we can discuss the situation."

He was pleading now, almost desperate.

Heidi was not one to question authority. The first eighteen years of her life had instilled in her a deep, reflexive faith in the status quo. The world made sense. Follow the rules and you will be rewarded. Putting down the phone, *not* calling the Viral Containment Task Force and immediately reporting a confirmed—no, *two* confirmed lupinovirus exposures—went against every fiber of her being. But . . .

Heidi wasn't stupid either. What he was saying made sense. Her mind flashed to the #WolfKill videos she sometimes saw the boys at school watching. These were compilations of smartphone footage set to music that showed VCTF officers slaughtering werewolves in particularly "cool" ways. She'd never seen a single video where they were peacefully taken alive . . .

"Okay," said Heidi at last. She lowered her phone.

The burglar breathed a sigh of relief.

Just then, they heard a voice blare through a loudspeaker outside on the street: "Warning: Lycanthropic activity has been reported in the area. Officers of the Viral Containment Task Force will be conducting a residence-by-residence sweep. Any resistance will be taken as evidence of infection."

The burglar took a quick peek through the curtain. "Damn it. Too late."

Heidi looked too. Outside the house, three VCTF BearCats were parked in the middle of the street, flashers on.

She watched as dozens of VCTF officers exited these vehicles. They had more than truncheons this time. They carried flamethrowers and automatic weapons loaded with silver bullets. In groups of two or three, these officers began to fan out through the neighborhood.

"Any second the Dogcatchers are going to be banging on

your front door," said the burglar. "We've got to go. Out the back. Now."

Heidi didn't know what to say. "I . . . I don't even know your name."

"I'm trying to save your life!" he hissed.

It was a moment of truth for Heidi. How could she decide in a split second to leave the life she knew behind and follow some criminal who'd tried to rob her house? She looked at the bite on her arm, already surrounded by a bright pink rash. She was infected now, and she had a dawning realization that none of the rules she'd tried to live by applied anymore.

"Okay," Heidi said at last.

And both of them ran out the back door and into the darkness beyond.

5

Officer Erik Balikian—call sign "Caveman"—quietly swept through the dark suburban neighborhood, Heckler & Koch MP5 submachine gun in hand. His eyes were peeled for any sign of a 10–91W. He was a rookie, just a year out of high school, in fact. This was only his second LCC (Lunar Cycle Curfew) and right now his heart was beating so fast it felt like it might smash its way out of his rib cage and flop out onto the pavement.

Last month he didn't get to do shit. He got stuck guarding some mall in Wedgwood. Nothing happened. And, as any real Dogcatcher would tell you, the twenty-seven days between LCCs don't even count.

Tonight felt different. There was something in the air. Deep down, Erik knew he was finally going to see some action. He'd get to do what he signed up for. Serve the community. Kick some ass.

Every so often, Erik stole a glance at his partner for this sweep. Corporal Jason Mottola—call sign "Reaper"—was only ten years older than Erik but he was already a legend. The necklace of fangs around his neck told you everything you needed to know: more confirmed kills than anyone else on the force. That's how you get a call sign like "Reaper." (By contrast, Erik had been christened "Caveman" by his academy classmates on account of his thick unibrow. Erik had since shaved it but he was leaning in to the nickname. Cavemen were strong as shit, right?)

If Erik could do half of what Reaper had done by age thirty, he'd be proud of his time on the VCTF. He really, *really* did not want to embarrass himself in front of this man.

As Reaper walked, he didn't seem nervous or excited. He seemed loose, almost bored. The big Angel of Death patch on his right shoulder gleamed in the amber glow of the streetlights.

"Look," said Reaper. He nodded at the ground. There was a spatter of something dark on the sidewalk.

Erik crouched and ran a gloved finger through the liquid. He smelled it. Definitely blood. And it was fresh.

"Fucker went that way," said Reaper, indicating some broken branches through an azalea bush. "Better call it in."

Erik spoke into his portable radio. "This is Caveman. We got blood and what appear to be tracks headed southeast into a wooded area between"—he checked the nearby street signs—"Elmwood and King. Over."

The dispatcher's voice crackled over the radio: "10–4, Caveman. You and Reaper hold position and wait for backup. Over."

"Copy that," said Erik. "Over and out."

Click. He ended the transmission. Reaper shook his head.

"Hold position while it gets away," said Reaper. "Like these fuckers can't run forty miles an hour. Unbelievable."

So Erik wouldn't see any action tonight after all. Reaper checked his phone as he lit up a Marlboro.

"Nah," said Erik. "Fuck that. I want to drop this thing."

Reaper paused. Then he cocked his head, perhaps reappraising the nameless rookie he'd been randomly paired with tonight. "Atta boy, Rook."

Reaper carefully stubbed out the cigarette and slid it behind his ear for later, then the two of them pushed through the bushes and into the woods.

Away from the streetlights, Erik and Reaper flipped down their night vision goggles. The trunks of the trees were now a luminous green. Their leaves glowed like eyes. As the pair trudged forward, Reaper silently pointed to a spot up ahead where the ground sunk down into a wash.

As they approached, they could see a trickle of water flowing into a five-foot storm drain tunnel. They quietly stalked down into the wash and took up positions on either side of the tunnel mouth.

Reaper took a quick peek inside. He gave Erik a nod. The meaning was clear: Yep, the thing's in there.

"Party time, Caveman," whispered Reaper. He patted Erik on the helmet and disappeared into the woods toward the other end of the tunnel.

Erik Balikian stood alone beside the pitch-black mouth of the tunnel. His adrenaline was pumping. His pulse was probably somewhere north of 120. He felt like he might be hyperventilating. Carefully, so as not to drop them in the muck at his feet, he put in his Bluetooth headphones. Then he cranked his music—the speed metal he always listened to while working out—way, way up.

This was it. This was what he'd signed up for. He was terrified. He was a stone-cold killer. He was a goddamn Dogcatcher.

Erik turned on his bodycam and kissed the silver cross on the chain around his neck. Then he pulled the pin and hurled a flashbang into the tunnel. An instant later, a deafening boom echoed off the cylindrical walls of the tunnel. A wisp of pale smoke billowed out of the mouth.

"Cry 'Havoc' motherfucker!" screamed Erik at the top of his lungs. "And let slip the dogs of war!"

Then he flipped down his night vision goggles and charged into the storm drain.

Almost instantly, Erik realized his mistake. Thanks to the smoky haze of the flashbang, he couldn't see anything, even with the goggles.

But Erik pressed forward anyway, sloshing through the ankle-deep water. As he advanced, he started to fire indiscriminate bursts from his MP5.

RATTA-TAT . . . RATTA-TAT . . .

The amplified echo of the shots was so loud he thought he might blow out his eardrums. He started coughing from the smoke of the flashbang.

RATTA—

Erik's MP5 jammed.

"Fuck," he said to no one.

Erik tried to clear the jam but he couldn't see. He flipped up the night vision goggles. It was too dark. His hands were shaking. His nerves were too jangled.

"Goddamn it. Fuck. Fuck . . ."

Erik took a step back. Every fiber of his being was flooded with primordial terror. It was the fear of the cave bear, and the fear of the mountain lion; the fear that connected ten thousand generations of humanity to this moment.

The decision was made by his autonomic nervous system. Erik turned to run. He made it two steps when a massive beast leaped out of the swirling smoke and smashed into his back like a freight train.

As he hit the ground, Erik had the curious sensation of watching himself. He saw bear-trap jaws snap around the Kevlar armor on his arm. With a flick of the beast's head, there was a muffled pop. It had dislocated his shoulder. A half second later, Erik heard himself scream.

With a snarl, the beast began to shake Erik like a rag doll, bashing him against the walls of the tunnel. His tactical armor might protect him from the bites but some strangely rational part of Erik understood that the human body couldn't survive this punishment for long.

"Over here, sweetheart."

The werewolf spun and a burst of silver bullets from Reaper's MP5 blew its lower jaw up through its brainpan. The werewolf wobbled, then slumped into a ragged heap. Dead.

As Balikian's hearing returned, he could hear Reaper laughing. The older Dogcatcher extended a hand and pulled Erik to his feet. "Got your bell rung, huh?"

Erik felt his arm hanging limp and useless, like a piece of uncooked bacon. He tried to say something but he was still too rattled to form a coherent sentence.

Meanwhile, Reaper used his flashlight to give Erik the once-over, checking to see if any of the bites had penetrated his VCTF tactical armor.

"Oh shit," said Reaper, his tone suddenly serious.

"What?" said Erik. He couldn't see what Reaper was looking at on his back.

"Fuck," said Reaper. "I'm sorry, dude. I don't want to have to do this."

Reaper raised his MP5.

"No!" screamed Erik, stumbling backward. "C'mon man, please—"

Reaper broke down laughing even harder than before. "Nah. You're clean. No bites. Congrats, kid."

He slapped Erik on the top of the helmet, friendly if a little too hard. Erik tried to laugh. The dull ache in his arm was becoming a throbbing pain.

"Bad news is," said Reaper, "my kill. Not yours."

Reaper crouched in the water beside the hairy carcass and produced a pair of silver-plated pliers from his belt. He reached into what was left of the thing's face and wrenched a bloody fang out of the werewolf's upper jaw. He grinned at the white tooth shining in the darkness—another one for the necklace.

"Your arm broke?" asked Reaper.

"I don't think so," said Erik.

"Should get some PTO anyway," said Reaper. "Now you know how we do it, Caveman."

The two of them walked toward the mouth of the tunnel. Reaper took the cigarette from behind his ear and lit it up. Then he radioed the dispatcher.

"This is Reaper. 10–91W located and neutralized."

"10–4, Reaper," said the dispatcher. "Nice job. We'll send in the cleanup crew."

Reaper took a long drag on his cigarette. Erik paused. He turned and shined his flashlight back toward the dead werewolf.

Instead, he saw the pale, naked body of an elderly woman lying in the dirty water. The top of her skull had been blown off, her lower jaw was a pulp, and there was now a gap where the upper left canine tooth used to be.

6

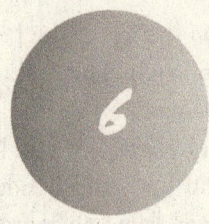

"How did you know my name?" asked Heidi.

"What?" whispered the burglar, startled by the sound of her voice.

"You called me by my name earlier. You said 'Heidi, put the phone down.'"

They'd been silent for minutes, crouched in the bushes on the edge of a large lawn. They'd heard gunfire in the distance and were listening for more. Heidi was terrified, but the waiting had given her a few moments to think.

"I don't know," he said, exasperated. "I probably saw it on a piece of mail or something. I'm Cam, by the way."

There was a moment of awkward silence.

"So I know your name and you know my name," he said. "Now we know each other."

"Okay. Nice to meet you . . . I guess?" said Heidi. "Do you think they killed it?"

"No idea," said Cam. "But we need to move."

With that, Cam started out across the lawn, striding with an awkward limp. But he only made it fifteen feet before he had to desperately scramble back to the bushes.

"Shit shit shit," he said.

A moment later, the searchlight of a passing VCTF BearCat

scanned the neighborhood. The beam passed right over the bush where they were hiding. The light blinded Heidi for a moment, and then they were in darkness again. Apparently, they hadn't been spotted. Heidi and Cam held their breath and waited for the vehicle to disappear down the block.

"All right," said Cam. "Now."

He started forward, but this time Heidi grabbed his arm.

"Wait," said Heidi. "Where are we even going?"

"This whole neighborhood is crawling with Dogcatchers. If we can get out of here, I know a safe place."

"Cascadian Estates is a gated community," said Heidi. "The only way out is through the gate."

"Not quite," said Cam. "Follow me."

Before Heidi could ask any more questions, Cam limped fast across the yard toward the street. They crossed two more lawns and once again plunged into one of the dark wooded areas that gave the neighborhood so much of its charm.

At last, Heidi and Cam reached the twelve-foot security fence that completely surrounded the neighborhood. It was made of vertical steel slats, six inches apart. There was no way to scale it.

"Told you," Heidi said.

"Hang on."

Cam turned and aligned himself with a light pole. He touched the fence and began to count slats as he walked forward. He stopped at the ninth one and shoulder-checked it. The bottom of the slat swung loose from the fence.

"It's how we got in." Cam held the loose slat aside. "After you."

The gap was narrow but just big enough for Heidi to squeeze through. Cam followed her.

The pair now found themselves on an empty wooded road.

After a quarter mile, they came to a car. It was a beat-up ten-year-old Kia, pulled off to the side and mostly hidden by the overhanging trees.

"My ride," said Cam.

Cam got into the driver's side, and Heidi moved to get into the passenger's side but paused when she saw the seat was filled with old fast-food containers and other trash.

"Sorry," said Cam, as he swept the trash onto the floorboard for Heidi to sit down.

He cranked the ignition. The engine wheezed and whined for at least three seconds before turning over. This momentary reprieve was enough for Heidi's terror to give way to rational thought.

"Wait, this is insane," said Heidi. "I'm going with a criminal to a second location. No, I can't do this."

"Too late," said Cam.

The tires of the Kia squealed as he pulled out onto the empty street.

"Seriously," said Heidi. "Let me out of the car. Right now or I'll scream!"

Cam looked at her. Then he shrugged and rolled the car to a stop. He leaned across and opened the passenger's-side door for her.

As the "door open" sound faintly chimed, Heidi was motionless and her mind continued to churn. What would happen if she went back? What would she tell the VCTF? What would they do? Had she already committed a crime by fleeing? Would she really never see her mom again if she got quarantined? Each outcome she imagined was worse than the last.

She didn't get out of the car.

"Yeah," said Cam, at last. "I didn't think so."

Cam accelerated, causing the passenger's-side door to close on its own. The Kia was now gliding through the darkness, headlights off. Heidi strained to see the road ahead.

"What about the curfew?" she asked. "Nobody's supposed to be out after dark."

"Exactly. That's why nobody will see us if we stick to the back streets and keep the lights off. Trust me, I've done this a million times before. It's why we picked tonight to . . ." He trailed off.

"To rob my house?" Heidi finished his sentence.

Cam shrugged and mumbled something Heidi couldn't make out.

Heidi had never been outside during a Lunar Cycle Curfew. She was afraid. But the world was oddly quiet. The full moon hung big and heavy, painting the trees silver. She'd never looked at the moon much. Tonight it was so large she felt like she could pick out every crack and crater on its surface.

Heidi realized she was scratching her arm. The bite mark was now painfully swollen and the area around it was bright reddish purple. She stopped scratching.

"Why are you helping me exactly?" she asked.

Cam kept his eyes on the road. "'Cause you need help. Obviously."

"Home invader with a heart of gold," said Heidi. "Sure."

Cam cracked a little smile. But it faded almost instantly as he saw something up ahead: red and blue lights dancing on the leaves of the trees.

"Damn it," said Cam.

Up ahead was a VCTF roadblock. The vehicles had their flashers on. There was nowhere for Cam to discreetly turn around.

"Turn on the headlights," said Heidi.

"But—"

"Turn them on."

Cam did.

The Kia rolled to a stop at the checkpoint. A VCTF officer in full body armor shined his 400-lumen LED flashlight right in Cam's face. Cam squinted and turned away.

"Why were you riding with your lights off?" asked the officer.

"We—"

Heidi leaned over so it was her that the officer was talking to. She gave him her brightest smile. Confidence was everything.

"Good evening, Officer," she said. "Are we in trouble?"

"You're violating curfew," he said. "You need to step out of the vehicle."

Heidi frowned. "Look, this is *totally* my fault. I accidentally left the back door open because I was burning some incense, and my cat Quinoa, she got out. He *totally* didn't want to, but I made him drive me around to look for her 'cause I'm scared, because what if, like, Quinoa gets eaten by . . . you know, one of those *things*? So, like, take *me* to jail, or whatever, but please don't punish him. He's just trying to be a good boyfriend."

Heidi clutched Cam's hand. Cam stared straight ahead.

The officer was quiet for a long moment. "Just get home. Now. It's not safe out here."

"Oh my God, *thank you*," said Heidi. "And if you see my cat Quinoa, she's an Egyptian mau, can you please, please text me?" She scribbled a phone number on a scrap of paper and handed it to the officer.

He stared at the number in silence. Then he pocketed it. "Will do. Move along."

Cam rolled through the checkpoint and continued down the

street. Once the roadblock was a half mile in the rearview mirror, he finally exhaled.

"What the *fuck* was that?" asked Cam.

"What?" said Heidi.

"You did some kind of rich-girl Jedi mind trick," said Cam.

Heidi frowned. "Fuck off."

"Do you think he's going to text you about the cat?" asked Cam.

"It was a fake number," said Heidi. "Just drive."

Cam cut the headlights again.

The Kia wound its way toward the poor side of town. Here, there were no high-tech security systems or armed gate guards keeping watch over these neighborhoods. Instead, people had protected their homes with makeshift barricades of barbed wire, old cars, broken furniture, and sharpened wooden stakes.

The lights inside most buildings were off—"excess illumination" was prohibited during Lunar Cycle Curfew hours—but makeshift torches and barrel fires blazed outside others. The infected were known to avoid open flames. The stink of oily smoke hung in the air from these ad hoc deterrents, making the neighborhood feel more like a medieval village than a twenty-first-century city.

"We're not far from my place," said Cam. "If we can get there, we should be— Wow."

Heidi saw it too. The road was splattered with red viscera and covered in hundreds of large green eggs. It took her a second to realize she was looking at watermelons. Many of them were crushed, spilling their juice and pulp onto the blacktop.

As they rounded a curve, a wrecked refrigerator truck came into view. The truck was flipped on its side, blocking the road ahead. Cam rolled to a stop.

Heidi stared at the scene, trying to make sense of what had happened.

Suddenly, a man covered in blood slammed himself against the passenger's-side window, startling Heidi and Cam.

"Help me!" screamed the bloody man, his breath fogging the glass. "My truck flipped. I need a doctor!"

His hand left a perfect print, in blood, where he'd slapped the window.

Cam hesitated. "Okay—okay, we'll get you to a hospital."

He leaned to manually unlock the back right door.

"Look!" cried Heidi. She pointed to movement in the shadows at the edge of the road. Several pairs of animal eyes gleamed in the moonlight beyond the streetlights.

"Fuck," said Cam.

He threw the Kia into reverse and hit the gas. The bloody trucker stumbled as the car slid away from him.

"Hey!" he screamed. "Don't drive away! Don't leave m—"

Suddenly, a big dark shape tackled the trucker off his feet. Heidi didn't look but she could hear the man's screams, even as the Kia sped away, going backward.

As Cam floored it in reverse, other werewolves—intermittently visible in the pools of light and shadow—began to run after the car. Heidi couldn't believe how fast they were. They had to be running at least thirty miles per hour.

Cam kept up a steady stream of curses as he drove backward. "Fuckfuckfuckfuck . . ."

"Turn around!" screamed Heidi.

Cam yanked the wheel and attempted to do a three-point turn at speed. Heidi's head suddenly slammed backward into the seat as Cam accidentally smashed the back of the Kia into a mailbox, crumpling the back bumper.

"Mailbox," said Heidi.

"Yeah, thank you, I see that now!" yelled Cam.

Cam swerved and the Kia was going forward now. He stomped on the gas and Heidi watched the speedometer needle push up to ninety. Without the headlights, the road ahead was a dark blur, invisible but for the occasional streetlight.

"Watch out!" screamed Heidi.

Cam swerved at a sharp curve in the road and narrowly avoided jumping the curb and wrapping the car around a light pole.

"Turn the fucking lights on!" said Heidi, who usually did not curse.

Cam did.

The road ahead was suddenly bathed in light. Twenty feet in front of the speeding Kia stood a woman with a short punk haircut wearing a leather jacket. Time seemed to slow, and for a fraction of a second, her gray eyes met Heidi's.

Cam jerked the wheel to avoid killing her and the Kia flipped.

7

The Kia spun through the air, rolling once, twice, and landing in a muddy ditch ten feet from the road. Miraculously, the car had landed on its wheels. Unfortunately, it was facing the opposite direction Cam had been driving.

Heidi blinked. For a moment, she didn't quite know where she was or what was happening. She looked over to see a young man in the driver's side beside her, his head slumped forward. Heidi tried to remember his name. Was it Luca? No, he had an even shorter name than that . . .

"Cam," said Heidi nudging his shoulder. "Are you okay?"

Cam groaned. He was alive. That was good. But . . . but they should be driving, thought Heidi. She remembered the dark shapes gliding through the shadows, running after the car.

"Come on," said Heidi. "Drive." She shook him harder. Apparently, he had hit his head on the steering wheel during the crash.

"They're going to catch up to us," said Heidi, thinking of the awful speed with which the things could move. "You have to drive the car. Now!"

"Okay . . . okay," said Cam, trying to shake off the brain fog.

He punched the accelerator but the Kia's wheels whined and spun uselessly in the mud.

"We're stuck," said Cam.

"Then—then we have to run," said Heidi.

Heidi stumbled out of the vehicle and nearly slipped in the mud. The car was sitting on a patch of yellow grass beside the road. On the hill above them, streetlights gleamed.

Heidi helped Cam out and the two of them clambered through the darkness and up the muddy hill. They climbed through the weeds and over a guardrail and found themselves on a street in what looked to be a run-down residential neighborhood. Most of the houses were shuttered, with their lights off.

Heidi stopped and listened. Just as she was wondering if they might not have been followed, after all, a howl rang out in the distance. She couldn't tell how far back. A moment later, it was answered by more howls. They sounded closer. The pack was on their trail.

"Maybe someone will let us in," said Heidi, trying to control her panic.

Cam said nothing. He still looked dazed from the crash. Heidi ran past several dark houses toward one with two fires blazing in the front yard.

As she got closer, she could see that barricades made of chicken wire and sharpened scrap metal had been affixed to the doors and windows. She had the embarrassing realization that she'd never even stopped to consider what people who didn't own top-of-the-line security systems did every full moon.

Heidi approached the house and called out: "Hello? Please! Let us in!"

From inside, someone yelled back: "Get the fuck out of here!" Whoever it was, they sounded as terrified as Heidi felt.

"We need help," said Heidi. "Please. There are—"

A gunshot rang out and Heidi heard the whiz of the bullet as it flew past her ear.

Before Heidi's mind could catch up to reality, Cam grabbed her by the elbow and they were running. Was that a warning shot? Or did they just miss?

"Where do we go now?" said Heidi.

"My apartment isn't far from here but I don't think we'll make it," said Cam, looking over his shoulder. "They'll catch up to us for sure."

Just then, they both heard a voice from down the block: "Over here."

Up ahead, the front door of a shabby row house had been opened eight inches. A hand extended from the sliver of darkness and waved them forward.

"Hurry," a woman's voice hissed from inside.

Heidi and Cam ran up the steps and into the house. A middle-aged woman slammed the door behind them and quickly triple barred the door with three heavy planks, old railroad ties by the look of them.

"Thank you," said Heidi. "We—"

"Shh," the woman said, "they're coming."

The woman pressed her eye to the peephole in the door. Heidi now saw that she was clutching a revolver in her hand. In addition to what she had loaded in the gun, three bullets stood upright on an end table by the door. Their tips gleamed silver.

Cam pressed his face against a gap in the boarded-up windows. Heidi shivered. They waited.

As Heidi's eyes adjusted to the darkness, she realized that she was being watched. A boy of about ten and a girl of six, brother and sister by the look of them, were sitting on the steps nearby. Both children were completely silent.

Heidi turned away. Then she looked back. The little girl was still staring at her. Heidi tried to smile and gave a little wave. The girl didn't smile or wave back. Heidi realized that she was looking at her arm.

Even in the darkness, Heidi could see that her wound looked puffy and infected. The outline of tooth marks was obvious. Everyone in America, even kids, knew how the virus spread. As casually as she could, Heidi angled herself away from the girl so that the bite mark could no longer be seen.

"There," whispered Cam.

Heidi peered through the gap. Out on the street, a number of dark shapes silently loped through the neighborhood. They kept to the darkness, avoiding the pools of light cast by the streetlights. They were on the hunt. Some of them moved on four legs, others on two. Heidi held her breath and watched as the pack continued on past the house and disappeared down the street.

Cam and Heidi kept their eyes locked on the street for several minutes longer.

"I think they're gone," whispered Cam, at last.

Heidi nodded. She glanced over her shoulder at the little girl. Still staring at Heidi. The girl leaned over and whispered something in her brother's ear. The boy's eyes darted to Heidi's arm. Heidi felt her wound throb.

"How far are we from your place?" whispered Heidi to Cam.

"About fourteen blocks," whispered Cam.

"It's safe there?"

Cam nodded.

"Then we should go," said Heidi, "before those *things* come back."

Cam hung his head in a mixture of fear and exhaustion. Then he took a deep breath. "Yeah. You're right." He nodded toward the kids. "We can't put them in any more danger." Cam turned and spoke to their mother. "Thank you. You saved our lives."

The woman clasped Cam's hands and nodded. "We've got to look out for each other. That's the only way through this."

She unbarred the door and Heidi and Cam quietly slipped out of the house and into the night. Just as quickly, she shut and barricaded it behind them.

Cam took off in an awkward, limping run. If Heidi's arm was bothering her this much, she could only imagine how badly his wounded legs must hurt.

"Can you make it?" she asked.

Cam gave a sour laugh. "Do I have a choice?"

They jogged through the neighborhood, down a hill, and onto a commercial street. Heidi routinely ran ten times the distance, but at the moment, she found herself sweating profusely. She was lightheaded and despite the exertion, she felt cold all over.

They passed corner stores, and dollar stores, and pizzerias all shuttered and locked with the best security measures their owners could afford.

"Not far now," said Cam. "We're gonna make it."

Suddenly, Heidi caught a scent, some pungent animal stench carried on the wind. As she ran, she turned and looked back down the street behind them.

The massive shape of a dark-furred beast was momentarily visible in the red glow cast by the LED ticker in a convenience store window. Just as quickly, the thing disappeared into the darkness.

"There's one still after us!" said Heidi.

Cam glanced over his shoulder. "Fuck!"

He turned and sprinted down a side street. Heidi followed and watched Cam quickly scale a tall chain-link fence surrounding a weedy vacant lot between two apartment buildings. He landed with a pained groan on the other side.

Heidi started to climb the fence too, but her sneaker slipped and she fell back to the ground.

Cam was on his feet now and scrambling up the other side to offer Heidi a hand. "C'mon!"

Heidi smelled the animal stink again. There was no time. The thing was closing on her fast.

She jumped to her feet and raced down a trash-filled alley. As the alley curved, she could see that it was a dead end. Desperately, she tried to open the rusty emergency exit of one of the buildings. Locked.

Heidi pounded on the door and screamed. "Somebody open up! Please!"

Then she felt herself go quiet. Before she even turned, she knew it was there: a hulking monster at the mouth of the alley, silhouetted against the streetlights beyond, its twisted shape casting a long shadow.

Heidi scrambled backward, catching her foot on a broken wooden pallet. She fell to the pavement. And before she could scream, the werewolf was on her.

8

Time passed in milliseconds. A scream started in Heidi's guts, but by the time it reached her throat it was only a choked whimper.

For some reason, though, her fear-addled brain still recoiled at the smell. The thing pinning her to the pavement reeked of musk and sweat and blood and decay. It was sickening.

The beast loomed over her, its hot, rank breath blowing in her face and ropy strands of saliva dangling from its crooked fangs. Its eyes glimmered in the darkness, faintly reflecting the streetlights at the end of the alley. Its posture was awkwardly hunched, an animal that was neither properly biped nor quadruped. The werewolf's elongated forelimbs ended in knobby paws—not quite feet, not quite hands. The toes (or fingers?) had hooked claws like the talons of a hawk.

With its weight on her legs, the werewolf stared at Heidi and gave a low, wet growl. At this moment, it occurred to the distant, rational part of her mind to wonder why she wasn't dead already.

Looking back into its misshapen nightmare of a face, Heidi perceived something she couldn't quite place. She realized the wolf's eyes were slate gray.

Fight or flight. In a burst of strength, Heidi squirmed backward on the ground, uselessly kicking at the beast. It only hooked its claws into the flesh of her calf muscle and dragged her back, as easily as a cat toying with a mouse.

Fight, then. Heidi reached in her pocket and pulled out the silver fork. With all her strength she levered herself up off the ground and tried to plunge it into the creature's eye.

But the beast was ungodly fast. It easily caught Heidi's forearm in an awkward iron grip. With its gray eyes still locked on hers, the wolf slowly tightened its hold around Heidi's wrist. She felt ligaments stretch, and bone grind against bone, and then she heard a muffled crack. Heidi felt a bolt of pure agony as her ulna snapped and her fingers involuntarily released the fork. This time she *did* scream.

The wolf swept the fork into a storm drain and pulled Heidi close for the killing bite.

But the bite didn't come. Instead, the wolf pressed its snout against her upper arm and sniffed at the puckered wound she'd gotten earlier.

And then, in an instant, the wolf released her and bounded off down the alley in a blur, disappearing from sight.

Heidi stumbled out onto the street a minute later, clutching her broken wrist. She scanned the area and saw nothing. The black-furred werewolf was gone.

Heidi took a few uncertain steps and realized she had no idea where she was going. Her heart was still pounding and she was shaking all over. For the second time that night, she'd been a hair's breadth away from dying. Heidi doubled over and tried to clear her swimming vision.

She heard a disembodied voice, somewhere between a whisper and a shout: "Over here!"

It was Cam. Thirty feet ahead, he crawled out from under a florist's van parked on the street.

"You okay?"

"I think my arm's broken," said Heidi. Though now the stabbing pain had faded to a throbbing ache. She realized she was probably in shock.

"That's all?" Cam sounded astonished.

"What, are you disappointed?"

"No, no, I mean, sorry," said Cam. "I'm glad you're okay. I just don't understand how come it . . . it just ran away."

Heidi started to answer but realized she couldn't. Why *hadn't* it killed her? She looked at the bite mark on her arm. Whitish pus now oozed from the punctured flesh. The sight of it made her feel dizzy. She wobbled and caught herself on a parking meter.

Cam looked concerned. "C'mon. My place is just down the block."

Soon, they were standing in front of an ugly gray two-story apartment complex that made Olivia's condo building look like the Ritz. For what it was worth, the complex seemed to have better lunar cycle security than some of the other buildings nearby. A graffiti-covered roll-down gate blocked the entrance to the inner courtyard.

Heidi felt a surge of panic. "Can we even get in?"

Cam nodded toward the gate. "It's padlocked from the inside. But there's another way."

He led Heidi around to the back of the building, past dumpsters piled high with trash, to a fire door.

"Doesn't opening that set off an alarm or something?" asked Heidi.

Cam chuckled. "Nope. Either the management company turned it off or they never installed it in the first place."

"Isn't that illegal?"

"Probably."

Cam reached in his pocket and pulled out a black Velcro wallet. Inside it was a set of small steel implements.

"Lockpicks?" said Heidi.

"Yeah, so?" said Cam, who suddenly sounded defensive.

"So nothing," said Heidi. She turned away and scanned the empty streets for any more danger.

A minute later, Cam had the door open. He led Heidi through a dank laundry room and up a fluorescent-lit stairwell to the courtyard and then up another set of outdoor stairs to apartment 2J.

His apartment, like all the others, had been outfitted with a flimsy outer security door made of aluminum. It didn't look like it would stand up to a strong wind, much less a werewolf. This time Cam at least opened it with a proper key.

Beyond was a small one-bedroom with a faintly stale smell that reminded Heidi of fried potatoes. The place was cluttered with delivery boxes and takeout containers, just like Cam's car. There were two large holes by the door, where it looked like someone had kicked the drywall.

Cam moved quickly to snatch a pair of boxer shorts up off the floor, which he subtly tried to hide behind his back.

"Sorry. Place is kind of a mess."

"You live alone," said Heidi.

"How could you tell?"

Heidi stepped in and Cam locked the door behind her. Her body felt heavy and achy but she didn't want to sit down, not on the ratty old polyester love seat. She didn't even want to guess what the gray stain on the cushion was.

"Is it cold in here?" asked Heidi.

"Thermostat's set at . . . well, the thermostat's been broken the whole time I've lived here," said Cam. "I can get out the space heater."

Cam disappeared down the short hall that led to the bedroom and came back with a small heater. He turned it on, and Heidi wrinkled her nose at the acrid scent of burning dust.

"Need anything else?" asked Cam. "You hungry? Thirsty?"

Even if her stomach wasn't already churning, the thought of eating anything in this apartment would've made Heidi queasy. She was thirsty though.

"Just a glass of water," she said.

"Sure. Is tap water okay?"

"You don't have to ask me that." Annoyance crept into Heidi's voice. "I don't need a San Pellegrino."

"Sorry," said Cam, who went into the apartment's small galley kitchen. "Didn't mean anything by it."

"Stop apologizing," said Heidi, repeating something her mother had said to her countless times.

Heidi heard Cam at the sink as she looked around the living-slash-dining room. The walls were covered with family photos—two young boys with a woman who was obviously their mom. One of the boys looked like Cam and the other had to be his brother.

A photo caught Heidi's eye. It was Cam—younger and skinnier—wearing glasses and an overstuffed backpack and smiling nervously in a sunny high school hallway. A hallway that looked very familiar.

"You went to Green Valley?" asked Heidi.

Cam handed Heidi a glass of water. "What? Oh, yeah. Ninth and tenth grade. No idea how my mom even got me in there. An hour on the city bus each way. Worst two years of my life."

"Wait, how old are you?" asked Heidi.

"Nineteen," said Cam.

"I'm a senior at Green Valley," said Heidi. "That means we went to high school together."

"Guess so," said Cam, his voice flat.

"I knew I recognized you!" said Heidi. It was coming back to her now.

Cam shrugged. "Don't take this the wrong way, but I have no idea who you are."

"Didn't we have a class together?" said Heidi. "Except you weren't Cam . . . you were . . ."

"I went by William back then. Cameron is my middle name."

"Oh my God, is that why you picked my house?" Heidi suddenly felt terrified to be alone in a criminal's apartment. "Have you been stalking me?"

"Get over yourself," said Cam. "I had no idea whose house it was. A.J. was the one who picked the place."

Heidi stared at him, looking for some clue that he was lying. But he seemed indignant. She took it for honesty, and relaxed a little.

"Okay, so, we made it here," she said. "What do we do now?"

Cam sighed. "I think we need to . . . get some rest. Think of something in the morning. When our heads are clearer."

"That's it? That's the master plan?" asked Heidi. "Go to sleep?"

"Look, I'm tired and my legs hurt and I feel like shit," said Cam. "No offense, but you look like you feel like shit."

Heidi's eyes went wide.

"I'm not saying you *look* like shit," protested Cam. "I'm saying you look like you *feel* like shit."

"Explain the difference."

"I don't know, but I'm sure I look like shit too! My skin itches like hell and I've got a splitting headache and I'm sweating through my clothes and I feel like I could throw up at any second."

Heidi wanted to argue, but instead she plopped down onto the couch. Her brain felt foggy and she had chills.

"I don't suppose you have spare sheets."

"I do, actually."

He retreated to the bedroom and came back with a clean set of twin bedsheets that he tossed to Heidi.

"I'm gonna hit the sack," said Cam. "If you need anything . . . you can probably find it yourself. The place isn't that big."

And then he disappeared down the hall.

Heidi unfolded the sheets—which were patterned with Spider-Man in different action poses—and started trying to fit them over the awkward shape of the love seat. Halfway through, she ran out of energy. Instead, she kicked off her shoes and wrapped herself in the top sheet.

Even though she was shivering, her hair was damp and runnels of sweat were snaking down her face and neck. The muscles in her legs, and then her abdomen, were starting to cramp. She tried to knead them out, but it was no use. Something hard was jabbing into her lower back through the cheap foam cushions of the love seat. She rolled over to get more comfortable and thought about searching the bathroom for some ibuprofen, but she realized she was too tired to get up. Instead, she rolled over again and found herself staring at a photo of Cam and his mom and brother at a water park. In the distance, she heard the intermittent snaps and pops of gunfire and a faint whining sound that was either sirens or howling.

* * *

Sunlight was pouring through the windows as Heidi woke up. She was in her own bed on her own queen-sized memory foam mattress fitted with eight-hundred-thread-count Egyptian cotton sheets. She'd lived her whole life without ever actually appreciating her own bed. Her bed was great, she now knew. Her bed was wonderful, in fact. She would never take it for granted again.

Heidi smelled something delicious downstairs. She made her way to the kitchen and found her mother, Madeline, apparently up for hours already, standing at the stove.

A pot of coffee was steeping in the French press and Heidi saw that she was making scrambled eggs just the way Heidi liked them. No runny stuff. Madeline worked the spatula with her left hand while in her right she held the international section of *The New York Times.* The sun coming through the window was so bright that Heidi had to shield her eyes.

"Good morning, sweetheart," said Madeline, "I thought you might sleep the day away. Are you hungry?"

The smell of the eggs suddenly turned Heidi's stomach. She shook her head.

"Mom, I don't feel so good."

Madeline put down the paper and pressed the back of her hand to Heidi's forehead.

"Poor baby," said Madeline. "Are you sick?"

Heidi had a sudden pang of fear. She'd made a mistake. She somehow knew that she shouldn't have told her mom anything about how she felt. She shouldn't tell anyone anything.

"I'm okay, actually," said Heidi. "I'm good."

Madeline smiled and shook her head. "No, sweetie. You're burning up."

"Am I?"

"Maybe you're sick because you didn't get into Harvard."

"What?"

Madeline shrugged. "I'm only guessing here, but maybe you feel bad because you're such a fucking disappointment."

Heidi blinked. She felt a lump forming in her throat and tears welling in her eyes. She didn't know what to say.

"I mean look around, sweetheart," said Madeline, indicating the beautiful kitchen and the well-tended lawn out the window. "Look at my career. Look at the life that I built, without anyone's help. Look at this house. I did all of this on my own. But you? You can't even get the simplest things right. You don't care enough to try."

"I *do* try!" shouted Heidi.

Madeline cocked her head and gave her daughter a wry smile. "Please. Don't feed me that. You wasted all your potential. You're pathetic, sweetheart. You're nothing."

Heidi started to cry. "I'm sorry."

"How many times do I have to tell you: stop apologizing all the time. Pardon my language, but I hate how much you *fucking* apologize," said Madeline. "You're nothing, so an apology from you means nothing. Do you understand me?"

"I'm not nothing."

"Oh yeah? Then what are you, sweetheart?" asked Madeline. "Please, it's been eighteen years. I'm dying to know."

"I'm something!" snarled Heidi and she lunged at her mother.

She caught Madeline's neck in her left hand and started to squeeze. Madeline's eyes bulged and she tried to cry out but Heidi held her windpipe closed. Madeline started to thrash and fight. She was a tall woman, strong from years of daily exercise. But Heidi's one-handed grip was unbreakable. Madeline's struggles were nothing to her.

Heidi smiled. "I am something."

Madeline was frantic now, fighting uselessly against Heidi's strength. With her right hand, Heidi took hold of the skin of her mother's face and started to pull.

Despite Heidi's crushing grip, a noise of desperate pain somehow squeaked out of Madeline's throat. Heidi pulled and the skin began to tear off her mother's face in a ragged, bloody flap. She saw muscle and bone underneath. Madeline thrashed wildly and then stopped struggling altogether.

Heidi flung her mother to the ground and looked at her hands, covered in blood. Except they weren't her hands. Her fingers were gnarled and misshapen. Disgusting. They ended in black claws.

Heidi looked up to see an intruder standing in her kitchen with a ski mask and a flashlight.

"Bad time?" said Cam.

Without thinking, Heidi moved toward him and pulled the mask up. Before Cam could say anything, she kissed him on the mouth, hard.

"Ow." Cam smiled. "Guess not."

Heidi kissed him again and he kissed her back. She kept going, moving down his neck, pressing her body against his, touching him and smearing his skin and hair with blood.

"What the fuck are you doing?"

Heidi turned to see Luca. He was standing in the kitchen, dumbfounded.

"Who is this guy?" asked Luca. His eyes were wild with fury.

Heidi laughed at his obvious pain. Cam shot him a sly grin.

"Fuck you! I'll kill you!" cried Luca as he charged toward Cam.

With a snarl, Heidi raked her claws across Luca's belly, tearing into his flesh. Luca shrieked and Heidi felt something warm and wet fall out. She'd torn a hole in him and his entrails were spilling out onto the kitchen tiles. Luca doubled over and slowly sank to the floor, trying in vain to hold his guts in his body.

Cam sniffed the air. "Damn. Something smells good."

The scrambled eggs were burning on the stove. The smoke alarm had started to beep.

"Mm-hmm," said Heidi.

She crouched down beside Luca. His eyes were glassy, staring out into nothing. She couldn't tell if he was still breathing and she didn't care. She rolled him over to expose the red ruin of his belly. She bent forward and sniffed the gash. The blood smelled good.

"Breakfast time," said Heidi.

Then, she started to eat. Cam knelt beside her and he ate too.

* * *

As Heidi emerged from the nightmare, she found herself in a room she didn't know, stuffing cold meat into her mouth by the handful. She was starving and the blood tasted so good. Cam was there beside her, crouched on the floor, gorging himself on the same flesh.

Heidi looked around with her mouth full, and remembered where she was: a strange apartment on the wrong side of town. Cam's apartment.

The refrigerator door was open. Heidi was kneeling on the dirty linoleum across from Cam. A package of uncooked hamburger meat was torn open between them and they were stuffing it into their mouths. Cam still looked like he was half asleep.

Immediately, Heidi's stomach ejected its contents in a spray of bloody vomit.

9

Heidi had been in the shower for forty-five minutes. She'd finally managed to stop crying but, every so often, she felt her stomach churn and she would dry heave again. Nothing came up except a few strands of pink saliva, quickly washed down the drain.

She straightened her body and kept on scrubbing. The images from her dream were still vivid in her mind: her mother's face, half torn off; Luca's furious eyes going dull; the pink coils of his intestines, glistening in the morning sun. She could still taste the iron tang of blood . . . Luca's blood . . . the hamburger meat . . .

She doubled over to puke up nothing again. Her stomach muscles hurt from clenching.

Her wrist didn't though. The werewolf in the alley had crushed the bone. She'd heard it snap. But as she flexed her arm and rolled her hand, her wrist felt okay. She looked at the bite mark on her upper arm. It was still swollen and painfully tender. The bite marks had closed into a collection of scabs.

Heidi picked at one and saw something underneath: A long wiry black hair was growing out of her biceps. Heidi plucked the hair out of her arm and started crying all over again.

When she'd finally finished up in the bathroom, she found Cam standing in the kitchen, staring out the window at the yellow grass of the apartment complex's dingy courtyard. He'd cleaned up the meat and the vomit and clearly sprayed some sort of air freshener but the stink still lingered.

"Hey," said Cam. "I'd offer you breakfast but . . . you know."

"Yeah, no," said Heidi. "Anyway, I'm thinking maybe we're not actually infected after all."

Cam opened his mouth. Then he closed it. "Heidi, we both got bit. We have the virus."

"That's not necessarily true," said Heidi. "When there's a flesh wound, the *Rabies lupinovirus* isn't *always* transmitted."

"The odds are over ninety-nine percent," said Cam. "Even I know that. Every single public service announcement says—"

"If it's not one hundred percent, then that means there's still a chance," said Heidi. "Unlikely things happen all the time. Don't they?"

Cam sighed. "I mean, I guess. But we got sick. I had a fever. I had cramps. Don't you feel . . . *different*?" He glanced at the spot on the kitchen floor, now clean, where the hamburger meat had been.

Heidi didn't answer his question. She didn't want to accept what he was saying. She repeated, "If it's not one hundred percent, then there's a chance."

Cam looked like he wanted to argue. Instead, he shrugged. "Okay, well, there's a pharmacy around the corner. I guess we can go grab a couple of spit tests."

Out on the street, Heidi saw people enjoying the nice weather. There were kids riding bikes, people shopping for groceries, buying fast food. The same neighborhood that had been a violent hellscape twelve hours earlier was now calm and boring in the morning light. It was surreal.

Inside the pharmacy, Cam grabbed two boxes labeled

GAINES RABIES LUPINOVIRUS RAPID TEST. Then he picked up a third.

"I'll get an extra, just in case," said Cam.

Heidi felt annoyed. He was humoring her.

"Do whatever you want," she said, and tried to act casual as they waited in the checkout line. She scrolled her phone and rolled her eyes at a clickbait article Marcie Love had shared claiming that apple cider vinegar was the cure for the virus.

Cam handed the tests to the cashier along with his credit card. She rang them up and her brow wrinkled.

"Card doesn't work," said the cashier.

"Seriously?" said Cam. "It should. Can you try it again? Sometimes the chip's a little temperamental."

She tried the card again and shook her head.

Cam turned to Heidi. "So, um, I may actually be, ahem, slightly short on funds at the moment—"

"It's fine," said Heidi, handing the cashier her own credit card.

Fifteen minutes later, they were back in Cam's apartment. They each opened a test kit. Inside was an individually wrapped swab as well as a small plastic vial sealed with a foil tab. As both of them had done countless times before, they each stuck the swab into their mouth and circled for fifteen seconds, then dipped it into the plastic vial and started to stir. Neither Cam nor Heidi said anything.

Heidi watched her phone timer, counting exactly thirty seconds of stirring. She hoped—prayed even—that somehow, *somehow*, she had escaped infection. Some people did. She'd read stories about them on social media. Sometimes they got interviewed on TV.

Once the stirring was done, the instructions said to wait a full nine minutes for accurate results. But within seconds, the white band on Heidi's test vial had turned pink—a pink so deep it could almost be called red. Heidi let out a single sob and then went quiet.

"Sorry," said Cam.

Heidi looked at the band around Cam's vial. It was white.

"I'm gonna go shower," said Cam. He disappeared down the hall and into the bathroom.

Heidi kept watching his vial as the seconds ticked by. One minute. Two minutes. Four minutes. Seven minutes. Still white.

She felt sick in the pit of her stomach. How could this happen? How was this fair? Cam had gotten mauled far worse than she had, but she was the one who had contracted the virus? Why? *Why?* She had done everything she was supposed to. It was Cam who should be infected, not her. Cam broke into her house. He was a thief and a criminal. Cam deserved to be sick. Not her.

At last, sometime around the eight-minute mark, the band on Cam's vial turned a faint shade of pink. As per the instructions, this was a positive result. Heidi felt relief, followed by a wave of guilt.

Cam returned from his shower, still drying his hair. He glanced at his positive saliva test.

"Yep," he said. He pointed at the third, unopened test kit. "You want to test yourself again?"

"No!" snapped Heidi.

"Easy," said Cam, as he sat down on one of his cheap plastic kitchen chairs. "You can get as mad as you want. It doesn't change anything."

"Sorry," she muttered petulantly.

"Look, I've been thinking. You and me, we're not from the same set. We pretty much have nothing in common. Aside from technically living in the same city, our lives couldn't be more different."

"We did actually go to the same high school," said Heidi.

"The exception that proves the rule. Anyway, regardless of our differences, we happen to find ourselves in the same boat. And it's obviously not a great boat."

Heidi listened but said nothing.

"This might sound dramatic, but for the moment at least, our fates are intertwined," said Cam.

"Why?" asked Heidi. "The sun's up. We could go our separate ways."

Cam frowned. "Don't you see? If one of us gets caught, that will lead them to the other."

"So we're stuck with each other?"

Cam nodded. "And I've been on my own for a long time, so I'm not used to being stuck with *anyone*. But whatever we decide to do, it has to work for both of us. You're rich, so you might think you know better than me, or you're in charge or something—"

"I don't actually think that," said Heidi. "You feel annoyed because I made us take unnecessary saliva tests. That's mistaking me being *thorough* for me being *demanding*. The way I solve problems is I'm thorough. I consider every option. That's just how I was raised."

"All right, then," said Cam. "As long as we understand each other." He cleared his throat. "So let's use this Heidi Mills Thoroughness Method and solve our problem."

Heidi crossed her arms. "No."

Cam looked at her like she'd lost it. "No? Why not, exactly? Do you have something more pressing you need to attend to?"

"I'm saying 'no' because I agree with you. Before we do anything, we *do* need to get on the same page. I'm not going to think up any plans. I'm not going anywhere or doing anything else, until you tell me *why*."

Cam rolled his eyes. "I told you last night. A.J. picked your house. He follows a bunch of rich people on social media and figures out when they're on vacation. Nobody was supposed to be home. And nobody expects to get robbed on the full moon. That's it. It was totally random. Could've been literally any address in that neighborhood."

"Not that," said Heidi. "I don't care about that. I want to know why you decided to help me. You just listed off all the reasons you shouldn't give a shit about me. How different we are. You could've run out that door alone, but you didn't. So why?"

Cam looked uncomfortable. "I have no idea. Maybe I wasn't thinking straight? To be perfectly honest, it was not the best decision I ever made, and that's coming from a guy who regularly breaks into houses. Dragging you along makes my life a headache. Suddenly, I'm forced to look out for another person who—"

"Excuse me," said Heidi. "I'm the one who pulled you out of your shitty Kia after you wrecked it."

"I swerved to avoid a pedestrian!"

"You'd be dead if it weren't for me," said Heidi.

"I'd have thought of something," muttered Cam. Though his voice sounded a little uncertain to Heidi.

"Dude. I'm not going to ask again. Tell me why you helped me, right now, or I'll call the hotline. I don't even give a shit." It was an empty threat, but Heidi was really annoyed now.

Cam shrugged. "What can I say? It was a mistake. I fucked up. I do that a lot. It's kind of my thing."

Heidi shook her head. "No. I don't believe you."

"Okay. Fine. You want to know? The reason I helped you is

that I know from personal experience how the virus will fuck up your life."

"Go on," said Heidi.

"You remember back when this whole thing started? When it was still crazy? Before everything got, you know, the way it is now?"

Heidi nodded. She was a lot younger then, but she remembered the months of uncertainty. Madeline and Ron panicking constantly but doing their best—which wasn't very good—to keep their anxiety hidden from her. Heidi remembered being told she couldn't do most of the things she wanted to do because of a deadly new disease she might catch. It was scary. But it was annoying and inconvenient, and most of all, it was really, *really* boring.

"In those first few weeks, nobody knew what the hell was happening," said Cam. "Some people were determined to act like everything was normal. Other people were scared to leave their houses. Lots of people hadn't even heard about any of it. And some people, like my mom, had no choice. They just had to keep going because werewolves or not, you've got to pay rent.

"Anyway, this was the early days. My mom was a nurse. One day she had this patient in the ER who was acting crazy. She tried to put an IV drip in and this motherfucker bit her on the hand. She slapped a bandage on it and finished her shift.

"A few weeks later my mom and I had an argument. We weren't getting along very well at the time, but I remember she seemed, like, extra pissed off that day. Like, she never got that angry. She told me I couldn't go out that night because I might catch the big bad virus everybody at the hospital was talking about. I said some shit to her I shouldn't have said and then I went out anyway. I was fifteen, how could she stop me? I just *had* to see my friends, you know?"

Heidi nodded. She remembered her own version of that fight with Madeline.

Cam continued, "Anyway, that night was a full moon. She changed. Right here in this apartment."

He nodded toward the gaping holes in the drywall that Heidi had noticed earlier.

"I was out, but my little brother, he was home when it happened and uh . . ." Cam trailed off, unable to keep going.

Heidi put a hand on his. "Cam, I'm so sorry."

Cam swallowed and continued. "The next morning I came home and I saw . . . I saw what she'd done. I called 911. They took Michael to Valley Medical but, uh, he didn't make it.

"They arrested my mom. She's been in the pound—sorry, she's been in 'indefinite quarantine' ever since. She's at the High Desert Recovery and Treatment Center out in Arizona. It's a shitty place but believe me, it's a hundred times better than the government version. It costs five thousand a month and insurance doesn't cover it, even if she had any. So it's up to me to pay the bill."

"So that's why you . . ." Heidi trailed off without saying *rob houses*.

Cam shrugged. "Can't exactly afford it flipping burgers. And before you ask, I still love my mom. I know she wasn't responsible for what happened. But she blames herself. She won't ever forgive herself for Michael's death. Something broke inside her that day and it will never be fixed."

Heidi didn't know what to say. "Cam, I—"

Cam cut her off. "Yep. I know. Boohoo, right? It's a real sob story. I know she'll never get out of the pound. It's a life sentence with another name. We'll never go to the movies again. We'll never go to Dick's Drive-In for fries. Hell, I'll never even get to hug my mom again. I've accepted it. She's almost as dead as my brother. But to answer your question: That's why I helped you. I don't know you, but what happened to my family is something I wouldn't wish on anyone. So, are you sorry you asked?"

"No," said Heidi. "I'm not."

Cam shrugged. "And here's the thing: Now that I told you, you don't get to pity me. You understand? I'm the low-life scumbag that broke into your house to steal your family's silver. I don't need your fucking pity. Got it?"

"Yes," said Heidi. "Got it."

Cam wiped his eyes with the back of his hand. "Damn. Stop looking at me like that!"

"Sorry." Heidi looked away.

Cam clapped his hands as if to provide a hard conclusion to the previous topic. "Okay, now that we got my tragic backstory out of the way, I will admit, I have no idea what we're supposed to do next."

"Me neither," said Heidi. "When I'm stumped I usually make a list."

"Of course you do," said Cam.

"Got something I can write on?" asked Heidi.

Cam rifled through a pile of unopened mail on the counter. He tossed Heidi a pink envelope from the cable company that said FINAL NOTICE on it.

Heidi frowned at the envelope. "Are you sure this isn't important?"

"I got bigger problems than Comcast now," said Cam.

"Okay," said Heidi. "So we've both been, ah, *infected.*" Even saying the word made her blood run cold. Still, Heidi made herself write it down and underline it. Infected. "So what are our options?"

"Do you happen to own a time machine?" asked Cam.

Heidi rolled her eyes. "It might seem silly, but the point of this exercise is to write down everything to see if there's anything we haven't thought of."

"Fair enough. Then I guess option one is to get shot by the Dogcatchers," said Cam. "Not sure how you feel about that one, but I'm leaning toward 'no.'"

"Yeah, I'll pass." Heidi wrote down "Get shot" and crossed it out.

"Option two would be to turn ourselves in peacefully," said Heidi.

"No way," said Cam. "I'm not going to the pound. I'd rather take option one."

Heidi nodded. She wrote down "Turn ourselves in" and crossed it out.

Cam took a deep breath and then looked at her. "Okay, this is honestly what I've been thinking since last night: We run."

"What, like together?" asked Heidi, incredulous.

"Yeah, I'm not excited about it, either," snapped Cam. "But if we split up and you get caught . . . I don't know if you'd do the right thing."

"Do the right thing?"

"Would you lie to the cops if they asked about me?"

Heidi paused. "Yes," she said, at last. "I'd lie to the cops."

Cam chuckled darkly. "You hesitated for *way* too long. You don't even sound comfortable using the word *cops*. You sound like you're worried you might get in trouble if you don't call them *the police*."

"I would too lie," insisted Heidi. "I already have. Remember my missing cat Quinoa?"

"That was pretty smooth," admitted Cam.

"But I don't want to go on the run," said Heidi. "I have friends and a boyfriend and a life that I can't just leave behind. Prom is in a couple of weeks!"

Cam looked at her like she was insane. "Prom? Right now, what you're thinking about is prom?"

Heidi instantly felt embarrassed. "Whatever, I'm not becoming a fucking fugitive, okay?"

Cam scowled. "It's an option, so you have to write it down. Your rules, not mine."

Heidi wrote "Go on the run" and resisted the urge to immediately cross it out.

"Option four is we try to keep the infection a secret," said Heidi.

"That's not really an option, right? We have to do it," said Cam. "Nobody gives a shit about me. What about you? Can you hide"—Cam nodded to the spot on the floor where both of them had woken up eating raw meat—"*this* from your family? From your boyfriend?"

Heidi thought about her mom and stepdad. Ron wasn't the sharpest tool in the shed. He was an avid bird-watcher and model train enthusiast who barely noticed half of what went on right in front of his nose. Madeline, on the other hand, was keenly observant. But Heidi lied to her often, as a matter of course.

Luca was another matter. He always paid extremely close attention to what she did and didn't do, who she spent time with, where she went. Heidi decided not to think about it.

"Yeah," said Heidi. "I can hide it from them."

"Are you sure? Most regular people, when they find out, they're going to call that hotline," said Cam. "Just like you wanted to."

Heidi wondered if Madeline would do that. Would she lock up her only daughter into indefinite quarantine? Heidi wrote down "Keep it a secret" and marked it with an asterisk.

"So obviously we've got to hide it," said Cam. "But that's just kicking the can. Only works until the next full moon."

"That gives us a month, at least," said Heidi.

"Twenty-eight days," corrected Cam.

"The way I see it, there's only one good option," said Heidi, as she wrote down what she was thinking at the bottom of the list.

"Yeah? Please. Tell me."

"We need to find a cure," said Heidi.

Cam burst out laughing. Heidi frowned.

"I'm sorry, did you get into my stash while I was in the shower?" Cam carefully looked into her eyes. "'Cause you sound pretty high right now."

"Tell me when you're done," said Heidi.

"You're— Oh my God, you're actually serious?"

"Yes, I'm serious," said Heidi.

"Find a cure," said Cam. "I mean, look, you do seem smart. Honestly. But, man, you don't seem to understand shit. *Find a cure.* My mind is blown. Goddamn. Is this the kind of optimism you get from growing up rich?"

"Tell me when you're done," repeated Heidi in a tight voice.

"Okay, all right, sorry. I'm done. Sure. Let's go ahead and find that cure," said Cam. He threw open a nearby cabinet. "Maybe the cure is, uh, old hot sauce mixed with um . . ." He opened the fridge. "Blue Gatorade?"

"I don't mean discover a cure in your shitty apartment. I mean do some basic research. Every year they spend billions and billions of dollars testing various drugs and therapies to see if they're effective against the virus. Pfizer. Merck. The Gaines Foundation—they're all looking for a cure. My mom told me the whole process takes years and years. There are scientific trials after scientific trials, and then there's the FDA approval process, which can take even longer. So what I propose we do is try to figure out if any of the drugs they're currently testing seem like they might be effective."

"How the hell will you know that?" asked Cam.

"I got a five on the AP Bio test!" snapped Heidi, who had finally had enough of Cam's bullshit.

Cam threw his hands up defensively. "Okay, okay!"

"If any of the drugs seem promising, then maybe—and I will admit this is a big maybe—maybe we can treat ourselves?"

Cam still looked skeptical, but he didn't say anything. Indeed, even as Heidi heard herself say it out loud it sounded like a long shot.

She held up the pink envelope. "I'm sorry, but do you see a better option on this list?"

"Not really," admitted Cam.

"Then quit arguing and go get me your computer," said Heidi. "If we only have twenty-eight days, then I might as well get started now."

Cam nodded and went to the bedroom and returned with a five-year-old laptop. He started to hand it to Heidi but hesitated.

"What?" asked Heidi.

"Okay. So. Uh. I just— Don't check the browser history," said Cam.

"Ew," said Heidi.

She took the laptop and opened up Google Scholar. In the search field she typed "lupinovirus cure."

"You're just gonna google it, huh?" said Cam.

"I'm using a dedicated search engine for academic research," snapped Heidi.

She clicked the search button. There were 46,192 results.

Heidi took a deep breath. She was diving headfirst into the most heavily researched scientific topic of the last decade. She chose a result at random and clicked on it, which took her to the abstract that summarized the paper. The technical terms that the authors used—*homology, glycoprotein, isomers, nicotinic acetylcholine receptors*—made her head swim. Despite her outburst about the AP Bio test, Heidi immediately knew she was way out of her depth.

But Cam was still behind her, looking at the screen.

"So what does all of this mean?" he asked.

"Can you stop looking over my shoulder, please?" asked Heidi. "Give me some space."

"It's a three-hundred-fifty-square-foot apartment," said Cam.

"Then go build a pillow fort or something," said Heidi.

Cam frowned. "I should grab my car anyway. If I'm remembering correctly, it's sitting in a ditch somewhere off Marginal Way. Possibly totaled. You cool to be on your own for a few hours?"

"I'll be fine," said Heidi.

"Great. If my Kia starts, I should be back soon," said Cam.

He walked out and locked the apartment door and the flimsy security gate behind him.

Heidi poured herself a glass of tap water, did a few quick neck rolls, and then forced herself to read a paper titled "Effectiveness of Intramuscular and Intracerebroventricular Administration of Monoclonal Antibodies in the Treatment of *Rabies lupinovirus*."

* * *

By the time Cam returned an hour and twenty-five minutes later, Heidi had found the cure. She would have called him, but she didn't have his number.

As he walked in the door, Heidi practically charged at him. "Cam, you've got to see this. I found something interesting. Like, really, *really* interesting."

"You didn't check the browser history did you? Because—"

Heidi cut him off. "No, just look at this."

She spun the screen of the laptop so that he could see what she was looking at. It was a PDF titled "Extiva Est un Traitement Antiviral Efficace du *Lupinovirus de la Rage*."

Cam read the title and nodded. "The fuck does that say?"

"Oh, sorry, it says that 'Extiva Is an Effective Antiviral Treatment for *Rabies lupinovirus*.'"

Cam cocked his head. "You can speak French?"

"What? Yeah," said Heidi. "Okay, let me explain the paper: So there's this drug called Extiva. It was originally developed as a weight loss drug. But it got discontinued back in the nineties."

"Discontinued?"

"Yeah, it happens all the time with new drugs," said Heidi. "The side effects outweigh the benefits, or the drug isn't as effective as they originally thought. The most common reason is that nobody is buying it, so there's no point in trying to sell it."

Cam nodded. "Okay."

"Anyway, earlier this year, these French scientists did a study to see if Extiva works against lupinovirus."

"And it does?"

"They found that it was ninety-eight percent effective as an antiviral!" Heidi was so excited she was almost screaming. "Ninety-eight percent!"

Cam scowled. "Heidi, if there's a cure out there, then why aren't they giving it to people?"

Heidi nodded. "That's the thing. These scientists posted their research online, but within forty-eight hours the paper got taken down. Thankfully, people keep reposting it on Reddit."

Cam cocked his head. "Why'd it get taken down?"

"Nobody knows," said Heidi. "One of the scientists has publicly said their research is being suppressed. Everybody online thinks it's because of the people who make money off the pandemic. They don't actually want it to end. Like, they don't want there to actually be a cure."

At this, Cam nodded. "The High Desert Recovery and Treatment Center charges five thousand dollars a month to keep my mom locked up in quarantine for the rest of her life. I imagine a cure would certainly cut into that margin."

"If you think about it, there's so much money in all of it," said Heidi. "It's like everybody online is saying: the saliva tests, the gear, and the vehicles that the VCTF use, all these scientific studies that don't ever produce any results."

"Okay, so if Extiva is an actual cure . . . how do we even get it? You said it's been off the market since the nineties. I'm thinking we may need that time machine after all."

Heidi shook her head. "It has been discontinued. But only in the US. Extiva is still available in China."

"So our lives depend on a Chinese prescription weight loss drug?" Cam didn't sound optimistic.

"Cam, we have twenty-eight days," said Heidi. "It's possible. We can do this!"

At that moment, both their phones buzzed. It was a push notification from the LC Countdown app that every smartphone in America was required by law to have. Heidi's heart sank as she read it.

EMERGENCY ALERT

Tonight a supermoon in your area will result in a second full moon. Curfew is in effect from 6:00 PM April 5th until 6:00 AM April 6th. Remain securely indoors and take all necessary precautions—VCTF

"The supermoon," whispered Heidi.

"We don't have twenty-eight days," said Cam. "We have ten hours."

10

Heidi put her face in her hands. She felt like crying again, but this time the tears wouldn't come. After all she'd been through, the whiplash of hope back to despair was too much. She felt like giving up.

Heidi had the sudden urge to call Madeline, to interrupt her Hawaiian vacation and tell her everything. Some childlike part of her thought her mother would know what to do, because Madeline always knew what to do. Madeline could do anything. She could fix anything.

Not this, though. Heidi felt a pang of sorrow as she imagined her mother calmly calling the Viral Containment Task Force to turn her in.

"C'mon, cheer up," Cam said, though he didn't sound very convincing. "Don't cry."

"Why did this have to happen to me?" asked Heidi.

Cam rolled his eyes. "Quit being dramatic. Things aren't that bad."

"I'm a fucking werewolf!" cried Heidi.

Cam considered her words. "Okay, yeah, when you put it that way . . . it's not *awesome*. The good news is: I have an idea."

"Is this an *idea* idea or just more bullshit?" asked Heidi.

"Look, we happen to need an illicit pharmaceutical. And

luckily, I am acquainted with a certain individual who specializes in procuring illicit pharmaceuticals."

"A drug dealer," said Heidi.

"It's a long shot," said Cam. "But what else are we gonna do?"

Outside, it was warm and sunny. Clear skies were rare this time of year and there was something unnerving about just how pleasant it was. Cam and Heidi crossed the patchy yellow grass of the apartment complex's courtyard and passed through the security gate out onto the street.

There, parked by the curb, was Cam's Kia. In the light of day, the car looked like shit, but Heidi wasn't sure which dents and scratches were from the wreck last night and which predated it. They climbed inside.

"She's not dead yet," Cam said as he kissed two fingers and pressed them to the dashboard. Then he cranked the engine and nothing happened.

Heidi put her face in her hands.

"Don't worry," said Cam. "This is absolutely normal. She does this sometimes. I just have to prove that I still love her . . ."

Fourteen minutes later, after a jump start from Cam's neighbor—an elderly man in a skullcap named Fazal—they were on the road.

They drove through the shabby residential sprawl of Cam's neighborhood. Out the window, Heidi saw the alley where she'd been attacked by the black wolf. A gyro truck was parked there now, with a line that stretched halfway down the block.

"How does everybody do it?" asked Heidi.

"One foot in front of the other," said Cam, eyes on the road. "Till you step in that manhole."

Heidi noticed a billboard towering over the street, with a message that she'd never seen in her neighborhood. The background showed the full moon. In the foreground was a pair of hands greedily clutching a fan of hundred-dollar bills. It said:

UP TO $10,000 CASH REWARD

For information leading to the quarantine of anyone infected with *Rabies lupinovirus.* Call the Viral Containment Task Force Hotline at 1-800-555-4949.

Heidi shivered and tried to think about something else. "So who is this drug dealer guy anyway?"

"Not a guy, for starters," said Cam. "Her name is Micaela."

Heidi waited for him to elaborate. He didn't.

"Okay, so . . . how do you know her?"

"She sells study drugs to the kids up at the college," said Cam. "You know, Ritalin, Adderall. And maybe some other stuff that's a little, uh, less academic. In the past I have occasionally helped her out with that."

"So you're a drug dealer too," said Heidi.

"Part-time!" said Cam defensively. "Anyway, sometimes the college kids put in weird requests and she manages to get the stuff. I dunno. Maybe there's a chance she can get us some Chinese diet pills."

Heidi nodded. "There's something you're not telling me."

Cam frowned. "Well, the only thing is, it could be a little bit awkward."

"Why?"

Cam sighed. "Micaela is my ex."

"And it didn't end well?"

"I might've . . ." Cam trailed off.

"Might've what?"

"I might've dumped her. By text."

"Jesus, Cam."

They drove north, past downtown and toward the university. Cam got off the freeway and soon they were passing dive bars and vape shops and cheap apartment blocks where students lived off-campus. He turned onto a leafy street called Paradise Way and pulled over in front of a small ranch house with stained siding and an overgrown lawn.

Instead of getting out, Cam sat in silence behind the wheel, staring straight ahead.

"What're you waiting for?" asked Heidi.

"Nothing," said Cam. He glanced at the house. "I hope her roommate's not home. The roommate never liked me."

"That must be tough," said Heidi. "Anyway, we're infected and the full moon is in nine hours so . . ."

"I know. I know. Just trying to, uh, organize my thoughts." Still, Cam didn't move.

"You want to text her before you show up at her door?" said Heidi.

"Yeah, that's probably a good idea," said Cam. He pulled out his phone but didn't type anything. At last he turned to Heidi. "Can you do it?"

"Dude," said Heidi. "Seriously?"

Cam nodded. He looked pathetic, like a hunted animal.

"Fine," said Heidi.

Cam handed her his phone and she saw that, indeed, the last text exchange was two sentences from Cam telling her it wasn't going to work out, and Micaela's response: the fuck? Cam hadn't written anything back.

"Jesus, Cam," said Heidi.

Then she took five minutes to compose an eminently thoughtful message apologizing for how things had ended, while subtly alluding to some unspecified emotional trauma that had led to his selfishness and cruelty. She asked if Micaela might be willing to meet up, and ended with a self-deprecating joke about how she (Cam) was a complete piece of shit.

"There," said Heidi.

Cam read what she'd written. "Damn, this is good. This is really good."

"Uh, thank you? I guess. I feel gross."

"I should call you whenever I need to break up with someone."

"No," snapped Heidi. "You should have the balls to do it in person."

"Right, yes, definitely," said Cam. "Okay, I'm gonna send it."

He did.

A second later, he got a text back. Cam frowned and showed it to Heidi.

> Is that your shitty car parked in front
> of my house?

Cam took a deep breath. "Okay. I'm going in."

"Should I come in with you?" asked Heidi.

"Definitely not," said Cam. "I'll be back in five."

Cam walked across the lawn. As he approached the house, Heidi could've sworn she heard the faint sound of a dog barking. The door opened and Cam stepped inside.

Heidi sat in the car and watched clouds crawl across the sky. Occasionally, a car drove past. A group of college kids in pajama pants and slides exited the house two doors down. They talked and laughed and looked at their phones. Heidi imagined that she was one of them—carefree, attending a mediocre local college, stumbling out the door with friends for a late-morning hangover cure.

Her phone buzzed. It was a push notification from the LC Countdown app—exactly 00:09:00:00 to moonrise. Every second they wasted here was a second closer to . . . Heidi couldn't bear to think of it.

Just then, she heard muffled yelling coming from inside the house.

Heidi turned to see Cam speed walking back toward the Kia. He climbed in and locked the door behind him.

"So does she have any Extiva?" asked Heidi.

"We didn't really get that far," said Cam.

He cranked the ignition and the engine started immediately this time.

"Hang on," said Heidi. "We can't just leave."

"I'm sorry," said Cam. "It's a dead end. I don't think she's going to help me."

"Well, then," said Heidi, "maybe she'll help *me*."

Before Cam could stop her, she was out of the car and crossing the yard. As Heidi rang the doorbell, again she was sure she heard the distant sound of a dog barking from inside.

A woman with faded sea-green hair and glasses, maybe three or four years older than Heidi, answered the door. "Yeah?"

"Hi," said Heidi, putting on the smile that had won her the French Club presidency. "My friend was just here and he—"

"Oh my God," said the girl with glasses. "Cam did *not* just send his new girlfriend to the door."

"What the fuck?" came an outraged voice from somewhere in the house.

A second later, Green Hair was joined by another girl about

the same age. She wore a faded Nirvana sweatshirt and an extremely pissed-off expression on her face.

"Who the *fuck* are you?" asked the girl in the Nirvana shirt, who Heidi guessed must be Micaela.

"My name's Dawn Suppley," said Heidi, making a split-second decision to go full alter ego. "I'm here because Cam—"

"Fuck Cam," said Micaela. "And fuck you too, Dawn Suppley. How old are you?"

"I'm, uh, twenty-seven," said Heidi.

At this, Green Hair burst out laughing.

Micaela eyed Heidi. "You look like you're in high school. This motherfucker dumped me for a high schooler."

"For the record," said Green Hair, "I never liked him."

"I'm afraid you've got it all wrong," said Heidi, trying to sound very reasonable, like how she imagined Dawn Suppley might. "I'm not Cam's girlfriend. In fact, I'm his social worker—"

"Enough of this bullshit." Micaela stepped nose to nose with Heidi and spoke very slowly. "Get the fuck off my lawn, you little bitch, before I fuck up your yearbook photo."

For an instant, Heidi felt thrilled. She saw herself grabbing this bitch by the hair. She imagined slamming her skull into the pavement until she stopped moving, while Green Hair watched helplessly and screamed.

Heidi blinked. The thought now made her queasy. She'd never been in a fight in her life. She'd never wanted to physically hurt anyone. At least, she thought she hadn't. That wasn't her, was it?

Instead of attacking, Heidi stepped back and threw up her hands in a gesture of submission. "I'm sorry. You're right. I *am* a high schooler. And Cam—Cam's an idiot. But we're not together. He's not even my friend. In fact, I barely know him."

Micaela cocked her head. "Go on."

"The thing is, we need drugs," said Heidi. "You sell drugs, right? I have money. So sell us some drugs and make some money. It's simple, really."

"It would be simple," said Micaela. "If it wasn't him."

"Okay, then," said Heidi. "Sell *me* the drugs and if you want . . . you can kick Cam in the balls."

Micaela laughed then caught herself. She turned to her roommate. "What the hell is even going on right now? I feel like I'm losing my mind."

Green Hair shrugged. "Ex-boyfriend psyop?"

Micaela turned back to Heidi, now sounding more amused than pissed. "No offense sweetie, but you seem like you might already be on drugs."

Heidi shrugged helplessly. "All I can say is Cam's in trouble. If you ever cared about him, now is the time to help."

"And what will help Cam is . . . drugs?" Micaela's voice dripped with disbelief.

"One drug," said Heidi. "Have you ever heard of a pill called Extiva?"

Micaela's face showed no recognition. She shrugged. "Nope. Sorry."

"Damn it," said Heidi.

"Well, this has been the strangest interaction of my life so far," said Micaela. "Please tell Cam I hope he dies in a fire—"

"What about your supplier?" asked Heidi.

"My *supplier*?" said Micaela. "What, do you think you're in an episode of *Law & Order*?"

"I don't know, whatever you call the person who gets you the drugs that you sell," said Heidi. "Maybe that person would be able to get us some Extiva."

Micaela's eyes narrowed as she stared past Heidi to Cam, sitting in the Kia.

"You know I was actually in love with that asshole," said Micaela.

"I never liked him," repeated Green Hair.

"Shut up, Gina," said Micaela. She turned to Heidi. "You wrote that text for him didn't you?"

Heidi stared at her feet. "Yeah. Sorry."

"No," said Micaela. "It's fucked up, but . . . I actually appreciate it."

* * *

"Her supplier's name is Chook," said Heidi as she climbed back into the Kia.

"Her *supplier*?" said Cam. "What, do you think you're in an episode of—"

"Save it. We don't have much time," said Heidi. "Micaela said he hangs out at the park on John Street and Ninth Avenue. But she made me swear we wouldn't mention her name."

"What, are you guys friends now?" asked Cam as he pulled away from the curb.

"Maybe," said Heidi.

"How the hell did you swing that?"

"Easy," said Heidi. "I promised she could kick you in the balls."

Cam nodded. "That tracks."

The Kia's tires squealed as Cam made the turn off Paradise Way heading toward the west side of the city.

The neighborhood they traveled to was bifurcated: million-dollar high-rise condos with vast homeless encampments on the streets below. Years ago, tech and finance workers had been desperately trying to gentrify it with axe-throwing bars and brunch restaurants on every corner. But the virus had made a mockery of all that. Now, half the condos were vacant and most of the bars and restaurants were closed. The gentrifiers who remained were waiting for property values to go back up so they could sell and get the hell out.

To Heidi, this part of town was where high school kids might go to drink without getting carded—not that *she* ever did that—and a place her mom had always warned her she might get pick-pocketed, or worse.

Heidi felt a jolt of adrenaline as they passed a VCTF BearCat parked at an intersection, subtly reminding the citizens that they were being watched. Always being watched. A day ago, the sight of that BearCat might have comforted Heidi, if she even noticed it at all.

"This is it," said Cam as he pulled over on the street next to a public park. It was crowded. Even in the middle of the workday, people were determined to take advantage of the good weather.

Beside the basketball courts, they found a small fenced-in area ringed with rolls and rolls of faded yellow caution tape. There was so much of it that you couldn't easily see inside. The plaque out front read NINTH AVE. PARK OFF-LEASH AREA. A much more prominent sign had been affixed to the fence years ago. In big block letters, it read:

DUE TO THE RISK OF CANINE VIRAL TRANSMISSION
THIS AREA IS TEMPORARILY CLOSED

Since dogs were found to be passive carriers of the virus, owning one had become strictly illegal. Dozens of dog parks around the city sat locked and unused. But the padlock and chain on this one had long since been clipped. Heidi heard music from inside the gate.

"So, Micaela said Chook can be kind of a scary dude," said Heidi.

"Don't worry," said Cam. "I know how to deal with guys like this."

Heidi and Cam stepped through the gate and saw a group of three men, enjoying the sun like everyone else. They'd clearly claimed the Ninth Ave. Park Off-Leash Area as their own long ago.

One of them—a pale, heavyset, bald man in sunglasses—sat in an old lawn chair. He sipped an energy drink and played music at top volume from a small Bluetooth speaker. The way he relaxed while the others stood made it clear who was in charge.

"Yo, you Chook?" said Cam. His tone was subtly deeper than normal. *Cam's own version of Dawn Suppley, perhaps,* thought Heidi.

The big bald man smiled. "Depends very much on who's asking."

"I'm Cam. I'm a friend of a friend."

Chook stood and stretched. He was over six feet tall and probably weighed 250 pounds. He rolled his neck and took a careful sip of his electric-blue energy drink.

"I don't have any friends," he said.

"Anyway," said Cam in a quieter voice. "I need some stuff."

Chook turned to Heidi. "No need to be shy. What's your name, sweetheart?"

One of Chook's cronies snickered.

"Dawn," said Heidi.

"Dawn," repeated Chook, talking right past Cam. "The light at the end of a long, dark night."

"Yep," said Heidi, "that's what the word 'dawn' means."

"A beautiful name for a beautiful girl."

His stare made her skin crawl.

"Yo, can we just do this?" asked Cam. "I got places to be."

Chook ignored him and spoke only to Heidi. "Don't tell me you're with him. I mean, damn. Look at his shoes. Look at those jeans. You need a man who can afford to buy you the finer things."

"Dude, I'm talking to you!" snapped Cam.

Chook kept his eyes on Heidi but spoke to Cam. "Speak then."

"It's called Extiva," said Cam. "You got any?"

Instantly, Chook's whole demeanor changed. The swagger was gone. He took his sunglasses off and turned to stare down Cam. "No, get lost."

"Seriously?" said Cam. "I heard you were the guy who could get anything."

Chook poked a finger into Cam's chest. "You think you're the first one to ask me about that shit? You don't think I don't know *why* you're asking?"

"What?" said Cam, poorly feigning ignorance. "No, man, it's not like that—"

"I don't want any part of the trouble you're in, okay?" said Chook, looking around. "Fuck that. I don't need the cops. I don't need the Dogcatchers. And I'm telling you: I don't have any Extiva. So get the fuck out of here before I do something hasty."

Chook stepped to Cam, getting right in his face. "Do I make myself clear?"

Cam backed off. "Yeah."

"All right, go on then," said Chook, waving dismissively. "Shoo fly. Get the fuck ou—"

With a cry of wordless rage, Heidi flew at Chook. She hit him in his midriff and knocked him off his feet. All 250 pounds of him came crashing down onto the packed dirt of the dog park. The impact knocked the wind out of him.

She used Chook's big soft body as a springboard and flew at one of his goons who was already running toward the fight. Her knee caught him right under his chin. She hit the sweet spot. The blow knocked him unconscious instantly.

Almost as quickly, the other one had an aluminum bat in his hands. He paused and took in the situation: two men down; Heidi and Cam still up.

Heidi snarled, which seemed to push him to a decision. The guy dropped the bat and turned to flee at top speed. In two seconds, he'd scrambled over the chain-link fence and disappeared into the park.

With Chook's goons out of the fight, Heidi turned back to finish him off. She grunted and lunged toward him. She was going to kill him.

Cam caught her by the shoulder and yanked her backward. "What the fuck?" he whispered.

Heidi spun and saw that his eyes were wide. Cam was afraid. Not of Chook or his crew; he was frightened of her.

She looked down at Chook. With his sunglasses off, Heidi could see that he was much older than he dressed. He was thirty, thirty-five maybe. He'd shaved his head because he was going bald—a middle-aged man who spent all day in an abandoned dog park selling drugs to teenagers.

Heidi put her foot on his neck. "Tell us where to get Extiva, or we'll kill you," she said. "If you know what kind of trouble we're in, then you know we've got nothing to lose."

Chook whimpered. "Look, I *told* you. I don't have any. I swear to God. I'm not lying."

Heidi ground her heel into his neck. Chook squealed.

"You don't have any Extiva," said Heidi. "But you know where we can get some."

"I don't!"

Heidi gingerly took her foot off his neck. Then she kicked him in the face. The bones of his nose shattered with a crunch. Cam flinched. Chook howled in pain, writhing on the ground and clutching his face as blood gushed out of his nostrils.

"Heidi," said Cam.

"Last chance," said Heidi.

"I don't know. I don't," wailed Chook, his voice now distorted by a broken septum. "But . . ."

"But what?" said Heidi.

"It might just be a rumor. But there's this lady," said Chook. "The Bitch."

Heidi's eyes narrowed. "Excuse me?"

"No! Don't get mad at me, that's what she calls herself!" cried Chook. "Or maybe she's not real. But she can get you some. At least that's what my cousin told me. Okay?"

"Where is she?" asked Heidi.

"I heard she lives in the woods north of the city. That's all I know, I promise you."

"Heidi, we should really go," said Cam. "Like, now."

The Ninth Ave. Park Off-Leash Area was secluded, but Heidi had just attacked two men in broad daylight.

Heidi glared at Chook. "In the future you should be more *polite* to your customers."

She turned and walked toward the exit. Cam quickly followed her.

The second they were out of the dog park, both of them ran. As suddenly as it had come on, Heidi's anger was gone. She was left with the strange sensation of remembering what she'd just done as though she had witnessed the actions of someone else. Had she really just attacked an armed criminal who was twice her size? That didn't seem possible.

Cam started the Kia and pulled onto the street.

"I don't know if assaulting a drug dealer was the best decision," he said.

"I did what I had to do," said Heidi.

"You can't just do shit like that. You've got to control yourself."

"Do I?" said Heidi. She wasn't asking the question rhetorically, she actually wondered.

"If you start acting crazy, you get caught. And if you get caught, then *I* get caught. Damn, I thought you were gonna kill that dude."

Heidi shrugged. She thought about hurting Chook more, or even killing him, and she felt nothing. No, not nothing. If she was being honest, she felt a strange sense of satisfaction. It was alarming.

"He told us where to find Extiva," said Heidi.

"He gave us some urban legend bullshit because he was scared for his life. Trust me, people will say anything in that situation."

"Still, it's the best hope we've got," said Heidi. She checked the LC Countdown app. "We have six hours to find this Bitch."

11

Cam got on the interstate, heading north. While he drove, Heidi frantically googled on her spiderwebbed phone.

"So . . . 'the woods north of town' isn't very specific," said Cam.

"I think he must mean the national forest," said Heidi.

"It's pretty big," said Cam.

"It's not big," said Heidi. "It's huge. Almost a million acres."

Cam sighed. "Any idea where we start looking for this lady?"

"I don't know," said Heidi, who was deep in the park's janky old website. "The visitor center?"

At this, Cam actually laughed.

"What? Do you have a better plan?" said Heidi.

Cam shook his head. "Nope. Sad to say that I don't. Let's start our search for this mysterious woman at . . . the visitor center."

The city gave way to suburban sprawl and then pine forests hiding intermittent houses. They got off the interstate and onto a four-lane county road. Soon the houses were gone altogether, and they were flanked on either side by a tall forest of Sitka spruce. A wooden sign, painted brown, marked the entrance to the national forest. Even though it was only early afternoon, the canopy of the trees blocked the sky, so that only scattered pools of sunlight found their way to the forest floor.

"You seem like a hiker," said Cam apropos of nothing.

"What the hell does *that* mean?" said Heidi.

Cam shrugged. "Isn't that what rich people like to do? Buy a four-hundred-dollar pair of boots to go stomp around in the woods and get mosquito bites?"

"You know, you're making a lot of assumptions about me," said Heidi, who did not want to admit that, yes, she really did enjoy hiking very much, in boots that may have, indeed, cost four hundred dollars.

"Sorry," said Cam. "I didn't say hiking was a bad thing."

"No, no. Please, tell me more about myself," said Heidi. "I'm dying to know."

"Okay, well, I'm guessing you've got a best friend named Chloe," said Cam. "Every year you two line up to be the first ones through the door at Starbucks on the day they start serving the pumpkin spice lattes."

Heidi tried not to laugh, but she did. "My best friend's name's Olivia, actually."

"Chloe? Olivia? I feel like I ought to get half credit," said Cam. "Let's see, what else. I don't know if you're valedictorian but you're definitely getting that Perfect Attendance Award."

"Shut up," said Heidi, but she wasn't angry. Not really.

"And I'm guessing Stanford's your safety school, because you're going straight to the Sorbonne."

Heidi's smile was gone now. She silently stared at her lap.

"What?" said Cam.

"Nothing," said Heidi. "Doesn't matter."

"Sorry, I think I make jokes when I'm stressed out," said Cam. "If you're not laughing you're crying, right?"

"No, it's just that right before all this, I found out I didn't get into Harvard." She instantly regretted saying it. Whining about not getting into the best college in the country was so stupid, so trivial compared to everything that had happened since then.

Cam was silent for a long moment. Heidi was certain that he was going to mock her for her irrational, childish feelings.

Instead he said, "Man, fuck Harvard."

As Cam and Heidi pulled into the visitor center parking lot, a ranger in a straw hat reminded them that the park would be closing at 6:00 PM today for the Lunar Cycle Curfew. Heidi and Cam thanked her for the reminder.

They grabbed a map of the park and still had no idea where to begin.

"It's fourteen hundred square miles," said Cam. "How could we possibly find her?"

"I guess we just ask people," said Heidi.

"Okay," said Cam. "And what do we ask them, exactly?"

"I'll figure it out,'" said Heidi, hoping she would.

The clock was ticking. They decided their best bet was to check the hiking trails nearby.

They approached a family of four in the trailhead parking lot. They were in the midst of climbing into their hatchback to head home.

"Here goes," said Heidi.

"Excuse me," she said as she approached the family, "have you . . . seen . . . a woman?" She tried to smile, but the weirdness of the question was unavoidable.

The mom cocked her head. "Well, yeah. Can you be more specific?"

"She lives here, in the woods." Heidi cleared her throat. "And they call her, uh . . ." She trailed off, unwilling to swear in front of children.

The mom was more patient than Heidi expected. "I don't

think anybody lives in the park. Except maybe some of the rangers."

Next, Heidi approached a teenage girl who seemed to be hiking alone.

"Nope," said the girl simply.

"Her nickname is the Bitch," Cam added.

The girl's eyes narrowed.

"No, it isn't," said Heidi. "Sorry to bother you."

They asked a dozen more people. No one knew anything and somehow, asking got more awkward each time, not less. A part of Heidi wanted to laugh at how ridiculous it all was. But the bigger part of her felt her panic growing as the seconds before moonrise slipped away.

Eventually, they made their way back to the visitor center. In desperation, Heidi asked the ranger manning the information desk if he knew anything about a woman who lived in the forest.

"Nobody lives in the forest," the ranger said flatly.

"Yeah, right, I didn't think so," said Heidi. "Sorry."

"I seen her."

Heidi turned to see an old-timer with a beard and a sweat-stained bandanna tying back his long gray hair. He had the ropy physique and jerky-like complexion of a serious hiker.

"Really?" said Heidi.

The old man nodded. Heidi's eyes flitted to the ranger, but he was already helping another park visitor locate the Panther Creek Trail on their map.

"Tell me."

"I was camping," said the old man. "Middle of the night, I had to take a piss. That's when I saw her. Out on the trail. Nothin' but her birthday suit. And those eyes. I had to check and see if I was hallucinating."

"Were you?" asked Cam.

The guy chuckled. "Not that time. Stone-cold sober. Well, pretty sober, anyways. I figured she was some kinda Wiccan or something. You know they do their rituals out in the forest. This was a few weeks back. Maybe it was the equinox?"

"Where?" asked Heidi.

"Not too far from here," he said. "Ocean Ridge Trail. She a friend of yours or something?"

But he got no answer. Heidi and Cam were already running out the door to their car.

They drove along the winding two-lane road through the park until they came to a tiny gravel parking lot. Cam's Kia was the only vehicle there. They got out and found that the forest around them was eerily quiet, though they could hear the distant sounds of waves lapping against the shore.

As they walked toward the trailhead, they heard the sound of another vehicle. A Chevy Tahoe, with the National Park Service logo on the side, pulled into the lot. The ranger rolled down his window.

"You two know the park is closing early, right?" His tone was friendly but firm. He checked his watch. "You've only got an hour and a half."

Heidi smiled and nodded, but said nothing. She felt sick. They both watched the Tahoe drive off, leaving them alone in the woods once more.

Heidi started walking but Cam didn't move.

"Heidi, what are we even doing?" He sounded tired.

"Maybe she's around here somewhere," said Heidi, who wouldn't allow herself to consider the alternative. "Maybe we'll find her."

"But—"

"What other choice is there?"

"I guess there isn't one."

"Yeah," said Heidi. "You can give up if you want. I'm going on."

"I'm not giving up."

Heidi grabbed a trail map from the waterproof box attached to the sign. The Ocean Ridge Trail was a seven-mile loop that skirted along the cliffs overlooking the sea.

It was close to 4:30 PM as Heidi and Cam started along the trail. They made their way uphill through the forest, following a rocky path that had frequent switchbacks as it gained elevation. More than once Cam wished aloud for a pair of four-hundred-dollar boots instead of his old worn-out sneakers.

The yellow blazes that marked the trail were faded, which made orienteering difficult. The path was overgrown in places, and the way forward wasn't always obvious. They were often forced to stop and carefully search the trunks of the surrounding trees for faint splashes of yellow. Twice they realized they'd missed a blaze, forcing them to backtrack until they found the trail again.

The woods were quiet. As they hiked, they searched for any sign of the Bitch, but they saw nothing. Heard nothing. They might as well have been the only two people in the world. Yet at times, Heidi felt the hairs on the back of her neck stand up, as though some unseen observer was watching their slow ascent. Each time, she scanned the forest to find it empty.

The sun sank lower in the sky as they continued their climb. As they rounded a hairpin bend, a blur of movement ahead startled them. A pack of four-legged beasts bounded across their path and disappeared into the underbrush. Heidi's heart leaped into her throat for the split second before she realized that they'd only surprised a herd of deer.

Cam and Heidi hiked on, mostly without talking now. The only sounds besides their own footfalls were occasional bird-calls and the growing white noise of the ocean waves. The sky above had turned orange, as the sun drifted down toward the horizon.

Once again, Heidi felt watched.

She stopped in the trail and screamed at the top of her lungs, "Hello! Are you out here?"

There was no answer. Her cry only succeeded in silencing the birds.

The trail took a steep uphill turn. It was hard going, and Heidi often had to grab on to tree roots or moss-covered rocks to keep moving forward. As they crested a ridge, the forest opened up to a hillside of massive limestone boulders. Tangled thickets of blackberry bushes sprouted between the rocks.

Heidi and Cam helped each other scramble over the boulders and up the hill. They reached the top and found themselves in a wide clearing on a tall bluff overlooking the ocean. The sun was setting, painting the water and the sky red, gold, and purple. The view here was incredible. So incredible that Heidi's first instinct was to take a selfie. The thought made her laugh.

"What's funny?" asked Cam.

Heidi shrugged. "If you're not laughing, you're crying."

She took a moment to absorb the scene: the sunset, the open water, the sea breeze ruffling the grass. From up here, she felt like she could see for a hundred miles. She closed her eyes.

"The moon will be up in twenty minutes," said Cam.

"C'mon. Let's keep going," said Heidi.

"Heidi."

"What are you waiting for? Let's move." She'd already started back along the trail.

"We're not going to find her," said Cam. He sat down on a wide, flat rock. "This is where it's going to happen."

Heidi didn't want to believe him. But she knew he was right. She took a deep breath, then sat down on the rock beside him.

"I guess the plan didn't work," she said. "Sorry."

"Not your fault," said Cam. "When your best hope is getting Chinese diet pills from an urban legend you heard about from a drug dealer you just beat up, I'm not sure the specific plan actually matters all that much."

Heidi laughed. Then both of them looked out over the ocean in silence. The sun was gone now. Darkness had fallen.

"We should probably undress," said Heidi.

"What?" said Cam.

"If we survive this, we'll want our clothes in the morning."

"Always thinking practically," said Cam. "I like that about you."

Cam turned away from Heidi and started to take his shirt off. Heidi stepped out of her sneakers and took off her socks. She took off her jeans and her T-shirt and carefully folded them.

Cam stripped down to his boxer shorts. They put their clothes, along with their phones, keys, and wallets, in the crook of an alder tree and sat back down on the rock, which now felt uncomfortably cold against Heidi's bare skin.

"Not how I was expecting to spend my Friday night," said Cam.

"I've read that it hurts pretty bad."

"Yeah. In the videos I've seen, it looks like it hurts." Cam shivered.

"Should've brought a blanket," said Heidi.

"Should've brought a book," said Cam. "How much time you think we've got before . . ."

"I'm not sure," said Heidi.

But she knew it wouldn't be long. She could feel that clearly. Even though her skin was covered in goose bumps, she was starting to sweat. Something was happening to her; in her.

"Want to play twenty questions?" asked Cam.

"Not really," said Heidi. "Want to play tic-tac-toe?"

"Sure."

"Too bad. No paper."

"Damn. Why you gotta get my hopes up like that?"

There was another long silence.

"Heidi."

"Yeah."

"I feel . . . scared."

"Me too."

Heidi's hand inched across the cold stone to find Cam's. She held it and she heard him breathe a soft sigh of relief.

It was dark now. Behind them a strip of silvery light peeked above the mountains as the full moon rose.

A ragged scream burst out of Heidi's lungs as the first wave of excruciating pain racked her body. She felt simultaneous cramps all over. Every muscle in her abdomen clenched, launching her involuntarily forward onto her stomach.

"It's going to be okay," said Cam, who still held her hand, even though she was now squeezing it as hard as she could.

A moment later, Heidi puked. She hadn't eaten much that day so all that came out was a thin stream of bile. Heidi tried to say something—apologize maybe—but all she managed was a long moan. The noise barely sounded human. Heidi tried to speak, but her jaw had locked and her mouth seemed incapable of forming words.

"It's going to be okay," repeated Cam. "It's going to be—"

He suddenly doubled over in pain, clutching his belly with a high-pitched groan. Even though Heidi was in agony herself, some part of her wanted to help Cam. She hated to see him endure such misery.

But Heidi couldn't help. She couldn't move. Her body was no longer obeying her brain. She was controlled by whatever was happening inside her.

She writhed in the puddle of her own bile as she felt her bones cracking, her hands and feet clenching tight against the pain. Her fingernails scrabbled on the rocks until they tore off. Something hard and sharp was pushing up from her fingertips, bursting from her skin like bloody flowers to replace them. She felt her jaws distending and her teeth lengthening. As her muscles tensed and bulged, her skin stretched and stretched, and then it began to rip. In the ragged holes where it tore open, patches of dark, wet fur burst forth, rank and repulsive.

Beside her, she heard Cam struggling to breathe, heard his heart racing in his chest. She smelled his sweat and his blood and his saliva. She somehow forced her cramping neck to turn and look at him and she wished she hadn't. He was an abomination now—a nightmare thing of flesh and bone. His eyes bulged and rolled in his misshapen skull.

The sight was unbearable. The sounds were unbearable. The smell was unbearable. But most of all, the pain was unbearable. And at last Heidi could endure no more. Her vision blurred as her mind slipped into blessed unconsciousness.

12

Erik Balikian counted the reasons he couldn't sleep.

Reason number one was that his shoulder still hurt like hell. Last night, back at the station, Reaper had helped him pop it back into its socket—almost as painful as dislocating it in the first place. After that, he'd even slipped Erik some pain meds that he had handy in his locker ("for emergencies"). Despite the codeine he'd taken a couple of hours ago, Erik still couldn't find a position on his—admittedly crappy—mattress that didn't eventually cause a burning pain to shoot up his arm and into his brain. He tossed and turned and never settled.

The second reason was that as a VCTF officer he worked nights. That was just the job. He still hadn't gotten used to going to bed at the exact moment the rest of the world was making breakfast. Everybody on the force told him he ought to take some money from his first paycheck and invest in a decent set of blackout curtains and a white noise machine. He'd bought a sick new pair of sneakers instead. And now sunlight was streaming into his bedroom through his cheap polyester curtains, and he could hear every noise out on the street.

The final reason Erik couldn't sleep was one that he didn't even want to admit to himself: Every time he closed his eyes he was back in that tunnel. He was blinded by the smoke of his flash-bang and blowing out his eardrums with his own MP5. His gun was jamming. And then the *thing* was there. He couldn't really remember what it looked like and he really didn't want to, only that it was a violent blur of fur, and muscle, and teeth. It was death incarnate.

Yet, somehow he'd cheated it. He'd lived. But now, as he lay exhausted on the cusp of sleep, half dreaming and replaying the night before, sometimes he wasn't so lucky. Sometimes the monster found one of the soft spots in his Kevlar armor—the gap between the helmet and the chest, his hands, the area under his arms that was thinner for increased flexibility—and it tore into him. It ripped out his jugular, or it tore his arm off, or it bit his fingers off. Sometimes it killed him there in the tunnel. And sometimes it left him alive, moaning and bleeding in the dirty water, and it was Reaper who finished him off with a grin and a silver bullet and then lit up a smoke afterward.

And then worst of all, sometimes it wasn't the beast at all he was facing in that tunnel. Sometimes it was a naked old woman, terrified and begging for her life before a silver 9mm round to her brainpan ended her pleading. She looked like Erik's neighbor down the hall, Mrs. Alvarez, or maybe his grandma Gadarine, who had died when he was four. Sometimes it was Reaper who casually blew her head off. Sometimes it was Erik.

Erik sat up and rubbed his eyes. He checked his phone. 12:26 PM. After last night—injury in the line of duty—he was fully entitled to some paid time off. But when the VCTF doctor had examined him, he'd laughed and joked and pretended he wasn't hurt at all. He could tell that Reaper approved. It was a supermoon, two nights of LCC in a row, and Erik Balikian would be clocking in again in a few hours for another shift. Unless he called in sick.

He thought about it. He thought about texting his girlfriend Leah. They'd been dating since tenth grade and decided to stay together even after graduation. Now they were a year out of high school. Leah had gone to college in Idaho and he'd joined the Viral Containment Task Force. When Erik talked to her she was worried about credit hours and exams. He didn't even know how he would explain to her what had happened to him down in that tunnel. Would she be proud of him? Afraid? Would she understand what it was like to come that close to a real-life monster? To wrestle with death itself? And if she didn't understand any of that, what then?

Instead of texting Leah, Erik wrote a text to Reaper ("Jason" in his phone but Erik could only think of him as Reaper) and sent it:

Yo thanks again man. I owe you.

He figured Reaper would be asleep. Instead his phone buzzed a second later with a message.

Can't sleep?

Nah. You?

Can a kid sleep on Christmas Eve?

Erik laughed at this. Dude was nuts. Before he could reply, his phone buzzed with another text.

Wanna go do something fun?

Erik didn't particularly want to go do something fun. He wanted to sleep. He wanted his arm to not hurt anymore. He wanted to forget the thing in the tunnel that looked like his grandma. He replied to Reaper.

Hell yeah

Reaper replied with the rock n' roll fingers emoji.

Twenty minutes later, Jason Mottola was idling out front of Erik's apartment building in his big black pickup. He wasn't wearing his helmet or the Kevlar armor and his notorious calling card—the necklace of fangs—was nowhere to be seen. Reaper was dressed in plain clothes with his badge on a lanyard around his neck, just as he'd instructed Erik to do. Hip-hop blasted on the radio.

"'Sup, Caveman" was all Reaper said as Erik climbed into the passenger's side.

"Nice truck," said Erik.

"I know," said Reaper. "You strapped?"

Erik patted his service weapon, a Glock-17, in his holster.

"Boy Scout," said Reaper as he pulled out onto the street. "Always be prepared."

Reaper drove through traffic, drumming the steering wheel in time to the music. People were out on the street: jogging, shopping, playing pickup basketball on an outdoor court.

"Look at them," said Reaper. "Nice day. They think they're entitled to it. Like they've got a right to be safe. They don't realize where safety comes from."

"Fucking chumps," said Erik, but he didn't really believe it. Part of him wished he was playing basketball too, or maybe just sitting on a park bench enjoying the sun.

"Safety comes out the end of what you got in that holster," said Reaper.

"Yeah," said Erik. "I understand that now. Especially after last night."

Reaper nodded. "About that: When something like what happened to you happens to somebody, there's two ways it can go."

"Yeah?"

"You can let it affect you. Or you can let it motivate you."

Erik nodded like he understood.

"There's no shame in letting it affect you," said Reaper. "Plenty of guys tap out. Go for a desk job. Go join the regular police. PTSD. Whatever."

"I don't have PTSD," said Erik.

"Personally, I find that you can take all that shit that you feel—the helplessness, the anger, and yes, even the fear—and instead of it being a burden, you can use that to light a fire under your ass. Dude, you weren't trapped in a tunnel with an infected civilian last night. You were in hell. Actual, literal hell on earth. You went toe to toe with the devil himself. And you're the one who walked out of there, bro."

There was something odd about calling that dead old lady "the devil himself," but Erik just nodded and said, "Thanks to you, dude."

"Don't thank me," said Reaper. "Just return the favor someday."

"You can count on me, bro," said Erik, though he couldn't possibly imagine a situation where Reaper—the *Reaper*—would need his help.

"After that shit last night, you know what that's like—facing down Armageddon," said Reaper. "Now you have a responsibility. It's up to you to make sure no one else is ever in that same position because one of these fucking *things* is running around loose." He waved his hand at the world whizzing by outside the truck. "If you and me didn't go in that tunnel last night—if we'd just followed orders and sat around with our thumbs up our assholes—maybe that 10–91W escapes?" said Reaper. "Maybe it's out there, running around tonight? And maybe it kills somebody. Or worse, maybe it *doesn't* kill 'em. Maybe it passes along the disease. And now there's two of 'em; and now there's four, and then eight, and sixteen, and so on."

Reaper was normally cool as ice, but Erik could see a fire in his eyes as he spoke.

"They call it a 'public health crisis' or a 'race for the cure,'" said Reaper. "That's bullshit. This is a war. And unfortunately it's an asymmetrical war. To win it, we have to get rid of them all. But they multiply like roaches, like they *are* a virus. All it takes to turn a little old lady into a killing machine is some saliva. There's only one cure."

Reaper aimed his finger like a gun and pantomimed pulling the trigger.

"I'd like to cure a few myself," said Erik.

Reaper nodded in approval. "For our side to win we need people with the guts and the will to do whatever it takes—people like me. Maybe people like you. But we're a dying breed, Caveman."

"People are all pussies nowadays," said Erik. He was excited Reaper had put him into the same category as himself, but he definitely caught the "maybe." Did he still have something to prove?

"Right now, you could be sitting at home on leave, getting paid to do nothing. But when I asked you to get off your butt and come help me, you were all in. That tells me something. That tells me you want to go the extra mile."

"Absolutely, dude," said Erik. "Whatever it takes."

Reaper nodded and kept driving. He wasn't smiling but Erik thought he looked pleased.

"So where are we going?" asked Erik.

"They IDed the dead doggie from last night," said Reaper. "Name's Dagamara Brodzińska. Age sixty-three. Born Wrocław, Poland. I'd like to learn a little bit more about her. Maybe figure out how she got bit."

"Contact tracing," said Erik. "Isn't that what Investigative Services is supposed to do?"

The VCTF had their own corps of detectives whose only job was to track the origins of confirmed infections.

Reaper snorted. "She's dead, so they won't even open a case."

"What?" said Erik.

"They can't interview her, so they won't bother."

"That's bullshit," said Erik. "They could talk to other people. They could do an investigation."

Reaper shrugged. "They *could*. But they won't. That's the problem with IS. They do the bare minimum because it's all people who already tapped out. They picked a day job. Picked safety. Very rarely do they go the extra mile."

Erik was shocked. Making detective was the dream of practically every new recruit who joined the Dogcatchers. Here, Reaper was calling Investigative Services lazy. Useless even.

Reaper pulled over in front of a tiny grocery store called White Eagle Polish Specialties.

"The only family I found stateside is her brother, Teodor Rosiński," said Reaper. "You like kielbasa?"

"Sure."

"Then follow me."

Inside, they found an older man standing behind the counter of a small deli. There was a refrigerated case filled with sausages, stuffed cabbages, pierogis, sauerkraut.

"Mr. Rosiński," said Reaper. "I'm Corporal Mottola of the Viral Containment Task Force. This is my colleague, Officer Balikian."

Erik nodded.

The old man had the naturally suspicious look of anyone who was unexpectedly being called their last name by an officer of the law. "Yes" was all he said.

"Mr. Rosiński, I'd like to talk to you about your sister."

"Sister?" said Teodor, confused.

Instantly, Erik understood. The old man hadn't been told his sister was dead yet. Erik felt sick. Did Reaper know?

Whether he did or didn't, Reaper didn't miss a beat. "I'm very sorry to inform you that your sister, Dagamara, passed away last night."

Almost instantly, the old man's reticence shattered and he broke down. Erik couldn't bear to look at him. Instead, he focused his gaze on the plastic containers of white borscht inside the refrigerator case.

"She died?" sobbed Teodor. "How? How?"

"Unfortunately she became infected with *Rabies lupinovirus*," said Reaper.

Erik would not have expected that a cowboy like Reaper would actually be good at something like this. But he was. The guy sounded official yet somehow comforting. You'd never guess from his gentle tone that he was the one who'd put a bullet in

Dagamara Brodzińska's head and then pulled one of her teeth out with a pair of silver pliers.

"Unfortunately, this pandemic continues to take a toll," said Reaper. "If there's anything you can tell us about how or where she may have become infected, we'd be very appreciative."

"I don't know," said the old man, violently sobbing. "I don't know."

"Did she have any friends?"

He shook his head. "All in Poland."

"A job?"

"She was housekeeper," said the old man. "Family called Mills."

Reaper copied down the address. Then he handed the old man a plain white business card that said JASON MOTTOLA—VIRAL CONTAINMENT TASK FORCE and his phone at the bottom.

"If you think of anything else, please reach out," said Reaper. "Once again, very sorry for your loss." He shot a quick glance at Erik.

"Sorry," mumbled Erik.

They left the old man in his store, crying and staring at the business card.

Out on the street, Reaper said, "Well, that was a waste of time."

"It was?" asked Erik. "Should we talk to the family she worked for?"

"Nah, that's where we were last night," said Reaper. "Cascadian Estates. Seven-figure houses. Best security money can buy. The transmission rate is basically zero in that zip code. She must've got bit somewhere around here."

Erik nodded.

They drove half a mile to Dagamara Brodzińska's house and knocked on a few of the neighbors' doors. Nobody answered, which wasn't unusual as it was the middle of a workday. They climbed back into Reaper's truck, having learned nothing. Erik couldn't stop thinking of Teodor Rosiński. When he willed himself to forget the old man, he instead saw Dagamara's ruined face, dead in the water. Erik wished he'd never agreed to do this.

Reaper seemed cheerful as he drove them north. Erik didn't know the neighborhood well, but they were somewhere near the university.

"Something came in on the tip line," said Reaper. "I want to check it out."

Reaper turned onto a street called Paradise Way and pulled his truck over in front of a small dingy house with a lawn that badly needed mowing.

"Neighbor anonymously reported that they've got a dog in there."

Reaper must've caught the look on Erik's face. He laughed. "What's the matter, Rook? Enthusiasm flagging?"

"Nah, man. The law's the law. Dogs are passive—"

Reaper killed the music. "This is what going the extra mile looks like. Sometimes it's boring as hell."

"I get it," said Erik. "Gotta do the legwork."

Reaper stroked his jaw. "Well I guess I did promise you something fun. I'll do my best to make this one interesting. Just for you, Caveman."

"Yeah?" said Erik.

Reaper shot him a mischievous grin. "This one's a shot in the dark, but sometimes you get lucky. And I happen to be a lucky man. Just remember: When we knock on that door, we're not going to say we're IS. But we're not going to say we're *not*."

"Got it," said Erik.

"Shake the tree and see what falls out."

Reaper walked across the lawn and stopped halfway to the door. He turned around and shot Erik a crazy smile. Then he let out a wolf howl at the top of his lungs. It was a perfect imitation of the real thing, and loud enough that anyone in the neighborhood could hear it. Erik wondered if he'd lost his mind.

Reaper stopped and before Erik could say anything, he pointed to his ear. A moment later, Erik heard it: a faint barking coming from inside the house. The sound was quickly cut off.

Reaper pounded on the front door. "Hello. Viral Containment Task Force. I see the lights on, cars in the driveway. I know somebody's home."

He pounded again. No response. He turned to Erik. "You want to do the honors, Caveman?"

Erik nodded. He took a step back and then he kicked the door, just like they taught him in the academy. The first kick splintered the jamb. The second one made the door fly wide open.

A woman about Erik's age—college girl; cute in a Nirvana shirt—was standing just inside the door, fists balled.

"What the fuck?" said the girl. "You can't just kick the door down and barge in!"

Reaper smiled politely. "We did knock, Ms. Esposito. Is it okay if I call you Micaela?"

"You have no legal right to be here," she said.

"What, are you pre-law?" asked Reaper, stepping inside and looking around. "Because my file says you dropped out of school. Makes me wonder why you even still live around the college?" He turned to Erik. "That's got to be a little depressing, right?"

"Yeah," said Erik. "Real bummer."

"Fuck you, Dogcatcher," said Micaela. "The virus is running rampant and *I'm* the one you're trying to intimidate. You fucking pigs are about to be famous."

Micaela raised her phone to film. Reaper turned to Erik and gave a disappointed shake of the head. Erik stepped forward and wrenched the phone out of her hand.

"Ow, my fucking hand," cried Micaela.

"Ow, your hand," repeated Reaper with a chuckle. "My guy had his arm yanked out of its socket by a 10–91W that was trying to tear his head off last night. But by all means: Please complain about your sore pinkie, snowflake."

"I'm going to sue the shit out of you," said Micaela, clutching her fingers. "You're a fucking fascist."

Reaper smiled, almost benevolently. "To answer your question of due process: Under the continued state of emergency, the Viral Containment Task Force has extraordinary powers under the law. We had probable cause to enter this domicile the moment we heard your dog barking."

Erik saw something flash across the girl's face.

"I don't own a dog," said Micaela.

"Lying to us is a crime," said Reaper. "Didn't you learn that before you flunked out of school?"

"Two cars in the driveway," said Erik. "You got a boyfriend?"

Micaela cocked her head and gave Erik a withering smile. "Are you asking me out?"

"You got a roommate?" asked Reaper. "Maybe it's her dog?"

"I don't own a dog," repeated Micaela.

Reaper nodded. "Yeah, we're gonna need to have a look around. Take a seat on the couch, miss."

"Give me my phone back," said Micaela.

Reaper didn't. He motioned for Erik to follow as they made a tour of the house's small kitchen. They checked the cabinets and the drawers. They looked inside the fridge: virtually empty, except some hot sauce and a few old takeout containers. Swap out the oat milk for 2 percent and it was eerily similar to Erik's own fridge at home.

"You think there's a dog in my refrigerator?" sneered Micaela from the other room.

Reaper and Erik ignored her and continued around the house. They checked the bathroom. The counter was cluttered with dozens of beauty and hair care products. By contrast, the medicine cabinet was oddly empty.

They worked their way to the bedrooms. There were two of them, and it was clear that two girls lived here. One of the bedrooms was kept in decent order. The other was a complete wreck.

"You take that one," said Reaper, nodding to the messy room. "I'll take this one."

"Sure," said Erik, trying not to frown.

Erik stepped into the pigsty. There were clothes all over the floor, and somehow even more beauty products on every flat surface. He didn't relish digging through someone else's dirty laundry, so he started by looking under the mattress, and under the bed. He found a pair of ice skates, an unused yoga mat still in the shrinkwrap, a bunch of mismatched, unwashed socks. In short, nothing.

He heard a whistle from the other bedroom. Erik saw that Reaper had pulled out the middle drawer of a chipped wooden armoire. There, hidden under the folded clothes, was a Tupperware container. Inside the container were a dozen yellow pill bottles.

Reaper stepped back into the living room. "My goodness. Quite the pharmacy you have here. I'm sure you've got prescriptions for all of these?"

Micaela said nothing.

"You find anything?" Reaper asked Erik.

"Not yet," said Erik.

Reaper smiled. "Keep looking. There's always something."

Erik went back into the messy room. He tried to imagine where somebody might put something they didn't want found. He slid open the door to the closet. Inside it was almost bursting with shoes and clothing. The closet was so shallow that the hangers were all turned at a forty-five-degree angle so the clothes would even fit.

Erik wondered who the hell would make a closet like this? It was too shitty, even for a rental house for college kids.

He grabbed an armful of clothes and tossed them onto the bed, exposing the bare gray wall behind. There was definitely something off about it. Erik pushed on the back wall and felt it give. He heard something in the darkness behind it, a gasp maybe.

"Yo," called Erik.

Reaper joined him in the bedroom. He smiled when he saw what Erik was looking at and said, "Oh, hell yes."

Erik pushed aside the false wall and saw the true back wall of the closet, maybe eighteen inches deeper. There was a dark, narrow space where a girl with green hair was crouching. She was hugging a small dog to her chest, with her hand capped over its muzzle.

"Good afternoon, miss," said Reaper very politely. "Why don't you come on out of there?"

Without speaking, the green-haired girl climbed out of the little hidden space. Tears glistened on her cheeks. The dog whined. It looked like a mutt with some terrier blood, maybe a bit of corgi. *Cute little guy*, thought Erik.

Reaper clucked his tongue and gave the green-haired girl a disapproving look. "This is not good."

"I know, I—I have anxiety," said the girl with the green hair. "And before the pandemic, I was able to have a licensed emotional support animal. But now—and I know he's not infected, I *know* he's not, because I test him all the time, and he doesn't come into contact with *any* other dogs. I don't even think he's *seen* another dog in years so there's no way he has the—"

Reaper put a finger to his lips and Green Hair went quiet. He knelt and whistled. The dog came toward him. Reaper grinned as he scratched behind the dog's ears and the dog licked his hand.

"What's his name?" asked Reaper.

"Bagel," said the girl.

"Bagel. That's cute," said Reaper. "Here's the deal. Federal law says this dog ought to be immediately euthanized."

The green-haired girl gave an anguished groan.

"But today's your lucky day," said Reaper. "I happen to be a dog lover. We had this border collie growing up. His name was Hunter. Best dog ever. Seriously. He was like part of the family. Smarter than some of my brothers. Goddamn, I miss that dog."

Reaper smiled as he stared off into the middle distance, perhaps reliving fond memories with his childhood pet, while giving Bagel a vigorous belly rub.

"So I'm gonna cut you a little slack today, miss," said Reaper. "If you tell me something useful, I might just forget I ever saw Bagel."

"What do you mean 'useful'?" asked Green Hair.

Reaper shrugged. "Tell us something that you think we would want to know."

"I . . . I don't know anything like that," said Green Hair.

"Don't tell them shit, Gina."

Micaela was standing in the door. Her eyes were locked on Gina's.

Reaper sighed. "Your friend has been less than polite to us, even though we're public servants simply trying to do our job."

"Uh-huh," said Gina.

"Look, I know the stats on dogs," said Reaper. "There hasn't been a verified case of canine transmission in the US in at least two years. And I believe you when you say you test him. I know you can order the kits online. But that doesn't change the fact that owning him is against the law. This is a federal crime we're talking about. So c'mon. Help me out, here."

Gina was quiet as she looked like she was considering something. "Okay, I think I know something."

"Don't," said Micaela. "These pigs are not your friends."

"We save lives," snapped Erik. "What the fuck do you do?"

"Okay, so it may be nothing," said Gina, "but these people came by earlier and they were asking about this drug called Extiva. Micaela had no idea what they were talking about but—but I'm pretty sure I know why they were looking for it . . ."

"Uh-huh," said Reaper, as he scratched under Bagel's chin. "Tell me more."

* * *

It was after 4:30 PM as they made their way back to Reaper's truck.

Erik's adrenaline was pumping. He had a huge grin on his face. He saw that Reaper did too.

"We got names," said Erik.

"This is the type of intel the IS pencil pushers never get," said Reaper. "Nice work in there, Caveman."

"Let's go find them," said Erik. "Two more 10–91Ws we can take off the street."

Reaper shook his head. "It's LCC tonight. We both clock in in less than an hour."

"Oh right," said Erik. "Almost forgot."

"How could you forget the main event? You ever hear that old song about the bad moon?" Reaper launched into an off-key rendition of a classic rock song Erik had never heard before.

Erik chuckled. "Nah, dude."

"Don't laugh at my singing," said Reaper with a sly grin. "You got any plans for your day off tomorrow?"

Erik smiled. "Going the extra mile."

"Hell yeah," said Reaper, "Tomorrow, let's go pay a visit to Dawn Suppley and Cameron Woodbine."

Reaper drove them both to the VCTF headquarters. Erik couldn't help but notice the looks he got from the other rookies—Cho, Caudell, and the others—as he walked into the station, laughing and chatting with Corporal Jason "Reaper" Mottola.

The officers gathered in the conference room, Styrofoam cups of burned coffee in hand, as Lt. Aoki gave out assignments for the evening—patrols, roadblocks, guard duty, and rapid response around the city. He stressed the importance, to much groaning from the assembled Dogcatchers, of activating personal bodycams in advance of an incident.

"And last of all, I need ten volunteers for a special assignment," said the lieutenant.

Reaper's hand went up faster than anyone else's. A few others raised their hands, as well. Erik was one of them. The lieutenant counted out ten.

"Great," said Aoki. "The rest of you can go suit up. Good luck and stay safe out there."

The other Dogcatchers filed out, leaving ten volunteers with the lieutenant. Aoki turned on his overhead projector, which showed a satellite map of a stretch of forest outside the city.

"We've received reports of elevated 10–91W presence in this area," said the lieutenant. "The supermoon gives us a unique opportunity to use this intel proactively and immediately. I want to deploy two-man teams to run BGG operations throughout this valley tonight."

"Caveman's with me," said Reaper.

"Noted," said Lt. Aoki. "And just to give the dead horse one more kick: Anything happens, I do want bodycams on. Questions?"

Erik barely listened to the rest of what the lieutenant said. He couldn't believe that Reaper had chosen him as his partner.

* * *

Forty minutes later, Erik was suited up in his helmet and Kevlar—along with nine of his fellow officers—in the back of a VCTF BearCat as it rumbled down the highway.

Erik was quiet while the others laughed and joked, showing each other funny videos on their phones. Pretending they were brave. The only person Erik was positive wasn't afraid was Reaper. The guy had actually nodded off during the ride. He was snoring with the necklace of fangs around his neck.

Erik had long since realized it was way too late to ask anyone what a "BGG operation" was, so he kept his mouth shut.

The BearCat rolled to a stop. Ten officers climbed out the back. They found themselves on an empty highway in the middle of a forested valley. Scenic hills rose on either side of the road. The sky was dusk purple, but the moon had not yet risen.

There was already a VCTF truck parked here, with a trailer hitched to the back. The trailer was the kind with air holes, used to transport police horses.

Reaper yawned and stretched. "Go on, Rook," he said to Erik. "Go get our assignment."

Erik didn't know how to ride a horse. Why the hell had he volunteered for this? He wanted to protest. But he didn't. Instead he stepped up to the back of the horse trailer and found that it wasn't carrying horses at all. A dozen goats bleated inside.

A VCTF officer named Unger handed Erik a nylon leash. On the end of it was a goat.

"Don't get too attached," said Unger.

Erik led the goat back to Reaper, who scratched it behind the ear.

"Careful," said Reaper. "These things bite."

Each of the five teams of two was assigned their own goat and they fanned out in different directions. Erik and Reaper climbed over the guardrail of the highway and into the forest. The dark canopy closed around them. Overhead, Erik heard a VCTF helicopter circling. Occasionally he saw its searchlight flash in the sky.

"Dude, what the hell is a BGG operation?" asked Erik.

Reaper laughed. "BGG is Dogcatcher slang: Billy Goats Gruff. We use the goat as bait. Then we wait for whatever comes out from under the bridge . . ."

It was dark now as they hiked up the hill through the forest. The full moon peeked through the leaves, bright enough that Erik didn't need his night vision goggles. He led the goat as Reaper started to sing the old rock song about the bad moon rising.

Suddenly Reaper went quiet. Then he chuckled. "About damn time," he said. "Bodycam, Rook."

Erik was confused. Had Reaper noticed something he hadn't?

The question was answered as a howl rang out through the valley. Erik turned his bodycam on and kissed his cross.

13

Heidi woke up face down in a ditch. She pushed herself up off the ground and looked around. She was in the forest, next to a trickling mountain stream as the morning sun filtered down through the trees. She had no idea where she was.

She picked a stick out of her hair and saw that her hands were covered in something dark and sticky. Dried blood.

Heidi fought the urge to scream. Instead, she knelt by the bank of the stream and frantically scrubbed off the blood as best as she could. Whose blood was it? What had she done? She struggled to remember, but all she had were disparate images. She wasn't sure if they were dreams or things she'd seen in movies or events that had really happened.

When her hands were clean, she called out, "Cam?"

No answer. Heidi took a deep breath through her nose and tried to calm herself and collect her thoughts. As she did, she smelled him.

Heidi followed Cam's scent a few hundred yards downstream until she saw him. He was lying on his back in a bed of ferns, motionless.

"Cam?" she said.

He didn't move. Was he dead? Heidi ran to him. As she got closer, she saw a wound on his neck. Blood on his face.

"Cam," she repeated with a tremor in her voice. She gently touched his shoulder.

"Ow," said Cam without opening his eyes.

"Are you okay?"

Cam sat up and looked around, blinking. It took him a moment to register his surroundings. Then he looked at Heidi and smiled.

"Damn," he said. "We're alive."

"Sure seems like it," said Heidi.

Cam moved to touch the cut on his neck and winced. "My neck hurts like hell," he said. "How bad is it?"

Heidi peered at the wound. The cut itself didn't look too deep—not much more than a scratch—but the skin around it was an angry shade of purple.

"Maybe infected," said Heidi.

"Great," said Cam. "Another disease. Do you remember anything?"

"Not really," said Heidi.

"Me neither," said Cam. "I know we didn't find what we came here for, but maybe having . . . the *change* happen way out here, away from anybody we might hurt, maybe that was an accidental blessing?"

"Uh-huh," said Heidi. She didn't mention the blood she'd just washed off her hands.

"Where the hell are we?" said Cam.

"Not sure, but I think I can get us back to the trail," said Heidi.

Heidi led the way. She didn't tell Cam, but every few hundred feet, she stopped to sniff the air. She was following their scent back the way they'd come.

It took them an hour of hiking, barefoot, to make their way

back to the Ocean Ridge Trail. They reached the overlook and found that their clothes and personal belongings were, thankfully, still in the crook of the alder tree, right where they'd left them.

As Heidi was getting dressed, she found something wrapped up in her shirt. It was a leather cord with twelve fangs on it. Who had put it here? She scanned the forest and saw nothing. But on the wind she caught the faintest hint of sour musk. She thought she recognized that smell from somewhere.

Before Cam saw it, Heidi balled up the necklace of fangs and threw it into the weeds. She finished getting dressed and rejoined him as he stood staring out over the ocean. The sky was overcast and the water looked as gray as slate.

"You think it was bullshit?" asked Cam.

"What?"

"You know, a mysterious woman who lives in the woods that can help us cure ourselves?"

Heidi shrugged. "When you put it that way . . . it doesn't sound very likely, does it?"

Cam eyed the tree line behind them. "Should we keep looking?"

Heidi suddenly felt bone-tired. "I need to get home. I'm exhausted."

"I should probably put a Band-Aid on this." Cam pointed to his neck.

It was late morning by the time they made it down to the trailhead parking lot. It was drizzling, as it did half the days of the year. Normally Heidi wouldn't have noticed, but today the rain chilled her.

Cam's Kia started on the second try, and soon they were driving out of the forest toward the interstate.

As they returned to cell service, Heidi's phone suddenly pinged with a dozen missed calls and messages from the past twelve hours: Olivia, Luca, her mom, other friends. Heidi didn't have the energy to look at them all. She stuck her phone in her pocket and watched the raindrops on the window slither up and backward across the glass as they sped down I-5.

Heidi looked over and was surprised to see that Cam had a big smile on his face.

"Why are you so happy?" she asked.

"Because we made it through the full moon. We survived it."

"Yeah," said Heidi.

"C'mon," said Cam. "This counts as a win. We bought ourselves some time. We have a month—"

"Twenty-eight days," said Heidi.

"We have twenty-eight days to get our hands on some Extiva," said Cam. "We can treat ourselves. We can do your plan. Race for the damn cure!"

Heidi was silent. All she could think about was the blood she'd washed off her hands. What had she done? Who had she hurt? Had she made that gash across Cam's neck? The thought made her shudder, but for the life of her, she couldn't remember. All she had were vague impressions: a light in the sky, the sound of gunshots, the taste of flesh, a ragged death cry. She thought of the necklace of fangs that she'd tossed into the weeds.

As Heidi's anxiety spiked, her mind shifted to what she remembered well: the transformation. She relived her body doing things it was never meant to do: the virus breaking her flesh and reassembling her into something different, something horrific. And in four weeks—656 hours, to be precise—it was going to happen all over again.

"We survived but . . . that was bad, right?" said Heidi.

"Zero stars," said Cam. "Would not recommend."

They traveled south into the city and Heidi began to give Cam directions to her neighborhood, before he stopped her to remind her that he already knew where she lived. Heidi felt mildly embarrassed as they reached the security gate for Cascadian Estates. Inside the booth, as always, was the up-armored security guard whose name Heidi never remembered.

He eyeballed Cam's—unknown, shitty—car with a scowl on his face. "Window down," he barked.

Cam rolled down the window, letting rain fall into the car. The guard looked inside and his expression instantly softened the moment he saw Heidi in the passenger seat.

"Good afternoon, Miss Mills," he said in an overly jovial tone. "How are you doing today?"

"Oh, just enjoying the weather," said Heidi with a fake laugh.

The guard returned an equally fake laugh and pressed the button to open the gate.

"Have a good one," he said as they drove through.

After a minute, Heidi spoke. "Sorry," she said.

"Sorry for what?" asked Cam.

"I don't know," said Heidi. "I didn't introduce you."

"Damn it," said Cam. "Now I'm going to miss out on a beautiful friendship with your fancy gated community's rent-a-cop. What was his name again?"

"Fuck off," said Heidi.

"Fuckhoff? What is that? Dutch?"

It wasn't until they pulled into the driveway of Heidi's house that they remembered.

Heidi opened the front door with a feeling of dread. The house was a wreck. Furniture was overturned and broken to pieces. She saw a ten-inch hole that had somehow been knocked into the wall. And even at the front door, she could smell it: a revolting stench of old blood, meat that was just starting to spoil, and human shit.

They found his body lying on the kitchen floor with his guts spilling out of the hole in his abdomen—the other burglar who'd tried to rob Heidi's house and had died in the first seconds of the werewolf attack. Somehow, even though the doors and windows had been closed up tight, there were already flies buzzing around the corpse. Heidi felt like she was going to throw up. Cam shook his head as he looked away.

"A.J.," said Cam.

"I'm sorry," said Heidi. "He was a friend of yours."

"Not really," said Cam. "I barely knew the guy. I don't even know what 'A.J.' stands for. He was a friend of a friend of a friend. But he wanted to get into the game, and he said he knew about an easy score. Ha-ha."

"Even so," said Heidi. "I'm sorry."

"Not as sorry as him," said Cam. "Poor bastard."

"What do we do now?" asked Heidi.

"You think I've ever been in this situation before?" asked Cam. "Because I assure you I have not."

"Can we call the police?" asked Heidi.

Cam said nothing. Heidi already knew the answer to her own question.

"Then we have to get rid of the body," said Heidi.

"Yeah," said Cam. "How?"

"I don't know. This is the type of neighborhood where everybody sits at home and peeks through the blinds, spying on everybody else." Heidi could feel herself starting to panic. "Shit, they're going to notice your shitty car in the driveway. You should move it."

"Too late," said Cam. "We passed through the gate. I'm sure my license place is already on camera."

"Fuck," said Heidi, as she sat down in a kitchen chair. "Fuck, fuck, fuck."

"I agree. Fuck," said Cam. "You got any orange juice?"

"I don't know," said Heidi, annoyed. "Check the refrigerator."

Cam went to the fridge and poured himself a glass of Florida's Finest Pure Premium 100% Organic Orange Juice.

He took a sip and made a face. "What is all this shit?"

"What?"

"There's, like, little bits of stuff in it." Cam put the glass down on the counter. "I think it's gone bad."

"What are you talking about?" said Heidi. "It's pulp. Have you seriously never had orange juice with pulp in it before?"

"Uh. Guess not?" said Cam. He took another tentative sip and frowned. "You *like* this stuff?"

"What? I don't know. No? Why are we even talking about this right now?"

"Because it's easier than what we *should* be talking about." Cam nodded toward the dead body on the floor.

"Maybe we could use my car," said Heidi. "If we could get him into the trunk. Maybe we could dump him somewhere."

"Moving a body is just another chance to get caught," said Cam. "Or so I've heard."

"Well, my mom is coming back *tomorrow*," said Heidi. "I think she might notice a fucking disemboweled corpse lying on her fucking kitchen floor!"

"Don't get mad at me," said Cam.

"Why not?" cried Heidi. "If you hadn't broken into my house, none of this would have happened!"

"If you hadn't lied to your parents, you'd be sipping a virgin mai tai at the Four Seasons in Hawaii right now."

"Yeah, but . . ." Heidi trailed off. "Okay, first of all, Ron is not my 'parent,' he's my stepdad." Even to herself, Heidi sounded like a child.

Cam shrugged. "I hereby formally apologize for breaking and entering. Unfortunately, that doesn't get either of us out of any of this. But if it makes you feel any better, I *definitely* wish I'd stayed home, gotten high, and played Xbox instead of robbing you."

There was an awkward silence.

"Thanks for saying sorry," said Heidi.

Cam shrugged. "The good news is that nobody besides me knew he was here."

"Yeah, nobody has any reason to look for him in this neighborhood," said Heidi. "But how do we get rid of him?"

She peeked through the curtains and saw that the neighbor's electric vehicle was in the driveway. Beyond, she saw her own family's backyard. At the far end of the yard was the Amish-built wooden shed Ron had put in two summers ago. She still remembered Madeline chiding him over the price.

"The shed," said Heidi, almost to herself.

Cam nodded as he joined Heidi at the window. "You said your mom would notice a dead body in the kitchen. She's not going to find one in the storage shed?"

"Nobody ever goes in there," said Heidi. "It's full of spiders and overpriced power tools Ron bought and then never touched. We could take up the floorboards and bury the body underneath it."

Cam gave her a sidelong glance. "You sure you haven't done this before?"

"Ha-ha," said Heidi.

"We'd still need to get him across your yard without anyone noticing. What about the nosy neighbors?"

"The yard backs up onto the woods there, so we're covered from the back. The Kramers are out of town. I think they're visiting family in Tucson or something." Heidi pointed to the house with the Tesla. "It's only the Washburns we have to worry about. I know how to handle the Washburns."

"Okay, then, let's get this place cleaned up," said Cam. He pulled out his phone and then paused. "Hmm. I feel like I probably shouldn't just google 'how to clean up dead body,' right?"

"Not going to look great if it ever comes up in court," said Heidi. "I think we just wing it."

Heidi found an old bedsheet in the basement beside Ron's model trains and they managed to get A.J.'s body on top of it. They wrapped the sheet around him and used duct tape to make sure it stayed on. Heidi then found the plastic tarp her family used to take on their camping trips and rolled the heavy bundle onto it.

With both of them working together, they were able to drag the tarp across the floor to the back door. Heidi was struck by just how difficult it was to move the corpse even fifty feet. The effort had both of them sweating.

Heidi then went to the closet under the stairs and found the large plastic bin where the family kept cleaning supplies for Dagamara. Heidi's mom was very particular about how she wanted the house cleaned, so they had everything on hand. Most importantly, they had a jug of bleach. From various true crime documentaries and podcasts, Heidi knew bleach was important because it destroyed DNA evidence. Or something.

Heidi and Cam donned rubber gloves and tied bandanas around their mouths. At first they tried mopping the kitchen, but it quickly became apparent that the old blood wouldn't wash away easily. Heidi noted with grim fascination how much stickier it was than the fresher blood she'd found on her hands this morning.

Ultimately, they were both forced to get down onto their hands and knees and use abrasive sponges and powdered cleaner to scour away the gummy stains. It took them hours to get the kitchen clean. All the while, they carefully collected all the paper towels and sponges they'd used in a white kitchen garbage bag.

In between exhausting bouts of scrubbing blood off the floor on all fours, Heidi began another project. She cracked an egg into a bowl of flour, baking powder, baking soda, and salt, and whisked it all together. Then she added chilled butter and sugar. She covered this dough in plastic wrap and put it in the refrigerator to chill.

With most of the blood scrubbed away, Cam was now able to mop the kitchen floor with a generous dose of bleach. Heidi was surprised at how efficient he was. Most boys she knew had never cleaned up after themselves in their lives. Even though her family had a weekly cleaning lady, Heidi was always expected to keep the house tidy. Her mother would tolerate nothing less.

While Cam mopped, Heidi spot cleaned the random blood spatter that had ended up on the counter, the side of the kitchen island, and, somehow, the door of the microwave. While she was scrubbing away at a low cabinet, she noticed something poking out from under the fridge.

It was A.J.'s snub-nosed revolver.

Heidi gingerly picked up the gun with her gloved hand. "Um. What do we do with this?"

Cam frowned. "I'll hold on to it until I can get rid of it, for real."

Cam grabbed a dish towel out of the drawer, wrapped the gun in it, and shoved it into his pocket.

By now the dough had chilled, and Heidi rolled it out and used her mother's cookie cutters to press it into the shapes of bells and stars and mittens. She put the cookies in the oven at 375 degrees to bake for seven minutes.

"Damn. Those smell good," said Cam. "Not sure I want to associate the aroma of fresh-baked cookies with, you know, cleaning up a murder scene."

"Could make Christmas weird," said Heidi as she placed the cookies on a rack to cool.

She and Cam moved on to the other rooms of the house, where they attempted to tidy up the aftermath of not only a fatal werewolf attack but an attempted burglary as well.

"Why do thieves just dump everything out when they rob a house?" asked Heidi, as she replaced the contents of an end table junk drawer that had been strewn all over the floor. "It makes such a big mess."

"I don't know," said Cam. "It's just faster."

"But if you kept things tidy, people might not even realize that they'd been robbed until months later."

Cam nodded. "As considerate as it is devious. You should start, like, a crime-consulting business." He held up the broken leg of a hand-carved Peruvian walnut chair. "So what are you going to tell your mom about this?"

Heidi shrugged. "That chair's old. I guess I'll say that I had Olivia over and she accidentally sat down on it too hard and it broke."

"What about that?" Cam pointed to the large hole that had been knocked in the wall.

"I don't know. I'll come up with something," said Heidi. "My mom always believes me for some reason."

Cam smiled and shook his head. "I could never get *anything* past mine."

Madeline always did believe Heidi's lies, but some small part of her suspected that it was because her mother didn't think Heidi was smart enough to deceive her. In this case, damage to the house would be extra plausible because it supported Madeline's preconception that Heidi was careless with nice things.

"Okay, the cookies are cool enough to ice," said Heidi. "You ready?"

Cam took a deep breath. "Yeah. Let's do this."

* * *

Heidi checked her phone: 3:14 PM. She patiently waited until it was 3:15 before she knocked on the Washburns' front door. Mrs. Washburn, a grandmotherly woman in her mid-sixties, answered the door.

"Heidi," said Mrs. Washburn.

"Hello, Mrs. Washburn."

"How are you, dear? I thought you were in Hawaii."

"I couldn't go, unfortunately," said Heidi. "Exams."

"Oh, I remember those days," said Mrs. Washburn. "Well, don't study too hard. You're a senior after all. This is when you're supposed to have fun, right?"

"Yes ma'am," said Heidi.

"Hear anything from Harvard?"

Heidi's smile didn't falter. "Not yet. Fingers crossed."

Mrs. Washburn smiled and nodded. "I'm sure you'll get in. You've always been a bright girl. Good at school. Not like our boys."

Heidi kept up the smile and nodded along.

"So what can I do for you?" asked Mrs. Washburn.

"Oh, well, I remembered how during the big storm you let us use your generator and I just wanted to thank you."

"That was two years ago, dear," said Mrs. Washburn.

"Well I figured it's never too late for 'Thank You' cookies," said Heidi, as she held up a tin full of iced sugar cookies.

Mrs. Washburn grinned. "My goodness! You really shouldn't have done all this."

"I remembered your husband likes cinnamon so I dusted a little extra on top," said Heidi. "Is Mr. Washburn around?"

"Well that is too sweet." Mrs. Washburn yelled back into the house. "Ed!"

Mr. Washburn shuffled to the door, confused, but his face lit up the instant he saw what Heidi had brought. "Christmas cookies in April?"

"Hey it's got to be Christmas somewhere, right?" said Heidi with a fake laugh.

The Washburns laughed too. And so Heidi stood, chatting with her neighbors on their front stoop—about school, and her parents, and their grandkids—until she felt her phone buzz in her pocket. She'd set a ten-minute timer—that was the amount of time Cam said he would need to drag a dead body across the back lawn and into the storage shed. By the time Heidi managed to extricate herself from the conversation, the Washburns had invited Heidi, her mom, and Ron over for dinner the following week. Mrs. Washburn was simply too polite to let the undeserved "Thank You" cookies stand.

Heidi walked back to her house. Praying the Washburns were in their kitchen putting the cookies away, she quickly slunk out the back door. Sure enough, Cam was inside the storage shed. A.J.'s body lay at his feet. The small space already reeked of death.

Heidi and Cam piled all the odds and ends that had accumulated in the shed over the years to either side. Then they set about working the nails out of the floorboards beneath them. Soon a strip of bare dirt was visible beneath their feet.

They each grabbed a shovel. In grim silence, Heidi and Cam started to dig. It took them four hours to make a hole that was deep enough. By the time it was done, Heidi's back ached and her hands were covered in blisters. Cam unceremoniously rolled the corpse into the hole.

"You want to say something?" asked Heidi.

Cam stretched his back and his vertebrae cracked. "Not really. I mean, sooner or later I guess this is where we all end up, right? The guy was kind of an asshole. I hope somebody out there loved him."

"I didn't think it was possible," said Heidi, "but you somehow just made this situation more depressing."

"I do what I can," said Cam.

Then they set about filling the makeshift grave back up with dirt from the two tall piles that flanked the hole. Once that was done, they carefully replaced the floorboards and tried to drive the nails back into the same holes. It took far longer than either would have liked and when they were done, Heidi thought the floor of the shed was conspicuously uneven. There was nothing to do about it now. She hoped that once the clutter had been replaced, no one would notice.

As they pushed the last of the storage shed contents back into place, they realized twilight had fallen. Both of them were filthy and worse, their clothes smelled like a dead body. After clocking that the Washburns' car was gone, they quickly scurried back inside the house.

"You want to take a shower?" asked Heidi. "You could borrow

some of Ron's clothes, I guess. How do you feel about pleated khakis and Tommy Bahama shirts?"

"I'm cool. I think I'm just going to head straight back to my apartment, take some Advil, and go to sleep for three days."

"That sounds amazing."

"So anyway, I guess we should, uh . . ."

"What?"

"Well, I should get your number, right?" said Cam. "We've still got to figure this whole thing out."

Heidi nodded and pulled out her own phone. "Okay, my number is—"

She was interrupted by the sound of the front doorbell.

14

Heidi was frozen with panic. There was someone at the front door.

"Answer it," hissed Cam. "Could be the neighbors. It's weird if you don't."

Cam quickly hid. Heidi swallowed and crept toward the front door, praying it was a package delivery or someone trying to sell her on a new religion. She stopped in the foyer and waited and listened. Maybe whoever it was had decided to leave.

But the doorbell rang again. And again. And again. Whoever had come was not going away.

Heidi quickly tried to brush the dirt off her clothes. She ran her fingers through her greasy hair and was acutely aware of how much she stank. There was nothing to do about it now. She made sure to smile before she answered the door.

Luca stood on the stoop. "I texted you."

Heidi's smile fell. "Luca. I didn't—I'm not—"

"Where have you been?" he asked. "Why weren't you at school Friday?"

"I—I was tired, so I ditched," she stammered.

"*You* ditched?" said Luca, clearly incredulous.

Heidi nodded.

"And you were so tired your thumbs didn't work?" He pantomimed typing out a reply on a phone.

"Sorry," said Heidi.

"Uh-huh," said Luca. He stepped into the house. "If you're going to disappear, you need to check in with me first."

Heidi felt a flicker of anger. "I need to check in with you?"

"Yes. I'm your boyfriend. I care about you." His tone didn't soften. "I care about your safety. When I don't know where you are, I get worried."

"Right," said Heidi.

"It's really inconsiderate," said Luca.

"Okay, I get it."

"Do you?" snapped Luca.

Heidi blinked.

Instantly, Luca's expression softened. "I'm just glad you're okay, that's all." Then he leaned in for a kiss.

"No!" shrieked Heidi, as she ducked away and shoved him back.

Luca looked shocked. Then angry. But he said nothing. There was a moment of tense silence.

Heidi's saliva carried *Rabies lupinovirus*. A kiss on the mouth would doom Luca to the same fate. She realized, for the first time, that until she was cured she would never be able to kiss her boyfriend again.

"Why did you do that?" asked Luca quietly.

"Sorry, I just—I haven't brushed my teeth yet today," she muttered.

"It's nearly 7:00 PM, Heidi," said Luca. "You need to get it together."

She shrugged. She wasn't prepared for any of this. Her excuses weren't making sense.

Luca's phone buzzed and he checked it. "Peter and Nils are here," he said.

"Why?" cried Heidi.

"What do you mean *why*?" said Luca. "The party starts in ten minutes."

"Fuck," said Heidi.

Heidi heard car doors slam, then Luca's two best friends, Peter and Nils, crossed the lawn and barged into the house.

"What up," said Nils, handing Heidi a six-pack of hard seltzer.

"Yo," said Peter as he walked past Heidi and jumped onto the couch. Nils found the remote and turned the TV on.

Luca crinkled his nose. "Jesus, can we crack a window? It smells like . . . What is that? Bleach?"

"It smells like a pillowcase full of wet assholes," said Nils as he flipped through the channels.

"Somebody should tell Ron to wash his balls," said Peter.

At this, both Luca and Nils laughed. Heidi didn't. Her mind was racing. She had completely forgotten the senior party, which she had volunteered to host. It was the main reason she'd skipped the trip to Hawaii in the first place. She was going to show the entire graduating class that she was more than just a good girl grinder by having everyone over to her big empty house to get drunk.

Luca eyed her. "What's the problem?" he asked. "You *did* get the booze, right?"

"Yes," said Heidi. "Sorry. Time just, uh, got away from me today, I guess. I . . ."

In a matter of minutes, a hundred kids from Green Valley would be crawling all over her house, going places where they shouldn't go, touching things they shouldn't touch, looking in places they shouldn't look. Had she and Cam cleaned up everything? Had they found every last spot of blood?

Heidi hadn't spoken for several seconds. Luca waved his hand in front of her face.

"Are you having a fucking stroke or something?" He lowered his voice so that his friends wouldn't hear. "No offense, but you look like shit. Is that the same outfit you wore to school on Thursday?"

"Yeah."

"It's Saturday," said Luca. "You need to take a shower."

Heidi nodded silently, still processing.

Luca pointed to the hard seltzer. "And you should probably put those in the fridge before . . ."

Luca trailed off. He was staring at Cam, who stood in the kitchen sipping orange juice.

"'Hello," said Cam.

"Hi," said Luca.

Luca looked at Heidi. Heidi said nothing.

"Uh, quick question, babe," said Luca. "Who the fuck is this guy in your house?"

"Oh, Luca this is Cam. Cam, Luca," said Heidi. "I invited him to the party."

The boys locked eyes and shook hands. To Heidi, it looked more like a test of strength than a friendly greeting. Cam had a sly grin on his face while Luca glared.

Then all of a sudden, Luca was all smiles. "*Enchanté,* my dude. Sorry, I guess I missed it: How exactly do you two know each other?"

Nils whispered something to Peter, and Peter snickered.

"Oh, Cam and I are just, uh . . . in the same . . . club," said Heidi.

"Uh-huh," said Luca, his eyes on Cam. "And what club would that be?"

Cam laughed. "Dude, c'mon. You don't even know what clubs your girlfriend is in?"

"Apparently not," said Luca.

"A word of advice," said Cam. "In every relationship, the most important thing is to listen."

"Thanks for that," said Luca. "What club?"

"Oh, well," said Heidi. "The club we are both in is, uh . . . Wildlife Club."

Luca cocked his head. Then he nodded. "Dope. I'm big into sea otters. You ever see the video where the sea otter is playing with the baby monkey? Fucking adorable. Man, I saw you standing there and I seriously thought some criminal had broken into Heidi's house. Isn't that funny?" Luca gave a loud, exaggerated laugh.

"Nobody broke into my house," said Heidi.

"Yeah, I know that," said Luca. "I was joking."

"Ha-ha," said Cam. "Good one."

"Cam's just a little early to the party," said Heidi.

"They call me Mr. Punctual," said Cam with a shrug. "If I'm not early, I'm late."

"So that must be your shit box parked out front?" asked Luca.

"That's my shit box," said Cam.

"Respect, dude. I could never drive a car like that," said Luca. "Fuck, man, you look so familiar. Doesn't he look familiar?"

"He looks familiar," said Peter.

"Your mom looks familiar," said Nils. "Well, just the bottom half."

"Shut the fuck up," said Peter.

Luca stared into Cam's eyes. "Seriously, I feel like I know you, somehow."

Cam shrugged. "Just got that kind of face, I guess." He turned to Heidi. "Anyway, I'm actually feeling a little tired, so I think I'm going to skip the party and head home."

"Okay," said Heidi. "So then, I'll . . . I'll see you at Wildlife Club."

Luca threw an arm around Cam's shoulder. "Dude, *what*? You can't leave now. You're going to miss the party of the year. You have to stay. Babe, tell him he has to stay!"

"You have to stay," said Heidi quietly.

Peter grabbed a hard seltzer. "We're gonna get wrecked on this shit. Only two grams of carbs per bottle."

"Awesome," said Cam.

"It will be," said Luca. "The social order will be inverted. Memories will be made. I don't want to overpromise, but tonight, Cam, you might even find love."

"Nikki Napolitano will give you a hand job," said Nils.

"Shut up, you fucking asshole," snapped Heidi.

Nils looked shocked. "Potty mouth," he muttered.

Luca ignored them. "The party is going to be fucking rad."

Cam turned to Heidi. "Well now, if it's going to be *rad* . . ."

"Yeah, you really should stay," said Heidi, trying to sound casual. "It ought to be fun."

Heidi raced upstairs and showered as quickly as she could. She snagged the green dress from the closet that she knew Luca liked but for some reason thought better of wearing it. Instead, she picked out a pair of jeans and a floral top. She hoped that in the fifteen minutes she was getting ready, Luca and Cam didn't murder each other.

By the time Heidi made it back down to the party, there were at least fifty people inside her house. Many she didn't recognize: friends of friends, kids from other grades, randos from other schools. Someone had commandeered the sound system and a SoundCloud rapper Heidi didn't know was blaring throughout the house, spitting fire about being depressed. Half-empty Solo cups were already covering every horizontal surface.

"Heidi!"

Heidi felt a surge of fury as she saw Marcie Love winding her way through the crowd toward her with a huge fake smile on her face.

"You weren't at school yesterday," said Marcie, as the pair gave each other air-kisses. "We all thought you were dead."

"Still alive," said Heidi. "That's an interesting shirt. Can I get you a drink?"

"Oh my God, yes," said Marcie. "I didn't even know you drank, Heidi. When I heard you were hosting the senior party, I was kind of expecting you to serve everyone milk and cookies."

"I drink," said Heidi, struggling to mask her annoyance. "I love to drink."

"Uh. Cool?" said Marcie.

Heidi led Marcie into the kitchen where a dozen bottles of alcohol and assorted mixers crowded the kitchen island.

"Screwdriver," said Marcie.

Heidi nodded.

"Oh, that's vodka and orange juice," added Marcie in a stage whisper, loud enough for everyone in the kitchen to hear.

"I know what it is," said Heidi. She started to mix Marcie her drink. As she did, Heidi noticed a dark spot on the countertop. It was a drop of dried blood she'd somehow missed. Heidi put an empty cup on top of it and mixed herself a screwdriver too.

"Who's *that* guy?" asked Marcie.

Across the room, Cam stood by himself sipping from a red Solo cup.

"No idea," said Heidi.

"Does he go to our school?" said Marcie, brushing her hair behind her ear.

"No," said Heidi. "He has a girlfriend."

"If you don't know who he is, how do you know he has a girlfriend?" asked Marcie.

"She was here earlier," said Heidi. "They were making out. It was disgusting."

"Well, she's not here now, is she?" said Marcie, collecting her drink. "Ciao."

Marcie turned to slither her way through the mass of partygoers toward Cam. Heidi felt a sudden urge to grab her mother's nine-inch chef's knife out of the block and plunge it into Marcie's back.

"Dude, are you okay?"

Heidi turned to see Olivia. She looked concerned.

"Olivia," said Heidi. "Hi. Yeah, I'm—I'm fine. God, I'm glad to see you."

She gave Olivia a hug.

"Where have you been?" asked Olivia. "I've been texting you nonstop for the past two days. I was starting to think it was Amber Alert time."

"I just had a lot on my mind," said Heidi. "You know, with—"

"Right," said Olivia. She raised her cup. "Fuck Harvard."

Heidi picked up the drink she'd just mixed. "Fuck Harvard."

Both of them took a swig. As Heidi lowered her cup she saw that Olivia was still staring at her.

"You sure there's nothing else you're not telling me?" asked Olivia.

Olivia was Heidi's best friend. She had been for nearly a decade. She could obviously tell that Heidi was acting weird. The two of them kept no secrets from one another. But this was different.

Could she trust Olivia enough to tell her what was really going on? It was a question she never would have asked herself before.

Heidi smiled. "No, Olivia. You know I tell you everything."

Olivia nodded but didn't look convinced. "Well, if you ever want to talk, you know I'm always here for you, right?"

"Of course," said Heidi.

"And when I text you, text me back," said Olivia. "So I know you haven't been chopped up in Goth Steve's basement."

"I will," said Heidi. "I'm sorry."

Olivia's eyes drifted over to Marcie Love, who was now laughing uproariously at something Cam had said. Cam had a bemused half smile on his face. He glanced at Heidi for a moment. Heidi smiled and shook her head.

Olivia sighed. "Marcie looks incredible. I hate her so much."

"Don't worry," said Heidi. "I poisoned her drink."

Just then, Peter blundered forward, clearly already drunk and sloshing a plastic cup full of thick red wine. "You guys tried the port? Shit is delicious." He drained his cup. "Screw hard seltzer. I'm a port guy now."

The night wore on and the house filled with high school kids—as many strangers as Green Valley students—eager for a last hurrah. Or maybe just a few beers. Heidi drank more than she usually did, and actually started to enjoy herself in a way that was rare for her at parties. She danced and laughed with Olivia and her other friends. It felt like a release valve for her stress, rather than an obligation or a performance. Luca and his buddies got progressively drunker. Somebody broke a traditional Chorotega pot that Madeline had brought back from a vacation in Costa Rica. Once or twice, Heidi looked for Cam again but she never found him. She realized that, at some point, he must have simply gone home. She understood that this wasn't his crowd, but she still felt a little hurt.

Around 1:00 AM, as Heidi danced to a K-pop song with Olivia, she saw blue and red flashers on the street outside. Her buzz vanished in a surge of adrenaline. It was the Dogcatchers. Heidi had ten, maybe fifteen seconds to act—

"It's the cops," said Nils, as he peered through the blinds.

"Which cops?" asked Heidi.

"What?" asked Nils, who was extremely drunk. "I don't understand the question."

"Which cops is it!" snapped Heidi.

"I don't know their names!" protested Nils.

Heidi looked through the window herself. A black-and-white cruiser was parked outside and two officers were walking across the lawn. It was the city police department, not the Viral Containment Task Force.

Heidi killed the music, to which a number of drunker party guests booed.

"Everyone shut up!" yelled Heidi, as she went to the door.

A young police officer stood outside, looking extremely uncomfortable. His partner hung back with his arms crossed.

"Hello, miss," said the young officer. "We've gotten a number of noise complaints from this address."

"Oh my gosh," said Heidi. "I'm super sorry. I just had a few friends over for my birthday. I guess we got a little loud, huh?"

The young officer glanced around at the dozens of cars parked up and down the block. Clearly more than a few friends were here.

"Uh-huh. You all been drinking in there?" He tried to look past her through the door.

"No, sir. Well, just soda, if that counts."

The young cop sighed. He looked at his partner, whose face was as unreadable as a statue. The older cop shrugged.

Heidi knew they knew she was lying, but considering the zip code, the multimillion-dollar homes lining the street, she was praying they wouldn't press the issue. They weren't Dogcatchers, after all. But any interaction with the police, no matter how trivial, was likely to result in a mandatory saliva test . . .

"Look, just keep it down, okay? Your neighbors are trying to sleep."

"I promise we will," said Heidi.

The old cop spoke up. "Don't make us come back here."

The police drove off and after a minute or two some deranged soul used Bluetooth to hijack the sound system and put on the original cast recording of the musical *Cats*. Meanwhile, Heidi went from room to room, turning on all the lights in the house. Even the most inebriated guests began to conclude that it was time to clear out. Heidi was suddenly bone-tired and was ready for the party to be over.

As Heidi poured herself a glass of water at the kitchen sink, a hand roughly grabbed her by the elbow. Instantly, she spun, ready to fight.

It was Luca. His eyes were glassy. He was clearly very drunk. In his hand was Heidi's phone. "What the fuck is this?"

Heidi yanked her elbow out of his grasp. "What is what?"

"This."

Luca showed Heidi what he was looking at. It was the email from the Harvard admissions office. Heidi felt a wave of shame, tinged with anger.

"Why are you looking at my phone without my permission?" said Heidi as she snatched it out of his hand. "That's private!"

"You got this email two days ago," said Luca.

"Yes. I know," said Heidi.

"Jesus. Get off her back," said Olivia. Heidi realized she was standing right beside her.

Luca ignored Olivia. His speech was slurred and he stank of booze. "Like I wasn't going to find out."

"You know what," said Heidi, trying to regain her dignity, "I've been thinking about it, and . . . I'm not actually sure I even want to go to Harvard."

"What? Why wouldn't you want to go to Harvard? It's fucking *Harvard*."

"Who cares," said Olivia. "It's possible to get a good education anywhere."

"Nobody is talking to you, you stupid bitch," said Luca.

Olivia's jaw dropped open. She turned to Heidi.

"Olivia," said Heidi. "This is between me and Luca."

"But—"

"Just shut the fuck up!" yelled Heidi.

Olivia stared back at Heidi, wounded. "Whatever," she said. "You two deserve each other."

And she pushed off through the thinning crowd of partygoers, who were studiously trying to ignore Heidi and Luca's fight.

Luca whistled and shook his head. "This is bad, Heidi. You fucked up big-time. I mean, maybe—maybe—you can transfer in after your first year. But the odds of getting in as a transfer are way worse."

Why was he telling her what to do? Why was he deciding what her life should be? Heidi imagined balling her fist and smashing it into his face. She imagined how satisfying it would feel to break his nose. She imagined grabbing him by the neck and using her hip to flip him backward, smashing the back of his skull into the corner of the countertop. How it would feel to hear his bones break, to feel his hot blood on her hands.

No, she didn't want to do that. Was she losing her mind? This wasn't her. Or had she always felt this way? Had the rage always been there? Had she just kept it hidden from everyone, as she hid so many things?

Heidi swallowed her anger, like she had often done for the past eighteen years of her life. Her voice became meek, submissive. Pleading. "I know, Luca. I don't know what happened. I'm sorry."

"I told you that you should've done early decision, like I did," said Luca. "Didn't I tell you that?"

"Yeah."

"Well, why the fuck didn't you listen to me?"

"I don't know."

"Did you even use the essay editing service that my dad recommended?"

"I used it."

Luca shook his head. "Writing was never your strong suit. Look, I can talk to my uncle. It's putting me in a very awkward position, but he knows the admissions people really well. It's a long shot but maybe there's something he can do to fix this."

"Uh-huh," said Heidi, who felt numb and humiliated. She stared at the floor. "Thank you."

She caught a glimpse of Marcie Love smiling at her as the rest of the guests cleared out.

Even Luca's drunk friends could tell how drunk he was. They called him an Uber and practically had to force him into it, thankfully sparing Heidi from any more of his hectoring or his advances. Soon she was alone in her house, which no longer smelled of bleach so much as sweat and the sour tang of spilled beer. Heidi dragged herself up the stairs to bed and fell asleep almost instantly.

* * *

She woke up around 10:00 AM and immediately sent an apology text to Olivia. No reply. She spent the remainder of the morning thoroughly cleaning her house for a second time. What had been done to the downstairs bathroom almost made her long for the murder scene.

It took her hours, but she got the place back to some sense of order and cleanliness. Heidi had just slumped down on the couch to rest when she heard the sound of the front door.

It was Madeline and Ron, who looked tan and happy from their Hawaiian vacation.

"Sweetheart!" said Madeline.

"Hi, Mom," said Heidi. "Hi Ron."

Heidi looked at them. And then she burst into tears. Ron looked confused. Madeline hugged her daughter tight.

"Oh, sweetie," said Madeline. "I'm sorry you didn't get to go."

Heidi buried her face in her mother's shoulder and sobbed like she was a child.

"Me too, Mom. Me too."

Madeline took a step back and inspected Heidi's face. "You look tired, Heidi. Are you still sick?"

Heidi pulled away, now feeling defensive. Angry. "I'm not sick. Why would you even ask that?"

Madeline rolled her eyes and seemed to resist the urge to say anything snappish. But Ron dug into his carry-on bag and pulled out a teddy bear wearing a hula skirt. It had on a little T-shirt that read LIFE'S A BEACH.

"Well," said Ron, "we got you a little souv—"

"Thanks, but I'm not five years old, Ron," snapped Heidi.

Madeline's eyes went wide. "Do *not* talk to Ron that way."

"It's okay," muttered Ron. He shrugged and looked at the floor as he stuffed the teddy bear back into his bag. "No worries."

"No, it's not okay," said Madeline. "Apologize to your stepfather. Now."

"Fuck this," said Heidi, and she ran up the stairs to her room.

"You come back here, right this instant!" Madeline called after her. "What the hell is this hole in the wall? Did you have a party while I was gone?"

15

It was Monday morning—25:11:47:06 till the next full moon. Heidi sat in her homeroom class. While other students chatted over the morning announcements playing on the classroom TV, Heidi stared at her phone under her desk and watched the seconds count down.

After her outburst the night before, she had apologized to Ron. He was always annoying, but Heidi had to admit he hadn't actually done anything wrong. She even took the stupid teddy bear and pretended she liked it. Madeline was livid that Heidi had apparently thrown a party while they were in Hawaii. Heidi apologized, of course, but a party was actually the best explanation for any unexpected property damage that Madeline might notice. She'd inadvertently created the perfect cover story.

As her mind drifted, Heidi thought back to waking up in the forest with blood on her hands, to Cam, to the beast that had smashed its way through her house . . .

"This weekend was insane, right?"

Heidi was startled out of her fugue. She turned to see Nikki Napolitano trying to talk to her.

"What?"

"This weekend was insane, right?"

"No, I . . ." Heidi stammered. "Not for me, no. My weekend was . . . yeah, just pretty average, I'd say."

"I'm talking about the party at your house," said Nikki. "I got so drunk . . . I think I kissed Devin, but I'm not even sure. Do you know if I did?"

"I don't know," said Heidi. "Sorry."

"How did you even convince the cops to go away?"

"Just lied my ass off," said Heidi.

"You're a lot more fun than I thought."

"Shh," said Ms. Okomura, gesturing toward the TV.

Nikki rolled her eyes.

"Sorry," said Heidi quietly.

On-screen, the two student anchors were running through various sports scores in a strained monotone.

"And on Saturday our own varsity baseball team defeated the Central High Bears five to one," said the male anchor, a junior with terrible acne. "Go Raptors."

25:11:44:56, now. Heidi had twenty-five days, eleven hours, and forty-four minutes to save herself.

The broadcast cut to the female anchor, a mousy tenth grader with teal-framed glasses. As she spoke, she somehow managed to sound wooden, nervous, and somber, all at once. "And now we would like to honor GVHS alumnus Corporal Jason Mottola."

On the screen was a photo of a fit, smiling man in his late twenties. His arm was slung over the shoulder of a woman, presumably his wife.

The girl spoke over a series of photos. "After graduating Green Valley High School ten years ago, Jason bravely served his country overseas. When the pandemic struck, he returned home to serve his own community as a member of the Viral Containment Task Force. Jason was known to be an exemplary officer.

Last year, he received the Law Enforcement Medal of Honor for acts of bravery."

Now there was a photo of Jason Mottola in uniform, receiving a medal from a red-faced man in a suit.

Heidi's scalp began to tingle. She had a creeping sensation of dread mixed with familiarity. The hairs on her arms were standing up.

"On Friday night, Corporal Jason Mottola made the ultimate sacrifice in the line of duty," said the student anchor with rehearsed gravity. "He gave his life to keep all of us safe."

Now there was a photo of Mottola looking heroic in his Viral Containment Task Force tactical armor, sans balaclava. An oversized patch on his arm depicted an Angel of Death with the word "Reaper" below. Around his neck, he wore a necklace of fangs.

At the sight of it, Heidi's unease curdled into a sharp pang of anxiety. The necklace looked like the one she'd found folded up in her clothes. Was it the same? But before she could tell, the picture had dissolved to another: a head-on portrait of Mottola, handsome in his crisp dress uniform, with the American flag behind him.

"Let us now observe a moment of silence for this fallen hero who truly embodied Raptor spirit," said the student anchor.

The class went quiet. Heidi's stomach turned. With no other sounds to drown it out, she could hear her own pulse pounding in her ears. She felt like she couldn't breathe. Why did she have a dead man's necklace? No, she told herself, it wasn't the same one. She shouldn't assume that. But what if the blood on her hands was—

The bell for first period rang and Heidi nearly jumped out of her seat.

She drifted like a ghost among the other students as they

made their way to their classes. It took her a moment to realize that Luca and Nils and Peter were walking beside her, chatting and laughing among themselves.

"Damn. I wonder how that Mottola guy got got," said Luca. "I searched #WolfKill but I guess there's no video."

"They only release the bodycam footage if it makes them look good," said Nils.

"The werewolf probably ripped his dick off and ate it like a fucking mozzarella stick," said Peter.

"That happened to you a while back, didn't it Peter?" said Nils.

Before Peter could think of a comeback, Heidi snapped: "A man died and it's actually sad, you asshole."

Nils looked taken aback. "Don't blame me. I didn't say the thing about the mozzarella dick! Get mad at Peter!"

Peter shrugged. "What's your problem, Heidi?"

"I don't have one," she said, though she could hear the edge in her own voice.

Nils started to whisper something to Peter, but Luca cut them off.

"Shut the hell up," said Luca, "both of you."

They did. Luca was the alpha of their little group and they knew it.

"It's fine," said Heidi. "You don't have to do that. I don't care. Sorry."

Luca shrugged. "You *do* care, and that's sweet. But I'm like: Is it actually sad?"

"What?"

"Like, is it sad that that guy died?"

"What are you talking about?" asked Heidi. "He was young. He had a wife."

"Yeah, I know, but the dude graduated from this high school," said Luca. "*This* high school. He could've done anything he wanted. He could've been an astrophysicist. Or restored classic cars. But instead, he voluntarily joined the Viral Containment Task Force. That was his choice, wasn't it?"

"He wanted to help people."

"You really think that's why?" said Luca. "There are lots of ways to help people. But not many jobs where you get to shoot guns and beat people up and pretend like you're the star of some action movie."

"You don't know what he was thinking," said Heidi. "And even if that's true it's still sad when *anyone* dies."

Luca shrugged. "Is it? We all bite it eventually, right? In the time it takes me to say this sentence I bet, like, three people in some third-world country are going to die. At least this VCTF dude went out doing what he loved—"

"I promise you he did not love getting torn apart by a monster!" yelled Heidi.

Luca's eyes went wide. Heidi never raised her voice. She definitely never raised her voice with Luca. Nils and Peter gave each other a not-so-subtle look, but they kept their mouths shut.

Instead of getting mad, Luca put his hands up in faux surrender. "Okay, okay, dude, chill. You know me. I just don't like the cops. They profile me because I drive a nice car."

"Uh-huh," said Heidi.

"What's with the attitude?" asked Luca. "Are you feeling okay?"

"I'm fine," said Heidi. "I think I'm still just a little hung over from Saturday."

"See, this is why you should drink port," said Peter. "Absolutely no hangover whatsoever."

Heidi was ready to be done with this conversation. "Sorry I got a little touchy. I'll see you guys later."

She gave Luca a quick hug and then hung back as the crowd moved on. Peter immediately whispered something to Nils, probably whatever he'd tried to say earlier. Nils snickered.

Heidi waited for Olivia, whom she'd spotted in the crowd behind her. As Olivia got closer, their eyes met for a split second. Olivia looked away.

"Hey, Olivia," called Heidi.

Olivia ignored her. So Heidi moved to stand directly in her path.

"Olivia."

"Excuse me," said Olivia sharply. She stared at the ground and tried to speed walk past.

Heidi grabbed her by the sleeve and pulled her aside into the doorway of the bio lab.

"Look, I'm *really* sorry about Saturday," said Heidi. "I should never have said that to you. I'm an asshole. I don't know what got into me."

"Eh, don't worry about it," said Olivia. "I understand. Your boyfriend is more important than me. Very simple, really."

"Luca is *not* more important than you," said Heidi.

"Don't get me wrong, I get why I'm necessary. You need to keep a loser like me around to help you feel better about yourself. Hopefully I did my job at the party." Olivia gave Heidi a sarcastic thumbs-up.

"Can you please stop being so dramatic?" said Heidi. "That's not what our friendship is, and you know it. I need you right now. I'm so stressed out. And I'm scared."

"Why?"

Heidi paused. "I can't actually tell you."

"Well can you tell me *why* can't you tell me?"

Heidi shook her head.

"Did something happen?" asked Olivia.

"Yes."

"Do you need help?"

"Maybe," said Heidi. "But trust me. It's just . . . it's better for you if you don't know. It's better for everyone."

Olivia's hurt and anger had given way to concern now. Heidi was torn. Through vague hints at her genuine distress, she'd manipulated her friend into sympathy. On the other hand, it had worked.

"I think—I think I might be losing it," said Heidi. "One minute, I feel like myself and the next I'm . . . I'm furious. With everyone."

"That doesn't sound like you," said Olivia. "You always hold it together, no matter what. If you're falling apart, what hope do I have?"

"I'm not perfect," said Heidi. "Please don't give up on me, Olivia. I'm a dumbass. I'll do anything you want. I'll eat a bug again, like in fourth grade."

Olivia sighed. "I don't want you to eat a bug."

"Are you sure?" asked Heidi. "Because I will do it. I think I could do an ant. Maybe a ladybug. Please not a house centipede."

"Shut up," said Olivia, rolling her eyes.

"I just want you to stay friends with me."

Olivia sighed. "Fine."

Heidi hugged Olivia. She felt better than she had in days. They walked together, arm in arm, toward their first-period class. Heidi glanced up at the lunar cycle countdown clock: 25:11:31:20 . . . 25:11:31:19 . . . 25:11:31:18 . . .

* * *

That afternoon, Heidi told Madeline and Ron that she didn't get into Harvard. Ron tried to console her but Heidi just shrugged off his awkward hug. Through clenched teeth, Madeline told her that it wasn't the end of the world and that it was possible to get a decent education anywhere. After all, she, Madeline, hadn't gone to an Ivy League school and yet she had become in-house counsel for a Fortune 500 company. She said Heidi would find her own path and land on her feet, as long as she stayed focused and didn't waste her time on frivolous things. Madeline was saying the right things, almost like she was checking off a list from a textbook, but Heidi could feel her disappointment. To Heidi, the implication was that she had *already* wasted much of her time on frivolous things.

After dinner, Heidi told her parents that she was going over to Olivia's house to study. Instead, she drove across the city to a residential neighborhood on a hill overlooking downtown.

She parked her Audi down the block and made her way to Dean Park: a few acres of grass dominated by a fifteen-foot abstract sculpture made of black steel. Heidi had walked past the sculpture a dozen times before without ever really stopping to look at it. Tonight, for some reason, she did. It was a stack of dark, undulating shapes called Metamorphosis. In the fading light, they looked almost human. Or perhaps animal.

Dean Park was famous for its panoramic view of the city skyline. Luca had brought Heidi here on their first date, in fact. Today, a few couples were taking selfies. An elderly man in layers of filthy clothes picked through the trash looking for cans. On a bench looking out over the lights of the high-rises, Cam was waiting for her. They'd chosen the park as a meeting point because it was equidistant from both their homes.

"Today sucked, right?" said Cam.

Heidi plopped down on the bench beside him. "Oh yeah. I

think Garfield may have been onto something with Mondays." She pulled out a small pad of paper and a pen. "Any progress?"

Cam shook his head. "I spent the whole day reaching out to every single shady character I know and a few that I don't. Nobody has Extiva."

Heidi nodded. "I looked everywhere online. Not available."

"Look, this is crazy," said Cam, "but could one of us, like, fly to China to buy some?"

"You can't get on a plane without a spit test," said Heidi. "And even if you could, China has had a travel ban in effect for the last five years."

Cam sighed and nodded. He spoke tentatively. "Okay. Then . . . I think I may have an alternative idea."

Heidi was surprised. "Well, that's good, because I don't."

"So . . . I've been reading about Canada. They don't use lethal force against the infected there. At least, they try not to."

Heidi spoke reflexively. "Cam, I'm not going to Canada—"

"I know, I know," he said, "but just hear me out: When we changed out in the woods, we didn't end up hurting anybody, right?"

Heidi nodded without speaking. She remembered the blood on her hands and the necklace of fangs that she'd found with her clothes.

"There are a lot of places like that up there," said Cam. "Big swathes of empty wilderness. Places where we'd be safe, where we wouldn't cause any harm."

"I can't just leave everything behind," said Heidi. "I have a family. I have a boyfriend."

Cam sighed. "Okay. Cross it off the list, then. And I guess we keep looking for the cure . . ."

They sat for a while in silence, staring out over the city below.

Each point of light shining in the evening marked someone else's life, someone with their own hopes and struggles. As she looked at the sea of glimmering lives, Heidi had the uncomfortable feeling she, too, was being watched.

But when she turned, the park was empty. Just the old man looking through the garbage.

16

The LC countdown clock mounted on the fence by the tennis courts read 20:11:32:09, the precise moment Heidi smashed her racket into the asphalt. With a single powerful stroke, she destroyed it.

On the other side of the net, Madeline lowered her own racket. She stared at her daughter with a look of shock, bordering on horror. "What did you just do?"

"Nothing," grunted Heidi. "It was an accident."

It hadn't been an accident. Heidi had missed what should have been an easy return, giving her mother the point. From out of nowhere her rage had exploded, and before she knew what she was doing, she'd demolished a $275 tennis racket.

"Don't lie to me, Heidi," said Madeline.

Heidi didn't know what to say. Other players on adjacent courts were staring at her, stunned or amused by the tantrum.

"It's just a tennis racket," muttered Heidi. "Who gives a shit?"

Madeline chuckled derisively. "Who gives a shit? That's very easy for you to say. You don't have to go to work every day to earn a paycheck."

"You buy a new racket every year!" snapped Heidi. "You have a garage full of them."

"Because I worked hard enough to become successful in my chosen field, I can afford to do that."

"You think I won't be successful?" asked Heidi. Despite her best efforts at control, her anger was flaring again. In her humiliation, she was lashing out.

"I did not say that," said Madeline. "But I know that you have had tremendous advantages in your life. Advantages that I never had. And yet you still—"

"If you didn't want me to have all these 'advantages,' then why the fuck did you give them to me? I didn't ask for anything from you."

"You ask for things all the time," said Madeline. "You effectively just asked me for a new tennis racket."

"I don't care! I fucking hate tennis!"

This wasn't true either. Heidi played with her mother most Saturdays, and she enjoyed it. Madeline was an excellent tennis player, still very fit into her forties and with years of practice. Heidi rarely won, but these days it was a close contest.

"Why are you swearing at me?" asked Madeline calmly. "You've been acting like a spoiled brat ever since we came back from Hawaii. What's wrong with you?"

"What's wrong with *you*?" yelled Heidi.

She saw a teenage girl staring at her through the chain-link fence. Heidi felt her neck burn with embarrassment. She definitely knew the girl from somewhere and now the story of her fit on the court would get back to other people she knew . . .

Madeline gave Heidi a condescending smile. "Very persuasive. You're really convincing me of your maturity. Bravo."

"Whatever."

"Maybe it's not missing a return that you're angry about,"

said Madeline. "Maybe you're mad at yourself for some other reason?"

"Why should I be mad at myself?" asked Heidi, her voice icy now. She felt sure her mother was talking about Harvard.

Madeline merely shrugged and pretended like she wasn't saying what she was saying. "I suppose the game's over. Can I trust you not to break anything else on the way home?"

Later, in the shower, Heidi noticed a patch of coarse dark hair growing on her shoulder. It was exactly the spot where she'd been bitten. She carefully shaved the hairs off and tried not to cry.

Her moods were becoming increasingly erratic. On Wednesday, when someone cut her off on her drive to school, Heidi sped up to catch the offender at a red light. She screamed the foulest obscenities she could think of out her open window. The middle-aged businessman in the other car looked completely terrified.

Later that morning, when Heidi walked into homeroom and saw a group of boys watching #WolfKill videos, she burst into tears.

None of the other kids seemed to know what to do as Heidi stood there sobbing uncontrollably until Olivia told them all to mind their own damn business. Out of the corner of her eye, Heidi saw Marcie Love smirking as she whispered something to her friends.

Heidi texted Cam every day, checking in to see if he'd made any progress and to report that she hadn't. It had been a week and, so far, they were stuck. As the clocks and apps and timers everywhere continued to remind Heidi, time was slipping away. In addition to their secret, they still had to deal with all the normal problems of their lives. Cam's struggles—like trying to decide whether to pay his rent or $400 in car repairs, when he didn't have money for either—put Heidi's own in perspective. They traded bleak jokes about their situation. Texting with him always made her feel a little bit better.

Heidi could tell that Olivia was concerned about her. Occasionally, she would very earnestly ask Heidi if she wanted to talk about whatever it was that was eating at her. Heidi tried to pretend that things were fine and that there was no reason for her friend to worry. She would change the subject to something like prom dresses or *Project: Hope*. Heidi often didn't reply to Olivia's texts, and soon Olivia stopped reaching out.

On Saturday, despite her best efforts to decline, Heidi was pressured into going to the movies with Luca. They saw something about a team of superheroes who were trying to get to the center of the earth for . . . reasons. Heidi could barely follow the plot. It was two and a half hours of colors and noises. She spent it brooding, lost in her own dark thoughts. Once or twice, Luca leaned over to kiss her, but she subtly ducked him without making it seem like she was ducking him.

In the parking lot, after the movie, Heidi knew it was coming again. As Luca closed his eyes and moved closer, she leaned away.

"What the fuck?" said Luca.

"What?"

"What is it? What's wrong with me?"

"Nothing, Luca. There's nothing wrong with you."

"You're not attracted to me."

"It's not anything like that. I swear."

"Then what is it? Why have you been acting so weird lately?"

"I haven't been," said Heidi. "I just can't kiss you, I'm sick."

Luca cocked his head. "Sick with what?"

"Mono," said Heidi.

Luca laughed. "You think I give a shit if I get mono? I had mono twice in ninth grade. Come here, babe. Give me some mono."

He moved to kiss her again but Heidi's hand on his chest stopped him.

"I just . . . I don't want to. Mono can be really serious. I'll be better soon. But I'd feel awful if I gave it to you."

For an instant, Luca looked furious, like a toddler who might throw a tantrum. But just as quickly the expression passed and he put on a casual smile. "Well, if we can't kiss, can we, you know, do something else?"

He put his hand on her leg. But before Heidi could say anything, he jerked it back as he physically recoiled.

"Dude, what the *fuck*?" cried Luca.

"What?"

Luca pointed at her leg. Heidi looked down and saw that a coarse, two-inch-long hair was growing out of her knee.

"Sorry," muttered Heidi. Mortified, she quickly plucked the hair.

Luca shuddered. "Wow. Okay, you win, Heidi. I do *not* want to fool around anymore."

"You can be really fucking mean sometimes," said Heidi.

Luca started the car. "Mean? I apologize, but that's just my natural reaction— Look, no offense, and feminism is great or whatever, but you ought to be a little more, ah, *thorough* when you're, you know, taking care of your personal hygiene. It's kinda gross. Not trying to be a dick."

"I'm sorry," whispered Heidi. She felt humiliated, disgusted with herself, and angry all at the same time. She balled her fists, feeling herself seethe.

Luca drove her home in silence. Heidi didn't want to talk, either, but once she calmed down, she felt like she should. The few times she tried to make polite conversation, Luca responded in monosyllabic grunts.

Luca pulled his BMW over to the curb in front of Heidi's house. She forced a smile onto her face and tried to be cheerful as she climbed out of the car.

"Good night. Sorry I'm so weird. I've just been a little stressed lately, but it's all good. I keep forgetting that it's senior year, and I should just relax. Anyway thanks for the movie. I had a lot of fun."

"How did you get mono?" asked Luca.

"I'm not really sure," said Heidi. She hadn't anticipated the question when she'd come up with the lie.

"They call it the 'kissing disease,'" said Luca. "I mean, that's how I got it in the ninth grade. So I'm wondering how *you* got it?"

"You don't necessarily get it from— I haven't been— What do you think I've been doing?"

"I don't know," said Luca. "That's why I'm asking the question."

"I don't lie," said Heidi. "I'm not a liar."

"You didn't tell me about Harvard," said Luca. "You didn't tell me about Wildlife Club, or whatever the hell it's called, and your new best friend. Now I'm learning you have a secret disease and you don't know how you got it."

"It's not a secret disease."

Luca rolled his eyes. "Okay, a *disease* that you're keeping a *secret*. How did you get it?"

"How do you get any disease? It's just random. It doesn't happen for a reason. It's just fucking random."

Luca frowned but said nothing.

"There's no law that says we have to tell each other everything all the time," said Heidi. "There are plenty of things that you keep from me, right? Stuff you do with your friends."

"You're right. I'm the one acting weird," said Luca. "Not sure why I thought honesty was the foundation of a healthy relationship."

"Luca."

"I'll see you later."

With that, he punched the gas and his tires squealed as he sped off down the street, leaving black marks on the pavement. Heidi flipped him off as he drove away.

She turned to notice Mrs. Washburn staring at her through her blinds. Heidi put on a fake smile and tried to turn the middle finger into a friendly wave.

* * *

It was a little after ten and Heidi was home alone. Madeline and Ron had gone out to some charity thing—puppetry programs for inner-city schools or maybe microloans for women farmers in the developing world, Heidi hadn't really paid attention. Her mother had attended events like these roughly once a week for as long as Heidi remembered. They tended to blur together.

Heidi couldn't stop thinking about Luca pawing at her and then having the nerve to call her gross. The memory of it nearly made her stomach turn: his slobbery mouth, his rotten breath on her neck . . .

"Fuck you!" snarled Heidi, as she pounded her fist on the countertop. To her horror, she realized that she'd somehow hit it so hard that she'd left a dent in the marble.

"Jesus Christ," said Heidi, marveling at what she'd done.

She quickly moved a vase of flowers to cover the hole in the counter—yet another thing she would have to conceal from everyone around her.

There was only one way out of this hell. The cure. The Extiva.

She texted Cam.

I just got so pissed off I punched a
hole in solid stone fml

Cam texted her back the muscle arm emoji and the smiley face with star eyes, which made Heidi grin. She typed back:

please tell me some good news

saw a thing on TV this morning that
says coffee isn't that bad for you. so
there's that.

Heidi laughed, then realized she was starving. She grabbed a bowl out of the cabinet for yogurt, but she knew it wouldn't be enough.

Heidi sniffed the air and caught the scent of something good. She opened the fridge and looked inside the meat drawer. There, she saw four six-ounce butcher's cut filets mignons. Ron sometimes ordered steaks from a specialty company in Nebraska (much to the chagrin of Heidi's mother, who was always on Ron about his diet).

Heidi sniffed again. Now she could pick out the iron scent

of blood, the oily smell of the fat marbling the meat; she even caught an earthy hint of the grass that, according to the label, these dead cows had exclusively fed on.

Heidi had never craved a steak in her life, but she wanted one now. She grabbed her phone and googled "how to cook a steak" and then immediately googled "how to cook a steak rare." She pulled up a seven-minute video on YouTube. While the pan was heating up on the stove, Heidi ripped through the plastic and sank her teeth into the raw meat.

17

Erik Balikian woke up in a room full of flowers. His head was throbbing, his mouth was dry, and his tongue was poking through a gap in his teeth that shouldn't be there. Something was beeping.

"Erik?"

He slowly turned his head and saw his girlfriend, Leah, sitting beside his hospital bed. She looked surprised, like she didn't expect him to be awake.

"Aren't you in Idaho?" said Erik quietly.

The next two hours were a whirlwind of activity. A series of nurses checked his vitals, drew his blood, and administered various cognitive tests that Erik felt like he passed, even though everything was still a little fuzzy. His body hurt. A doctor explained to him that he'd been in a coma for days—ever since he had suffered severe blunt force trauma to the head. She told Erik that even though he was awake now, he could expect to experience symptoms such as headaches, nausea, and loss of equilibrium for months to come. As for his missing tooth, he was assured that could be remedied with a dental implant once he was out of the hospital.

His mom and dad showed up later that day. So did a representative from the Viral Containment Task Force: Linda, a public relations officer in a power suit who constantly checked her phone. Erik had never met the woman before, but she thanked him for his service and told him that the state attorney general's office had been in touch. They were considering him for the Law Enforcement Medal of Honor.

"Why?" asked Erik.

"Well, they award this medal for exceptional meritorious conduct," said Linda.

"What was the meritorious conduct?" asked Erik. "What did I— What happened to me?"

The woman's eyes went wide when she realized that no one had yet told him anything about how he'd come to be here. She cleared her throat. "You were wounded in the line of duty."

"By a werewolf?"

She nodded. Erik remembered nothing. One moment he was leading a goat through the dark woods and the next moment he was here in this hospital room.

"So, I got attacked," said Erik, "but I'm not . . ."

"No, they've tested you multiple times," she said. "You're not infected."

Erik breathed a sigh of relief. "And now I get a medal?"

"I'd be surprised if you didn't," said Linda.

Erik nodded. He still didn't really understand how getting his ass handed to him was "exceptional meritorious conduct."

"Where's Reaper?" he asked.

Linda shifted uncomfortably in her seat. "Corporal Mottola . . . well, he didn't make it, Erik."

She put her hand on his. Erik recoiled.

"What the hell are you talking about?" said Erik. Reaper had more confirmed kills than anyone else on the force. He was a living legend. No way he got smoked by some random-ass 10–91W.

"Apparently, he was killed instantly. So, at least he didn't suffer," said Linda. "I'm very sorry for your loss."

"Bullshit," said Erik. "There's got to be some mistake."

Erik's family looked nervous as he tried to push himself up out of his hospital bed.

"Easy, sweetheart," said his mom, putting a hand on his shoulder. "You need to rest."

"Jason Mottola made the ultimate sacrifice to keep all of us safe," said Linda. It sounded like she'd used this particular phrase a lot in her career. "He will, of course, be posthumously receiving the Medal of Honor, as well. His second, I believe."

Erik blinked back tears. He wasn't about to let himself cry in front of this woman. He struggled to remember what happened, but it was all still a fog.

"Did they kill it, at least?"

Linda frowned. It was clear that she was debating how to answer him. At last, she shook her head. "No. The infected individual who assaulted Corporal Mottola fled the scene."

Erik felt his sorrow and guilt turning to outrage. "How the—How did they let it get away? We had a goddamn chopper in the air!"

"I don't know the details," said Linda. "You should speak with Lieutenant Aoki."

Erik sunk back down into his hospital bed. He was reeling. Reaper was gone and the 10–91W got away. Erik was supposed to have his back. Reaper had been counting on him . . .

Linda cleared her throat. "I am sorry to ask this, right now, since you're grieving for your friend, but . . . would it be possible for me to take a few photos for our social accounts?"

"Seriously?" said Erik.

Linda gave him a smile that didn't seem particularly sincere. "A lot of people out there are pulling for you, Erik."

She snapped a few pics of Erik with her smartphone, and then she was gone.

* * *

Erik spent the next few days in the hospital undergoing physical therapy and enduring the crippling headaches that came on once or twice a day. The doctors were impressed at his progress. They told him that if he kept at it, he stood a good chance of making a full recovery. Leah and his parents came every day during visiting hours, which Erik found almost as exhausting as his PT.

Leah, in particular, kept trying to get Erik to open up and tell her how he felt about everything that had happened to him. She was always sort of vague, but she meant "almost dying." Erik didn't see the point of talking about his feelings, because how he felt about anything wouldn't change it.

Still, he tried to do what she wanted. He told her the main thing he *felt* was that he wanted to get back to work. From her reaction, she didn't seem to think this was the right answer to her question.

At last, Erik was officially discharged from the hospital. He could walk on his own by then. He could pick up a glass of water and take a sip without spilling (much). His parents expected him to come home and stay with them, but Erik told them all he was fine in his own apartment. Leah had already missed a lot of school. But she promised to stay an extra night, just to make sure he was okay at home.

When they got to Erik's place, there was a letter from the VCTF waiting in his mailbox. The department was giving him two months paid time off. For some people, getting paid to do nothing was the dream. Erik crumpled up the letter.

"Fuck that," he said.

"Fuck what?" asked Leah.

"Nothing."

His bed wasn't any more comfortable now than before he'd been put in a coma. Erik tossed and turned the whole night, struggling in vain to remember how it had all gone down. Wondering if there was anything he could have done differently . . .

Leah got up early the next morning to head back to college in Idaho. Erik kissed her goodbye and had the unshakable feeling that this was the last time he would ever see her. He probably ought to be sad about that, but for some reason he wasn't. Leah didn't understand him and she never would, he decided.

After she left, Erik put on his uniform and drove himself to work. He still felt stiff and sore in ten different places and he had a monster of a headache coming on, but as he entered the VCTF station, he made sure to hold his head high and hide the pain. Erik arrived in time for roll call. As he walked into the conference room, the other officers gave him a round of applause and a standing ovation. It was the most respect that Erik Balikian had ever gotten at this or any job. He almost smiled.

He could tell Lt. Aoki wasn't happy, though. After the other officers had received their daily assignments—breaking up a homeless encampment that had built up around a bunch of the recent condo buildings downtown and patrolling various neighborhoods that had been designated as lupinovirus "red zones" by the governor's incomprehensible color-coded alert system—they were dismissed. Erik didn't get an assignment.

Lieutenant Aoki took him aside and told him point-blank, "You should be at home and in bed, Caveman."

"Nah, L.T. I feel fine," said Erik. "I don't need PTO. I'm ready to get back to work. Keep people safe. Kick some ass."

"From my experience, if you push yourself too hard after an injury, you just end up hurting yourself again," said Lt. Aoki. "Even if it's not physical, you can burn out, mentally. What happened to you wasn't a little thing."

"Mentally, I'm one hundred percent," said Erik, trying to keep the edge out of his voice. "What's the status of the 10–91W that got Reaper?"

Lt. Aoki sighed. "We're looking for it, Caveman. Investigative Services is working some leads."

"What leads?"

Lt. Aoki's brow furrowed. "Leave it to the detectives, Officer. They do their job and we do ours. You know this."

"Can I see the bodycam footage?"

The lieutenant shook his head. "I can't show you that. You're not a part of the investigation."

"C'mon, L.T.," said Erik. "It happened to *me*."

"Then why do you need footage?"

"Because . . ." Erik was reluctant to admit it. "Because I can't remember shit."

Lt. Aoki looked pained, but he stood firm. "Reach out to the detectives—Mendez and Patino. It's their call. Maybe they'll let you review the footage."

Erik fought the urge to roll his eyes. "Look, before he died, Reaper and I were doing an, uh, independent investigation."

"Aw, Christ," said the lieutenant.

"We got the names of two, uh, infected individuals—"

"I don't want any of Reaper's names."

"Excuse me?"

Lt. Aoki frowned. "Look, Balikian, I'm going to tell you

something because you're a rookie, and this is when bad habits are formed."

"Bad habits, sir?"

"The rules exist for a reason. Understand? I know everybody worshipped the ground Jason Mottola walked on; God rest his soul. I get it. He did have his talents. The guy had guts. But Mottola never did things the right way. Ever. He was always charging around like a bull in a china shop, threatening and coercing citizens, running his own 'investigations.'"

"He was going the extra mile."

"He cost the VCTF millions of dollars in lawsuits: property damage, false arrests, extortion, and personal injury."

"He was doing the job that Investigative Services is too lazy to do," said Erik, his voice rising.

"Maybe he told you that," said Lt. Aoki, "but what he was actually doing was undermining our mission by scaring innocent people. If the public doesn't believe we're here to help them, then they won't cooperate when we need them to."

Erik crossed his arms. He wasn't going to listen to this. The lieutenant had always seemed like a stand-up guy, but Erik could now see he was part of the problem—another do-nothing who was punching a clock and collecting a paycheck until retirement. He wasn't half the Dogcatcher that Reaper had been.

Erik left and went home. He did his physical therapy exercises then he sent an email requesting to see his own bodycam footage from the night of Reaper's death. Almost immediately, he received an email back thanking him for his request.

He tried to search for any news articles with more information about Reaper's death but there wasn't much. The few that existed were vague, and focused mainly on Corporal Jason Mottola's career accomplishments as an exemplary officer of the Viral Containment Task Force. It only took Erik a few minutes to realize this was a dead end.

He checked his email again. Nothing from Investigative Services yet. He tried to watch TV but he kept changing streaming shows after five minutes until he turned it off. It wasn't even lunchtime yet. He had nothing to do, and he would officially have nothing to do for months. The prospect was unbearable. He could feel his headache getting worse.

Erik rubbed his temples and the bridge of his nose. If he was stuck at home, he might as well go the extra mile. He grabbed his laptop again and typed two names into the search bar. The first was "Dawn Supple." The second was "Cameron Woodbine."

18

Heidi was on her way to English class, checking the LC Countdown app—17:06:45:86—when the question came.

"Where were you last night?" asked Luca.

Heidi froze, caught off guard. It took her a moment to answer. "Yesterday? Oh, I was at home, watching *Project: Hope*," Heidi lied. "That show is so ridicu—"

"At home?" said Luca, his eyes hard. "That's weird. Because I called your landline and your mom said you were out."

Heidi *had* gone out. She'd met up with Cam at Dean Park—it had become their default meeting place—a scenic spot to compare notes and try to strategize about what they should do next. Though each time they met up, they had less to report. Neither of them were having any luck in the search for Extiva. What once had seemed like a ray of hope was now beginning to feel like a mirage. Or a cruel joke.

"Why did you call my landline?" sputtered Heidi.

"Because you didn't answer your phone."

Heidi was caught in a lie, but she felt indignant too. "What, are you stalking me?"

"I can't stalk you," said Luca. "You're my girlfriend."

"Yes," said Heidi. "I went out for a little bit. So what?"

"So where did you go? Who did you go with?"

"Christ, can you calm down?" asked Heidi.

"Maybe when you tell me the truth."

"I hung out with Olivia for a while," said Heidi. "That's all."

"So if I ask Olivia, she'll confirm your little story?"

"Confirm my little story? Is this a police investiga—"

"You can try to keep lying but I *will* find out the truth," snapped Luca. "Eventually."

"I'm *not* lying," said Heidi in a wheedling voice.

Luca glowered. He looked like he might explode. Instead, he spoke very softly. "I don't want you spending any more time with him."

"Him?" Heidi feigned ignorance. "Who are you talking about?"

Luca stared at her for a moment with cold fury in his eyes. But he said nothing.

"Fuck you," snarled Heidi, surprising herself. "Don't tell me what to do."

Luca flinched at the guttural sound of her voice—perhaps that was what she wanted—but he offered no response. Instead, without a word, he broke off and headed for his desk. Over his shoulder, Heidi saw Marci Love smirking at her from the hall. She gave a little wave before heading on her merry way.

Heidi's heart was still pounding as she found her own desk. So stupid. She couldn't afford to lose control. Not here. When she glanced back at Luca, he was laughing and talking with Peter and Nils like nothing had happened. He didn't make eye contact with her.

Thankfully, Mr. Hirsch didn't ask Heidi any questions about *Nicholas Nickleby*. She spent the period alternately seething, racked with guilt, and worried someone had noticed her outburst. Who was Luca to tell her who she could or couldn't spend time with? But . . . why had she felt compelled to lie to him? Luca was her boyfriend and she loved him, right? And Cam was . . . what was Cam? A stranger? Not anymore. Cam was the only other passenger on the same sinking ship. He was cursed. Doomed. Just like her.

Heidi made up her mind. She decided to apologize to Luca. But as the bell rang, he was out the door before she could catch up to him.

Heidi's mind was racing. She could feel the tightness of anxiety squeezing her chest. She realized she'd been worrying, nonstop, for weeks. She decided to go for a run after school. Cross-country was her sport, and exercise usually had a way of calming her and clearing her mind.

* * *

A quarter-mile track encircled the Green Valley football field. Heidi stretched out, feeling the pull in her quads and calf muscles.

Her normal run was twelve laps. But today she set out at a brisker speed than usual, hoping she could somehow outrun the demons in her head. But even as she ran, her racing thoughts kept pace. She pushed herself harder, increasing her speed. Still, she thought of Luca. She thought of the High Desert Recovery and Treatment Center. She thought of a necklace of fangs. Her mother's disappointment. Getting shot in the head with a silver bullet. Heidi ran faster.

She realized she was almost running at a full sprint now, and yet her body wasn't getting tired. Not even a little bit.

Members of the boys' track team, warming up before practice, were staring at her in disbelief.

Heidi consciously forced herself to run slower. Still, almost without trying, she finished three miles in just under seventeen minutes. It was her best time ever, by more than a minute. As she slowed to a walk, she'd barely broken a sweat. Heidi grinned, despite herself.

But her smile fell as she saw Luca standing beside the track ahead.

"Hey," he said.

"Hey," said Heidi.

"Doesn't look like mono is slowing you down."

Heidi merely shrugged.

"So . . . I talked to Olivia."

Heidi felt her pulse quicken. "Yeah?"

"She confirmed what you said," said Luca. "That you two hung out last night."

Heidi was flooded with a sense of relief. She also felt a pang of guilt for forcing Olivia to lie on her behalf. Olivia hated lying.

"So, I just wanted to say, uh, I'm sorry," said Luca. "I screwed up."

Heidi took a deep breath. "I did, too. I shouldn't speak to you that way. I apologize for losing my temper."

Luca grinned. "It's okay. I kinda like the new feisty Heidi." He held out his hand. "I just wanted to tell you: I'm here for you, babe. No matter what."

Heidi took his hand. The two of them walked together toward the parking lot. For a few minutes Heidi felt normal. She forgot she was sick.

They stopped at her Audi.

"You're not going to hang out with him anymore, are you?" asked Luca. His voice was pleading, his expression hurt.

"I won't," said Heidi. She hated herself for saying it. She hated how pathetic she sounded.

* * *

Madeline insisted on having a family dinner once a week, though she never cooked. That night Ron made a particularly gloopy and underseasoned meal for Heidi and Madeline. Heidi barely touched her food.

"I thought you liked polenta," said Ron.

"Maybe if this *was* polenta, Ron," said Heidi.

"Don't talk to your stepfather like that," said Madeline.

"Sorry," said Heidi, her voice dripping with sarcasm. She took a huge forkful of bland polenta and shoved it in her mouth. "Mmm. This is delicious."

"Stop that," said Madeline. "Don't be rude. Act your age."

"You know what? You're right: I suck," said Heidi. "May I be excused, now?"

Without waiting for an answer Heidi rose from the table and stomped out the front door. The tires of her Audi squealed as she pulled out onto the street.

Heidi ignored her buzzing phone as she drove. Without making a conscious decision, she realized she was heading south. Half an hour later, she pulled over to the curb in front of Cam's run-down apartment building.

What was she even doing? Why had she come here?

Heidi ignored the six missed calls from Madeline and sent a text to Cam:

Can you meet up?

Cam texted back almost immediately.

Sure. Dean Park, tomorrow?

Heidi swallowed, suddenly a little nervous.

How about right now?

Five minutes later, Cam exited the security gate of his apartment complex and climbed into the passenger's side of Heidi's Audi.

"Damn," said Cam. "Nice car."

"My parents gave it to me for my eighteenth birthday," said Heidi, almost wanting Cam to judge her.

"Cool" was all he said. "So what was so urgent?"

Heidi had no answer. "I—I don't know. Nothing. I just—I can't calm down and . . ."

Cam nodded. "Yeah, same."

"Cam, what if it's hopeless? What if we don't figure out how to—"

"We will figure something out," said Cam. He put his hand on her arm and squeezed. "You want to grab a bite to eat?"

"Sure," she said. "That'd be great."

As they drove, Heidi's phone kept buzzing with more missed calls.

"You, uh, just going to ignore that?" said Cam, at last.

"It's my mom. She's acting like a bitch."

Cam nodded. "Mothers tend to worry."

Heidi suddenly felt guilty. Her mother wasn't locked away in some quarantine prison three states away. Madeline was only calling because she cared about Heidi.

"Yeah, I'll text her when we get there to let her know I'm okay," mumbled Heidi.

At Cam's direction, Heidi drove to an industrial stretch of the waterfront where a handful of food trucks had set up shop. They waited in a twenty-minute line and bought way too many tacos ("Best in the city," Cam boldly declared) before continuing on to Dean Park.

It was a particularly beautiful evening—clear and a little chilly—as they found their usual bench. The city skyline spread out before them in a twinkling panorama.

Cam inhaled deeply. "Mmm. Smell that?"

"You talking about the day-old piss in that bush over there?" said Heidi, nodding toward a shrub on the edge of the path. The acrid odor burned her nostrils.

"No." Cam nodded toward a big bearded guy in a flannel shirt a hundred feet away. "I mean smell that dude's feet."

Heidi laughed. But she *could* smell the rank vinegar stench of his sweaty socks. She could smell the protein bar in a passing jogger's backpack. She could smell squirrels hiding acorns in the trees. She could smell everything, all the time. It was disgusting but . . . fascinating too.

"I'm costing my family hundreds of dollars a week because I keep eating my stepdad's premium steaks," said Heidi. "Raw."

Cam considered this. "I caught myself looking at a pigeon out the window this morning and wondering how it would taste."

"I bet it would be stringy," said Heidi, "but . . . strangely satisfying."

Cam glanced at a flock of pigeons eating breadcrumbs on a brick path. "You save room for dessert?"

Heidi laughed and then shook her head. "Damn, this whole thing sucks," she said. "I don't feel like myself. I feel angry all the time. And afraid. And most of all, I feel alone. But I can't tell anybody anything. I have a boyfriend but I can't even kiss him."

"That must be hard." Cam paused. "You love him?"

Heidi was blindsided by the question. She paused to consider.

Then she realized she was pausing and blurted out, "Of course I do."

Cam nodded. "What do you like about him?"

"He's . . ." Heidi struggled. "He's kind." Immediately after she said it, she knew it wasn't right. Another lie. "Why are you aski—"

"Hey!"

A disheveled man yelled at them from across the park. He was carrying a homemade cardboard sign that read #PLANDEMIC on one side and #WEREWOLVESARENTREAL on the other. Heidi made the fatal mistake of direct eye contact. She immediately turned away, but it was too late. The man made a beeline straight for their bench.

"Great," said Cam quietly. "One of those people."

The man's eyes bulged as he ranted at them in a high, reedy voice. "The virus is a false flag operation to take our constitutional freedoms! The videos you've seen online have been doctored! It's all Hollywood special effects. They use crisis actors on the news! Read your history and wake up!"

"I'll do that," said Cam, hoping to cut the interaction short. "I'll read my history and wake up."

But the man wasn't satisfied, because of course he wasn't. In fact, it wasn't clear if he was even listening to Cam at all. "Let me ask you one question: Whose agenda does this so-called 'virus' serve?"

Cam sighed. "I'm gonna guess: somebody bad?"

"The globalist elite," cried the man. "It's all about levers of control. The endless lockdown is all about taking away choice and forcing us to accept a planned economy."

Heidi glanced around at the people milling around the little park. "We're *not* actually locked down."

"When you submit to the state-mandated saliva tests they collect your DNA," screeched the man. "All that information goes into a massive computer database located in the headquarters of the World Economic Forum in Cologny, Switzerland."

"Yo, shut the fuck up." The guy in the flannel shirt with the smelly feet had made his way to them.

Heidi could see now that he was huge and muscle-bound. Veins bulged in his thick neck.

But the ranter didn't break eye contact with Heidi and Cam. "That's what they want. They want my voice to be silenced. They want to deplatform me. They want the truth to be suppre—"

Flannel Shirt lunged forward and shoved the #PLANDEMIC man onto the ground. "I said shut up, motherfucker!"

Heidi leaped to her feet and put herself between the two men. "Hey! C'mon. Stop it!"

"I can't *stand* people like that," said Flannel Shirt.

"Just calm down," said Heidi. "It's not worth it. We're all in this shit together, aren't we?"

Flannel Shirt stalked off across the park, swearing. Heidi looked at the man on the ground. He had a huge smile on his face.

"I've been targeted by the agents of globalism. They don't want me to spread the truth. But I'll never give up. This is 1776. Give me liberty or give me death!"

He picked up his ratty cardboard sign and, thankfully, continued onward to spread the truth.

After the rant and the sudden altercation, Heidi could feel that the mood between her and Cam had shifted. Their food was gone and all that was left were the greasy wrappers. They sat in glum silence now.

"Look," said Cam, "it's been almost two weeks and we

haven't found any Extiva . . . Maybe we should start thinking about Plan B?"

"What, like run away together?"

Cam stared at her but didn't say anything.

"Ha-ha," said Heidi. "Good one, dude."

Now he gave her a smile, tinged with sadness. "I should probably get back home. It's my mom's birthday today, and I ought to give her a call."

"Yeah, I need to get home too."

Heidi dropped Cam off at his apartment and made the long drive back to her own neighborhood. By the time she got home Ron and Madeline had already turned in for the night. Heidi tiptoed up to her room and quietly got ready for bed.

She lay awake in the darkness and felt certain that sleep wouldn't come. A few minutes after she'd turned off the lights, her bedroom door quietly opened. Madeline came in and sat down on the corner of her bed.

"Where did you go?" asked Madeline.

"I just met up with a friend," said Heidi.

"Olivia?"

"No, a friend you don't know."

Madeline nodded. "You don't have to be cruel to Ron just because you're angry with me, you know. I can take it. But he doesn't deserve to get caught in the crossfire."

"Sorry. You're right. I'll apologize to him in the morning."

"Saying 'sorry' stops meaning anything if you keep doing the things you're sorry for, Heidi."

"I know. Sorry."

"You've been out of sorts for weeks. I understand that it's a major disappointment that you didn't get in to Harvard. Believe me, I get it."

"It's not that."

Madeline ignored her and pressed on. "When you're sure you've got it all figured out, life kicks you in the teeth. You had a setback. Okay. So you pull yourself up. You dust yourself off. And you move forward."

"What if it's something that you can't move forward from?" asked Heidi. "What if something happens and there's no fixing it? What are you supposed to do then?"

"You're young, and that's just how young people think. Everything seems so significant. But life marches on whether you want it to or not. You know, I didn't grow up with all of this. I didn't have a stable home life. I didn't go to a good school. I had to work like a dog for everything, with no help from anyone. I tried my best to make sure you didn't have to struggle like I did, but I worry it's made you . . ."

"It's made me what?"

"It's just—I worry that you haven't ever not gotten exactly what you wanted."

Is that true? Heidi wondered. Had she simply been handed everything in life?

"Anyway. Harvard's out. But you still haven't heard from Brown, UCLA—"

"It's not just college, Mom."

Madeline waited for Heidi to elaborate. But Heidi didn't.

"Well, whatever it is you're going through, I'm sure I've been through it too," said Madeline. "We may butt heads sometimes, but you know you can talk to me about anything."

Heidi wanted to tell her right then and there. She yearned to reveal her secret to her mother and have Madeline hug her and tell her everything was going to be okay. That it was silly to even be worried about it. That she wouldn't be locked away. That Heidi could be fixed.

But Heidi didn't tell her. She couldn't.

"I know, Mom," said Heidi quietly as tears welled in her eyes. "I know."

19

Heidi regarded herself in the mirror. She wore a black off-the-shoulder mermaid gown studded with silver beads.

"That one's good, right?" said Olivia. "You look like a hot witch."

Madeline glanced up from a work email on her phone. "I like it. You look beautiful."

"I don't know," said Heidi. She turned and looked at herself from the side.

Madeline frowned. "You know, you do actually have to pick one of these dresses eventually."

"Heidi's just holding out for the best, Mrs. Mills," said Olivia. "She's a perfectionist, just like you."

Madeline grunted and went back to her phone.

"It is really cute," said Olivia to Heidi with a tone of exhaustion in her voice. "And it's true that there are only so many prom dresses in the world."

Olivia had already settled on a blue sequined gown almost two hours ago. Since then, Heidi had tried on eleven different prom dresses. She didn't hate any of them. But she didn't like any of them either. In fact, when she looked at herself in the mirror, she felt nothing.

Because it doesn't matter, thought Heidi. *None of this matters.*

But if it didn't matter, why couldn't she just pick one of the dresses and be done with it?

This was normally the sort of thing she loved: shopping with her best friend. It was supposed to distract her. It was supposed to stave off the anxiety that was gnawing at her every minute of every day. But it wasn't making her feel better. She'd agreed to this to convince Olivia and her mother—and maybe herself—that things were normal. But it wasn't working. Why wasn't it working?

Heidi shook her head. "I don't think this is the one."

Olivia sighed and slumped forward. "You're right."

In the full-length mirror, Heidi saw a dark-haired girl, about her age, browsing the rack of gowns behind her. She looked familiar somehow. But more than that, Heidi realized, the girl *smelled* familiar. For an instant, their eyes met in the mirror.

Heidi turned but as she did, the girl moved on to another rack.

"Who is that?" asked Heidi.

"Who? Her?" asked Olivia. "I don't think I know her."

"I do," said Heidi.

Heidi remembered. She'd seen the girl on the next tennis court the day she'd smashed her racket in a fit of useless rage. But . . . she'd seen her somewhere else too. Where?

Heidi started walking toward the girl.

"Heidi, where are you going?" asked Madeline.

Heidi didn't answer. As she approached, the dark-haired girl grabbed a gown off the rack and made for the dressing room.

"Hey," Heidi called out. "Excuse me."

The girl didn't hear Heidi. Or if she did, she ignored her. She ducked through the fitting room door.

Heidi followed her into a short, dimly lit hallway, with five changing room doors on either side. Three of them were empty, their doors swinging open, loose hangers on the floor. Heidi sniffed the air. The girl was in here.

Heidi knocked on one of the closed doors. "Hello?"

"Occupied," came an older woman's voice from inside.

Heidi knocked on another door. There was no answer.

"Are you following me?" Heidi asked through the thin plywood door.

Silence. Heidi jiggled the handle, but the changing room door was, of course, locked.

"Who are you?"

Still nothing.

"I know you're in there," said Heidi. "Just tell me what you want from me."

The girl said nothing.

With a grunt, Heidi forced the door open, splintering the jamb with a loud crack. But the dressing room behind it was empty.

"Heidi?"

Heidi turned to see that Olivia had followed her. She was staring, mouth open, at the door Heidi had just broken through.

"Is everything okay?" whispered Olivia.

A woman in her sixties stepped out of the first door Heidi had knocked on, dressed in an ill-fitting pantsuit, utterly confused. "What the hell's going on?"

"Everybody okay in here, folks?" barked a store security guard from the doorway.

It was all Heidi could do not to force open another one of

the locked doors. The dark-haired girl was behind one of them. Hiding. The guard's eyes were locked on Heidi.

She took a deep breath. "Yes, I'm fine. I think I may have, uh, accidentally broken the door."

"Uh-huh." The guard watched her the whole time as she walked out of the dressing room.

"What was that?" hissed Olivia when they were out of earshot.

"Nothing. Just an accident," said Heidi. It wasn't much of an explanation. "I got confused."

"About what?"

Heidi didn't answer. She made her way back to her mother and grabbed a random gown—purple satin—off the rack. "This is the one. Let's go."

Madeline looked up from her email. "Finally."

* * *

The question of who the girl was nagged at Heidi. It wasn't until later that evening that she started wondering whether she might have been some sort of undercover Viral Containment Task Force agent. Did they even have undercover agents? Heidi texted Cam, but he didn't know (though he wouldn't put it past them).

If they were following her then it was only a matter of time now. That night Heidi barely slept, half expecting her door to get kicked in before dawn. She'd read somewhere that's when they usually conducted raids. A half dozen times she considered waking Madeline up and telling her the truth. Or walking out the front door of her house and never coming back.

But she didn't. And the morning came without incident.

Heidi went to school and passed the hours in a fugue state of anxiety and exhaustion. Between the fear she was going to get caught at any moment and raging emotions she could barely contain, she could feel herself unraveling. Was it her imagination, or were the other kids smirking and whispering behind her back? They could tell something was wrong with her. Or maybe she was simply losing her mind, seeing things that weren't there.

At lunch, Heidi sat in the cafeteria, silent, uselessly racking her brain to remember how she knew the girl from the store. Luca and Olivia sat with her. They were bickering, as they always did whenever they were within one hundred feet of one another.

"I cannot *believe* I'm going to prom alone," said Olivia.

"You've still got five days to find a date," said Luca. "You should go with Goth Steve."

"Shut up," said Olivia.

"It would be perfect," said Luca. "You two could form, like, a powerful witches' coven."

Olivia laughed, despite herself. "God, you're a dick. I think you may actually be a sociopath. You know there's a test you can take online."

"Unnecessary. Sociopaths don't care about the feelings of others, but I simply want you to have an unforgettable senior prom." Luca elbowed Heidi. "What do you think, babe?"

Heidi realized that someone was talking to her. Expecting a response.

"Uh, sorry. What?" said Heidi. "I . . . wasn't paying attention."

Luca shook his head. "You kids with your phones. I'm asking who you think Olivia should go to prom with?"

Heidi shrugged. "It's fine if she wants to go alone."

"But that's just it: She doesn't *want* to go alone. Look in her eyes. She's dreaming of a magical evening on the arm of a strapping young man. Our friend Olivia is ready for love."

"Eat shit," said Olivia.

"Ooh, how about Nils?" asked Luca. "He's single."

Olivia frowned. "He's single because he's repulsive."

"Interesting. And why do you think *you're* single?"

Olivia answered by flipping him off.

Luca grinned and threw an arm around her shoulder. "Don't get mad at me. I'm the one trying to help you. We can put a pin in this for now, but don't you worry. I'm going to make this happen for you. We're gonna *Never Been Kissed* this thing."

"Get the fuck off me," said Olivia as she shoved his arm away.

Something wasn't right. The hairs on the back of Heidi's arms stood up. Amid the cacophony of high school lunch—yelled conversations and utensils clattering on trays—she heard the staccato clack of boots on linoleum; she smelled Kevlar and gun oil.

Instantly, Heidi was on her feet, adrenaline pumping. Her body entered fight-or-flight mode a split second before the doors of the cafeteria flew open.

Four Dogcatchers in full tactical armor burst in with truncheons in their hands. Somebody screamed.

20

Heidi had pictured this moment countless times already. Often it happened while she was at home, asleep. Sometimes she was at school. Sometimes at the movies with Luca, or at Dean Park with Cam. But they always caught up to her. And now they were here. They'd finally come to take her in.

Time seemed to slow as Heidi started to run. But out of the corner of her eye, she saw that across the cafeteria, the custodian, Mr. Santangelo, was running too.

One of the Dogcatchers tackled him to the ground. But somehow Mr. Santangelo threw the man off, and in a moment he was back on his feet, eyes wild. Another Dogcatcher bashed him across the neck with a truncheon while two more dove for his legs. Mr. Santangelo went down again, and the first Dogcatcher piled onto his back.

Mr. Santangelo wailed as the Dogcatchers overpowered him. One of them wrenched his arms behind his body while another zip cuffed him. As he struggled, they jerked a black spit hood down over his head and cinched it around his neck.

Kids were crying. Others had their phones out, trying to film, but in a matter of seconds it was all over. Mr. Santangelo lay motionless and limp on the floor of the cafeteria, still making that horrible wailing sound in the back of his throat. Without a word, the four Dogcatchers picked him up by his arms and legs and carried him out of the cafeteria.

Kids ran to the door and pressed their faces and phones up against the windows for a final glimpse of Mr. Santangelo's fate as he was taken away by the Viral Containment Task Force.

A nervous silence had fallen over the cafeteria. Heidi was lucky. Everyone's attention had been focused on the fight and the arrest. It seemed that no one had noticed her jump to her feet in a panic and start sprinting for the exit.

But now the students began to talk among themselves, anxiously trying to process what they had just witnessed.

"That was insane. You see that shit?"

"Mr. Santangelo was a goddamn werewolf?"

"He fought, like, four guys."

Ms. Okomura shook her head as she spoke quietly to Mr. Hirsch. "Did they have to do it here in front of the kids? Couldn't they have just waited till he got off work?"

Luca whistled and turned to Olivia. "Sorry, Olivia. I guess you won't be going to prom with Mr. Santangelo."

This time Olivia didn't laugh. "God, you're an asshole."

The PA system crackled and the school principal, Mrs. Porras, spoke over it. Her voice sounded shaky. "Good afternoon, Raptors. As many of you know there was an unexpected incident in the, uh— Due to, um, potential exposure, all students, faculty, and staff, please report to the auditorium for lupinovirus testing. Immediately. Thank you."

This raised a collective groan from the students in the cafeteria. For years they'd been subjected to the regular indignity of random saliva testing. It was the defining annoyance of their young lives.

"Saliva test? God, I'm tired of strangers shoving things in my mouth," said Luca. "Hey, there's a sentence you'll never say, Olivia."

"You're disgusting," said Olivia. "How do you even have friends?"

"Everybody loves me," said Luca with an angelic smile.

Both of them rose to join the crowd slowly making its way toward the school auditorium. Testing everyone in school would take the rest of the day, which would at least get them out of class.

But Heidi was frozen, panicked.

Olivia turned back and must've seen something in her best friend's face. "Everything okay?"

"Mm-hmm," said Heidi.

"You coming?" said Luca.

"I'll catch up," said Heidi. "Just need to pee first."

Heidi turned and walked toward the girls' restroom until she was sure Olivia and Luca were no longer watching. Then she ducked into a stairwell and waited. Once the coast was clear, she quickly darted out an emergency exit.

It was all she could do not to break into a run as she crossed school grounds toward the parking lot. There had been regular saliva testing at school at the start of the pandemic but such measures had been phased out years ago, especially in low-risk "green" zip codes.

But it was clear now that Heidi wasn't safe at Green Valley anymore. She wasn't safe anywhere. She climbed into her Audi and cranked the ignition, ready to peel out of the parking lot. But she saw her hands shaking and stopped herself. Probably not a good idea to be driving during the middle of a full-blown panic attack. So, instead, she sat in her vehicle, trying 4–7–8 breathing to calm herself down. She watched as a VCTF van squealed past the parking lot and drove off with its flashers on, carrying Mr. Santangelo toward indefinite quarantine.

Heidi tried to think calming thoughts: sleepy cats, fresh-baked scones, a quiet forest glade—

Suddenly, it hit her where she recognized the girl from. Heidi texted Cam and asked if he could meet her immediately.

* * *

Heidi sat on the bench at Dean Park, ignoring the view of the city and the slate-gray thunderheads on the horizon. She alternated between searching her phone and scanning the park, wondering if she'd been followed. When Cam arrived, Heidi was surprised at how relieved she was to see him.

"Got here as fast as I could," he said, sitting down beside her. "I left a load of clothes in the washer, so I hope this is good."

"You remember the girl who was following me the other day?"

"A Dogcatcher?" He involuntarily glanced over his own shoulder.

"I don't think so. I saw her twice before. Once on the tennis court with my mom and today I remembered the other time: when we were in the forest, asking people about the Bitch."

Cam nodded. "Right. I remember. That girl hiking alone. But . . . it could be a coincidence?"

"It's not," said Heidi. "I know it's her. It has to be. I think it's the Bitch."

Cam cocked his head. "Didn't we decide the—uh, is it better if I say 'b-word'?"

Heidi shrugged.

"Didn't we decide the b-word was an urban legend?" asked Cam.

"We did. And I might still think that, if I hadn't found this."

Heidi showed Cam a picture on her phone. It was a scan of an old-fashioned topographical map with a few buildings delineated on it. The label said FORT MCMILLAN.

"What exactly am I looking at?" asked Cam. "This map's from 1941."

"It's the national forest," said Heidi. "Well, it's the area that eventually became the national forest. Back then, all the land was owned by the army."

"Okay. I'm still not following."

"This fort was decommissioned way back in the 1950s. But it must still be there. In the woods."

Cam understood. "You think that's where she lives?"

Heidi nodded. "Look."

Heidi dragged a saved jpeg of a trail map onto the image of Fort McMillan. Then she decreased the transparency and resized it until the two maps matched. Fort McMillan was just off the Ocean Ridge Trail.

"Damn," said Cam.

As they made their way to Heidi's Audi, Heidi recognized someone down the block. "Shit," she said as she quickly ducked into her car.

"What?" asked Cam.

"Nothing."

Heidi pulled out and five minutes later, they were speeding north on the interstate. She only hoped that Luca's friend, Peter, hadn't seen her too.

21

Heidi pulled into the small gravel parking lot. As thunder rumbled in the distance, she and Cam started along the Ocean Ridge Trail—the same trail they'd hiked two weeks ago.

Almost immediately, they met a hiker coming the other way, a red-haired woman in her thirties. "Careful," said the woman. "Storm's coming."

"We know," said Heidi as she strode past.

Heidi and Cam saw no one else on the winding path that led up and into the darkness of the forest. Their pace was rapid, almost desperate.

Twenty minutes into the hike, Cam broke the silence. "I still owe you an explanation. I didn't tell you the whole truth."

"The whole truth about what?"

"That first night, you asked me why I decided to help you. And, yeah, most of it was because I personally know what happens to people who get infected and quarantined. But there was something else."

Heidi stopped on the trail and turned to face him. "What do you mean?"

"I recognized you," said Cam. "We did have a class together when I was at Green Valley. Bio with Mr. Bishop. I was in tenth grade. You were a freshman."

"I'm sorry, I don't really remember much about that class."

Cam shrugged. "You mean you don't remember much about me. I don't blame you. I was a quiet kid. Glasses. Braces. I don't think I ever talked to you. Except for that one day Mr. Bishop made us lab partners. You remember the dead mice?"

Heidi did remember now. "Oh my God, you were the kid who was scared to dissect a mouse."

"I wasn't scared," said Cam, defensively. "It's just nasty, and I stand by that. It's also, like, cruelty to animals. Why the hell are we murdering all these innocent mice anyway? I guess Mr. Bishop made me your lab partner because he knew you were a stone-cold killer."

Heidi shrugged. "The mice were already dead. And we got through it. I remember you even managed to get the liver out."

"Not a lot of people were nice to me at that school, but you were. So when I recognized you I . . . I don't know. I just, I wanted to help you like you helped me that day. And I . . ." He seemed like he wanted to say something else, but trailed off.

Heidi smiled. "I'm glad I got to know you, Cam. Even if it was like this."

The forest opened before them. They'd reached the cliffs that looked out over the ocean—the place where they had their change. The brewing storm looked closer now, racing in from the water.

"It shouldn't be far from here," said Heidi.

Heidi pushed into the darkness of the woods and Cam followed. As their eyes adjusted, they soon saw a chain-link fence topped with rusty razor wire that encircled a series of crumbling concrete structures, overgrown with weeds and brush. It was only a few hundred feet from the trail.

Heidi and Cam approached the fence and saw that it was

covered in signs that were so badly rusted, they were hard to read. As they got closer, they could make out messages like RESTRICTED! UNAUTHORIZED PERSONS KEEP OUT! and US ARMY PROPERTY. NO TRESPASSING. VIOLATORS WILL BE PROSECUTED.

Whether any such violators had ever been prosecuted was unclear, but it was obvious that many before them had defied these warnings. The ground had enough litter—candy wrappers, chip bags, old beer cans—to suggest many generations of trespassers. They could see now that under the vines and dead leaves, the concrete walls were covered with countless layers of faded graffiti.

The fence was more of a notional barrier than a physical one. They found one of the many spots where it had rusted loose and they passed through.

The contours of a complex of ruined buildings became clearer now, though the forest had done its best to swallow them whole. Heidi's emotions were mixed. She felt the hope of knowing she was on the right track, mingled with a growing sense of dread. Thunder growled on the wind.

Cam shivered. "Why do I feel like I'm walking across somebody's grave? Or somebody's walking on mine?"

They picked their way through the underbrush and across half-buried concrete slabs. Ahead Heidi spotted a corroded plaque embedded in a fallen wall. The words FORT MCMILLAN were visible.

"It's the right place, at least," said Heidi.

"Except I don't see any mysterious criminal masterminds who look like they could help us," said Cam. He sat down on a toppled pylon wreathed in vines. "We got our hopes up for nothing. Again."

"I don't think so," said Heidi.

What remained of the fort did appear thoroughly deserted. But something—some subtle clue on the edge of her senses—told Heidi it wasn't. A damp moldy scent caught her nose. She pressed forward and saw it.

"Look," said Heidi, almost in a whisper.

There was a door in the ground—a square of pitch black that was darker than the forest gloom. Beyond the threshold were concrete steps that disappeared into the darkness.

At the sight of it, Cam shook his head and quietly swore to himself.

"There were bunkers underneath the fort," said Heidi. "This must lead to them."

"Abandoned tunnels," said Cam. "Great. You know old tunnels fill with toxic gas right? And then people go stomping around in them and that mixes the gas with the clean air and they asphyxiate."

"Are you having second thoughts?"

"Yes! I'm having second thoughts," said Cam. "I'm having third thoughts. Hell, I'm having some fifth thoughts." Cam pointed at the door. "I've seen enough horror movies to know what happens when you go into a door in the ground."

"I don't want to either," said Heidi. "But what choice do we have?"

She moved toward the steps and something crunched under her feet. Heidi looked down and saw that she'd crushed the bleached skull of some small mammal. She now saw that entrance to the tunnels was carpeted in hundreds of small bones.

Cam saw what she'd stepped on. "Jesus Christ."

"Just animal bones," said Heidi.

"You sure about that?" asked Cam. He nudged a longer, thicker bone that was half buried in the dirt.

Heidi was afraid now too. This wasn't just a tunnel. It was a lair. Something lived down there hiding from the light, something that ate meat. A primal instinct told her to turn and run away as fast as she possibly could.

Instead, Heidi started down the steps. A few feet in, and it was clear how many trespassers had been here before her. A scrawl of graffiti covered every surface of the concrete walls—so many individual messages layered on top of each other that you could barely read any of them.

Heidi yelled as loud as she could into the bunker, "Hello?"

The sound echoed its way down into the concrete tunnels, dying at last.

"What the hell are you doing?" whispered Cam, still standing outside.

"If somebody is down there, it's probably better if we *don't* surprise them, right?" Heidi called into the tunnel again, "Hello!"

Again, nothing.

Cam shook his head. "Nobody here. Let's go."

"It's too late for that," said Heidi.

Before Cam could argue, Heidi walked down the stairs into darkness.

"Well, don't go alone," said Cam, who hastened to catch up to her.

Fifty feet down the concrete steps of the old bunker, it felt to Heidi like they'd entered another world. The glowing square of daylight at the entrance had disappeared from view behind them. It was pitch-black down here in these tunnels. They could only see by the blue-white glare of their phone flashlights—weak against the darkness, yet somehow blinding when you inadvertently looked directly into them.

What they mostly saw was graffiti, and lots of it. Decades of scribbled and spray-painted words—competing on every wall—made the place disorienting, an underworld of mixed messages. Heidi chanced to read a more recent sentence that stood out in red paint: YOUR IN HELL NOW.

They kept going down. Their footsteps echoed weirdly on the concrete. Heidi stopped to listen and, for a moment, heard something that sounded like music but couldn't have been. She smelled the air and her nostrils burned with the damp scent of mold. Beyond it was a more pungent hint of something rotting in the darkness. She could feel Cam's nervous energy behind her, like static electricity tickling the back of her neck.

"Can you back up?" said Heidi. "Give me some space."

"Sorry," said Cam. He took a step backward, up the stairs. "This place is clearly empty, anyway."

"Then what're you so worried about?" said Heidi. Her words sounded braver than she felt.

Cam sighed. "Nothing. Lead the way."

The stairs ended at a flat perpendicular hallway. A puddle of dark liquid glinted in the light of their phones. It took Heidi a moment to realize that it was only water, being fed by a steady drip from the ceiling. She listened for the music again but heard nothing.

"Which way?" asked Cam, his voice barely a whisper.

Heidi had no idea, but she tried to sound confident when she said, "Right."

They walked along the concrete tunnel, passing a number of doorways that branched off into smaller rooms. They shined their lights into these chambers as they passed. Most looked like they hadn't been disturbed in years. Some were heaped with rubble where parts of the concrete wall had cracked and collapsed, burst inward by tree roots questing for water. Others held piles of moldering furniture. In one, Heidi saw an almost fully intact mid-century office desk. It looked pristine, save for the clumps of thin white toadstool mushrooms that sprouted from the waterlogged laminate desktop.

Heidi's confidence was ebbing and her fear was growing. She tried to distract herself by imagining this place in its heyday, a hundred years ago: a series of busy, well-lit offices and storerooms for the soldiers manning the fort.

Just then she heard something behind them—a grunt or a growl. Heidi froze.

"Did you hear that?" she asked Cam.

"No," said Cam. He spun and shined his phone light behind them. There was nothing in the tunnel but dancing shadows.

"What did it sound like?" asked Cam, his voice tight with tension.

Heidi didn't answer him. "Hello?" she cried again.

Her voice visibly startled Cam. The sound echoed back down the hallway the way they came. There was no answer. But as it faded away, Heidi felt the hairs on the back of her neck stand up. She heard something: a sound so faint, she thought it might be her imagination. From the darkness there came a low, continuous growl.

"We're being followed," whispered Heidi.

"We are?" said Cam. He frantically shined his light at every dark corner.

Heidi saw something on the edge of the darkness move—a

shifting blackness, a glint of something white. Or was it a trick of the light?

"Run," yelled Heidi.

The way out was cut off. So Heidi sprinted as fast as she could in the opposite direction. She hit another T-intersection and turned right again. She heard Cam's footfalls behind her. Their phone lights swung back and forth as they ran, making the darkness strobe. Were there other footsteps too? Heavy breathing? The sound of clicking against the concrete?

Something was chasing after them. She was sure she could hear it now. She was sure she could smell it too. Musk and sweat and blood and decay.

Heidi chanced a look over her shoulder, but Cam's phone light blinded her. She hit a patch of wet concrete that was slick with scum and her feet flew out from under her. Heidi hit the ground hard enough that she yelped in pain. Her own phone flew out of her hands, bouncing away into the darkness and landing in a puddle, flashlight down.

"Leave it!" screamed Cam, as he grabbed the back of her shirt and hauled her back to her feet.

Now Heidi was running after Cam with no light of her own. She heard the thing behind her clearly now—breathing and snorting. Its stink filled her nostrils. Heidi dared not stop to look back, because if she did, it would catch her. Cam was faster than Heidi, and as he sped forward the darkness behind him closed in around her.

It *was* going to catch her. Any second, the thing was going to catch her.

"This way!" cried Cam as he darted sideways through an open doorway.

They found themselves in a long, narrow chamber with a rounded half-pipe ceiling and walls. But it was a dead end.

Heidi spun just in time to see a heavy metal door slam shut behind them, sealing them inside the vault.

22

At first they were quiet, huddled in terror in the far corner of the bunker, waiting for the door to swing open and for whatever had been chasing them to burst in.

But it never did.

Seconds passed. Then minutes. The only sound was their panting breath, amplified by the bare concrete and the silence around them. The sharp smell of their sweat began to overpower the damp mustiness of the bunker. At last, Heidi spoke.

"Is it gone?"

"I have no idea," said Cam.

They approached the door and found that it was, of course, locked. The door itself was made of heavy steel covered in countless layers of black paint. Heidi pressed her ear to it and listened, but heard nothing.

"Let us out!" she screamed at the top of her lungs.

Heidi charged at the door and slammed her shoulder into it. It rattled but didn't budge. She backed up and threw herself against it again. And again. The third time, Cam grabbed her by the arm to stop her.

"Heidi, that door was probably made to withstand bombs."

With a snarl, Heidi broke away and slammed into the door as hard as she could. It didn't give.

"Chill," said Cam, stepping between her and the door and putting his hands up. "Just chill."

Heidi nodded and tried not to panic. She walked to the other end of the bunker, where, for the first time, she noticed the room's lone decoration: a water-stained poster taped to the wall. It showed a crown with big block letters: KEEP CALM AND CARRY ON.

Heidi burst out laughing. There was a touch of hysteria to it. She moved to rip the poster down.

"Leave it," said Cam. He slowly slid down the wall to a sitting position and held up his phone. "I'm at eight percent."

"Do you have a signal?" asked Heidi. She already knew the answer.

Cam closed his eyes and shook his head. "I know it's not great, but . . . I should probably turn the flashlight off before the battery goes completely dead. Are you going to be okay with that?"

Heidi nodded and sat down on the cold concrete floor beside him. Cam turned off his phone and the darkness around them was absolute.

"Probably should've charged it before doing this," said Cam. "Live and learn."

"Hopefully."

"What do you think is going to happen?"

"I guess whatever it is—whoever it is—doesn't want us dead quite yet. Maybe that's a good thing?"

"Maybe they just want us to starve to death down here. Prolong our suffering."

"Cam, don't be ridiculous," said Heidi. "We'll die of dehydration way before we starve to death."

"Ah, okay. Good to know."

"Or maybe we'll lose it and kill each other first?" said Heidi.

"How long do you think that would take?"

"I feel like I've got another twenty minutes before I lose my mind," said Heidi.

Cam laughed. "Okay, I'll set a timer on my phone. Wait, no. Damn it."

Hours passed. They heard nothing, saw nothing. Their fear was too intense to be sustained indefinitely, and gradually it faded to numbness and even boredom. They played "I'm Thinking of an Animal" and worked together to come up with the rules for something called "The Ultimate Movie Game." They moved around the country, state by state, trying to name the capital city and attempting to do their best (ridiculous) version of whatever the local accent was.

Both of them tried to recount their entire autobiography from birth until the present day, in maximum detail, so as to take as much time as possible. Cam's funny stories of his brother and mother were heartbreaking to Heidi, now knowing what had happened to them in the end. With whatever time she had left—which didn't seem like much—Heidi resolved to appreciate her family more. Even Ron.

Time and darkness stretched out to infinity. Sometimes Heidi cried. Sometimes she laughed, for minutes at a time, at the absurdity of her predicament or perhaps nothing at all. Locked in a bunker in the middle of the woods. What a way to go! With nothing else left to do, Heidi fell asleep.

But her sleep was fitful, troubled by violent dreams. She was running through the forest, not a person but not a beast either. A goat bleated in the darkness. Gunfire lit up the trees around her. Blood was everywhere.

Heidi awakened with a gasp. It took her a moment to realize her eyes were open because the darkness was total. Her heart sank as she remembered she was still trapped in the same concrete hell.

"Sorry, I woke you up," said Cam. "You sounded like you were having a nightmare."

"Thank you," said Heidi. She stretched her sore neck and pulled herself into a sitting position. "Nobody came to kill us yet?"

"No," said Cam. "I promise I'll let you know if they do."

"Thanks. Appreciate it."

There was a long pause. Cam cleared his throat. "Heidi."

"Yeah?"

"There's something I think you should know."

"What is it?"

"I'm in love with you. I have been for years. Ever since that day in tenth grade with the dead mice. For an hour that day, you showed me who you really were. And I think you saw the real me. It was a long time ago, and I did kind of forget about you. But I was still in love with you, if that makes any sense."

Heidi didn't know what to say.

"Sorry," said Cam. "I know it sounds like I'm delirious or something. And this definitely isn't the ideal time to bring this up. But I mean it. And I just figured I should tell you before . . . well, before whatever is going to happen happens."

"Cam," said Heidi softly.

She felt Cam shift beside her. Heidi shifted too, unable to see him, but moving toward the warmth of his body. She closed her eyes and felt his face close to hers, as he leaned in to kiss her—

Metal scraped against metal. The door's rusty hinges groaned as it swung open. Heidi and Cam leaped to their feet and were blinded by light.

"Rise and shine," said a female voice from behind the beam of a high-powered LED flashlight.

Heidi involuntarily turned away, blinking back tears. She couldn't see, but she recognized the scent.

"You—you've been following me around for weeks," said Heidi.

"Ding ding ding."

The flashlight lowered. As Heidi's eyes slowly adjusted she could see that, indeed, it was the girl from the store and the tennis courts, from the hiking trail. She appeared to be roughly Heidi's age, perhaps even younger.

"Are you . . . *her*?" asked Cam.

The girl gave a harsh laugh. "I'm Xuying. Follow me." Without another word, she turned and stepped back out into the hall.

Finally Heidi's emotions caught up to her. She rushed the girl and grabbed her by the shoulder. "Hey! Why the fuck did you lock us in there?"

Xuying turned and stared at Heidi with an icy expression. "Didn't know if we could trust you. Still don't."

"Who's we?" asked Cam.

"You'll see," said Xuying.

She led them through a twisting maze of underground tunnels—some flooded with inches of water, others half collapsed, their walls burst inward by the pressures of the earth.

At last, they saw light ahead. A faint tinkling sound floated through the air. It was the music that Heidi had heard before, clearer now.

A section of the concrete hallway was filled with furniture. Folding chairs and cots lined the walls. Heidi saw a tall pyramid of canned food beside a battered camp stove. The stink of unwashed bodies mingled with the damp, fetid smell of the tunnels. A small Bluetooth speaker was playing classical music at a barely audible volume, something by Rachmaninoff.

There were people here too. By the dim light of a propane lantern, she saw an older man in a wrinkled suit sitting on a milk crate. He played cards with a red-haired woman.

Another man—a big, muscular guy in a flannel shirt—sat on a cot by the wall, reading by a small LED light. It was a dog-eared copy of *Manufacturing Consent* by Edward S. Herman and Noam Chomsky.

Heidi was overwhelmed by a sense of déjà vu. She had the vague but certain sense that she knew all these people, despite the fact that they were strangers. Heidi took an involuntary step backward.

"Are we prisoners here?" she asked.

The old man scowled at her. Then he spoke with a surprisingly refined British accent. "Trust that all will be made clear. In the meantime, do be so kind as to keep your voice down."

He nodded toward the far side of the encampment, and Cam and Heidi saw a bearded man asleep on a dirty sleeping bag at the edge of the lantern light.

The big guy went back to reading his book. The old man and the red-haired woman returned to their card game. Several long moments of unsettling silence passed.

"Are we prisoners?" repeated Heidi.

Xuying merely chuckled.

"Okay. Then we're leaving," said Heidi.

She turned to go, but Xuying stepped in front of her.

"Not so fast," said Xuying.

"Gin," said the red-haired woman.

"Blast it all," said the old man, tossing his cards down on the wooden cable spool that served as a makeshift table.

"Get out of my way," said Heidi.

Xuying grinned but didn't budge. Her expression said: "Make me."

"Move!" said Heidi. She tried to sound firm, but there was a tremor in her voice.

Now the man on the cot stood up. Heidi could see just how big he was—six foot five at least, with a bodybuilder's physique. He reeked of sour vinegar. The guy rolled his neck and Heidi heard vertebrae crackle.

"Is there a problem?" he asked.

"There's about to be," said Cam, stepping toward him.

"Everyone, calm down."

A woman had emerged from somewhere deeper in the encampment. She wore boots and jeans and a black leather motorcycle jacket. Heidi's first thought was that she was attractive, but not at all in the way that Heidi had ever aspired to be. She was muscular and androgynous, with a short, severe haircut and striking eyes that were the color of steel. Her age was impossible to guess. She might have been twenty-five or forty-five. There was something fascinating about her, but something threatening too.

The moment she appeared, Xuying and the big guy seemed to deflate.

The woman clucked her tongue at them. "Come on. Where are your manners?"

"Sorry," muttered the big guy, staring at the floor.

Xuying merely grunted.

The gray-eyed woman turned to Heidi and Cam. "I apologize. We don't get a lot of visitors, so our social skills can get a little rusty."

"You're the Bitch," said Cam.

The woman's eyes went wide. "*Excuse* me?"

Cam sheepishly cleared his throat. "I mean, we were, uh, told you call yourself that."

The woman squared up with Cam, and Heidi could see that they were about the same height. She looked right into his eyes with a horrified expression on her face. After a moment, Cam looked away.

The woman burst out laughing. "Nah, I'm just messing with you. You're right. I'm her. But please, call me Rhea."

Heidi couldn't stop staring at the woman. She knew those eyes.

"We've met before," said Heidi.

Rhea nodded. "That we have. Are you two hungry? This way."

Rhea led them past the underground encampment and into one of the small side chambers. It was stockpiled with non-perishable foods—packages of ramen, sacks of rice and dried beans, jugs of water, silver foil packets that contained military surplus MREs—all stacked on wooden pallets to keep everything off the damp floor. In the center of the dark room was a stained card table and three metal folding chairs. An unlit candle sat in the middle of the table.

"This is the break room," said Rhea, with a chuckle. She used an old-fashioned Zippo lighter—the kind Heidi's grandpa used to have—to light the candle, bathing the room in warm, flickering light.

"Much better," said Rhea.

Then she rummaged around in a nearby cardboard box and came back with two protein bars and two bottles of water, which she handed to Heidi and Cam.

"Sorry," said Rhea. "I know it's not much of a breakfast."

"Breakfast?" asked Heidi. "How long have we been down here?"

"Awhile," said Rhea. "My friends and I had to come to a decision. We're a leaderless organization, so building consensus can take time."

"A decision about what?" asked Cam.

"What to do with two trespassers."

Cam tensed but Rhea put a hand on his arm.

"Don't worry," she said, "my side won."

"What would have happened if the other side had?" asked Heidi.

Rhea merely grinned. There was another awkward silence.

"So, what do you want with us?" asked Heidi.

Rhea shrugged. "Technically, you're the ones who found me."

Rhea was right, of course, Heidi realized. "Well, because we heard that you can help . . . people . . ."

Rhea raised her eyebrows. "People?"

"People . . . like us," said Heidi.

Rhea made a face of mock confusion. "And what are you *like*, exactly?"

Heidi swallowed. She couldn't bring herself to say it.

"Infected," said Cam. "You know we're infected."

Rhea nodded. "Ah. So you're bloodthirsty monsters, then?"

"No," said Heidi. "We're not monsters."

Rhea put a hand on Heidi's wrist. Her touch was firm and calming. "Yes, you are. You're wanted: dead or alive. I could call the Dogcatchers right now and get a twenty-thousand-dollar reward for turning the two of you in. Why would the government pay me that much money if you're not monsters?"

Cam shook his head and turned to Heidi. "C'mon. This is bullshit. Let's go."

"No," said Heidi. She locked eyes with Rhea. "I think the reward money is to let everyone know they're being watched. So they think they're safe. Even though, maybe, nobody's ever actually safe."

"Smart girl," said Rhea. "Then again, I already knew that."

"Because you've been watching me, haven't you?" said Heidi.

It wasn't just Xuying that Heidi remembered following her. She'd realized that she'd seen the others before. The old man was picking through the trash in Dean Park. The big guy was the one who'd started a fight with the #PLANDEMIC conspiracy theorist. Most recently, they'd passed the red-haired woman hiking the opposite way along the Ocean Ridge Trail.

"We have to protect ourselves," said Rhea. "I knew you were looking for me, but I didn't know who you were. Now I do."

"And yet, we still don't know who you are," said Cam. "Or what the hell any of this is."

"You could think of us as a mutual aid society," said Rhea. "There's nobody looking out for us, so we look out for each other. We call ourselves the Underdogs." She paused and slowly smiled. "The name's kind of a joke."

Heidi nodded. "So can you help us, or are we wasting our time?"

Rhea considered. "I can try. But you need to understand, nothing in this world comes for free."

Cam scoffed. "Tell me something I don't know."

Rhea turned to Heidi. "How about you? Do you understand what I'm saying?"

"I understand," said Heidi.

"Good," said Rhea. "So, what is it that you want from me?"

"Extiva," said Heidi. "Enough for both of us."

An expression passed across Rhea's face, too quick for Heidi to read. "That's what everybody wants, these days. It won't be easy. It'll take some time."

"We only have two weeks," said Heidi.

Rhea shrugged, then nodded. "The only thing I can promise is that I'll do my best."

For some reason her words put Heidi's heart at ease. For the first time in weeks, she felt like things might be okay.

"If that's all," said Rhea, "I can show you the way out."

They followed the light of Rhea's candle through the labyrinth of bunker tunnels. The whole place was much larger than Heidi could have imagined. She found herself lagging behind Rhea and Cam as they walked ahead in silence. At a T-intersection, Rhea turned right. Heidi looked down the left tunnel and saw light pouring through a cracked door.

The plaque on the door said C6. Heidi opened it a little and peered inside. She saw a small room with a blueprint tacked to a bulletin board. It was hard to make out much at a distance, but the floor plan was labeled GAINES MUSEUM—that was the big downtown art museum.

"Nosy nosy," said Xuying.

Heidi turned. She hadn't even realized she was being followed.

"I got lost," said Heidi. She hurried to catch up with Rhea and Cam, leaving Xuying standing in the dark, watching her go.

By some circuitous route, they had arrived at the familiar graffitied steps that led to the surface. Heidi followed Rhea and Cam up. As she stepped outside, the morning air was fresh and cool against her skin. Patches of blue sky peeked through the rustling leaves above. Rhea closed her eyes and took a deep breath.

"Very few people know about this place," said Rhea. "Please keep it that way."

"We will," said Heidi.

"So you'll be in touch, when you get the Extiva?" said Cam, as he pulled out his phone. "You have a phone number?"

"No," said Rhea.

"Shit," said Heidi, suddenly remembering that she'd dropped and left her own phone in the bunker tunnels.

Before she could explain, Rhea reached into the pocket of her motorcycle jacket and handed Heidi her spiderwebbed iPhone.

"Okay. How about an email, then?" said Cam. "Mailing address?"

Rhea gave an enigmatic smile and shook her head. "I know who you are. I'll be in touch." She turned back toward the bunker stairs. "It's rough out there. Good luck."

"Wait," said Heidi.

Rhea paused and regarded her with those striking gray eyes.

"Thank you," said Heidi.

Rhea nodded. "We've got to look out for each other. That's how we get through this."

And with that, she disappeared back down the dark steps.

23

"You think she's full of shit?" asked Cam, as they hiked down the Ocean Ridge Trail.

"No," said Heidi. "For some reason, I trust her."

Cam nodded. "Sure. A lady with no last name who lives in a sewer in the woods. Nothing suspicious about that at all."

"I don't know how to articulate it. But she seems . . . *sincere*. I think she'll come through," said Heidi. "Honestly, this is the first good news we've had in weeks. Can you just let me enjoy it?"

"My bad," said Cam. "Expect the worst and you'll always be pleasantly surprised. That's always been my motto. Anyway, you want to play the Ultimate Movie Game?"

Heidi sighed. "Please no more anime."

"Fine. Then no more early-2000s rom-coms!"

They laughed and talked all the way down to the trailhead. Neither one of them mentioned Cam's confession or the kiss that had almost happened inside the bunker. The thought of bringing it up felt strange to Heidi—too heavy, too consequential. She didn't want to dampen the mood.

They reached the parking lot and were soon driving south toward the city. Once they were back in cell service, Heidi's heart sank as she saw that she had dozens of missed calls from Madeline.

Heidi sighed. "My mom must think I'm dead."

"None of my business," said Cam, "but you should probably tell her you're not."

Reluctantly, Heidi dialed Madeline.

"Where are you?" was how her mother answered.

"I'm fine, Mom. I was . . . I was with Olivia."

"No you weren't. I called Olivia's mother. That's not where you were."

Heidi silently cursed herself. She didn't know what to say. "Sorry. I messed up."

"You're sorry? You messed up? Heidi, I was sitting here for the last eighteen hours thinking you might never come home."

"I was safe the whole time. I was fine." Two more lies.

"And you didn't think I'd like to know that? You didn't think I'd be worried sick, imagining the worst? Are you even capable of considering how your actions might make someone else feel?"

There was no arguing, no way to let her mother know the truth.

"It won't happen again," said Heidi softly.

"Damn right it won't," said Madeline. "I'm taking your car away."

A sudden surge of anger boiled up inside Heidi. Her body tensed, but Cam put his hand on her shoulder and shook his head. She knew he was right, of course.

Heidi swallowed. "That's fair."

"I'm glad you think it's fair." Madeline's voice was acid.

"I'll be home in an hour. We can talk then," said Heidi. "I love you."

Madeline said nothing as she hung up the phone. Heidi glanced over at Cam.

"She's just worried," he offered. "But, yeah, sounds like you're in for it."

Heidi said nothing. They drove in silence through the city, toward Dean Park. Heidi pulled over next to the corner where Cam's Kia was parked.

"I think we did it," said Heidi. "We found the cure."

Cam's face looked pained, like he wanted to say something.

"What is it?" asked Heidi.

"So, yeah, about what happened last night in the bunker—"

"Yo!" came a voice from down the street.

In the rearview, Heidi saw the door of Luca's silver BMW fly open. Luca got out of his car and started toward them. He had an iced latte in his hand and a furious expression on his face.

"Jesus," said Heidi. She climbed out to intercept him as he approached.

"What the hell is going on here?" yelled Luca.

"Nothing's going on."

"It's time to stop lying. You disappeared yesterday. You went to the bathroom and you never came back. Where were you?"

"I can explain everything. Just please calm down."

"After you ditched school, Peter said he saw you with *him*." He pointed to Cam.

Now Cam got out of the car too. "Yep. She was with me. Is that a problem?"

"Yeah, it's a big fucking problem," said Luca as he moved toward Cam.

"Luca, stop!" cried Heidi.

Luca didn't. Instead, he lunged forward and threw his iced latte all over Cam, soaking him in sticky, milky liquid.

Cam was motionless for a moment. A slight smile crossed his face. Then he gave a bestial growl and shoved Luca, hard. Luca flew backward and bounced off the driver's-side door of a parked Nissan. The impact left a clear dent in the car.

Luca scrambled to his feet, fists up, ready to fight, but Heidi put herself between the two of them.

"Calm down! It's not what you think!" She turned to Cam. "Can you just go? Please?"

There was a fire in Cam's eyes. He clearly wanted a fight. But instead he took a big step back and put his hands up. "Okay. Fine."

Heidi kept her hand on Luca's chest as Cam got into his Kia—still dripping with iced coffee. He peeled out and sped off down the street.

"What the fuck was that?" said Heidi.

"It was assault," said Luca. "That fucker assaulted me."

Luca pulled out his phone and started to dial.

"What?" cried Heidi. "You started it!"

"Maybe *you* started it. Ever think of that?" said Luca as he put the phone up to his ear. "What's his last name?"

"Why are you asking me?"

"Because I'm calling the police."

Heidi's voice got quiet. "Don't do that, Luca."

"Fuck you. Don't tell me what to do."

Luca dialed. Heidi heard the faint tone of the phone ringing in his ear.

"Please. You don't know what you're doing," said Heidi. "If you do this you'll—you'll kill him."

Something passed across Luca's eyes, like he finally understood something. "What are you talking about?"

"Just put the phone down."

Luca's eyes went wide. "He's in some kind of trouble, isn't he? Like, real trouble."

"No."

"You're trying to protect him. Aren't you?"

"911, what's your emergency?" asked the operator.

Luca paused. "Yes, I'd like to report an—"

Heidi punched the phone out of Luca's hand. It clattered down the street and slid under a parked car.

Luca clutched his hand. He stared at Heidi in disbelief—half angry, half stunned. "Why the fuck did you do that?"

It was everything Heidi could do not to lunge at him right then and there, to choke the life out of him and smash his face into the pavement until he stopped moving. She wanted to shut him up forever.

Instead, she said, "I think . . . maybe . . . we both need a little space right now."

The shock and fear in Luca's eyes became something else. "*What?*"

Heidi was desperate to stay calm. She saw other people on the street—a woman walking her French bulldog, an elderly couple sipping boba tea on a bench. They were all watching the drama unfold. Heidi couldn't afford to draw any more attention to herself.

She swallowed. "We're going to be at different colleges. Different states. You don't need to be tied down. You should be free. You'll meet someone new."

Luca shook his head. "No. You don't break up with me. Not for . . . *him*."

"Luca, it's not working," said Heidi. "And it's my fault. I admit that. You know that I care about you, but—"

Luca's expression turned to anguish. "If you break up with me, I *will* call the cops on him!"

The words hung heavy between them.

"What?" said Heidi. "Well, that doesn't matter because he's not—"

"Bullshit," said Luca. "If you break up with me, your friend Cam is done for. Within an hour the police will be kicking in his door. Understand me?"

"He's not in any trouble," said Heidi weakly.

Luca gave a harsh laugh. "You always sucked at lying."

Heidi tried to order her racing thoughts—to come up with a plan, any plan, for a way out. "Why are you doing this?" she whispered.

"Because I love you," said Luca.

Heidi nodded. "Okay."

"Okay . . . you're still my girlfriend?"

"Uh-huh," said Heidi. She hated herself for saying it but she saw no other way.

"I love you," repeated Luca. He waited as though he expected Heidi to respond.

"I love you too," she said.

"Good," said Luca. "Now go pick up my phone."

24

"Whoa," said the dispatcher on duty.

She was unable to hide her reaction as she saw Erik Balikian walk into the Viral Containment Task Force station for the first time in weeks.

Erik knew he looked like hell—greasy hair from not showering, bags under his eyes from not sleeping, and enough stubble that it had become a patchy beard. He didn't care.

"Afternoon," said Erik. "Is Lieutenant Aoki around?"

"He's not working today," said the dispatcher.

"Too bad," Erik said, knowing full well Tuesday was the lieutenant's usual day off.

"Is it something Sergeant Lowery could handle?" asked the dispatcher.

"Maybe so," said Erik. *That was exactly what he had been hoping for.* The lieutenant was a hard-ass. Everybody knew Lowery was a pushover.

"Okay, I'll tell him you're here to see him." The dispatcher paused with a look of concern on her face. "You doing okay, Erik?"

He smiled, revealing the gap where his tooth used to be. "Never better."

Erik poured himself a Styrofoam cup of weak coffee and sat down on one of the plastic chairs in the waiting area. A few minutes later, he was called back.

Sgt. Lowery—a round, red-faced man—sat behind Lt. Aoki's desk, filling in for the day.

"Good to see you, Caveman," said Lowery, shaking his hand. "Enjoying that PTO?"

"Oh yeah," Erik lied.

"How's your girlfriend?"

"Studying hard," said Erik. He hadn't spoken to her since she went back to school.

"So," said Sgt. Lowery, leaning back in his swivel chair, "what can I do you for?"

"Well, see, today was the day that I was supposed to come in and review the bodycam footage with the lieutenant."

Sgt. Lowery looked confused. "Investigative Services signed off on that?"

They hadn't. In fact, they'd never responded to Erik's email, or his many follow-up calls. They didn't give a shit. Still he nodded. "IS said it's cool."

"Huh," said Lowery, looking a tad uncomfortable.

"I mean, I guess I could wait till L.T. is back," said Erik. "It just sucks 'cause I drove all the way across town . . ."

"You know what?" said the sergeant. "I can pull up the footage."

"For real?" Erik feigned surprise. "That would be great."

"Yeah, give me one sec." Sgt. Lowery logged in to the lieutenant's clunky desktop computer. "Okay. Here we go."

He turned the monitor around so they could both see. Erik could feel his heart racing now, as Sgt. Lowery cued up the footage. He realized he was gripping the arms of his chair so tight that his hands were hurting.

Lowery clicked play. The video was surprisingly sharp, shot from the standard-issue VCTF camera that Erik (and all other Dogcatchers) wore clipped to their right shoulder. It showed the woods, illuminated by the full moon. Up ahead, he saw Reaper's back, his black helmet glinting in the moonlight. The long leash Erik had been holding trailed away into the darkness. At the end of it he heard, but didn't see, the bleating goat.

"Something there," said Reaper.

The camera jostled, as Erik fumbled to get his MP5 up while maintaining his grip on the leash. There was a moment of quiet, followed by a violent commotion in the bushes. The leash snapped out of Erik's hand and whipped away into the underbrush. There was a high-pitched scream that sounded almost human—the goat's death cry.

"Light 'em up!" yelled Reaper, and he fired a burst from his MP5 into the trees.

Erik raised his MP5 and got off a single shot. From the video, it was impossible to know whether he hit anything or not.

"Oh shit," said Reaper.

Suddenly, a blur barreled out of the leaves right at the camera, and now it was pointing straight up at the night sky, unmoving—an angle that didn't show anything useful.

"What the hell?" asked Erik, leaning forward in his chair. "Can you go back?"

Lowery scrubbed the player backward a few seconds. Then he moved forward, frame by frame, as the blur launched itself toward Erik's bodycam.

"Pause it," said Erik.

The clearest frame showed a splayed, four-legged form flying through the air toward Erik. It wasn't a werewolf that had pounced on him. The goat's bloody carcass had been flung at him. Erik swallowed.

"Play," said Erik.

The bodycam stayed aimed at the sky. This was the point at which Erik had been taken out of the action. A dead goat had put him into a coma. But the bodycam was still recording audio. Erik strained to hear the faint sounds of a struggle and then there came another scream—this one clearly human—lasting several agonizing seconds until it trailed off into silence. Jason Mottola had just been killed.

Erik closed his eyes. He felt sick. The public relations woman's lie echoed in his mind: *"At least he didn't suffer . . ."*

"You okay, son?" asked Lowery as he stopped the video.

Erik nodded, but he wasn't okay. He'd only fired a single, shaky shot and he'd clearly missed his target. He could have saved Reaper—he *should've* saved Reaper—but he wasn't good enough. He choked because he was weak. Useless. Reaper died because of him. Erik felt himself sinking down into a well of despair.

"Erik?" said Sgt. Lowery.

Erik took a ragged breath. "Can I see Reaper's bodycam footage?"

Sgt. Lowery went pale. "You don't want to do that. Believe me."

"Yes. I do."

"Why?"

"Because I want to know if there was . . . something I could've done."

Lowery gestured toward the footage. "What happened here

wasn't your fault, son. Nobody thinks you did anything wrong. Hell, they're going to give you the Law Enforcement Medal of Honor."

His words meant nothing. Erik had to know the truth.

"Please," said Erik quietly. "Show it to me. It's all I ask."

Lowery swallowed, for some reason unable to deny Erik's request. "Okay," he said. "Okay."

He went back into the antiquated database to try to pull up the file. Then Erik saw him frown.

"What?"

"No, it's just . . ."

"Tell me." Erik's words came out harsher than he meant.

"There is no footage," said Lowery.

"What do you mean?"

"All I have is a note here that he wasn't wearing a bodycam," said Lowery.

"But that's not true," said Erik. "He *was* wearing one. He told me to turn mine on. What the hell?"

Lowery shrugged. "I don't know. I guess just ask Investigative Services. Maybe they could—"

But Erik was already up and out the door. He didn't want to wait for the elevator. Instead he walked, then ran, up the stairs to the third floor to the Investigative Services offices. He was told the detectives assigned to investigate Reaper's death, Inspectors Mendez and Patino, were both out. Erik wanted to scream. He wanted to smash something. Hurt someone.

He slowly walked out to the street and quietly sat down on the curb. It was his fault. It was his fucking fault. He had to do something. He needed to put all this right. There had to be something. Anything.

And so, Erik Balikian decided to do the only thing he could think of.

He got in his car and drove back to his apartment. Inside, he grabbed his Glock-17 off the top of the fridge and checked the magazine: seventeen silver-tipped 9mm rounds worth about $2500—courtesy of the US taxpayer. Then he snatched his VCTF badge off his dresser and got back in his car again.

In the weeks since he'd been discharged from the hospital, his days had been empty. Every morning, after his physical therapy exercises, if he wasn't having a headache, Erik would call Investigative Services for an update on their investigation. He got nothing. His calls went straight to voicemail. Reaper was right, Erik had decided. These people had already tapped out. They didn't care anymore.

It made Erik crazy. Without anything else to do, he'd turned his attention to the names that he and Reaper had found.

Searching "Dawn Suppley" had turned up nothing. The woman was a ghost. As for Cameron Woodbine, he'd found a few of them. But there was one in particular, one who was probably the right age. His name came up as "William Cameron Woodbine" in a single news article, apparently the teenage son of a frontline worker who'd been infected at the very start of the pandemic. The details of the story were stomach-turning. Since then, Erik had been able to find an address in the city and a vehicle registered in his name.

This was the guy. In his bones, Erik knew it. After seeing the video, Erik decided he wasn't going to wait anymore. It was time to act. Time to do what Reaper would've done.

* * *

Dusk was falling as Erik arrived at a run-down apartment complex in a crummy neighborhood. Sure enough, parked down the block he saw the ten-year-old Kia registered to William Cameron Woodbine. The car was somehow in even worse shape than he could've imagined.

Without a warrant or any probable cause to enter the building, he'd need to be careful. Maybe, *maybe*, if he was on duty he could get away with it. But he was on his own now. Erik would have to play it cool and use his head, which he could admit wasn't always his strong suit. He sat in his car and watched and waited till he saw someone coming out of the apartment's security gate.

It was an old man in a skullcap, pulling a grocery cart. As he exited, Erik sprinted toward the gate.

The old man stopped and blocked Erik's path into the apartment complex. He looked Erik up and down. "You don't live here."

"Oh, yeah. I'm actually a friend of Cameron's. He said he'd buzz me in when I got here but he's not answering his phone. No idea what's up."

"Cameron?" said the old man.

"Cameron Woodbine?" said Erik. "He lives in apartment 2J, right?"

The old man shrugged. "You tell me. He's *your* friend."

"Right, I know," said Erik, caught off guard by the pushback. "I've just never been to his place. That's all."

The old man eyeballed him for a long moment and then grunted. "I don't know the neighbors. They come and go."

Yet still, the old man wasn't moving. There was an awkward silence now. Erik's strategy wasn't working. Time to adjust. He quickly flashed his badge. He wasn't wearing a uniform, so he was hoping the guy might take him for a plainclothes detective.

"I'm going to need to get past you, sir," said Erik, instantly changing his tone from "friendly" to "law enforcement scary."

The old man stared at him for another moment, defiant. Then he stepped aside. Erik slipped through the security door and heard it clang shut behind him.

"You have a good evening, sir," said Erik without looking back.

The courtyard beyond the gate was empty. Erik scanned the area, on the lookout for anyone the right age to be Cameron Woodbine—only a few months younger than Erik, in fact.

He supposed he could play the long game: wait in his car and watch the Kia, or wait in the courtyard and stare at the apartment door until Cameron Woodbine came or went, but he didn't have the patience for that. He'd already waited long enough.

Erik ducked into the stairwell. Between the first and second floor, he pulled his gun. He moved quickly and deliberately along the balcony, past apartment after apartment . . . 2M . . . 2L . . . 2K . . .

He stopped in front of apartment 2J and listened. The TV was on inside. Moment of truth. Erik took a deep breath. This is what Reaper would've wanted.

"Cry 'Havoc,'" said Erik to himself, "and let slip the dogs of war."

He pounded on the outer security door and stepped aside so he wouldn't be visible through the peephole. Then he listened. He thought he heard someone moving around inside, but it might have just been whatever was happening on TV.

If he knocked again, he'd lose precious seconds. Instead, Erik stood back and kicked open the useless security door.

He found himself in a small, cluttered one-bedroom apartment. There was a dingy living room area with a tiny galley kitchen. On the stove, a teakettle was just starting to whistle. Cameron Woodbine was home.

"Viral Containment Task Force!" bellowed Erik at the top of his lungs. "Get on the floor!"

He heard someone down the hall. Erik charged forward, Glock out. He kicked the door open and saw a tiny bedroom in disarray. No one there. But the small window that looked out onto the street was wide open.

Erik rushed to the window and looked down. Twenty feet below, Cameron Woodbine was running as fast as he could, away down the block.

Erik took aim . . .

"Fuck!" he said, as Cameron Woodbine ducked around the corner and out of sight.

Erik lowered his gun, filled with self-loathing. He'd never catch him now.

Erik walked back into the kitchen. He calmly turned off the shrieking teakettle. Then he slapped an empty mug off the countertop.

"Stupid," he snarled. "Worthless."

He'd blown it again. He'd let a 10–91W get away and now he'd never catch him. Despair once again began to overcome him. Erik felt himself sinking back down the well.

But something caught his eye. On the table, there was a paper pharmacy bag. Erik looked inside it and found a small cardboard box—a Gaines Rabies Lupinovirus Rapid Test. Further confirmation that he and Reaper had been right.

But Erik noticed something else in the bag. It was a credit card receipt for $67.30. Three saliva tests, apparently. At the bottom Erik saw a name with a clean, legible signature above it. It wasn't "Cameron Woodbine." It wasn't "Dawn Suppley," either. The receipt read "Heidi Mills."

25

It had been a week since they'd found Rhea's bunker. Heidi had heard nothing since. It had started to gnaw at her. Maybe Cam had it right? Maybe it was insane to trust their fate to some stranger they barely knew. The worry kept her up at night. More than once, Heidi considered going back up to the forest to ask where the hell the Extiva was.

It wouldn't have been easy. Madeline was watching her like a hawk now. Ever since the night Heidi hadn't come home, her mother made it plain that she didn't trust her anymore. As promised, she had taken away the keys to Heidi's car. Now, anywhere Heidi wanted to go, anything she wanted to do, was met with a series of increasingly suspicious questions. The only silver lining was that, for the moment, she had an excuse not to go out with Luca.

But at school, Heidi had to pretend like everything was normal. She acted like Luca's girlfriend. She hung on his arm, held his hand, laughed at his shitty jokes. She played the part, but it made her sick inside. She tried hard to behave like she didn't hate him. But, now, there was no escaping that she did. At first, she was worried it would be obvious to Luca how she really felt. But soon she realized that he didn't actually seem to care.

The only thing he cared about was that she didn't break up with him, and that she wasn't seeing Cam anymore. Luca was more suspicious than Madeline. He grilled her constantly about where she had been, what she'd been doing, who she'd been doing it with. Heidi answered his questions. It was pathetic and maddening and it filled her with self-loathing and rage. But she was terrified that the moment she pushed back, Luca would call the police to kick down Cam's door.

She worried about Cam too. But he wasn't texting her back. Ever since his altercation with Luca, he'd been incommunicado. She missed him. Maybe because he was the only person who might've understood how she felt. At first, she was hurt by his silent treatment, but then she was scared. She was afraid that Cam had already been captured. She half wondered if Luca hadn't already gotten him arrested, but she was afraid that if he hadn't, asking about it might prompt him to do just that.

In truth, Heidi had never felt so alone in her life. It was 07:04:03:24 on her Lunar Cycle Countdown app as she texted Cam the same message she had seven times before.

Are you ok?

No answer.

"Ron asked you a question," said Madeline.

"What?" said Heidi, looking up from her phone.

Ron appeared distinctly uncomfortable. "No worries. Just wanted to know if tuna casserole's okay for dinner."

"Sure," said Heidi. "That's fine."

She checked her phone again. Cam still hadn't replied. Heidi started to type another message. Something different from before. She started to tell him how much she missed him. How important he was to her. How she needed him. Before she could send the text, Madeline spoke:

"All you ever do is stare at that thing. Maybe I should confiscate your phone too."

"I'm sorry," said Heidi without really meaning it.

"It seems like 'sorry' is all I ever hear from you, these days," said Madeline.

Heidi sighed and closed her eyes. "Can you just please lay off me for one minute? I'm just—I'm going through some stuff right now."

"What? What are you going through?" asked Madeline, exasperated. "I assume you're still sulking because I took your car away, which is, technically, *my* car, by the way."

"That's not why I'm upset," said Heidi, feeling her anger bubbling. "Whatever. Doesn't matter."

"It *does* matter if you're going to use some unspecified stress as an excuse to be rude to your family," said Madeline. "Just tell me what is happening with you and perhaps I can help."

"Uh, maybe I'll go start on dinner," said Ron as he quickly disappeared into the kitchen.

"I'm going to take a walk," said Heidi.

"Oh, no, you're not," said Madeline. "If I let you walk out that door, you might disappear to God knows where."

"I can't leave the house now?"

"Not until I can trust you."

"Do you remember being my age at all?" asked Heidi. "Do you remember how hard it was?"

Madeline actually laughed. "You think *your* life is hard?"

This pushed her over the edge. Heidi felt her fury building. The beast was trying to claw its way out.

Madeline pressed it. "By all means, tell me the hardest thing you went through today. Go on. I'll wait."

Heidi gritted her teeth. Madeline looked back at her with a contemptuous smile. The answer to her mother's question came into Heidi's mind clearly. The hardest thing she did all day, every day, was to hold back, to not give in. She had to fight herself every moment to keep the beast in check.

But there was a limit.

And now Heidi could feel her muscles tightening, her adrenaline rising. She couldn't do it any longer. She couldn't hold it back. The beast was about to explode. Heidi moved toward Madeline, ready to wipe the smirk off her face—

And that was when the doorbell rang.

Heidi stopped herself and took three slow, deep breaths. "I'm going to answer that."

"Thank you, I would appreciate it," said Madeline sarcastically.

Heidi opened the door and was stunned to see Rhea standing on her doorstep, hands in her pockets.

"Hi," said Rhea.

Heidi's eyes went wide. She was paralyzed. Before she could say anything, Madeline joined her at the door.

"Can I help you?" asked Madeline.

Rhea extended her hand. "Hi, I'm Heidi's teacher. My name's Rhea."

"Hello," said Madeline, tentatively shaking her hand. "Is there something you need?"

Rhea looked concerned. "Heidi didn't tell you?"

Madeline turned to Heidi. "No, she did not. There's a lot my daughter doesn't tell me these days." She turned back to Rhea. "Is Heidi in some sort of trouble?"

Rhea laughed. "What? No. She's a good kid."

Madeline nodded, still obviously confused. There was a long

moment of awkward silence. Heidi felt it too. It seemed to her that Rhea relished making people uncomfortable.

"Would you like to come in?" asked Madeline, at last.

Heidi subtly shook her head "no" to Rhea.

Rhea ignored the signal. "Thank you, Mrs. Mills. That would be lovely."

Five minutes later, Rhea was sitting in Heidi's living room with Madeline and Heidi. Ron put out a tray with crackers and hummus.

"Forgive my bluntness," said Madeline, "but why are you here, exactly?"

Rhea grinned, her mouth full of crackers. "First off, you have a beautiful house, Mrs. Mills."

"Thank you," said Madeline with a flat tone. "I apologize for the mess."

Rhea chuckled. "You should see my place."

"Mmm," said Madeline.

"Second," said Rhea. "I just wanted to tell you what an amazing daughter you have."

Madeline blinked, caught off guard. "Yes, thank you. Heidi . . . does have her strengths."

"I see a lot of potential in her," said Rhea. "She's smart. She's tough. She's much braver than I was at her age. And I think Heidi's a natural leader, too."

"Really?" said Madeline.

Rhea nodded. "You must be very proud."

"I am proud," said Madeline.

To Heidi's surprise, in that moment, it sounded as though her mother really meant it.

Rhea ate another cracker. Then she turned to Heidi. "So do you want to tell your mom about our secret project?"

"Wh-What?" stammered Heidi. "I— You know, maybe it's better if you do."

"Sure," said Rhea. "Heidi is doing an independent sociology study, sort of a survey of the existing literature."

"What's the topic?" asked Madeline.

"She wanted to figure out what effect the pandemic has had on young people."

Madeline shifted in her seat. "That's a very interesting question. What have you found so far?"

It took Heidi a moment to realize that Madeline was talking to her.

"Oh," said Heidi, "well, I'm not deep enough in the research to draw any conclusions, but . . . overall, it seems like increased levels of stress. Feelings of isolation. Depression."

Madeline nodded gravely. "That all makes sense. I can't imagine what it must be like for children to have to make sense of . . . all of this."

"Empathy too," added Heidi. "It's hard to measure but it seems like maybe the pandemic has given them a little more empathy for other people."

Madeline sighed. "What a way to come by it. The cure can't arrive soon enough."

Heidi was about to say that the cure might've already been found, but Rhea put a hand on her arm and spoke first.

"Anyway, I got permission from the university for Heidi to access the sociology library. I understand Heidi's not driving at the moment, so that's why I'm here: to give her a ride."

"Thank you, Rhea," said Madeline. "That's very kind of you."

"It's my pleasure to work with a student like Heidi." Rhea checked her watch. "Speaking of which, we should probably hit the road."

Madeline walked them both to the door.

"It was a pleasure to meet you, Rhea," said Madeline, shaking her hand.

"Likewise," said Rhea. "I don't say this to every parent, but I really do believe your daughter is going to do great things."

Madeline smiled and nodded. "I think you might be right."

"I guess I'm going to miss dinner," said Heidi.

"Don't worry about that," said Madeline. "We'll save some tuna casserole for you."

"Please don't," said Heidi quietly.

Madeline cracked a smile, despite herself.

After she closed the door, Heidi gave it ten seconds. Then she turned to Rhea and hissed, "What are you doing, coming to my house?"

"I told you I don't do phones," said Rhea.

"You stick out like a sore thumb," said Heidi. "It's a huge risk for you to be here."

Rhea grinned and shrugged as she regarded the homes on the block. "I guess. I've always wanted to see how the other half lives."

"How did you even get past the gate guard?" asked Heidi.

"You mean Melvin?" asked Rhea. "He just seemed to trust me."

"Melvin," said Heidi to herself, making a mental note to remember the name.

Rhea pointed to a shiny black muscle car parked on the street, a 1973 Plymouth Barracuda. "This is my ride."

"You've got to be kidding me," said Heidi.

Rhea pulled a pair of Wayfarer sunglasses out of her jacket pocket. "If you're going somewhere, why not go in style?"

* * *

Easy listening played on the radio as Rhea drove Heidi through the late-afternoon traffic, going twenty miles per hour over the speed limit. The Barracuda weaved in and out of the other cars with little regard for politeness and less for the law. It was all Heidi could do not to tell her to slow the hell down and stop driving like a lunatic.

Instead, Heidi said, "You . . . like this music?"

"Yeah. Keeps me on an even keel, you know?" Rhea floored it and pulled across the double yellow lines. "Before I rang the doorbell, it sounded like you were getting into it with your mom."

"She . . . she doesn't understand," said Heidi. "How could she?"

"Doesn't understand what you're going through? Or doesn't understand you?"

"Both, maybe."

"To me, it didn't sound like she was really trying," said Rhea. "Ever wonder what it would feel like to finally stand up to her?"

"What are you talking about?" asked Heidi.

Rhea grinned. "You know. Give her the ol' Chook treatment."

"I don't want to hurt my mother," said Heidi. "I don't want to hurt anybody."

"Really? Not even that little shit of a boyfriend you have?" Rhea grinned as she zoomed past three cars. "C'mon, you can tell your old pal Rhea the truth."

"How do you know anything about Lu— about my boyfriend?"

"I know everything," said Rhea flatly, avoiding the question. "I know you want to smash Luca's face in."

Heidi was about to argue when she realized she *did* want to hurt Luca. A part of her wanted it more than anything.

"It's wrong," said Heidi, "but sometimes, I get so angry . . ."

Rhea swerved back into the right lane, narrowly avoiding a head-on collision with a mail truck. The other driver laid on the horn behind them, as the Barracuda sped on.

"You realize, you don't have to take any more shit from anybody," said Rhea. "You have the power. You're in control."

Heidi gave a dark laugh. "Really? I'm in control?"

"Yes," said Rhea.

"Every time I get upset, I feel like I might murder someone," said Heidi. "In fact I'm actually terrified that I will. And when I'm not angry for no reason, I'm hiding from my friends and family, like some kind of criminal. I constantly look over my shoulder in case somebody wants to rat me out or lock me up or kill me. Meanwhile, I'm counting down the days until I turn into a mindless beast against my will. So forgive me, but it doesn't particularly feel like I'm in control."

"True control is letting go," said Rhea.

"Very profound," sneered Heidi. "Did you read that on the inside of a yogurt lid?"

Rhea laughed. "I really do like you. You're spicy."

Heidi looked out the window of the car. They were in a suburb she'd never bothered to visit, an ugly sea of strip malls and parking lots and big box stores. "Where are you taking me?"

"You'll see."

"You've got a real flair for the dramatic, huh? You just love keeping people in suspense." Heidi finally lost it and raised her voice. "Do you have the Extiva or not?"

"Don't worry," said Rhea. "I haven't forgotten what we discussed."

"That's not an answer to my question," said Heidi. "You couldn't have contacted me, at some point, in the last week? Just to give me an update. 'Hey Heidi, hope you're doing well. No need to worry. Just wanted to let you know everything's going according to plan.'"

"Beasts aren't mindless."

"What?"

"You said earlier that you're 'counting down the days until you turn into a mindless beast,'" said Rhea. "But beasts aren't mindless."

"Okay, cool."

"You're right that what's inside you can't be suppressed. You won't ever tame it."

"I don't want to tame it, I want to kill it! I want the cure!"

"Here's the thing," said Rhea. "You were angry before you caught the virus. The beast was always there. Even if you cure yourself, the beast will remain. It's a part of you. But you can master it."

Heidi considered what Rhea was saying. She thought of the dark wolf with the gray eyes that sniffed her in the alley, the beast that chased her and Cam through the underground bunker tunnels. The wolf was Rhea.

"You've mastered it," said Heidi.

Rhea merely smirked.

"You figured out how to change whenever you want," said Heidi. "Not just on the full moon. How?"

"Took me years," said Rhea. "Years of suffering. Just like you, I tried to suppress it. I tried to fight it. Tried to deny who I really was and be something other people wanted me to be. But then, one day, I understood."

"Can the others do it too?" asked Heidi. "The Underdogs."

"Not yet. But none of them have your potential."

"What potential?"

"The beast is stronger in you." Rhea turned to face Heidi, pale gray eyes visible over her sunglasses. "I can smell it."

Heidi shifted in her seat, uncomfortable in Rhea's direct gaze. "It's just a virus. It's submicroscopic bits of protein using the cells of my body to mindlessly replicate. It's not me."

"The virus only makes people do what they always wanted to do, but were too afraid to," said Rhea. "When the moon is full, werewolves aren't mindless. They go where they always wanted to go, kill who they always wanted to kill, have sex with who they always wanted to have sex with. Free from fear. Free from shame. No apologies. Wouldn't it be nice to stop apologizing?"

"I don't want to kill *anybody*!" said Heidi.

"You sure about that?" asked Rhea. "Luca thinks he has a right to tell you what to do, who to spend time with, what to think. He thinks he can tell you who you are. Why?"

"Because he's . . . a rich, entitled prick," said Heidi, admitting to herself what she'd known for a while now. "He thinks he can own everything. Including me."

"But when you knocked that phone out of his hand, for one beautiful moment, you showed him that he doesn't own you, didn't you?"

"How did you know about that?" said Heidi, almost immediately realizing the answer to her own question. "Right. Because you're still spying on me."

"Don't change the subject."

"Look, I—I could've just told Luca," said Heidi. "I could have broken up with him months ago. I *should* have! Violence isn't the way we solve problems."

"Maybe it shouldn't be. But in this world that we've all been forced to live in, it is."

"People can talk to each other. We can compromise."

"We are facing the worst pandemic in six hundred years. How has our society collectively decided to respond?"

At that moment they drove past another one of the billboards that Heidi had seen in Cam's neighborhood before: $10,000 reward for reporting the infected to the Viral Containment Task Force.

"Violence," said Rhea.

They rode awhile in silence, until Rhea pulled into a nondescript office park. She drove across a wide parking lot, now emptying as the workday came to a close. Rhea parked near a set of generic-looking offices. Situated between a hot tub showroom and a telemarketing company, there was a door with a small sign that said M&K CATERING.

"Here," said Rhea. "This is your secret mission."

Heidi was confused. "What are you talking about?"

"I need you to go inside there and get something for me."

"I . . . no." Heidi crossed her arms. "I'm not going to do that. I could get in trouble."

Rhea smirked. "People like you never get in trouble."

"No," said Heidi. "Enough games. This is bullshit. I'm not doing anything, unless you tell me why I should."

Rhea took off her Wayfarers. "Sure, I'll tell you. You'll do it because I have something you want."

She reached into her jacket pocket and pulled out a prescription pill bottle with Chinese labeling. Heidi recognized the only English phrase: EXTIVA 50MG.

26

The golden bottle glowed in the late-afternoon sun. Rhea shook it a little, causing the pills to rattle. Heidi grabbed for the bottle, but Rhea moved it out of reach.

"Not yet," said Rhea. "First, I need you to go in there and get me the shift schedule for May third. I'd do it myself but . . . I can't really pass for a nine-to-five civilian." She ran her fingers through her short spiky hair. "Too cool."

Heidi was more confused than ever. "Why would you possibly need the shift schedule of some random catering company?"

Rhea merely raised her eyebrows. "You sure you want to know?"

Heidi realized she didn't. She shook her head. "So this is the price?"

Rhea nodded. "This is the price."

Heidi got out of the car and walked toward the office. She regarded her own distorted reflection in the dark glass of the door. She didn't look like she worked at a catering company any more than Rhea did. In fact, she looked like a nervous high-schooler.

Still, Heidi pulled her hair into a ponytail and tried to, at least, assume a professional demeanor. How would her mother walk into a place like this?

Heidi stepped inside to find a small waiting area—three chairs and a few bridal magazines arrayed on a cheap glass coffee table. A middle-aged receptionist sat at a large desk. Behind her was a hallway that, judging by the heavenly smell of baking bread, led to the catering kitchen.

"Mmm," said Heidi. "Smells good in here."

The receptionist smiled. "You're telling me. I'm gluten-free, so every day it's slow torture. Can I help you with something?"

"Definitely," said Heidi. "I was hoping I could talk to someone about catering a graduation party?"

"That would be Marsha," said the receptionist. "Let me see if she's available—" She started to dial an extension on the office phone but caught herself. "Oh, sorry, I know it's super annoying, but we do actually need a saliva test for all outside visitors. We're required to follow all the federal guidelines for food preparation."

She handed Heidi a lupinovirus test kit. Heidi's mouth went dry. But she kept a smile on her face and nodded cheerfully as she picked up the box. "No worries, better safe than sorry."

"Right?" said the receptionist.

Heidi swallowed as she opened the small box. Inside, as expected, was a folded instruction sheet, a long cheek swab, and a plastic vial of testing solution. Heidi slowly unfolded the instruction sheet, playing for time.

The receptionist looked up at her expectantly. "You just swab it around in your mouth for thirty seconds and then stick it in the vial," she offered helpfully.

"Right, yes, of course," said Heidi. "I was looking at the Spanish side anyway." She chuckled and carefully refolded the instructions. With no other way to stall, she ripped off the plastic wrapper and began to swab her mouth, silently counting to thirty at one-quarter speed in her head. As she tore the foil tab off the little container of testing solution, she intentionally let it slip from her fingers and fall to the carpet.

"Oh shit. I'm sorry!" said Heidi. She grabbed a handful of Kleenexes from a box on the desk and stooped to mop up the spilled fluid. "I do this every time."

"No worries," said the receptionist. "I've got more test kits right here. One sec." She spun her chair to unlock a metal filing cabinet.

While the woman's back was turned, Heidi stayed low and crept past the desk and into the hallway. Then she rose and jogged toward the catering company's industrial kitchen. Once she'd turned a corner, Heidi slowed to a purposeful stride. She popped in earbuds to minimize the chance that someone might try to strike up a random conversation.

At the end of the hall, Heidi saw a handful of clean, white aprons hanging on pegs. She grabbed one and put it on. Now she could maybe pass for someone who worked here. Maybe. She pushed through a set of double doors.

The back was a clean, spacious industrial kitchen, with red tile floors and brushed-steel prep tables. Two caterers were loading big trays packed with dough into a massive oven.

Not far away, Heidi saw a pastry chef at a table filling éclairs with cream. She had her own earbuds in.

"Hi, sorry," said Heidi to the pastry chef.

The woman paused her music. "Yeah?"

"Sorry, I'm new. Do you know where they post the schedule?"

The woman looked confused. "Jeff didn't email it to you?"

Heidi shook her head and shrugged. "Guess he forgot. So Jeff, right?"

The woman laughed and nodded. "Down the hall, there's,

like, a T-intersection. Should be on the wall, right there. Blue clipboard."

"Thanks," said Heidi.

"Wait," said the chef.

Heidi froze. "Yeah?"

The pastry chef was staring at her now. "What's your name?"

"Dawn Suppley," said Heidi. She extended her hand.

The woman shook it. "Welcome aboard, Dawn."

Sure enough, Heidi found the clipboard on the wall. But when she checked, it seemed to be the previous week's schedule.

She stopped a young guy with a man bun wearing a chef's jacket as he walked past her toward the kitchen.

"Jeff forgot to email me the schedule for next week," said Heidi, hoping to preempt any questions. "Do you know where I can find a copy?"

The guy shrugged. "Maybe in his office? He's gone for the day, though, I think."

"Damn it," said Heidi.

It didn't take her long to find what had to be Jeff's office. Sure enough, the lights were off. She waited till she was sure no one was around, and then ducked inside.

On Jeff's desk, she found a drab-looking spreadsheet had been printed out for each day of the week. Heidi quickly flipped to May third. M&K was catering the Gray Ribbon Gala at the Gaines Museum of Fine Art. Heidi used her spiderwebbed phone to snap a pic of the schedule.

She made a quick retreat back through the kitchen before anyone could realize she wasn't supposed to be there. On her way through the reception area, the receptionist leaped to her feet.

"Hey, where'd you go?" she asked.

"Oh, sorry," said Heidi, as she made straight for the exit. "I got lost looking for the bathroom."

"Do you still want to talk to Marsha?"

"No, I think we're just going to order pizzas," said Heidi as she walked out the front door of M&K Catering. "Thanks anyway."

Heidi crossed the parking lot toward the Barracuda, heart pounding. But a part of her felt giddy, too. She almost wanted to laugh.

"Did you get in trouble?" asked Rhea with a smile.

"Turns out lying comes easily to me. Who knew?"

Heidi held up her phone and showed Rhea the photo. Rhea looked at it and nodded. She started up the Barracuda and pulled out of the lot and back onto the highway.

"You got balls," said Rhea.

"Uh. Thanks, I guess?"

"So our deal is done." Rhea produced two pill bottles from her pocket and tossed them to Heidi. "His and hers."

Heidi clutched the Extiva like a lifeline. This was it. This was the end of her waking nightmare. Inside these yellow bottles, there was a normal life. For her, and for Cam.

"Thank you," said Heidi as she stuffed the Extiva into her own pocket.

They drove back across town as the sunset behind them painted the streets in orange light and deep blue shadow. Rhea, if anything, drove more recklessly than before. Heidi hardly noticed. She was too busy imagining her life—she still hadn't heard from Brown, Columbia, or UCLA—ranked #12, #14, and #17, respectively. For the first time in a long time, the thought of her future made her happy.

"Now that you've got the pills," said Rhea, "I have to ask: Do you actually want to be cured?"

Heidi nearly laughed. "You're kidding, right?"

Rhea said nothing. The engine of the Barracuda growled as they sped down the road and onto an overpass.

"I don't want to be a monster anymore," said Heidi.

"You sure about that?" said Rhea. Then she jerked the wheel and drove the car off a bridge.

27

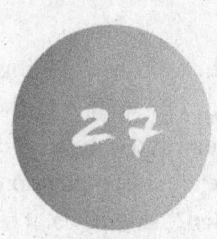

The Barracuda smashed through the barrier and flew off the overpass. For an instant, the vehicle soared through the air before plummeting twenty feet onto a frontage road below the highway. It hit the pavement hood-first at eighty miles per hour. The forward momentum flipped the car seven times before it smashed sideways into a telephone pole.

At some point, Heidi was flung through the windshield. She bounced forty feet across the asphalt, like a rag doll, taking much of her skin off in the process.

And in a split second it was over.

I'm dead, thought Heidi, before the cuts, shattered bones, and severe abrasions had even registered in her nervous system. There followed an exploding universe of pain, rapidly expanding to encompass every inch of her body.

I'm dead, she thought again. But if she was in pain, she couldn't be dead.

Heidi opened her eyes and blinked. Something dark was leaking into them and causing them to sting—motor oil or blood, maybe.

Heidi realized, now, that she was lying in a heap on the shoulder of the road, at the edge of a liquor store parking lot.

She screamed. It was a sad, ragged sound that almost died in her chest. When she tried to push herself up off the ground, she screamed again. Heidi looked at her skinless palms, muscle and bone shining through the blood.

Behind her, someone was laughing. Heidi heard the vertebrae in her neck grind as she slowly turned to look.

Broken glass and bits of black metal littered the ground. The Barracuda was on its roof, slowly spinning like a child's toy in the middle of the road. Flame and dark smoke billowed from its engine block.

Through the haze, Heidi saw a lone figure moving toward her, walking with a lurching, stumbling gait. It was Rhea. And her laughter was louder than the crackle of the engine fire.

Heidi could see the Bitch clearly now. There were bits of broken glass embedded in her face. Her left leg was broken—a jagged white shard of femur poked through her jeans. The pinky and ring finger of her right hand dangled, attached to her body by a thin shred of skin. She leaked blood from a dozen places as she walked.

Rhea stood over Heidi now, still laughing. She crouched and offered her left hand. Heidi took it and Rhea pulled her to her feet. To her surprise, she found that she could stand.

"Whoopsie," said Rhea.

"Why . . . did you do that?" asked Heidi.

"Practical demonstration." Rhea pressed her nearly amputated fingers against the bloody meat of her hand. "Everyone knows you need silver or fire to kill a werewolf. But they don't think about what that really means."

"What does it mean?"

"It means basically nothing else does."

Rhea bent over and grabbed her thigh with both hands. With a grunt, she popped her bloody, broken femur back into place. Then she slowly stood upright.

"We're not monsters, Heidi. We're gods."

Rhea grabbed Heidi's own shredded hand and forced her to look at it. The abrasions that had taken the skin off her palms were smaller now. Heidi's wounds were healing. New skin was already growing under the blood.

"Look at this! It's a miracle! You see this and you still want to return to your *normal* life?"

"Yes," sobbed Heidi.

"A life of weakness and subservience. A life of fulfilling the expectations of others while your own are denied. A life where *everything* can hurt you."

Heidi yanked her hand away. The pain of her injuries was already fading. Soon the hurt would merely be an unpleasant memory.

"Right now, we hide in the shadows or we're locked in cages," said Rhea. "This is so the rich can stay rich. So the powerful can stay powerful. To prop up the last crumbling vestiges of the world they prefer, because they're the ones on top. But nobody told them that world died five years ago." Rhea smiled at the burning car. "You may think you're one of them, but you're not. Not anymore. You're one of us, Heidi." She grabbed Heidi's shoulders. "And you're strong. Maybe the strongest I've ever seen."

"I just want this to be over," said Heidi.

"But it's only just beginning."

In the distance, emergency sirens started to blare. Cars were stopping in the road as the Barracuda burned. Heidi turned away from Rhea and began to run. But Rhea called after her.

"The meek shall inherit the earth. And soon the hunters will become the hunted. When that day comes, I don't want you to be on the wrong side . . ."

Heidi kept running.

* * *

Heidi sat on the bench at Dean Park, looking out over the city lights. Her bloody shirt and jeans had been nearly torn to pieces by the crash. But her skin had healed. Her bones had knitted themselves back together. She balled her hand into a fist and didn't so much as feel a twinge of pain. It was incredible.

Heidi stuck that hand into her pocket and touched the bottles of Extiva. Miraculously, the pills had survived the crash unharmed.

"Hey."

Heidi turned to see Cam. When she'd texted asking him to meet up, he'd responded immediately. She felt an overwhelming sense of relief that he was okay.

"Hey," she said.

Cam was staring at her ragged, filthy clothing. "What happened to you?"

"Long story short," said Heidi, "I hung out with the Bitch."

Cam's eyes went wide. "And?"

"Not very chill," said Heidi. "Why haven't you been texting me back?"

Cam sat down beside her. Heidi could see now that he looked like he hadn't slept for days. His clothes were dirty and rumpled. He'd gone through something too and she could tell he was worried.

"Sorry," said Cam. "I've been busy. Things haven't been great recently."

"Well that's very specific," said Heidi. "You know I've been worried sick about you."

"You don't have to worry about me," said Cam. "I can handle myself."

Heidi stared at him and she had the sense that there was something more he wanted to tell her. But he wasn't going to.

"Well, this should make you feel better." Heidi tossed Cam a bottle of Extiva.

Cam's eyes went wide. "Holy *shit*!" He stared at the pill bottle, then he suddenly hugged Heidi.

Heidi put her head on his shoulder and hugged him back.

Just as suddenly, Cam broke away. "Sorry about that. I didn't mean to, I just . . . I feel a little overwhelmed right now." He wiped the corner of his eye with the back of his hand. "How about this damn pollen, huh?"

"Don't be sorry. I cried, like, six different times already." Heidi opened the cap of her pill bottle and tapped out a small blue tablet onto her palm. "But I wanted to wait for you before I did this."

Cam got a pill out for himself too. He stared at it between his thumb and forefinger. "All right then. Down the hatch."

"See you on the other side," said Heidi.

They swallowed them at the same time. There was a long moment where neither of them spoke. Heidi and Cam looked at each other.

"You feel anything?" asked Cam.

Heidi nodded. "I think so. Maybe? A little?"

Cam breathed a sigh of relief, as he turned to look out over the city. "Damn. I'll be so happy when I no longer smell dog shit at five hundred yards."

Heidi laughed. "I'm excited to stop shaving my back."

"Some part of me will always wonder what raw pigeon tastes like," said Cam.

Heidi shook her head. "I don't know what I'm going to do

with myself if I'm not secretly spending all my free time scheming at a random public park with you."

Heidi could immediately see from Cam's face that he didn't take it as a joke.

"Right," said Cam. "Makes sense. Of course, in the real world someone like you wouldn't want anything to do with someone like me."

"What? No—I obviously didn't mean it like that. I just meant that now we can get back to our actual lives. I won't be texting you every day to tell you I ate a pound of raw meat. We won't be poking around abandoned bunkers looking for mysterious—"

"I get it, Heidi. You can go back to your boyfriend. I can go back to robbing houses. Happy ending."

"That's not it. I'm not—I don't want to be with Luca."

"But you *are*, though."

Heidi paused. She wanted to say "to protect you" but she stopped herself. She felt guilty that she'd put Cam in danger. She didn't want him to worry anymore.

"I don't understand," said Heidi. She held up her Extiva bottle. "This is exactly what we wanted, isn't it? An end to all this?"

Cam nodded. His voice was cold. "Yeah. I guess it is."

"Then what are you so upset about?"

Cam sighed. "You're going to make me say it? Heidi, I told you how I feel about you, and you . . . said nothing."

"When we were locked in the bunker? Sorry if I was a little distracted. If I recall, we both thought we were going to die."

"And now we're not. And it's okay. You just don't feel the same way. That's all." Cam gave an exaggerated shrug. "The virus was the only thing we had in common. Anyway, thanks for the cure."

He stood up from the bench and stared at her for a moment,

giving her a chance to speak. But Heidi hesitated. Cam turned and started to walk away.

"Cam, wait," said Heidi, at last.

But he didn't.

28

Heidi looked at herself in the mirror. She wore a floor-length A-line dress made of deep purple satin. The one she'd randomly grabbed off the rack had, ironically, turned out to be quite flattering. Her hair was pulled up in a high bun and her makeup was perfect. But beyond all these surface changes, Heidi looked different. She couldn't have said how, or why, but when she regarded herself, she barely recognized her own face.

It was something about her eyes, maybe. They were older now; harder. Or maybe clearer?

In the days since she'd started taking the Extiva, she'd felt her mood swings subside. She hadn't picked any pointless fights with Madeline. She was texting Olivia again about silly stuff—inside jokes or the latest outrageous plot twist on *Project: Hope.* She'd even stopped checking the Lunar Cycle Countdown app on her phone. Things were returning to normal.

But Heidi didn't feel normal. She wasn't the same as a month ago. The odd thought that came to mind was that she was a different person wearing her own skin.

And now that person dressed as Heidi Mills was going to senior prom with Luca Spiro, the cute, rich boy that all the other girls in her class wanted. Heidi had dreamed of this day for months. Years maybe?

Heidi gave a dark laugh. She might be cured, but she was still lying, still pretending. She despised Luca now, but she had to keep up the pretense for a little while longer until she was absolutely sure that all of this was finally over and done. She had to do it for Cam's sake.

Thinking of Cam made her feel unbearably sad. She hadn't texted him since the night he'd stormed off. He hadn't texted her either.

Cam had told her he was in love with her. Was she in love with him? She certainly cared about him. She wasn't thinking about it at the time, but she enjoyed being with him. She missed his jokes and his smile. In the preceding weeks, he was the only person she felt she could be herself around, whatever that meant now.

So when he asked her how she felt, why had she hesitated? Was it because what he said was true? Was the virus the only thing they had in common?

Heidi checked the clock on her phone and sighed. It was time to go. She went to her desk drawer and grabbed the pill bottle from where she'd hidden it inside a box of old costume jewelry. She tapped out another blue pill, her daily dose of Extiva, and swallowed it dry. Then she hurried downstairs.

"Wow. *Très* chic," said Ron. He gave Heidi a big thumbs-up.

Heidi smiled politely. "Thanks, Ron."

Somehow her mother had married the most awkward man on the face of the planet.

Madeline stood by the front door, arms crossed. "He's really not coming to pick you up?"

"No, Mom," said Heidi. "It's just easier if I meet him there."

"This is a special night," said Madeline. "You'd think he would want to—"

"I can't do this right now," said Heidi.

"Do what?"

"Can't take any criticism from you," said Heidi.

"I'm not criticizing you," said Madeline. "I just—I think you deserve someone who treats you with respect."

"Don't you see how that *is* a criticism of me?" For the first time in days, Heidi felt herself getting angry with Madeline. "Like, I'm too pathetic and weak to pick a boyfriend who isn't an asshole?"

"That's not what I think."

Heidi took a deep breath. She wasn't going to let herself lose her temper. Not now. She just had to get through tonight. "Whatever. I'll see you later."

As Heidi climbed into her car, she realized that she mostly felt annoyed because she knew her mother was right. Luca hadn't changed. He'd always been the same person—selfish and cruel. It's just that Heidi was the last one to notice it. Or had she known all along and pretended she didn't?

* * *

The Green Valley senior prom was held in a nondescript event center next to an Applebee's. Heidi's heart sank as she saw Luca's BMW in the parking lot. Still, she pulled into the spot next to him.

When Heidi tapped on his window, he glanced up from his phone.

"You look nice," said Luca as he climbed out of his car.

"Okay," said Heidi. She'd tried to keep her voice flat, but she'd let a little anger slip in.

Luca frowned. "You're not going to be sulking, are you?"

Heidi resisted the urge to snap at him. Instead, she shook her head and forced a smile onto her face.

Luca smiled back at her. "Good. Because this is our special night."

They walked inside, hand in hand. The touch of his skin made Heidi want to scream. But she didn't. Just a few more hours and she would be done with this. Done with him.

They were greeted by a cardboard cutout of the Eiffel Tower, boldly announcing the prom's theme, which was, for some reason, "A Night in Paris." Beyond was a large ballroom filled with crepe paper and awkward teenagers, marking the first and last time in their lives that any of them would wear a wrist corsage. The DJ was already blasting his Top 40 playlist. Big, shiny Mylar letter balloons spelled out the word BIENVENUE. Heidi had never actually been to Paris, but she guessed the tuxedos there probably fit better.

Heidi's heart leaped when she spotted Olivia.

"I'm going to go say hi," she said to Luca.

"Don't be too long," said Luca.

Heidi rushed to Olivia and gave her a huge hug.

"Uh, thanks. I love you too," said Olivia. "Everything okay?"

"Yeah," said Heidi. "It's just—I'm so glad you came."

She and Olivia made the rounds, effusively complimenting other girls on how "amazing" or "incredible" their hair and dresses looked. These girls, whom Heidi considered friends, returned the compliments, but she had the strange sense that she didn't actually know them at all. Or they didn't know her. The awkwardness of it made Heidi's skin crawl.

"Hey, you want to go dance?" Heidi asked Olivia.

They did. But it didn't provide the catharsis that Heidi was hoping for. The stink of hair spray and cheap cologne sweat was making Heidi feel lightheaded. After four or five interchangeable pop songs, she and Olivia found themselves sitting at a table watching the dance floor.

A moment later, Luca plopped down next to them. It was clear he'd been drinking.

"Saw you two dancing out there," slurred Luca. His breath smelled flammable. "Why don't you kiss?"

"Dude, shut up," said Olivia.

"C'mon," said Luca. "I'll give you three hundred bucks." He pulled a handful of twenties out of his wallet. "I know you could use the money, Olivia."

"You're such a dick," muttered Olivia.

Heidi put a firm hand on his arm. "Why don't you go drink some water?"

"Nah, I'm good." Luca leaned in to kiss Heidi on the mouth, but she turned her head away.

There was a tense moment as Luca glared at her.

Heidi glared back at him, no longer able to mask her contempt. "Maybe later," she said quietly.

"Fuck this," said Luca. He stood, knocking over his chair. Then he staggered across the dance floor toward Peter and Nils.

Heidi watched him cross the room. "I . . . hate him."

Olivia's eyes went wide. "What?"

"How did I date someone like that for two whole years?"

Olivia shrugged. "He's rich. He's handsome. He's popular."

"Those reasons are pathetic."

Olivia smiled. "We all make mistakes. He's Harvard's problem now. C'mon, this is my jam."

Olivia jumped to her feet and tried to pull Heidi back to the dance floor, but Heidi shook her head.

"Sorry, I'm . . . going to sit this one out."

Olivia looked disappointed. “Okay, well, maybe I'll go dance with Carmen and Delphine, then?”

Heidi made herself smile again. “Sure. Go have fun.”

And so Olivia skittered off to the dance floor to join some girls she knew from marching band. Heidi sat at the table and watched her classmates—awkward slow dances, boys clowning on each other, girls whispering and giggling, everyone taking their last shot. Even Goth Steve seemed to be in high spirits. He was surprisingly good at popping and locking.

This was the world Heidi was leaving behind. No, this was the world she'd already left behind. Heidi didn't want to be here, but she couldn't leave either. Not yet. She pulled out her phone and sent Cam a text.

I miss you.

Then she stood and rolled her shoulders. She had to get away from the noise and the lights and the smell. She stepped out into the hall and, without a better place to go, slowly walked toward the bathroom.

As she passed the men's room, she heard familiar voices inside.

“It was gnarly, dude . . .”

Luca was talking to someone. At this point, she couldn't imagine that there was anything Luca Spiro could say that Heidi was interested in hearing. But for some reason, she paused to listen.

“I'm not kidding, a three-inch pubic hair growing right out of her knee.”

“Jesus Christ,” said Nils.

“Fuck me,” said Peter.

"I'm telling you, I can't even grow leg hairs like this. This was disgusting, like, grandpa-at-the-beach-type shit—"

Heidi cut the boys' laughter short as she stepped into the men's room.

"Hello," she said.

There was silence as Nils and Peter looked at her, horrified and ashamed.

"Hey, babe," said Luca. He smiled but there was no warmth in his eyes.

"Were you talking about me?"

Luca shrugged. "I'm not sure that it's any of your business, but I will say that I talk to the people in my life about the things that are important to me. Aren't men supposed to share their feelings too?"

Heidi was honestly a little surprised that Luca still had the capacity to hurt her, to make her feel small. She turned to Peter and Nils.

"Leave," she said.

Something in her tone sent them both scurrying out of the bathroom.

Luca clucked his tongue, still grinning. "Trying to cut me off from my friends? You know that's one of the signs of an emotionally abusive partner."

Heidi felt her pulse quickening, her adrenaline pumping. "You found the hair on my leg disgusting?"

"As a matter of fact, I did," said Luca. "I wanted to fucking vomit."

"You want to know what I find disgusting about you?"

"What's that?"

"You."

With a guttural snarl Heidi lunged forward and shoved Luca

with both hands. He flew backward and bounced off a bathroom stall, landing hard on the tile floor.

Luca's grin was gone now. He looked up at her in terror. Heidi watched him there on the floor, helpless as a worm on a hook. She relished his fear. She wanted to attack him again—to feel his bones break and his flesh split open and his blood spill out. She wanted to finish the job and destroy him completely. Instead, she spoke.

"We're through, you and me," growled Heidi. "If I ever see you again, it will be too soon."

With a soft whimper, Luca crawled on all fours to the bathroom door, leaving Heidi alone.

She turned and saw herself in the mirror. Her eyes were angry slits, her lips were pulled back in an animal snarl. Her face was barely recognizable. Or maybe *this* was what she really looked like.

At that moment Heidi's phone pinged. Cam had texted her back.

I miss you too.

Heidi felt a surge of panic. What the hell had she just done? She felt another surge of rage at her own weakness, and she punched the monstrous face in the mirror, shattering the glass and slicing open her knuckles.

"Fuck," said Heidi.

She grabbed a wad of paper towels and pressed them to her bloody hand.

Heidi walked out of the bathroom and didn't stop. Without a word to anyone, she passed through the front door of the event center and across the parking lot to her car. She got in and cranked the ignition. But instead of peeling out she gently rested her head on the steering wheel and started to sob. What was happening to her? Why had she lost control? Why was she like this again?

She clenched her teeth as she pulled the bloody paper towels away from her lacerated knuckles. There was no pain. The cuts had already healed.

29

Heidi sat on her usual bench at Dean Park. It was 2:23 AM, and the park was deserted. After what happened at the prom, she didn't know where else to go.

The moon hung heavy in the sky—bright but not yet full—and the city spread out before her. But Heidi's attention was focused squarely on the glow of her phone. Tears rolled down Heidi's cheeks as she read a *New York Times* article:

Researchers Admit to Falsifying Results in Controversial Lupinovirus Study—Online Conspiracy Theorists Still Cling to Weight Loss Drug as Miracle Cure

She'd already read the story four times hoping she had somehow misunderstood what it was saying, hoping that it didn't mean what it obviously meant. The French scientists had fabricated the results of their Extiva study. Under threat of criminal prosecution by the European Union, they been forced to admit as much and issue a public apology.

She didn't want to believe it at first. In the subs where she'd originally read about how Extiva was a suppressed cure for the virus, no one was deterred. The posters simply viewed the researchers' ("coerced") admission as more evidence of a nefarious international conspiracy to hide the real truth about *Rabies lupinovirus* from the public.

But she knew they were wrong. She hadn't been cured. The virus was still inside her. The Lunar Cycle Countdown app said she had 05:20:11:16 until the moon was full.

She typed a text to Cam.

It's bullshit. It's not a cure. It's nothing.

Cam took only a second to reply.

I know.

Heidi texted him back, hurt and angry.

She had to have known. The Bitch lied to us.

This time Cam didn't answer. Heidi closed her eyes and listened to the wind rustling the leaves on the trees. She felt a wave of exhaustion and despair wash over her. She didn't have the strength to go on. To keep on hoping. This was it. This was the end.

"I knew you'd be here."

Heidi opened her eyes and saw Luca, standing on the path near the bench. The streetlight behind him cast his face in shadow.

"This is where you liked to meet up with him, right?" he sneered. "Even though I was the one who took you here first."

Heidi closed her eyes again.

"Don't fucking ignore me!" said Luca.

"You sound like you're still drunk," said Heidi.

"Don't pretend like you weren't just crying," said Luca. "I saw you."

"You think I'm crying over you?" Heidi actually laughed.

"Stop laughing!" yelled Luca.

"Go away," said Heidi. "I told you: I don't ever want to see you again."

Luca spoke in a low and dangerous voice. "You should really be nicer to me, Heidi."

"Why's that?"

"Because I figured out what happened back there. I know why you lost your mind and tried to kill me. For weeks, you've been acting weird. Lashing out. Lying about everything," said Luca. "You thought nobody noticed you freak out when they arrested Mr. Santangelo. But I did." He paused dramatically. "You don't have mono. You have the virus."

Heidi stared at him for a long moment. "Took you long enough, genius."

"Fuck you!"

"No, seriously. Harvard really made the right choice. You're very, very smart."

Luca pulled out his phone. "I should call the VCTF hotline and have you locked up right now."

Heidi nodded. "Maybe it's better if you do. I was thinking of calling them myself but I didn't have the guts to go through with it."

Luca froze. Heidi could tell that this wasn't how he thought this conversation was going to go.

"Well? What are you waiting for?" asked Heidi. "Call them."

"I will!" sputtered Luca. But then the look on his face changed, as though he finally understood something. "That's why you were sneaking around with him, isn't it? You're both *diseased*."

Heidi rose from the bench. "Leave Cam out of this."

Luca smiled. He'd finally touched a nerve. "Wow, you really care about him, huh? That's so sweet. But I'm afraid he's a public health risk now. And for the good of society he needs to be quarantined. Or worse."

"This is between you and me," said Heidi. "Cam doesn't need to be dragged into it."

"But you already dragged him into it, Heidi. You know what? I think I'll actually call the VCTF on him first." Luca started to dial the number. "Hang on a sec."

Heidi's adrenaline surged. She had to protect Cam. The rage was boiling up inside her. In a split second, she was going to explode.

"Put the phone down," said Heidi.

Luca didn't. "It's not me you're never going to see again. It's him."

"Put it down," growled Heidi.

Luca pressed the call button. Then he held the phone to his ear. "Yes, hello, I'd like to report—"

Heidi rushed at him. As she did, she felt herself changing—her skin stretching, her teeth growing, claws bursting from her fingertips. . .

30

When Heidi came to her senses, she saw blood everywhere. Luca was lying face down in the grass. Her first impulse was to try to help him. But somehow, she knew she couldn't. He was already dead.

Heidi turned away in horror. Whatever had killed Luca had torn him to shreds.

She noticed that her own prom dress was ripped, the seams burst. Her hands, too, were covered in blood. It took her a moment to realize that "whatever had killed" Luca . . . was her.

Heidi let out a single ragged cry. She felt like she was going to vomit but stopped herself. Some cold, analytical sliver of her brain chimed in to tell her that she shouldn't leave any more of her DNA at a murder scene than she already had.

The park was dark and empty. She sniffed the air and smelled no one. But still, some random passerby might come along at any second.

Heidi found Luca's smashed phone in the weeds. She turned it off and stuffed it into her pocket. Then she slung his body over her shoulder and carried him a short distance down the block to her car. Heidi popped the trunk and dropped him inside, praying nobody had seen her.

Heidi noticed the trail of dripped blood she'd left behind her.

She saw Luca's BMW parked down the street. Her mind was racing, thinking of all the loose ends, everything that could lead back to her.

Heidi used an exercise towel to wipe the blood off her hands as best she could. Then she called the only person she could think of.

Cam answered on the first ring. "What's up?"

"I need you." Heidi explained to him what had happened.

"Okay, stay there," said Cam. "I'm coming."

Heidi huddled in her car for fifteen agonizing minutes, as the reality of what she had done sank in. She'd killed someone. No, not just someone. She'd killed her boyfriend, a person she'd once loved. At least, she'd thought she loved him. But she'd done it to save someone else that she loved . . .

Down the street Heidi saw headlights. She sank low in her seat and felt indescribable relief when Cam's Kia pulled up.

Cam climbed out and Heidi resisted the urge to hug him.

"Thank God you're here," she said.

"Came as quick as I could," said Cam. "And . . . I brought someone with me."

Then the passenger door of Cam's car swung open, and Rhea climbed out.

At the sight of her, Heidi's first impulse was fury. "*You?* You lied to us!"

Rhea raised her eyebrows. "Whoa. Not even a 'hello'?"

"The cure was fake!" Heidi felt the rage swelling again, threatening to consume her.

Rhea sighed. "I said I could get you the pills. I never said Extiva was a cure. That was your idea."

"But you let us believe—"

"We believed what we wanted to believe," said Cam.

Heidi ignored him. "I trusted you."

"You're strong-willed," said Rhea. "I knew you wouldn't just take my word for it. I figured it was better for you to come to this conclusion for yourself. But I'll say it now, just to be perfectly clear: Extiva is not a cure because there is no cure. There will never be a cure."

"They're working on it," said Heidi. Her words sounded pathetic as they escaped her lips.

Rhea actually laughed. "Yes, always working on it. Yet the cure never seems to materialize, does it? Even though they keep getting billions of dollars to—"

"Now is not the time for this," hissed Cam.

"You're right," said Rhea. "I came here to help."

"Why?" asked Heidi.

"Because I believe in you, Heidi," said Rhea. "Is what Cam told me true? That you changed even though . . ." Rhea nodded to the gibbous moon, a little over half full.

Heidi nodded.

Rhea suddenly hugged Heidi tight. Heidi was taken aback. She resisted for a moment, but then she felt herself hugging Rhea too. The mercurial irony and the manic aggression of the Bitch were gone. The person who held her felt like a protector, like a mother. Deep down, Heidi wanted someone strong to fix everything. She wanted to be saved from this waking nightmare.

"Don't you worry," whispered Rhea. "It's all going to be okay."

Just then, there came a thump from inside Heidi's trunk. Heidi tensed, thinking she'd imagined it. But she listened and heard the sound again.

"He's—he's still alive," whispered Heidi.

Her heart leaped. She might be a bad person. She might have tried to kill Luca. But she hadn't succeeded. She wasn't a murderer. He was alive.

There was another thump, a little louder.

Heidi noticed that Rhea was staring at her. "So, what do you want to do?" asked Rhea.

Heidi was confused. "We have to get him to a hospital."

Rhea nodded. "And then what?"

"What do you mean?"

Rhea looked at Cam. Cam looked at Heidi.

"What I mean is," said Rhea, "can he be trusted?"

Heidi considered the implications of Rhea's question. At last, she shook her head.

"But you still want to save him?" said Rhea.

Heidi nodded.

Rhea considered this. "Okay. Then you two have to go."

"Right," said Cam.

She turned to Heidi. "Are you okay to drive?"

Heidi nodded.

"Pop the trunk," said Rhea.

Heidi did. Luca lay in a bloody heap inside. It was hard for Heidi to look at what she'd done to him.

Luca's eyes were closed, but he gave a rasping moan. "Help . . . me . . ."

"I'm going to take care of you," said Rhea, matter-of-factly.

She reached in and hauled Luca out of the trunk and onto his feet. It was immediately clear that he couldn't stand on his own. Rhea held him up like a rag doll as he oozed blood from a dozen wounds. She reached in his pocket and pulled out his car keys. She pressed the unlock button, causing the lights of his BMW to flash.

"Nice car," she said. Then she carried him to it and buckled him in the passenger's side. Rhea climbed into the driver's side and adjusted the mirrors. "You can relax. We're just going to take a little ride."

Luca didn't answer. He had already slipped back into unconsciousness.

Rhea pulled out and then rolled down the driver's-side window. "Take the Audi somewhere and clean it up."

"Got it," said Cam. He turned to Heidi. "Follow me."

Luca's BMW disappeared down the block. And a few minutes after that, Heidi pulled onto the highway, following Cam's Kia north, out of the city.

They made one stop, at a rural, self-service car wash with no security cameras. Heidi and Cam took twenty minutes to wash and vacuum her Audi—trying their best to clean the blood out of the trunk—before getting back on the road.

They were driving through forest now. Before Heidi lost cell service, there was a call she had to make. She didn't want to do it, but she knew it was necessary. An hour before dawn, Heidi dialed her mother.

"Heidi, where are you?" asked Madeline. She sounded both worried and tired. Like she'd waited up all night. "I thought you were coming home."

"No," said Heidi. "I'm staying over at Olivia's."

"Okay," said Madeline.

"In fact . . . I'm probably going to stay here for a while."

"Why?"

Heidi didn't want to say it. But she had no choice. She saw no other way. "Because—because I hate you. You don't respect me. I don't even think you like me."

Heidi expected her mother to push back, to sneer or ridicule her, as usual. But she didn't.

"It breaks my heart that you believe that," said Madeline quietly. "But I have only myself to blame. When you're ready to come back, I'll be here."

Heidi could tell that her mother was crying. She couldn't think of another time that Madeline had ever cried, not even when her own mother had passed away.

Heidi hung up without another word. Then she turned off her phone and burst into tears herself.

The sky was growing subtly brighter as she followed Cam's Kia along the twisty two-lane highway through the national forest. At last, he parked at the Ocean Ridge Trail lot.

Dawn was breaking as they hiked up the trail to the abandoned fort.

Heidi arrived at the old fort to find that the Underdogs had prepared her a change of clothes and a bed—soft fleece blankets on a new cot. Rhea wasn't here, but the others asked her if she needed anything.

She told them she didn't, and then she lay down and fell into a deep and dreamless sleep.

* * *

Heidi awoke to find Rhea sitting beside her cot.

"Is Luca . . . ?" asked Heidi.

Rhea smiled. "It's done. You don't need to worry. Everything's been taken care of."

Heidi sat up. The darkness down here was disorienting. She rubbed her eyes. The night before seemed like a bad dream. "What time is it?"

"You slept the day away," said Rhea. "If you feel up to it, I'd like to formally introduce you to the others."

The rest of the Underdogs had been gathered in the wide intersection of tunnels that served as their makeshift common room. They waited expectantly for Heidi.

"Xuying you already know," said Rhea.

Xuying gave a curt nod. "Long time no see."

Rhea indicated the big guy who looked like a bodybuilder. "This delicate flower is Dale."

He grinned and shook Heidi's hand with an iron grip. "Pleased to officially meet you."

"Pranjit and Nora," said Rhea.

"Hi." A man with a dark beard gave a little wave.

"Hello," said the red-haired woman, smiling.

"And of course, bringing a touch of sophistication to our uncouth band, we have Henry."

"Oh, bugger off," said the old man in the rumpled suit.

"You already know the newest member of our little club," said Rhea.

Cam smiled. "I'm not much of a joiner, Heidi, but these people are all right."

"Thank you for your glowing endorsement, young Cameron," said Henry.

"Everyone, while Heidi is here with us, please make her feel at home," said Rhea. "Heidi, you can stay as long as you like. We have food and water."

"The food's not great," said Dale.

"Not to brag, but we also possess a complete deck of fifty-two playing cards," said Henry. "Have you ever played gin, my dear?"

And so Heidi sat down to a card game with Henry and Nora. Cam soon joined her, offering unhelpful tips that made Heidi laugh and seemed to annoy Henry to no end. After a few hands, Heidi found herself able to relax.

"Can I ask . . . how you got infected?" asked Heidi, surprising herself with the question.

It was met with an awkward silence. Heidi instantly felt self-conscious. "Sorry. It's okay. You don't have to tell me."

"No, no. I shall," said Henry. "'Twas a dark and stormy night out upon the moors . . ." He paused dramatically. "Not really. I got blackout drunk at a work conference in Cincinnati and the next day I woke up feeling awful. I suspect I may have kissed the wrong wayward gentleman. I have always been unlucky in love."

"I was an EMT," said Nora, as she shuffled the deck. "Had what I thought was a tweaker having a full psychotic break. After she bit me, I had to revise my diagnosis."

"Damn," said Cam. "That's what happened to my mom."

"What about you two?" asked Nora.

Heidi and Cam looked at each other, then told them the story. But somehow, as they recounted it, it seemed funny rather than horrific. Both of them laid on the comic details, causing Nora and Henry to laugh uproariously.

"Wow," said Nora, after they'd finished. "What a meet-cute."

The Underdogs ate dinner together at a long folding table. It was Xuying's night to cook and she'd prepared two different types of MREs: chili and macaroni or lentils in masala (two of the Underdogs were vegetarians). As promised, both choices were awful, but the conversation was lively. Dale told them a hilarious story about how, as a teenager, he tried to impress a girl in his church youth group by inviting her to go kayaking, but he ended up peeing his pants in the boat.

When dinner was winding down, Rhea stood and addressed the group. "Okay, I hate to cut this short, but we have some planning left to do."

Heidi stood to join them.

"Sorry," said Rhea. "This is members only."

Rhea and the others, including Cam, made their way to another part of the underground complex, leaving Heidi alone.

* * *

Time passed strangely underground. Often, Heidi wasn't sure if it was day or night. The Underdogs came and went. Heidi got to know each of them a little. They were friendly, by and large (though Xuying remained a bit standoffish). All of them seemed to be idealists, even Henry, who claimed to be a complete cynic and a misanthrope. Despite their differences in age and background, Heidi found them to be warm and welcoming. She liked being around them.

She spent a lot of time with Cam, too. Rhea warned them not to stray too far, but she approved them taking daily walks in the woods near the entrance. Cam seemed to have grown lighterhearted, happy to be a part of a group. It was hard for Heidi to admit, and even harder to understand, but she felt this way too. She didn't know how long the feeling would last, when the real world would intrude again. She tried not to think about it.

On the afternoon of the third day, Heidi took Rhea aside.

"What is it that you're doing here?" asked Heidi.

"Running the world's weirdest group home," said Rhea.

"For real," said Heidi.

"It is a refuge. And a family of sorts. But you're right. We want it to be something more." Rhea paused. "You're going to laugh when I say it."

"I promise I won't."

"We're going to change the world," said Rhea.

"How?"

Rhea stared at her. Then she shook her head. "I can't tell

you that unless I bring you all the way in. Do you want to be part of it?"

"I . . ." Heidi trailed off.

"We could use someone like you, Heidi," said Rhea. "A leader."

"I don't know."

"Tell me when you're sure," said Rhea. "But don't wait too long. It's happening tomorrow."

That night, after dinner, the others went to their daily meeting. Heidi sat on her cot and tried to read a dog-eared paperback spy thriller—one of the few books the Underdogs possessed—but she was restless. The story couldn't hold her attention.

She crept through the twisting hallways. She knew these dark corridors better by now—though the complex was far larger than she first realized. She made her way to the door marked C6. The light was on inside. Heidi gently pressed her ear to the door and listened.

". . . imagine someone manages to call," said Henry.

"They won't," said Nora. "That's why we have a jammer. It'll scramble 3G, 4G, 5G, Wi-Fi 2. Hell, it'll even jam a walkie-talkie, if anybody tries."

"Nora, my dear, one must always hope for the best and plan for the worst," said Henry, a touch condescendingly. "Indulge me."

"I'll be distracting the local precinct," said Dale.

"Yes, but imagine they call the VCTF. Do we have any reliable estimate of a response time?"

"They're not prepared for anything like this," said Pranjit. "It'll be half an hour at least."

"Where are you getting that?" asked Rhea.

Pranjit chuckled. "The numbers are buried in the Dogcatchers' own website. They did an internal audit last year. Average response time: thirty-two minutes. I'm guessing that's generous."

"The lazy bastards are used to working one day a month," said Xuying. "When it's not the full moon, all they do is beat up homeless people."

"Hey c'mon. That's not *all* they do," said Dale. "They also sit around scrolling their phones for hours on end."

At this the others laughed. As the sound trailed off, Heidi heard Rhea's voice again.

"Have you heard enough, Heidi?" she asked.

Heidi took a step back.

The door swung open and Xuying stood on the other side. She clucked her tongue. "Nosy nosy."

31

All eyes were on Heidi. The faces of the Underdogs were unreadable.

"Sorry," said Heidi. "I didn't mean to—my curiosity got the better of me."

"No need to apologize," said Rhea. "Please. Come in."

Heidi stepped into the room. The Gaines Museum blueprint was still tacked to the wall. On a rack nearby, she saw hanging garment bags. Nora and Pranjit had laptops open. On a corner of the table was a porcupine of black antennas protruding from a thin metal box—Heidi guessed that was the jammer that Nora had mentioned.

"Now you know what we're planning," said Rhea.

"No, I only listened for a second," said Heidi.

The group looked at one another. Something silently passed among them.

"You heard enough," said Rhea. "Can we count you in?"

Heidi shook her head. "I'm not sure what you have in mind but . . . I don't want to hurt any innocent people."

"We're not going to hurt any innocent people," said Rhea.

"But you're going to hurt somebody, aren't you?"

Rhea merely stared at Heidi with her piercing steel-gray eyes.

"I can't do that," said Heidi.

"Yes, you can," said Rhea. "I've seen you hurt people, Heidi. I've seen you kill."

"I didn't kill Luca," protested Heidi. "I attacked him but—he was alive. You took him to the hospital."

Rhea cocked her head. "Are you really that naïve?"

"What?"

"I put him somewhere nobody is ever going to find him," said Rhea. "But . . . you knew that's what I was going to do."

"No, I didn't!" cried Heidi. "I wanted you to save him!"

"What you *wanted* to do was tear him limb from limb, Heidi."

Heidi wanted to argue, but she couldn't. "I did it to protect Cam, but I lost control . . . It was a mistake . . . "

"You killed Luca, just like you killed that Dogcatcher."

"What?"

"The first night you changed," said Rhea. "Not far from here. You eviscerated a man named Corporal Jason Mottola."

Heidi felt like the floor was crumbling beneath her feet. "I don't remember that."

"But you do remember waking up covered in blood, don't you?" said Rhea. "It's okay. He was going to kill you, so you killed him first. No judgment. That's just how it is. Kill or be killed."

"Did that really happen?"

"I was there, Heidi. I saw it."

"No, I—I don't believe you," said Heidi. "You've lied to me before."

Rhea shrugged. "You don't have to take my word for it. I made sure to take his bodycam so the VCTF wouldn't find you." Rhea nodded to Nora. "Show her."

Nora rummaged through a nearby file box and came out with a small black digital camera.

"Why don't you bring it up on your laptop for all of us to watch," said Rhea.

Xuying gave a sardonic clap. "Movie night."

Nora plugged a USB cable into the camera.

"No," whispered Heidi.

"You don't want to watch the footage, Heidi?" said Rhea. "You don't want to witness exactly what you did to him? I hope this isn't too much of a spoiler but: closed casket funeral."

Tears welled in Heidi's eyes now. "I don't want to see that!"

"It is quite graphic," said Rhea. "Since you don't remember anything, I do have another little memento. I managed to save it from that night, even though you tried to get rid of it."

She reached into the pocket of her motorcycle jacket and pulled out something. As Rhea held it up toward the light, Heidi recognized it. It was the necklace of fangs that she'd found folded up in her clothes, the same one from the photo she saw of Jason Mottola.

"This was his. You can count the teeth. He slaughtered twelve of us. Twelve innocent people—people with hopes and dreams. People with families. People who happened to catch a virus through no fault of their own. He killed them and he was proud of it. So proud that he wore pieces of them around his neck. Somehow that makes him a hero?" Rhea shook her head. "No. Not anymore. I say you're the hero, Heidi."

Rhea ceremoniously put the necklace around Heidi's neck.

"I didn't choose to do it," cried Heidi. "I don't want to hurt anyone. I wasn't in control."

"I think you were in control, Heidi. I think you're a monster. Just like me."

"I have a disease!"

Rhea frowned. "No, we have a gift—a chance to actually

change things. To split this rotten world open and let the pus ooze out. That's what has to happen before anything can heal. We have to lance the boil. Right now, they chase us and shoot us and throw us in cages, because they're parasites who profit from our suffering. It's kill or be killed out there. They made us all understand that." Her voice was rising in tone and pitch, almost like a sermon. "But tomorrow, we fight back, Heidi. The virus is God's gift to us. We will not be cured." She put a friendly hand on Heidi's shoulder. "So I'm going to ask you one more time: Will you join us?"

Heidi wiped the tears away. "You're nothing but a manipulator and a megalomaniac. Listen to yourself. You sound insane."

"Heidi," said Cam.

Rhea smiled. "Insane is thinking the world can just continue along as it always has, in the face of everything that's happened in the last five years. That idea is delusional." She paused. "So that's your final answer?"

"My final answer is: Fuck you."

Rhea nodded gravely. "Unfortunately, that means it's kill or be killed."

"What are you talking about?"

"I obviously can't let you leave here knowing what you know. If you're not with us, I'm going to have to kill you. Or you will have to kill me. So, go on. Do it. If you can."

Heidi shook her head and took a step backward.

"Kill me!" shrieked Rhea. With an inhumanly strong shove, she sent Heidi sprawling to the floor.

"The moment I met you, I could smell it," said Rhea. "You're filled with anger."

"I'm not," whimpered Heidi, "I'm—"

Rhea kicked her hard in the stomach. It knocked the wind out of Heidi.

"Hey!" cried Cam. He moved to intervene, but Henry and Xuying stood to stop him.

As Heidi gasped on the floor, struggling to catch her breath, Rhea crouched beside her. She spoke softly now, almost kindly. "You are angry. You don't want anybody to know it, but you're even angrier than I am." Now Rhea smiled and gently brushed the hair out of Heidi's face. "I don't blame you. It's a good thing, Heidi. The more you have bottled up inside you, the easier it is to let it all spill out. That's how you master the change, like I have. You just have to let go. You have to accept it."

She slapped Heidi across the mouth. "Let it out," said Rhea.

"No," croaked Heidi.

Rhea hit her again, this time with a closed fist. Heidi briefly saw stars.

"Let the beast out. Forget the rules. Become yourself. Become the real you."

Heidi shook her head. "I'm not an animal."

Rhea frowned. Then she grabbed a handful of Heidi's hair and effortlessly yanked her to her feet.

"Fire and silver. That's how they murder us by the dozens. But there's another way to harm our kind that they don't much talk about. The fangs and the claws of another werewolf can kill us too."

Rhea raised her other hand, and Heidi saw that it had changed. It was now grotesquely muscled, covered in coarse black fur. The misshapen fingers ended in hooked two-inch talons.

"You could change right now," said Rhea. "You could tear

me apart. In fact . . . I insist on it." With her changed hand she grabbed Heidi's shoulder in a vise grip. Rhea's claws punctured Heidi's flesh with a similar burning agony.

"Kill or be killed," said Rhea.

She squeezed Heidi's flesh and Heidi felt blood running down her arms from the searing wounds where the claws pierced her.

"Stop it! You can't do this!" cried Cam as he broke free. "Whatever you think about Heidi, she's still one of us."

Rhea's eyes narrowed. Her voice was deep and guttural. "She's weak."

"It took me a while to get it too," said Cam. "But we can't fight among ourselves. That's what they want us to do. It only helps them!"

"This is a war," said Rhea. "Tomorrow, we strike back. I have no time to coddle fools."

"Do it for me, then," said Cam. "For my sake, spare her. Please."

"It's too important. I can't risk her interfering with our plans."

"She won't!" cried Cam. "You can make sure she won't."

Rhea grunted and flung Heidi to the floor. "Lock her up."

"With pleasure," said Xuying. She and Dale grabbed Heidi by the arms and dragged her backward out of the room.

"Cam, help me!" screamed Heidi.

For a moment, her eyes met Cam's. But he turned away.

Heidi struggled and fought in vain, but she couldn't outmatch the two of them. Xuying and Dale dragged her to a dark doorway and threw her inside. Heidi leaped to her feet, but she wasn't quick enough. The heavy metal door slammed shut, once again sealing her inside the vault.

32

Heidi was alone in the darkness. She pounded on the door and called for help until her throat was ragged and sore. She cried until she couldn't cry anymore. She was trapped.

One way or another, Heidi figured that she would probably die down here. But there was nothing to do but wait. She sat down on the cold concrete.

They hadn't bothered to take her phone away—no reception a hundred feet underground, so what was the point. Heidi turned it on and started to scroll through her old photos. She went back years, until her phone was almost out of charge. The pictures were bittersweet now. She saw herself and Olivia making faces for the camera. Pictures of her mom and of Ron. Selfies with Luca at the beach—

Suddenly, Heidi saw herself attacking Luca. Tearing at his face. Biting his throat out. Luca screaming in agony. Heidi turned off her phone and realized how truly exhausted she felt. She lay down on the floor and fell asleep.

Now, she was in her own bedroom, in a multimillion-dollar house, in one of the most expensive gated communities in the city. Outside, the sun was shining. Birds were singing in the trees. Someone was mowing their lawn. Heidi lay in bed and enjoyed the indescribable feeling of being young and healthy on a perfect day. The dream did not turn to violence or fear, which made it all the more painful to wake up from.

Heidi opened her eyes to utter darkness, unsure of how much time had passed. In her mind's eye she saw the irritating poster she knew was taped to the wall here: KEEP CALM AND CARRY ON.

Wasn't that what she'd tried to do for the last eighteen years? Until a random twist of fate had changed everything, as it did for everyone, all the time.

Hours passed. Or maybe days. Sometimes, Heidi screamed at the top of her lungs and at other times she barely moved. The line between sleep and waking began to blur.

She sometimes passed the agonizing minutes by trying to imagine every version of the life she would've had if she'd never been bitten. Would she have successfully transferred to Harvard after a year? Would she have broken up with Luca? Or would she have married him and had his kids? Become a doctor? Become an art historian? (Was that even a job?) Had an affair with a guy at work? Died of brain cancer?

She replayed mauling Luca in her mind over and over again, from every gruesome angle, until she wasn't sure if it was a memory or not. The fact that she thought she was saving Cam didn't make it better. Luca didn't deserve to die. Just like Jason Mottola didn't deserve to die. Just like Heidi didn't deserve to get infected. Just like Heidi didn't deserve the fancy house she grew up in or the luxury car her mother had given her for her eighteenth birthday, either. And on and on it went.

The more Heidi thought about everything, the less sense it made. She cried thinking about her mother. The last thing she had said to Madeline was that she hated her. But it was a lie. She loved her and only craved her respect. And Madeline loved her too, Heidi knew, she just didn't always know the right way to show it. Perceiving her mother's flaws so clearly didn't make Heidi angry toward Madeline. It made her mother more human—another person who needed help.

Why did you only seem to realize what was important once it was too late? Heidi wondered. Why did the world have to be like this?

Maybe Rhea will change that too, thought Heidi with a dark chuckle. But it put her on a new line of thinking. She hadn't stopped yet to consider what exactly the Underdogs were planning to do.

Heidi thought back to what she'd heard and seen: garment bags, a cell phone scrambler, a blueprint of the Gaines Museum.

Something jogged Heidi's memory. She turned on her phone again—it was at 1 percent charge—and found the newest photo. In fact, it was the only one she'd taken since she'd contracted the virus: a slightly blurry pic of M&K Catering's shift schedule. Heidi zoomed in. There, at the top of the spreadsheet, she saw the address of the event they were catering—the Gaines Museum of Fine Art. It was the Gray Ribbon Gala.

At that moment, the phone went dead.

The Gray Ribbon Gala was an annual charity ball to raise money for the lupinovirus cure. Madeline and Ron attended it every year.

It was late afternoon now. She'd been locked inside the bunker for almost an entire day. The gala was tonight, happening in a few hours.

Heidi fought the urge to panic. Her mother was going to die.

"I can still stop them," said Heidi to no one.

But she had to get out of the bunker first.

Heidi leaped to her feet and slammed herself against the door. The heavy steel slab barely rattled. She charged again. And again. Her frail human body crumpled against the thick metal. The door didn't budge.

Heidi sunk to her knees, crying. It wasn't going to work. The door was made to withstand bombs . . .

Heidi gave a howl of impotent rage. Her sorrow barely sounded human.

Yet at that moment, Heidi knew what she had to do. She had to give in. Just like Rhea had told her: She had to let the beast out.

Heidi howled again, louder this time. And then she let go. She let go of her old life and her past ideas and all hope of ever returning to normal. Heidi gave in to the emotion and she began to change. It was easy, just like Rhea said it would be.

She felt the agony of her body breaking down and reassembling itself—muscles swelling, tendons stretching, fur sprouting—as her conscious brain went dark . . .

* * *

When Heidi regained her senses, she found herself standing in the hallway outside the vault. The steel blast door lay on the floor beneath her feet amid a pile of rubble. She had smashed it clean off its hinges.

Heidi touched her hands and her face and realized she was herself again. She'd been expecting a fight on the other side of the door—there was no way they didn't hear her burst out of a sealed vault. But the hallway was empty. She sniffed the air and smelled no one close by.

Still, they might be waiting in ambush, hiding in another part of the bunker. Heidi crept forward as quietly as she could.

She needed to make it out to call for help. And to call for help, she'd need to charge her phone.

Heidi made her way to room C6 and found it was empty, too. The garment bags were gone. Both the laptops were still on the table. Heidi breathed a sigh of relief as she found a phone charger plugged into an extension cord running from God knows where.

Heidi plugged in her phone and waited.

She noticed that Nora had left her laptop connected to Jason Mottola's bodycam.

Heidi made a decision. She had to know the truth of what Rhea had told her. And if she had really killed someone, she wanted to accept responsibility for what she had done. Her hands trembled as she queued up the footage.

On the laptop, Heidi saw a forest at night. A goat on a long leash stood in a dark clearing, bleating pitifully. Suddenly, there was a commotion. A shape moved with unnatural speed through the shadows. It was impossible to see it clearly until it burst out of the underbrush and sank its jaws into the goat's neck.

The goat let out a scream that sounded human.

Heidi paused the footage. In this grainy frame, she could almost make out a werewolf. Something about it looked familiar—the tilt of its head; the way it stood.

"Cam," whispered Heidi.

She unpaused the video.

"Light 'em up!" cried the voice of Jason Mottola.

He fired a burst from his submachine gun, but the bullets went wide. A second Dogcatcher fired a single shot from out of frame. Cam winced as the bullet grazed his neck.

Now, another werewolf burst out of the forest, bigger and more frightening than Cam. In fact, it was the largest one Heidi had ever seen. Instantly, Heidi knew it was her. A shiver of terror ran through her. It was a strange sensation, to feel fear of oneself.

"Oh shit," squealed Jason Mottola, at the very sight of her.

With a snarl, Heidi hefted the bloody goat carcass and flung it in the direction of the off-camera shooter.

Jason, and his bodycam, turned and started to run through the woods.

Heidi tensed. This was it, she thought, the moment she killed him. She wanted to look away, but she forced herself to keep watching.

Jason Mottola, unseen, panted and swore as he ran for his life. Suddenly, there was a werewolf in front of him . . . but it wasn't Heidi. It was a big, dark-furred beast with pale gray eyes.

Rhea snarled and leaped on him. The body camera was face down in the dirt now, but it was still capturing audio. Jason Mottola screamed in agony for several seconds before the sound trailed off to nothing. The body camera was suddenly facing the leaves above. And a moment after that, a hand closed around the lens and the footage abruptly ended.

Heidi realized she was panting, almost gasping for breath. She hadn't killed Jason Mottola. Rhea had. Heidi had done so many other things she regretted, made so many mistakes. She'd mauled Luca. But she hadn't killed. She hadn't killed . . .

Heidi's phone was at 4 percent now. Good enough. She grabbed it and started to run. But then she paused and took the bodycam too.

Two minutes later, Heidi burst out into the cool evening air. The setting sun made the ocean look like blood.

Heidi held her phone up, searching for a signal. Nothing. The clock was ticking. The gala was starting soon. Heidi took off down the Ocean Ridge Trail at a full sprint.

She made it to the parking lot in forty-five minutes. Heidi felt indescribable relief to see that her car was still there. There was only one other vehicle in the lot.

Heidi pulled out her phone again. Still no service.

"Damn it," she said, and raced toward her car.

"Step away from the vehicle."

Heidi froze. She turned to see a young man, dark-haired with a patchy beard and thick bushy eyebrows. He stared at her with cold, dead eyes.

"Are you Heidi Mills?" he asked.

Heidi didn't respond.

"I'll take that as a yes," said the man. "You ever go by the name Dawn Suppley?"

Heidi eyed the man as he moved toward her. He had one hand in his jacket pocket. His other hand held a pair of zip cuffs.

"What do you want?" asked Heidi.

"I believe you're infected with *Rabies lupinovirus*."

Heidi took an involuntary step backward. "Who are you?"

"My name is Officer Erik Balikian of the Viral Containment Task Force. And I'm detaining you for testing and possible quarantine. Any resistance will be taken as evidence of infection."

33

Heidi slowly put up her hands. "How did you know I was here?"

"Found your name on a receipt. Realized I remembered it from somewhere. Mills is the family Dagamara Brodzińska cleaned for. That's how you got infected, isn't it?"

Heidi didn't answer.

Erik continued, almost smug as he explained, "It was easy enough to pull an address from that. That's how I put a tracker on your car, because I figured you might lead me to Cameron Woodbine. Then I could pick up both of you before the full moon. Two birds, one stone." He scanned the woods behind her. "Is he here somewhere by the way? Your friend Cameron?"

Heidi ignored his question. "Look, if you're with the VCTF, there's something you need to know: There's going to be an attack—a werewolf attack on the Gaines Museum of Fine Art. It's happening tonight. Right now."

Erik scoffed. "Werewolf attack? It's the night *before* the full moon. You think I'm that stupid? You're not going to worm your way out of this one with a bunch of lies."

"I'm not lying," cried Heidi as she took another step back. "I swear to you I'm telling the truth!"

Suddenly Erik's eyes went wide. "Where did you get that?"

Heidi saw that he was staring at her neck. She realized she was still wearing the fang necklace.

"It—it belongs to a dead man," said Heidi.

"No shit!" yelled Erik, who no longer sounded cool and controlled. "Why the fuck is it around your neck?"

"Look, I'm sorry but I have to go—"

Erik pulled a gun out of his pocket. But before he could aim it at her, Heidi lunged forward. She twisted it out of his grip and pointed it at his face.

"I have to go," Heidi repeated, quietly.

Erik stared down the barrel with quiet anger in his eyes. "So, you're the one who did it, huh? You're the one who killed Reaper."

"I didn't," said Heidi. "I know you won't believe me. But for what it's worth, I'm sorry."

Heidi moved toward her car, but Erik stepped to block her.

"If you want to leave, you're going to have to shoot me," said Erik. "This is a war, and I'm prepared to die. Just like Reaper."

"Get out of my way," said Heidi. She shoved Erik aside, keeping the gun on him. "Don't follow me!"

"I *will* follow you," said Erik, his voice barely more than a whisper. "I'll follow you to the ends of the earth. I'll follow you to the gates of hell if I have to. I won't stop until you're—"

With a snarl, Heidi swung the gun and cracked him hard across the side of the head. Officer Erik Balikian went limp and slumped to the ground, bleeding from his temple.

Heidi didn't have time to feel bad for what she'd done. She checked his pulse: heart still beating. Good enough.

She left Officer Erik Balikian unconscious on the ground as she climbed into her car and sped away south toward the city.

* * *

"You've reached the personal cell phone of Madeline Mills. Please leave a message and I'll return your call." On the recording, as always, her mother spoke with perfect enunciation.

"Damn it!" cried Heidi, pounding the steering wheel. She was driving ninety miles an hour on the highway.

The voicemail beeped and Heidi spoke. "Mom, you and Ron need to get out of there. It's not safe. Something terrible is about to happen!"

This was the sixth time Heidi had called Madeline in the two minutes since she'd gotten back into reception. Of course her mother would have her phone off at an event like the Gray Ribbon Gala. Ron's phone was going straight to voicemail too. Or maybe it was the jammer she'd heard the Underdogs discussing. There was no way for Heidi to get in touch with them directly.

Heidi found the number and dialed the museum's landline. But whoever answered immediately put her on hold. Heidi waited a solid minute before hanging up. She had no time for this.

Heidi took a breath and tried to collect her thoughts as the interstate curved and the city came into view ahead.

She called Cam's cell phone. It rang a few times before going to voicemail as well.

"This is me. You know what to do," said Cam's recorded voice.

"Cam, if you're with them right now, you have to stop it. Please. My parents are there!"

Time was slipping by, minute by minute, second by second. It might already be too late. Heidi drove faster, weaving past other cars on the road like they were standing still. She called the police.

"911, what's your emergency," said the calm voice of an operator.

"There's going to be a werewolf attack at the Gaines Museum. At the Gray Ribbon Gala." Heidi tried to keep the panic out of her voice. "Tonight."

"I can transfer you to the Viral Containment Task Force—"

"No! I already tried to tell them, but they didn't believe me!"

There was a long pause before the operator spoke again. His tone was polite, but Heidi thought she could hear an undercurrent of condescension. "Ma'am, the full moon is *tomorrow* night."

"I know that!" said Heidi. "They're not going to be wolves when they do it."

"I'm sorry. I'm . . . not sure I understand what you mean then."

"They have a plan to attack the night before the full moon," said Heidi, who was fully aware of how unhinged it sounded. "Because nobody will be expecting that."

"Werewolves . . . with a plan?" said the operator. By now, incredulousness was overriding his professionalism.

"Look, I know it sounds crazy, but you just have to believe me," said Heidi. "They're not mindless beasts. They're people, like you or me. Don't you understand? Werewolves are just . . . people."

The operator kept his voice neutral but by this point Heidi knew that he didn't believe her. "You know, this pandemic has put lot of stress on all of us. If you like, I can refer you to our free mental health hotline for—"

"Can you please just send someone to check it out?"

"To be perfectly honest, ma'am, all available units are responding to a bank robbery downtown that's turned into a hostage situation—"

Heidi hung up. Bank robbery? She cursed as she remembered the distraction Dale had alluded to. They'd thought of everything.

Desperate, Heidi called the Gaines Museum once again. This time she got through to someone who claimed to be a member of the event planning team. Heidi told this woman, as calmly as she could while going forty miles an hour over the speed limit, what she thought was about to happen.

"We take event security for the Gray Ribbon Gala extremely seriously and we do make all guests test for the virus before they enter the building," said the woman curtly.

She wasn't listening. Heidi hung up, frustrated. It was up to her.

* * *

Her tires squealed as she pulled into the museum parking lot ten minutes later. It was a massive neoclassical building, artfully lit up to gleam in the night like the crown jewel of the city. Long banners hung between its marble columns. Each showed a gray ribbon and words in block letters: A CURE WITHIN REACH.

She saw muscle-bound security guards in black ties guarding the front entrance. A few late arrivals, in their masks and formal wear, were leaving their cars to the valet and scurrying up the grand front steps toward the revelry inside.

Heidi breathed a sigh of relief. Whatever was going to happen here hadn't happened yet. She wasn't too late.

For the first time, Heidi wondered if she'd somehow gotten it all wrong. Was she making connections that weren't there, like the raving man with his #PLANDEMIC sign or the posters who'd convinced themselves that a diet drug from the '90s was the miracle cure that humanity had been looking for?

Maybe. But Heidi felt the hairs on the back of her neck standing up. She had the vague but persistent sensation on the edge of her senses that something was wrong here. In the past month she'd learned to trust this animal feeling. So far, it had never let her down.

Heidi drove around the back of the museum where she saw a refrigerator truck parked at the edge of the lot with the words M&K CATERING painted on it. As Heidi passed the truck, she noticed that the back door was ajar. Something was very off.

Heidi got out of her car and approached the truck. There was no one in the cab. As she got closer, she saw dark liquid dripping from inside the refrigerated trailer. It didn't look like hot sauce.

Heidi took a deep breath and opened the back. The scene of carnage inside the trailer was unimaginable. Four people in catering blacks had been torn to shreds. Their innards had been pulled out, their skin torn off. Their blood had painted the inside walls. One of them seemed to be missing their head.

Heidi swallowed the bile that had risen in her throat. She wasn't wrong after all. There was no doubt in her mind who had done this. Heidi could still smell her here.

Heidi ran toward a service entrance at the back of the museum. The door was locked, so she kicked it, splintering the jamb and sending it flying open.

Heidi stepped into the building and came face-to-face with Cam. He was dressed in catering blacks—the same as the bodies in the truck—with a black domino mask over his eyes. He stood blocking her path. For a long moment, they stared at one another.

"I'm not supposed to let anyone in," said Cam.

"I have to stop her," said Heidi.

"Heidi, she's right," said Cam. "She's right about everything."

"I know that," said Heidi. "But something awful is about to happen. And I don't want you to be a part of it. You're not a bad person, Cam. And I won't let you become one."

"It's too late to back out now," said Cam, his voice wavering. "I'm already a part of it."

"No," said Heidi. "It's not too late."

Heidi tried to move past him, but Cam put a hand on her shoulder, holding her back.

"Cam, please." Heidi's voice broke as she said it. "My mom is in there."

34

The attendees of the Gray Ribbon Gala filled the art museum's large central atrium, lavishly lit and decorated in an avant-garde, Goth-chic style. Philanthropists, scientists, politicians, and even a number of celebrities had gathered tonight for the charity event of the season. They donned masks and drank cocktails and gobbled hors d'oeuvres as they laughed and talked among themselves. A stage had been raised at one end of the room, where the Gaines Foundation's chosen speakers would offer their remarks before dinner. A dinner that for Ron Vandemark could not come fast enough.

A young cater-waiter, a girl in a simple black mask who looked like she was barely old enough to drive, passed by Ron carrying a tray of hors d'oeuvres. Ron checked his six. Madeline was chatting with some guy she'd introduced as Toby, a senior vice president of community affairs at some social media company. She wasn't watching.

"What're those?" Ron quietly asked the cater-waiter.

"I dunno," said the young woman, somewhat brusquely. "Crab cakes, I think."

The waiter's face was locked in a perpetual scowl. Ron got it. These fancy events weren't his thing either. He would've preferred to be almost anywhere else. At home watching TV, in the basement working on his model trains, or perhaps on the back deck with a filet mignon from Nebraska sizzling on the grill. But this sort of event made his wife happy. Well, not *happy*, exactly, but energized somehow. Most weeks Ron accompanied Madeline to at least one of these things, sometimes more.

"I'll take one crab cake, please," said Ron to the cater-waiter. He glanced over his shoulder again. Madeline was still deep in conversation with Social Media Toby. "Actually, I'll take three."

The caterer held out her tray for Ron to take as many crab cakes as he wanted. She clearly didn't care what he did. He reached for them.

"Put them back, Ron," said Madeline.

Ron sighed. Classic mistake. Madeline was *always* watching.

He turned to face his wife with a smile. "Well, it's just that I'm actually, you know, pretty hungry. I mean it's already a bit late so—"

"If you're hungry that's a good sign. It means you're actually sticking to your diet," said Madeline. "We said no snacks and no drinks until dinner."

"Uh-huh," said Ron. "Right. I remember that."

In fact, *we* hadn't said anything. Madeline was the one who'd said it. She was concerned about Ron's blood pressure and his cholesterol—both way too high—and so she had decided he would eat healthier. When Madeline Mills decided something, Ron had learned that was the final word. It was liberating, in a way, to let somebody else take the wheel.

"Sorry," said Ron to the young caterer, as he put the crab cakes back onto her tray.

The cater-waiter shrugged and then disappeared into the crowd.

"How's Toby?" asked Ron.

"Sounds like content moderation is a nightmare these days," said Madeline. "Apparently, misinformation spreads three point seven times faster than the truth, and there's nothing they can do about it."

"Really?" said Ron, a little confused. "There's nothing they can—"

Before Ron could finish his thought, a voice echoed out over the crowd.

"Good evening!"

The Gray Ribbon Gala's emcee—a handsome comedian who'd starred in a beloved sitcom that was canceled before its time—spoke into a microphone. The murmur of the crowd quieted as people sipped their cocktails and listened.

"Welcome to the fourth annual Gray Ribbon Gala," said the emcee. "Wow. I haven't seen this many rich people in masks since the orgy room at Davos."

A little off-color, but it got a laugh.

"Everybody having fun?" asked the emcee, as all emcees must.

The crowd whooped and cheered. The cocktails had been flowing freely since the doors opened at seven.

"Well, this is gonna make your night even better. Tonight, you'll be happy to learn that we have raised over three million dollars for the Gaines Foundation's Gray Ribbon Initiative. So I just want all you beautiful people to please give yourselves a big round of applause. You deserve it."

The crowd heartily applauded themselves. Ron checked his watch. Dinner was supposed to be at 8:00 and it was already 7:53. Goddamn charity gala. Goddamn diet.

"Before we eat, I want to show you a little of the amazing work that the Gaines Foundation is doing with your support," said the emcee.

The lights dimmed and the emcee turned to look at the digital screen above the stage.

The presentation began with an upswell of inspirational music playing over various images of scientific and social progress. A female scientist in a hijab poured colorful liquid into a test tube in an ultramodern laboratory.

The narrator—an actress with an instantly recognizable voice, who was far more famous than the emcee; too famous to attend in person in fact—spoke with maximum gravitas. "Last year, the Gaines Foundation issued grants totaling more than one hundred fifty million dollars toward lupinovirus research."

Now there were happy schoolchildren lining up to receive Gaines Foundation saliva tests from a smiling nun outside a rural church somewhere in Latin America. Verdant jungle mountains soared in the background.

The narrator continued, "We deployed more than seven million rapid tests to the developing world."

Back in the first world now: A class of fresh-faced Viral Containment Task Force cadets listened intently to their instructor. A smiling cadet in a dress uniform raised her hand to ask a question.

"And we funded fifty thousand hours of advanced training for frontline workers, right here at home."

Now, against a blank white backdrop, the scientist, the schoolchildren, and the VCTF cadet all stared at the camera with intensely neutral expressions on their faces.

"Through innovation and dedication," said the narrator, "we know that a better world is within reach."

The presentation ended with a close shot of a gray ribbon. The words dramatically appeared below: A CURE WITHIN REACH.

The lights came up and the audience applauded lightly. The emcee took the mic once more. "Wow. Just incredibly inspiring work. Let's give it up for the folks at the Gaines Foundation."

The audience did, indeed, give it up.

"And now," said the emcee, "before you get to soak up those five martinis you drank with some beef medallions in Périgueux sauce . . ."

The audience laughed. Ron didn't.

". . . it is my great pleasure and honor to introduce tonight's keynote speaker: Dr. Gregor Gottschall, head of the Johns Hopkins Center for Lupinovirus Research, and one of the luminaries who is working tirelessly to end this pandemic once and for all."

The crowd applauded as the emcee left the stage. Ron sighed. It was past 8:00 and the keynote speech was just starting. He should've grabbed a stealth cheeseburger on the way here. No, he should've eaten a crab cake. He should've eaten ten crab cakes. He should've stuffed them in his face right in front of Madeline.

The applause petered out awkwardly. The stage was empty. Dr. Gregor Gottschall did not appear. An annoyed chatter broke out among the crowd.

"Extremely unprofessional," Ron heard Madeline mutter.

"If they run the gala like this," a white-haired man in a tuxedo whispered to his date, a woman half his age, "it does make one wonder where all the money is going?"

In his years with Madeline, Ron had observed that the rich were an extremely impatient breed. They believed that wasting their time was the greatest of sins.

But before there was a general revolt, someone did take the stage: a woman in a spectacular black ball gown. She wore a dark gray half-mask styled to look like a wolf.

The woman leaned into the microphone. "Sorry for the confusion. I'm not Dr. Gregor Gottschall."

The crowd was quiet, if more confused than ever now.

"I ripped his guts out backstage."

This elicited some nervous laughter. But Ron had ceased to worry about dinner and was starting to truly wonder what the hell was going on here.

The woman grinned from behind her wolf mask. Even at this distance, Ron could see that her eyes were a very striking shade of gray.

"You think I'm joking," she said.

The thin laughter died.

The woman surveyed the crowd. Ron saw contempt in those eyes. "Whoops. Did I bring down the mood? Sorry, everybody. I know. Why don't you all give yourselves another round of applause?"

She smiled down from the stage as the gala attendees once more clapped for themselves on command.

"You're all good people, right? You're the ones who care. After all, you paid to be here. Another couple million bucks toward the cure that never seems to come."

Her words stunned the crowd. Ron wasn't even sure he'd heard her correctly, but apparently, she had said what he thought she had. In all his years getting dragged along on the charity circuit, he'd never seen anything like this. Things were getting interesting.

"You're here," said the woman onstage. "And the people you

want to save—the ones who actually have the virus—are locked in quarantine prisons or hunted down like dogs out there."

The crowd was getting agitated now. Who was this woman and why was she bringing all of this up right now?

"You live in your personal fortresses, protected by the full, lethal force of the US government. Just like you always have. Honestly, the pandemic might as well not exist for you. Except for when you come here and pat yourselves on the back for profiting off the status quo enough to make a charitable donation that will ultimately lower your tax bill. Because you care."

"Shut the hell up!" yelled someone in the crowd.

"Who are you?" cried another.

The gray-eyed woman spoke over them, unperturbed, that wolfish grin still on her lips. "People think that this virus broke the world. It didn't. It just showed us what was already broken. That's why I believe it's a gift."

"Madeline, we should go now," said Ron, tugging on his wife's sleeve.

"I'm sorry but who does this woman think she is?" asked Madeline, utterly indignant. "There is a proper time and place for protest. This isn't it."

"Can somebody get security?" yelled the white-haired man to no one in particular.

Ron looked around and saw confusion in the room. Some people were trying to leave now. Some were pouting. Some were yelling, making a scene. He saw the young crab cake cater-waiter drop her tray and dart toward the exit, a dark object glinting in her hand. Was it a gun?

"Madeline please!" hissed Ron as he tried to pull her toward a different exit. "Let's get out of here."

"We can't just cede the public square to these extremists," said Madeline.

Ron wasn't sure if she hadn't seen the gun or if she simply didn't care. With Madeline it was a toss-up.

"They love to criticize," said Madeline, "but what are they contributing, exactly?"

"I think we're in danger, Madeline," said Ron.

As he dragged her through the crowd, he saw a bearded man in catering blacks blocking another exit. He was holding something close at his side. Ron couldn't see what it was but he had a guess. One of the gala guests was yelling in the caterer's face, but the man didn't move. He didn't even flinch. Something very wrong was unfolding.

Ron could see it now. Everyone who attended the Gray Ribbon Gala was being trapped here, in the atrium. These people weren't going to let them leave.

Some guests had their phones out now: calling the event coordinators to demand an explanation, or trying to summon their personal security teams from wherever they were waiting nearby, or perhaps even dialing 911. These were people used to always getting their way. But their phones weren't working.

Ron tried to call too. He had no signal, either. "Do you have any bars?" Ron asked Madeline, panic spiking in his voice.

"No," said Madeline, staring at her own smartphone. This finally seemed to snap her out of righteous-anger mode and awaken her to the mounting threat.

From the height of the stage, the gray-eyed woman watched the crowd scramble and yell with an amused look on her face.

Far too late, the emcee tried to retake control. He mounted the stage to snatch the mic away from her. "You need to get off the—"

With lightning speed, the woman grabbed the emcee by his perfect hair, freezing him in his tracks. She held him in place as she calmly spoke into the microphone.

"So many rich and powerful people, here in this room. If you wanted a *better world*, you could have it. But you don't. This is exactly the world you want. Dancing and drinking while the rest of us die."

The emcee struggled in vain against the woman's implacable strength.

"Deep down, none of you even think the infected are human. It's okay. You can admit it. In fact, I actually agree with you. We're not human. We're predators. And humans are our prey."

And then she sank her teeth into the emcee's throat. The man let out a strangled scream before the woman pulled her head back, ripping out a chunk of flesh. Red sprayed all over her and the stage and down onto the people closest to it. She grinned with bloody teeth.

There was an instant of stunned silence as the crowd realized that no one was coming to save them. Then all hell broke loose. The gala attendees flew into a full-blown panic. But Ron's eyes were glued to the stage. He couldn't look away. The gray-eyed woman dropped the thrashing, shrieking emcee and bent over double. Her muscles bulged, her dress ripped, her face lengthened. Fangs burst from her gums as dark fur sprouted from her skin. A monster now stood on the stage before them in all its terrible majesty.

Ron was transfixed. The moon wasn't full. This wasn't supposed to happen. It *couldn't* happen. But it had. The woman had become a beast.

The panicking crowd rushed for the exits now, pushing

and shoving and fighting each other to get out. But the caterers, clearly in league with the monster onstage, had pulled out handguns and were firing warning shots over their heads scaring people back.

Ron saw Social Media Toby—a big, fit man in his late forties—rush the crab cake cater-waiter.

"Get out of my way!" he bellowed. "I don't want to hurt you!"

"Can't say the same," said the girl.

Toby shoved her aside and tried the doors. They were locked.

"Open it!" bellowed Toby.

"Make me," sneered the girl.

Toby hauled off and cracked her across the face. The girl staggered but didn't fall. She turned back to face him, a streak of blood dribbling from her nose. She was smiling.

The girl raised her handgun and pulled the trigger. No warning shot. The bullet hit Toby in the kneecap. He fell to the ground squealing like some sort of animal. Ron felt himself starting to panic. He couldn't move. He couldn't breathe. He didn't know what to do.

"Down here," cried Madeline.

His wife was crouched under a table. Madeline usually kept her head in a crisis. Ron got down on his hands and knees and hid there beside her as the chaos and the carnage unfolded around them.

The werewolf sprang off the stage and landed in the midst of the terrified crowd. She took an elderly woman's arm in her jaws and whipped her head, flinging the poor woman twenty feet across the room.

A balding man in glasses tried to run past her and she raked her claws down his back, opening a massive wound. He fell to the ground, writhing and howling in pain. The werewolf stepped on him as she barreled forward, knocking tables and chairs aside like they were made of paper.

"Oh God," said Ron involuntarily.

The beast was coming right for them.

35

The werewolf flicked aside the table as though it weighed nothing. Madeline and Ron crouched on the floor, exposed and frozen in terror. The creature's lips peeled back to show yellow fangs as it moved for the kill.

Suddenly, a shriek of terror ran through the crowd as a set of doors on the far side of the room burst inward. A second werewolf, more massive than the first, landed in the atrium. It raised its muzzle and let out a deafening howl.

The first werewolf was frozen mid-kill—claws reared back, an instant from disemboweling Madeline. Instead, it turned to face the other wolf.

For a moment the two monsters stood staring one another down across the crowded atrium: Rhea and Heidi.

With a giant leap, Rhea sprang over the heads in the crowd. The ground shook as she landed twenty feet from Heidi. Fury burned in her gray eyes. Her claws were bloody. She meant to kill.

But the rage had overcome Heidi too. She hadn't tamed the beast. She had given in. She had discarded her humanity and let the protective instinct she felt for her mother turn into the impulse to rend, to maim, to annihilate. This time she had barely felt the pain as her body broke and remade itself.

At the same instant, the two wolves charged. Their massive forms thundered across the floor and their clash resounded throughout the atrium.

Rhea's claws ripped across Heidi's torso, flinging her to the ground. Heidi yelped. The pain was excruciating. The wound burned. She snapped her jaws but missed as Rhea bore down on her, grabbing her throat with a clawed hand.

Heidi thrashed and struggled beneath her, but Rhea was strong. Heidi's vision blurred as Rhea crushed her throat. Out of the corner of her eye, Heidi saw Madeline rise and pull Ron to his feet. They started to run away from the danger and some tiny sliver of rationality in Heidi's animal brain pinged relief.

Rhea must have seen it on Heidi's face. She turned and saw what Heidi saw. Then with a malicious glint in her eye, she sprang toward Madeline. She meant to kill her mother before Heidi's eyes. Madeline turned and screamed as she saw Rhea coming at her.

But in a split second, Heidi closed the distance between herself and her enemy. She smashed into Rhea and sent her tumbling.

Rhea was up in a flash, ignoring Madeline now, focusing only on Heidi. It was a fight to the death and they both knew it.

Rhea lunged and clawed at Heidi's belly, drawing more blood. But Heidi was unfazed. She barely felt the wound. The rage was flowing through her now, the rage that had always been there, even before she'd ever been infected with the virus. The small fragment of her reasoning brain that still held on was watching from outside now, as though this were a movie.

As Rhea clawed her again, Heidi snapped her jaws and caught Rhea's arm. Then she bit down, hard, breaking the bone with a muffled crack.

Rhea yelped in agony—the first time Heidi had ever seen her register pain. From the corner of her eye, Heidi saw that Madeline had managed to get away from the fight. With her mother safely out of the way, she could dispense with restraint.

Rhea wrenched her body and managed to free herself from Heidi's fangs, though her bloody forearm now dangled uselessly at a sickening angle. Yet, before she could counterattack, Heidi was on top of her again, savage and unstoppable. She slashed and kicked and bit at Rhea's back and head as Rhea curled away to protect her face and belly. Rhea struck back at Heidi, raking her with her talons.

The rest of Rhea's pack—the Underdogs—came now. They couldn't change form, like Rhea and Heidi, but they were armed and ready to kill.

Pranjit ran toward Heidi now, unloading a pistol. The bullets stung Heidi like mosquito bites. But they weren't silver. She kicked Pranjit in the chest, sending him careening backward, straight into Henry. Both of them landed in a heap on the floor.

Rhea tried to wriggle out from under Heidi now. But Heidi hooked her talons into Rhea's flesh and lifted her body over her head. With a roar, she flung Rhea ten feet, directly into a museum display case filled with Roman artifacts. The case, and the two-thousand-year-old pottery inside, shattered as Rhea passed through it.

The rage subsumed Heidi now, guiding her, strengthening her. Every action and every impulse were bent toward a singular goal: to destroy the Bitch. Before Rhea could get to her feet, Heidi pounced onto her again and bit into her neck for the kill.

As Heidi crushed Rhea's throat, she felt a sharp pain in her side. She shifted to see that Nora—the former EMT she had played cards with—had buried a tactical knife between her ribs.

The pain only angered her more. Without letting go of Rhea's neck, Heidi backhanded Nora with her gnarled fist. The jackhammer force of the blow sent Nora sailing backward into the wall, where she fell to the floor and didn't get up.

A second later, Xuying leaped onto Heidi's back, scratching and hitting and snarling like an animal herself, desperate to protect her leader. Heidi shook her off as one might shake away a fly.

She bit down harder on Rhea's neck. They couldn't save her. No one could.

Rhea flailed and kicked. Her body writhed and struggled. The effort was useless. Heidi was stronger. Her jaws crushed the life out of Rhea. At last, as her desperate flailing reached a crescendo—Rhea shifted back into her human form. She was covered in wounds, nearly naked in the tattered fragments of her ball gown. She looked weak and fragile on the floor.

But still her gray eyes were defiant. Even as she was dying, Rhea somehow grinned. Through sheer force of will, she pushed enough air through her teeth to whisper, "Go on . . . do it . . ."

The bloodlust was overwhelming Heidi. She wanted to tear the Bitch's head off.

But she didn't. Instead, she released her jaws. And then, without really knowing how she was doing it, Heidi transformed back into a human.

They were both people once more, tired and wounded. Heidi looked down at Rhea lying on the floor, bloody and pathetic.

She shook her head. "Everything you said is true. You're right. It all has to change. People like this—people like me—we messed everything up. And we didn't notice we were doing it . . . But kill or be killed? That never ends."

"You're weak," croaked Rhea. "You're scared."

"No. You're wrong," said Heidi. "Someone once said to me that we've got to look out for each other. That it's the only way through this. She was right."

Heidi turned her back on Rhea and found herself facing the crowd. They'd gone quiet, now, and they were looking at her, gobsmacked. A werewolf had attacked them and another had saved them. They stepped aside and stumbled backward as Heidi, barefoot and covered in blood, her clothes torn to shreds, searched for her mother.

She found Madeline standing with Ron in the wreckage of the attack. Both of them stared at her, wide-eyed and silent.

Heidi wanted to run to her mother. She wanted to hug her. But she stopped herself. "I'm sorry, Mom," said Heidi, choking back tears. "I—I think I have to go now."

Then she turned away, unable to face the look in Madeline's eyes, and made for the exit.

Heidi heard nothing as Rhea silently rose from the floor behind her, transforming as she moved. It was Madeline who cried out. Heidi turned to see Rhea lunging toward her, charging in for the kill—

Bang!

A single gunshot rang out. Rhea blinked and then stumbled forward. Heidi saw now that there was a circular hole in the center of her chest. A second later blood began to bubble out of it. Rhea dropped to her knees. Then she fell forward onto her face.

Heidi turned to see Cam standing in the open doorway. In his hand, he held the pistol she'd taken from Erik Balikian. A tendril of blue smoke curled from the barrel. He'd fired a single silver bullet.

An instant later, a bullhorn blared from somewhere outside

the museum: "This is the Viral Containment Task Force. Any resistance will be taken as a sign of infection."

Heidi saw the Underdogs scrambling. Xuying leaped to her feet. She pulled Nora up. Henry and Pranjit were already racing for the exits.

"I think you're right, Heidi," said Cam. "We've got to go. Out the back. Now."

Both of them ran for the door, down the hallway toward the service entrance.

"Heidi, wait!"

Heidi turned to see that Madeline had run after them. She caught up to Heidi and hugged her tight. In her mother's arms, Heidi felt her problems and her fears and even her pain disappear. She wanted to hold on to Madeline forever.

"Don't go, sweetheart," said Madeline. "Don't run away."

"I have to, Mom. I don't have a choice."

Madeline held on. "I love you, sweetheart. I haven't always been the best mother. I'll try to do better. I swear to you. We can make sure you're taken care of. We can get you help—"

"No, Mom . . . I think—I think this is just who I am now."

Madeline brushed Heidi's hair aside and stared into Heidi's eyes. "Then take my car. It might buy you some time." Madeline pressed her keys into Heidi's hand. "When you're somewhere safe, let me know if there's a way to help. I'll try to slow them down as best I can."

Heidi nodded.

"I'm proud of you," said Madeline. "Now go."

And so, Heidi and Cam did.

* * *

Erik Balikian's head was still bleeding as he kicked his way into the Gaines Museum of Fine Art with four Viral Containment Task Force officers behind him. He hadn't had time to bandage it since the 10–91W, Heidi Mills, had gotten the drop on him.

When he woke up on the ground with his head throbbing, he knew where she'd gone. He'd even thought about coming here alone. But when he saw what had happened to the event security, he was glad he hadn't. They'd found them in the front entryway, spread all over the walls and floor.

"Goddamn, Caveman," said Officer Monica Caudell, call sign Starchild. "You were right."

"I know," said Erik.

He heard one of the other officers throwing up behind him. Erik looked at the carnage around them and felt nothing beyond the singular desire that had brought him here.

He'd had a hell of a time convincing VCTF officers on duty that there was a situation they needed to respond to on the night before the LCC. But somehow he had. And when they'd rolled up on the museum and found no security and the doors locked, chained, and padlocked, it was clear something was amiss.

"You want to hang back, Caveman?" asked Officer Vinny Cho, call sign Lefty. "You're naked, bro."

"Naked" was Dogcatcher-speak for not wearing the standard Kevlar ceramic body armor that VCTF officers wore during Lunar Cycle Curfew.

"Fuck that," said Erik. "I'm gonna put down the dog that did this."

They proceeded, guns out, to another locked door. The others stood back as Erik kicked it open. Then the five of them burst into a brightly lit atrium.

The event was in disarray. It looked to Erik like someone had driven a truck through the museum. Tables were overturned, champagne flutes broken, trays of food scattered across the floor. Men in dinner jackets and women in gowns stared back at the officers, shell-shocked. Others sat on the floor crying, hugging their knees.

Immediately, Erik noticed a Glock-17 lying on the ground. *His* Glock-17. Erik picked it up and holstered it.

"There!" shrieked a woman in a torn dress. "She's over there!"

Erik pushed through the crowd toward the center of the atrium. "Back off!" he yelled at them. "Let me through!"

The crowd cleared and Erik saw her. Lying on the floor in a pool of blood was a woman wearing the tattered remnants of a black ball gown.

"It was her! She did all of this!" said a man with white hair. "She's infected!"

The other Dogcatchers surrounded the woman with their MP5s pointed at her. The woman on the ground didn't move.

"She's dead," said Starchild.

"Not quite," came the woman's voice, barely more than a whisper.

With incredible effort, the woman rolled herself over, blood dribbling from her mouth. Erik could see that she was shaking. It took him a moment to realize that the woman was laughing.

"What's so fucking funny?" asked Erik, his SMG trained on her forehead.

"The food . . ." whispered the woman between fits of rattling laughter. "We spit in the food . . ."

"I'm sorry, what did she just say?" asked the white-haired gala attendee.

A murmur ran through the crowd as it collectively dawned on them exactly what her words meant. The catering staff was all infected. *Rabies lupinovirus* spread through saliva. If they spit in the food then . . .

"Welcome to the revolution," said Rhea as she sprang to her feet.

Before she took a single step, Erik Balikian shot her clean through the forehead with a silver bullet.

By the time she hit the ground, he already had out a pair of silver-plated pliers.

36

Heidi leaped into her mother's Mercedes and cranked the engine. Cam climbed in after her. As they sped northward, Heidi saw the flashers—police cars and ambulances—heading in the opposite direction. She steeled herself to be pulled over and arrested.

But the convoy of emergency vehicles disappeared into the rearview mirror. Her mother's intuition had been right. Changing vehicles had bought them some time. Hopefully it would be enough.

Heidi spoke at last. "You saved my life back there."

"I think you saved mine too." He paused for a long time. "Heidi . . . I'm so sorry."

"For what?"

"I'm sorry that I went along with her. I'm sorry I couldn't see that it was wrong."

"Don't apologize," said Heidi. "You said it yourself: Rhea had a point."

"But she missed something," said Cam. "Love is stronger than hate. I want to believe that, anyway. But I was just so angry. And that made me blind. I think—I think I was looking for a mom or something to make it all better." Cam shook his head. "Pathetic."

Heidi put her hand on his. "It's not pathetic. It's human. We're still human, no matter what else we are."

They passed through the national forest and kept going north through the night.

Around 2:00 AM they came to the border crossing. After a cursory look at Heidi's driver's license—or rather, Dawn Suppley's—a somewhat sleepy Canadian border agent waved their vehicle through.

They kept going until the sun came up, when they pulled off the highway and got a room in a cheap motel for a few hours' sleep. They awoke in the early afternoon and immediately got back on the road.

By evening, they had made it to the edge of the vast temperate rainforest that stretched hundreds of miles up the Pacific coast—one of the largest areas of protected wilderness in North America. The sun slid toward the horizon, painting the sea scarlet, and the full moon rose.

Cam was afraid, but Heidi tried to calm him. She welcomed the change this time. Both of them let go, and they ran as beasts along the cliffside paths, where the forest rose above the water, until dawn glowed on the mountaintops, and they were people again.

During the night, they had killed. Blood and viscera stained the grass at their feet. The mangled, partially eaten carcass of a deer lay in the clearing before them. Heidi could still taste the animal's flesh in her mouth.

They were far from civilization now. They found an icy stream and, unpleasant though it was, they washed themselves as best they could before continuing their long journey northward.

It was a beautiful, cloudless spring day. As Heidi drove through the pristine old-growth forests of British Columbia,

Cam fiddled with the satellite radio. As he raced through the stations, something caught Heidi's ear.

"Wait, leave it here," she said.

It was a Canadian news broadcast. "The effects of the recent lupinovirus super-spreader event continue to ripple throughout America today," said the newscaster. "The Viral Containment Task Force, the US public health agency granted extraordinary powers to fight the pandemic, has enacted sweeping crackdowns around the country as both a show of strength and to preempt any similar attack before it can happen."

"Holy shit," said Cam.

The newscaster continued, "Yet at the same time, a growing number of critics have already begun to question the agency's methods and even its goals. Many of the Gray Ribbon Gala guests—among them celebrities, politicians, and CEOs—must now contend with a new reality: They have been infected with *Rabies lupinovirus.*"

Heidi looked out the window of the car. Through the trees to the west, she caught intermittent glimpses of the sun sparkling on the ocean.

The voice of the Gray Ribbon Gala emcee now spoke. "Personally, the way I've been treated in the short time since contracting this disease is simply inexcusable. It's inhuman. And we, as a society, must fundamentally change our approach to this pandemic."

The newscaster continued, "Members of Congress have already introduced a new bipartisan bill calling for greater oversight of the for-profit lupinovirus quarantine facilities that have proliferated in the wake of the initial outbreak five years ago . . . In other news, tensions continue to rise across the Middle East as—"

Heidi turned off the radio. "Damn. She actually did it."

"It's never that simple," said Cam.

"It's a start," said Heidi.

"Maybe. But I bet things get bad before they get better."

"Expect the worst and you'll always be pleasantly surprised?" said Heidi.

Cam laughed. "So, theoretically, what's the worst that would happen if I kissed you right now?"

Heidi frowned. "Could be catastrophic."

"Yeah?"

"I could get so distracted that I drive off the road and wreck the car."

Cam frowned and sank back in his seat. "Sorry, I didn't mean to presume any—"

Heidi cut him off by leaning across to the passenger's side and kissing him on the lips. She held the kiss for a moment before turning back to the road ahead. They didn't wreck.

"That wasn't too dangerous," said Cam.

Heidi smiled and shrugged. "Either way, I figured we'd survive."

"Yeah," said Cam. "I bet we would."

Outside, the green landscape rolled by as they drove north toward the future.

EPILOGUE

"Thank you for taking the time to meet with us," said the pale man in the gray suit, who'd simply introduced himself as Jim.

Erik shrugged. "Didn't really seem like I had much of a choice."

They were in a nondescript conference room on the fourteenth floor of a federal building downtown—nowhere near VCTF headquarters, which struck Erik as odd. Jim, and a handful of subordinates, sat across the table, staring at Erik like he was a zoo exhibit.

"After the super-spreader attack, we're in the midst of a comprehensive internal review," said Jim, "to determine just how badly the VCTF messed up."

"That's going to be a long report," said Erik.

Jim nodded. "Throughout it all, though, there is one name that keeps popping up: Erik Balikian."

Erik took a sip of the weak coffee he'd been offered. He had a monster of a headache coming on. "Let me guess, you want to lecture me about how I didn't do things the right way. Well, I'll tell you what I've told everyone so far. I had two names that I tried to give to the VCTF. Nobody cared. But if those names had been investigated earlier, none of this would have happened. You want to sit in judgment of me—"

"Quite the contrary, Officer Balikian." Jim gave an unsettling yellow smile. "There is a faction within our organization who believe our efforts to stop this pandemic have heretofore been misguided, that we have not gone far enough. After the disaster at the Gaines Museum, this faction—of which I count myself a member—is, shall we say, ascendant."

"Cheers," said Erik.

"Personally, I find the initiative you took here to be inspiring," said Jim. "You ignored the red tape. You disregarded bad orders. You did what you had to do to protect the public. And you took down the terrorist responsible."

"The others got away," said Erik.

Jim cleared his throat. "Still. Your reasoning is sound. If your superiors had only listened to you, it's quite possible this whole mess could've been avoided."

"So . . . I'm *not* getting canned?"

"Far from it," said Jim. "The Gaines Museum changed everything. It's more than a pandemic now. Our country faces a new threat, Officer Balikian: organized viral terror. Congress has approved the formation of a top secret Special Action Group within the VCTF. This will be an elite team dedicated to winning this war, using any methods necessary. I have been chosen as the first head of this Special Action Group."

"Mazel tov," said Erik, raising his paper cup of lukewarm coffee in a mock toast.

"The SAG will have total autonomy. Unlimited funding. Access to the latest technology. We will not be constrained by bureaucracy. We will not be hampered by procedure or outmoded laws. We will do whatever it takes to destroy our enemies and take our country back."

"And why are you telling me this?" asked Erik.

"Isn't it obvious?" said Jim. "I want you to join us. We need men like you: strong, smart, deadly. So, what do you say, Caveman?"

Erik stared at Jim. Inside his mouth he ran his tongue over his new dental implant. The silver tooth was smoother and sharper than its organic neighbors.

"What do I say?" repeated Erik. "I say: Go fuck yourself."

Erik Balikian placed his Viral Containment Task Force badge on the table and slid it across to Jim.

Jim stared at the badge, dumbfounded. "Excuse me?"

But Erik didn't elaborate. He got up and walked out of the conference room.

Yet another nine-to-five pencil pusher with big plans and no follow-through, somebody who tapped out a long time ago. Erik Balikian wasn't about to help the Viral Containment Task Force clean up the mess it had made. And he had no intention of selling his soul to an organization that would throw him under the bus the first chance it got. Let the VCTF burn.

Erik stepped out of the federal building and onto the sidewalk. He walked down the block, past happy citizens enjoying a nice spring day. It was just like Reaper said: None of them had a clue what it took to keep them safe. They never would. But now Erik knew.

He'd traded in his car for a four-cylinder motorcycle, leaner, faster, nimbler. He'd sold nearly everything he'd owned, too, and used all the money he got to buy ammunition. Silver ammunition.

Erik threw a leg over his bike and cranked it. The engine

roared. He smiled and his silver tooth glinted in the morning sun. He wasn't Caveman anymore.

Erik put on his helmet. On the back of it was a custom design he'd paid a pretty penny to have laser-engraved: a hooded skeleton holding a sickle and hourglass. Beneath it was a word in Gothic letters: REAPER.

And so, Erik Balikian sped off to find the ones who got away.

ACKNOWLEDGMENTS

It takes a lot to bring a book snarling and howling into this world. I will be forever grateful to have gotten the chance to spend all day making stuff up about werewolves. Pretty much the definition of a dream job.

I was inspired in my approach to the material by the films of George Romero, John Carpenter, and Robert Eggers. And I don't think I'd even know how to begin writing a book if not for the invaluable advice offered in Stephen King's *On Writing: A Memoir of the Craft* and Elmore Leonard's essay "Writers on Writing: Easy on the Adverbs, Exclamation Points and Especially Hooptedoodle."

I'd like to thank Sara Goodman for giving me this opportunity and pushing me hard (but in a nice way) to make the story better, and everyone else at Wednesday Books for their efforts to improve and support the book.

I'd like to thank my agent Noah Ballard at Verve, who's had my back since the very start of my writing career. Noah saw the potential in this idea and helped find it a fantastic home. Likewise, I'd like to thank his colleagues Nicky Mohebbi and Chris Noriega at Verve, as well as my manager, Zach Cox, at Circle of Confusion, who all offered helpful advice on how to approach this story.

ACKNOWLEDGMENTS

I'd like to thank my friends Ed Herro and Nick Amadeus for reading an earlier version of this idea and telling me what they thought about it (mostly positive!) and my friend Greg Distelhorst for being on call to answer all my Pacific Northwest regional questions.

I'd like to thank all the people who stepped up to help the rest of us when an unknown virus really did turn the world upside down. Some folks seem to want to forget the whole thing ever happened, but I never will.

I'd like to thank my father and mother who taught me that books were an important part of life. And my sister for always telling me I've got a great idea, even when that is debatably true. I'd also like to thank my in-laws, Anne and Gary, and my stepmother, Teresa, for being consistent sources of support throughout the years.

Most of all, I'd like to thank my wife, Colleen, for always believing in me even when I don't quite believe in myself. And I'd like to thank my kids, Spikey and Suzanna, who remind me of the joy of storytelling every single day. Also, they're just plain funny as hell.

ABOUT THE AUTHOR

Randi Rosenblum

Tom O'Donnell is the author of the Homerooms & Hall Passes and Hamstersaurus Rex book series. He's written for *The New Yorker* and McSweeney's as well as for film and TV. Find him at www.tomisokay.com.